KIZUMONOGATARI

WOUND TALE

NISIOISIN

VERTICAL.

KIZUMONOGATARI
Wound Tale

NISIOISIN

Art by VOFAN

Translated by Ko Ransom

VERTICAL.

KIZUMONOGATARI

© 2008 NISIOISIN

First published in Japan in 2008
by Kodansha Ltd., Tokyo.
Publication rights for this English edition
arranged through Kodansha Ltd., Tokyo.

Published by Vertical, Inc., New York, 2015

ISBN 978-1-941220-97-9

Manufactured in the United States of America

First Edition

Vertical, Inc.
451 Park Avenue South, 7th Floor
New York, NY 10016

www.vertical-inc.com

CHAPTER ZERO KOYOMI
VAMP

CHAPTER ZERO
KOYOMI VAMP

KISSSHOT
ACEROLA ORION
HE ARTUNDE RBLADE

0 0 1

I suppose I need to get around to talking about Kissshot Acerolaorion Heartunderblade. I probably have a duty to do so. During the spring break between my second and third years as a high school student—I met her. It was a shocking meeting, and it was a catastrophic one. In any case, I must have had terrible luck—of course, in the same way that I was unable to avoid that bad luck, even if I somehow had, I doubt someone else would have met that fate. It actually seems extremely irresponsible to talk about my bad luck here. Maybe I should just be upfront and say that it was my fault. In the end, I think it was a chain of events only made possible because I was me.

A chain of events.

Actually, while I used those words just now without giving them any particular thought, I wouldn't be able to tell you what events bookend this chain. Where this incident began, what path it took, or how it ended—I can't declare the precise truth of the matter. It could be that it has yet to end, even now, or perhaps it hasn't even started. And I say that not as a form of pretention or wordplay; that is what I honestly believe.

Ultimately, I can only observe the incident from my own perspective, so I will never be able to know what that chain of events truly meant to anyone else—or what it didn't mean. Asking "them" may allow me to come to some degree of understanding of the circumstances, but even then, there's no way for me to know if their words are true.

What I have is not the truth, but an understanding.

And perhaps that's enough.

But to begin with (and this is the one thing I *can* say definitively), such is the nature of the girl at the center of this all—Kissshot Acerolaorion Heartunderblade.

Someone who only holds meaning for the observer.

Someone whose meaning changes depending on the observer.

Someone whose meaning cannot be agreed upon by her observers.

A vampire.

Of course, I probably don't need to give you a detailed explanation of what a vampire is. Whether in comics, movies, or games, that is a vein long since mined dry. The majority of Japanese people must be closely familiar with them, even though they aren't creatures born from the culture of this country. You might call them a bit of an old notion.

Still, spring break.

I was attacked by a vampire, one of these notions we now consider dated twice over.

You could say it was stupid.

In fact, I think I was stupid.

And it was due to the stupidity of none but yours truly that I ended up experiencing two weeks of hell—a hell that took up the entire stretch of spring break, end to end.

If it was one big joke, it sure felt like hell; if it was hell, it sure felt like one big joke.

Like I said earlier, it will forever be a mystery to me when this chain of events began, where and how it transpired, and in what manner it ended. But while that may be an unsolvable dilemma, I am absolutely certain of when my own personal hell began and when it ended.

March 26th to April 7th.

Spring break.

I would come to learn that creatures such as her—Kissshot Acerolaorion Heartunderblade—are known as "aberrations."

Aberrations.

Monsters.

Inhumans.

In that case, the one thing above all others that caused me to experience hell was the fact that I observed her—at that moment, at that location, in that fashion.

I was a woefully unsuitable observer.

And yes, a stupid one.

While telling you about her would, by necessity, entail fully exposing my own stupidity—an act you may see as masochistic—I do think I have to talk about that vampire.

About the story of the wound I received from her.

About the story of how I wounded her.

I have to talk about it.

I have a duty to speak.

That is my responsibility.

…This preamble has gotten quite long, but I'd like to ask for your understanding here—though I've pompously gone on about responsibility and whatnot, it's merely the responsibility of a stupid jester. There's no telling when I'll founder—while it's a timid thing to say, I honestly do not have the confidence to finish telling this story. That is why I've been dragging out these proper-like preliminary remarks.

Even so, I couldn't possibly go any longer. And after I finally begin the story, it could become like a rock rolling down a hill so that it'll be harder to stop. But to be sure, just in case it turns out that I lack the resolve, allow me to divulge how it ends here in advance.

This story about a vampire has an unhappy ending.

11

It concludes with everyone becoming miserable.

And that's just the hell's ending. The chain of events may not yet be over, and in any case, my responsibility to her will be a lifelong affair.

002

Making friends would lower my intensity as a human.

I think I said something of the sort.

As to when, it was right before spring break: Saturday, March 25th, in the afternoon of the day our school held its closing ceremony. I was wandering around aimlessly near the school I go to, Naoetsu High.

We're talking about me, who has zero affiliation with any school club.

I really was just wandering around, for no reason whatsoever.

If you're wondering if I was thrilled that spring break would start the next day, I was by no means excited.

As a rule, students are happy about any cluster of days off. Not just spring break, but summer break, winter break, Golden Week, and so on. Even I was happy for the most part that our third trimester was over and that spring break had begun, but at the same time, long vacations also meant having far more time on my hands than I knew what to do with.

Especially spring break, since we don't even have homework.

Staying at home would feel a bit odd.

Anyway—with closing ceremonies over, I went to my classroom to receive my report card, and we were dismissed with an okay, see you next school year, but I hesitated to go straight home. Yet it wasn't as if I had anywhere else to go, which meant loitering around school like some sort of suspicious fellow.

I had no particular goal.

I did it less to fill time than to kill time.

While I bike to school, my bicycle was actually still parked in the school lot—another expression of my intention to not go home yet.

You could say I was going for a walk.

Of course, I'm not the health-conscious type.

While it may have seemed like a good idea to kill time inside school if killing time is what I wanted to do, just as I found being at home odd, in its own way it was odd being at school too—though it may have been the afternoon after closing ceremonies, a lot of people were in the middle of their club activities.

I don't like people who try hard.

Well, it's not like the students at my school are that enthusiastic about their clubs. The only real exception was the girls' basketball team after this monstrously huge rookie joined as the result of some sort of mistake. Most of the other clubs, even the sports teams, were the kinds of outfits that were actually happy to receive participation trophies.

And that's why (well, there's not any actual *reason* why) after aimlessly circling around the school a few times, I had begun to think that yeah, it really is about time for me to pick up my bike from inside the school and head home—I'm hungry, after all—when I came across an unexpected individual.

With it already being spring break, I frankly don't know whether to describe myself at that time as a second-year or a third-year, but in any case, a celebrity in my grade—Tsubasa Hanekawa—was walking straight toward me.

I wondered for a moment what she was doing, with both of her hands held there behind her head, until I realized she seemed to be adjusting the position of her braid. She wore her long hair behind her in a braid. While braids themselves are already rare to begin with these days, she also wore her bangs in a straight line.

She was wearing her school uniform.

A completely unaltered skirt falling four inches below her knees.

A black scarf.

A school sweater on top of her blouse as designated by school regulations.

White socks and school shoes as designated by those same regulations.

The very picture of a model student.

A model student among model students, a class president among class presidents.

She and I were in different classes during both our first and second years, so I doubted she knew who I was, but I had heard about her class-presidential ways and doings.

Since the rumors had gone so far to find their way to me, someone grossly ignorant of school gossip, even taken with a grain of salt those ways and doings must have been quite something.

She would no doubt continue to be class president as a third-year.

Plus, she had good grades.

While it's an odd way to put it, I'd heard that she was freakishly smart. Getting perfect marks in all of her classes was like nothing to her. Sure, when all the students take the same test, someone ending up in first place is as much of a given as someone else ending up in last place, but for two years, Tsubasa Hanekawa had always maintained her spot on top.

Though I had managed to get into a private prep school, Naoetsu High, I soon found myself in a position that you might call "left behind," which meant there was a world of difference between us. In a way, you could call us polar opposites.

Hmph.

And so, she caught my attention for a moment.

We were in different classes, after all, so while I may have known of her, I rarely saw her—yet it was her who I happened to see at that moment, right after closing ceremonies had ended, and that did surprise me a little.

Well.

A rare coincidence, that's all.

She seemed to have just left through the school gates, so upon further consideration, it wasn't that strange to come across her, considering how I'd been loitering around the school for all that time.

Naturally, Hanekawa didn't even notice me.

I didn't seem to be in her field of vision, as engrossed as she was in fixing the position of her braid—and had I happened to be in it, Hanekawa and I wouldn't normally so much as nod at each other, given our relationship (or lack therof).

Hah hah hah.

In fact, I thought that a model student like Hanekawa probably hated people with the kind of devil-may-care attitude that I had.

She was serious, and I was not.

Better if she didn't know about me.

I'll just let her pass by, I thought.

No reason to run away, either.

I kept walking forward, not missing a step, as if I hadn't noticed her—and right as we were only five or so steps away each from passing by without incident, it happened.

I...doubt I'll ever forget that moment as long as I live.

Out of absolutely nowhere—a gust of wind.

"Ah."

I hadn't been able to stay silent despite myself.

The front of Hanekawa's rather long pleated skirt, hanging four inches below her knees, flew straight up in the air.

I assume that under different circumstances, she would have reflexively pushed it back down into place—but thanks to some unfortunate timing, both of her hands were behind her head, engrossed in

16

the complex operation that was fixing the position of her braid. From where I stood, she almost looked like she was putting on a mildly affected pose, her hands clasped behind her.

And it was in that situation that her skirt was flipped up.

Its contents were put into plain sight.

They were certainly not gaudy—but they were the kind of elegant undergarments that refused to release one's gaze once a pair of eyes was attracted to them.

They were a tidy and pure white.

It was not as if they were suggestively shaped. In fact, they seemed to be on the higher end of the surface area spectrum. A wide article, made of thick cloth—by no means lascivious, and in fact, if one were to speak of them in that way, it would be reasonable to call them demure.

Yet they were so white it was dazzling.

And they were anything but plain.

In the center, white string had been used to sew a complex embroidered pattern over a white canvas—no doubt intended to evoke flowers. The pattern, with its bilateral symmetry, acted to bring a sublime balance to the piece as a whole. And toward the top-center of the embroidery sat a small ribbon.

This one ribbon worked to further cement the impression of the whole.

What's more, visible just above that small ribbon was her abdomen and her cute bellybutton. Yes, her skirt had been flipped so far up that those parts of her were now immodestly exposed. Had I wanted to, I could even have scrutinized the tails of her blouse, tucked into her skirt. I never knew that the shirttails of a blouse could appear so salacious.

The lining of a skirt was another fresh sight to my eyes. While I frequently caught sight of skirts, they seemed to be inviolable, mysterious existences—but I now felt as though, for the very first time, I understood the structure of this garment.

But most of all, it was exquisite how only the front section of her skirt was flipped.

Next to her pure-white undergarment stood something else so proudly white it was as if the two were in competition: her thighs, which had no small amount of meat on them. Sitting behind the two, her navy blue skirt placed them in relief and emphasized the contrast. You could say her skirt, longer than the average girl's, was now serving like a blackout curtain to accentuate a graceful work of fine art. Even the skirt's pleats came across like they might be made of a fine velvet.

And when coupled with that pose of hers, her hands joined behind her head, it practically seemed as if she was showing off her vaunted underwear to me. That was how she appeared in effect.

She—Tsubasa Hanekawa, did not move so much as a finger.

She must have been taken aback.

She stood in that pose, allowing her skirt to stay flipped, with everything down to her expression frozen in place.

In reality, I doubt that a solitary second went by.

But for me, it was like an hour—no, it felt so long I even began to imagine that my life might reach its natural end before this glimpse was over. This is absolutely not an exaggeration. In that moment, I experienced a lifetime.

My eyes were so captivated by her lower half that I felt as though my eyes were about to grow dry.

Of course, I understand—the gentlemanly thing to do in this kind of situation is to avert your eyes.

Of course I understand that.

In most cases, I probably would have done so. I even try my best to look down at my feet the entire while if a girl happens to be in front of me when I climb the stairs.

But at that moment in time, I was not so polished a man that I could promptly behave in said manner, utterly unprepared, upon being visited by such a blessing out of the blue.

It was like that image of Hanekawa was being burned into my retinas.

If I were to die at that moment and if my eyes were transplanted to another person, that someone would probably be haunted by visions of Hanekawa's underwear for life.

That is how shocking it was.

The underwear of a model student.

"........."

Hold on.

How long did I just go on describing a model student's panties?

While I did return to my senses, by the time I did, Hanekawa's skirt was already back in place.

It really had been an instant.

As for Hanekawa—she still looked taken aback. And she was looking at me.

She was staring at me.

"...Um."

Ack.

How was I to respond?

What was I supposed to do at a time like this?

"I...didn't see anything, you know?"

I tried a bald-faced lie.

But my bald-faced lie received no reply from Hanekawa. She only continued to stare at me as she finally finished adjusting her braid and brought her hands down to pat her skirt a few times.

Really? Now?

For just a moment, she took her eyes off of me and made as if to implore heaven. Then she looked at me again and said:

"Teheheh."

A bashful laugh.

...Wow.

She laughs?

What a broad-minded woman, indeed a class president among

class presidents.

"I don't know what to say."

Hop, hop, hop.

Hanekawa kept both of her feet together as she bounded toward me, seeming to use nothing more than the joints of her knees for movement.

We had been ten steps away from each other, but now we were down to three.

A bit on the close side.

"For something that's meant to hide what you don't want seen, skirts really are low security. Maybe I need the firewall of a pair of bike shorts after all?"

"Wh-Who knows…"

Her metaphor left me at a loss.

So what did that make me, a virus?

Fortunately for her—or possibly not, I'm not sure—no one else was around, including any other students from Naoetsu High.

It was just me and Hanekawa.

In other words, I was the only one to see her panties. While the fact made me feel a mild sense of superiority over the rest of mankind, let's put that aside for now.

"A little while back, people liked talking about Murphy's Law. Maybe I should chalk it up to that: The front of your skirt only gets flipped when your hands are behind you. You're normally careful about the back of your skirt, but the front is actually more of a blind spot than you'd expect."

"Yeah… Maybe."

How should I know?

Or rather, yikes, how awkward.

I didn't know if it was Hanekawa's intention to make me feel like she was berating me in a roundabout way, but that's how I felt. That said, and while it may not sound very convincing to you after I had looked that carefully at them, the fact that I had witnessed, even unintentionally, something that girls "don't want seen" made me feel undeniably guilty.

Not only that, she was being so smiley…

Trying to make something out of it—please, stop!

"W-Well, don't worry. I might've lied when I said I didn't see them, but I couldn't see them very well because they were shaded."

Of course, that was another lie. I saw them ridiculously well.

"Hu-u-uh."

Hanekawa tilted her head to one side.

"As a girl, it would make me feel much more at ease if you just said you got a good look at them if you really did."

"W-Well, I really do wish I could say that to you, but I simply can't tell you anything but the truth."

"Is that so? You can't?"

"Yeah. It's too bad I can't make you feel at ease. If only I could lie to you."

Words from a man speaking nothing but lies for a while now.

"So this feeling I have that you spent about two pages giving a precise description of what was under my skirt, down to the fine details, is all my imagination?"

"Totally your imagination. Super-duper all your imagination. Until just now, I was painting a beautiful visual landscape using words pregnant with emotion."

This, technically, was not a lie.

"Well, I should get going," I said, casually raising a hand to signal to Hanekawa that I had no intention of continuing our conversation, and began to step forward.

I walked away with quick steps.

Ah, I don't know.

Hanekawa was probably going to head home, but I wondered if she was going to send a text message or something to her friends on her way back about how I saw her panties. While part of me doubted that a model student would do something like that, another part of me thought that she would do it precisely because she was a model student. No, Hanekawa probably didn't know my name...but she would have to at least know that we were in the same year, no?

As rather overly self-conscious thoughts ran through my head, I began to slow my pace a bit, when—

"Wait up a second!"

I heard a voice from behind me.

It was Hanekawa.

She seemed to have chased after me, of all things.

"I finally caught up to you. You're a fast walker."

"...Weren't you heading home?"

"Hmm? Well, I'll go home eventually. And what about you, Araragi? Why are you heading back toward school?"

".........."

She had my name down.

Whaat?

It's not like I was wearing a name tag.

"...Um, well, I was going back to pick up my bike," I said.

"Aha! So you bike to school."

"Well, yeah... My house is a little on the far side, and—"

Hold on, that wasn't the issue. Though it did seem like she hadn't known that I biked to school.

"...Why do you know my name?"

"What? Of course I know it. We go to the same school, don't we?" Hanekawa said, like it was the most obvious thing in the world.

The same school...

She said it in the exact same way that someone might talk about knowing people in their own class. Who does that?

"Well, Araragi, you might not know about someone like me, but you're pretty famous, after all."

I couldn't help but go, "Huh?"

No, you're the famous one.

And me, of all people? My position within Naoetsu Private

High School was like that of a rock on the side of the road—
I wasn't even certain if my own classmates knew my full name.

"Hm? What's wrong, Araragi?"

"…"

"Araragi, with the 'A' written with the left radical for 'mound'
together with the first character in 'possibility,' the two 'ra' written
with the 'good' in 'good boy,' and the 'gi' you use to write 'arbor.'
Your given name is Koyomi, as in the character for 'calendar,' right?
So, Koyomi Araragi."

"………"

Not only did she know my full name, she knew the exact characters used to write it.

Seriously?

She knew my name and my face. If she had a Death Note, I'd
be dead…

Well, I was in the same position with regards to her too.

"You're—Hanekawa."

It wasn't in the way of retaliation, nor was I trying to hold my
own, but what I did was to utter those words to her without even
acknowledging what she'd said.

"You're Tsubasa Hanekawa."

"Wow!"

Hanekawa looked honestly and plainly surprised.

"I'm amazed that you know someone like me," she said.

"Tsubasa Hanekawa, who during final exams of the first trimester of our second year got only one answer wrong, a fill-in-the-blank,
across every subject including health and PE as well as art."

"What? That's…hey, why do you know so much about me?"

Hanekawa grew only more surprised.

It didn't seem to be an act.

"Wait… Are you stalking me, Araragi? Hah, maybe putting
it that way makes it sound like I have too much of a persecution
complex?"

"…No, not really."

It seemed as if she didn't realize she was famous.

She thought she was "normal."

A regular girl who had nothing to recommend her but being on the serious side? Was that it?

Add to that the fact she was treating *me* like I was someone famous and it got a little nasty—of course, I did recognize that I had somewhat of a reputation as a washout.

But even so, why call her out on it?

I decided to just give her a bullshit answer.

"I heard about you from an alien friend."

"What? You have friends, Araragi?"

"Ask about the alien bit first!"

I'm not the kind of person who normally flings retorts at people I'm meeting for practically the first time, but she managed to draw one out of me.

Even if she didn't intend any malice by it, what a terrible thing to say.

"Er, well," Hanekawa said uncomfortably. Even she must have realized what she'd just said. "You're always alone, so I had the impression that you lived up in a world apart from everyone else."

"You don't *actually* think I'm that cool, do you?"

She did seem to know a little bit about me.

But not too much.

"Well, you're right that I don't have any friends. Which makes you so famous that even a friendless loser knows who you are," I said.

"Oh, stop it."

Hanekawa sounded a little bothered by this. Her, a woman who quickly shrugged off with a single embarrassed smile the contents of her skirt being exposed for the world to see.

"I don't like jokes like that. Please don't make fun of me."

"…Oh."

24

I decided to just nod, as objecting seemed likely to launch a full-on argument.

Sheesh.

The pedestrian crossing facing the school gates was red, and so I stopped there—and Hanekawa stood next to me.

…

Why follow me?

Did she forget something at school?

"Hey, Araragi," she began to speak just as I was wondering why. "Do you believe in vampires, Araragi?"

"………"

What in god's name was she talking about?

Then, a moment later, I came upon the answer.

Oh. While she was acting calm, she was actually embarrassed that I'd seen her panties.

That was no surprise, of course.

While I was not by any means famous, Hanekawa did know who I was—and she even understood the state of my personal relationships (that I had no friends).

She had probably heard rumors, and not good ones.

So it wasn't strange for a model student to feel as though she'd made a slight blunder in allowing me a close, hard look…er, a happenstance glimpse of her underwear.

I came to the conclusion that she was following after me in order to deal with it.

Instead of parting ways right after I'd seen her panties, she was plotting to overwrite my memories by following me and talking to me like that.

Hah.

Nice try, model student.

Tossing out a bizarre topic like vampires wasn't going to erase my memories.

"What about vampires?" I asked.

Sure, if that was going to make her feel better, I'd play along and discuss whatever she wanted. Talking to her for a short while about a fruitless topic was a small price to pay for getting to see her panties.

"Well, there have been some rumors lately that there's a vampire here in town. They say not to walk around alone at night."

"What a vague...and phony rumor," I said, letting slip my honest impression. "Why would there be a vampire in a town in the middle of nowhere like ours?"

"Who knows."

"Vampires are foreign *yokai*, right?"

"I don't think that's exactly what they are, but go on."

"Whether you walked alone or with a group of ten people, if you had to face a vampire, I don't think the outcome would change very much."

"Well, that's true."

Ahaha, Hanekawa let out a little laugh.

A lighthearted laugh... It somehow didn't seem like the kind of laugh she'd have.

I realized that I'd been feeling as though something was off for a while now.

I'd imagined Hanekawa to be a more self-important type after hearing people call her a model student, a class president among class presidents and all that.

If anything, she was weirdly affable.

"But there've been a lot of eyewitness reports," she said.

"Eyewitness reports? Now that's funny. Round up these gentlemen."

"Well, these aren't gentlemen."

She explained that it was something being said among the girls at school.

"And not just the girls at our school—all the girls who go to school around here have heard about it. Actually, it's a rumor that's only spreading among the girls."

But a vampire?

I was amazed that a rumor like that had taken root.

"They say the vampire is a beautiful blond woman, but with eyes so cold they make your spine freeze."

"Those are really specific details, but how does that make her a vampire? Couldn't she just be a normal person who stands out because she has blond hair?"

After all, we were in a boring suburban town.

A town out in the sticks, away from everything else.

You didn't even see people with their hair dyed brown.

"But," Hanekawa said, "according to them, when she was under a street lamp, though her hair was blindingly bright…she didn't have a shadow."

"Ah…"

Vampire.

While the word sounded old and hackneyed to me, it wasn't as if I was that familiar with vampires. But I did recall hearing something like that, now that she mentioned it—vampires don't cast shadows.

Why was that again? Because they don't like the sun?

But then this had been at nighttime.

So she was in the light of a street lamp, but it still sounded like some trick of the eye—and besides, didn't that very street lamp cry out that it was a made-up piece of scenery?

Made-up, or maybe just cheap.

"Well, yeah," Hanekawa agreed. Despite my churlish reaction, she didn't seem particularly offended.

She was good at talking and at listening.

"I think it's a ridiculous rumor, too. But it's good from a safety standpoint. Thanks to it, girls aren't walking around by themselves at night anymore."

"Well, I guess you're right about that."

"But personally," Hanekawa said, lowering her voice a bit, "if there's a vampire, I'd like to meet her."

"...Why?"

It seemed as though my prediction may have been off.

I'd assumed she had brought up a fruitless topic in order to erase my memories of seeing her panties—but Hanekawa was sounding a little too enthused for that to be the case.

And anyway, telling a uniformed male student about a "rumor that's only spreading among the girls" seemed odd when I thought about it.

"Won't she suck your blood and kill you if you do?"

"Okay, I don't want to get killed. So maybe it's not accurate to say that I want to meet her. But I just thought it'd be neat if someone like that existed—an existence greater than humans."

"An existence greater than humans? Like a god?"

"It doesn't have to be a god." Hanekawa went silent for a while, as if she was trying to pick her words carefully. Eventually, though, she said, "Because in so many ways, where's the reward otherwise?"

Without my noticing...

The light had turned green.

But Hanekawa and I both stood there.

To be honest?

Not only did I have no idea what Hanekawa was saying, I didn't even know what she was trying to say. It felt almost as if her reply had nothing to do with my question.

"Oh no, oh no," she began to say, flustered. Had my expression betrayed my thoughts? "You know, Araragi, you're surprisingly easy to talk to. My tongue slipped and I feel like I ended up saying something that didn't make much sense just now."

"Y-Yeah. Well, you don't need to worry about it."

"It's strange that you don't have any friends when you're this easy to talk to. Why don't you make some?"

It was a direct question.

She probably didn't mean ill. I knew that much.

I hesitated to give an equally direct answer: The issue wasn't my not making friends, it was my not being able to make any.

Which is why—I gave that answer.

"Making friends would lower my intensity as a human."

"...What?" Hanekawa asked with a confounded expression. "Sorry, I don't really understand."

"Er... Well, you know, it's like..."

Crap.

I had tried to say something cool, but didn't have anything to follow it up with.

"In other words, if I had friends, I'd have to start worrying about them, right? If my friends were hurt, I'd feel hurt too, and if they felt sad, I'd feel sad too. You end up with more weak points, so to speak. I think that's the same as becoming weaker as a person."

"...But you have fun when your friends have fun, and you're happy when your friends are happy, so it's not all about becoming weaker, is it? You might gain more weak points, but you'd gain advantages, too."

"No," I replied, shaking my head, "I'd feel envious when my friends were having fun, and jealous when they were happy."

"...How petty of you," she nailed me.

Leave me alone.

"Even if what you said was true, that would average out to zero," I said. "It wouldn't make a difference whether you had friends or not. No—there are more bad things that happen in this world than good—so it'd be a net negative in the end, wouldn't it?"

"Now that's a cynical thing to say."

Hanekawa took back what she said about me being easy to talk to.

What a limited-time evaluation, I thought—but that was fine.

It's best to clear up those kinds of misunderstandings as soon as possible.

"You see, I want to become a plant," I said.

"A plant?"

"That way I wouldn't have to talk. Or walk, either."

"Hmm." Hanekawa did give me a cursory nod. "But you still want to be a living thing."

"Huh?"

"In that case, you normally say that you want to become something inorganic. Like stone or iron."

I felt as if something unexpected had been pointed out to me.

I wasn't lying—I had honestly felt for a long time that I wanted to become a plant—but I hadn't anticipated a counterargument from that angle.

I see. Inorganic, huh?

She was right, plants are alive.

"I was thinking of going to the library," Hanekawa said.

"Hm?"

"While I was talking to you, I started to feel like I wanted to go to the library."

"......"

What sort of mental circuitry was I dealing with?

She did say that she was going to go home eventually, so she must not have had any particular plans. While she had time, just as I did, you could either kill it wandering around outside of school or go to the library.

Maybe that was the wall separating the flunkeys from the model students.

"It'll be closed tomorrow because it's a Sunday, so I need to go by there today."

"Hunh."

"Do you want to come with me?"

"Why?" I asked with a sarcastic laugh.

The library.

I didn't even know we had one of those things in our town.

"What're you going to do at the library?"

"What else? Study."

"'What else'?" This time I was flabbergasted. "Sorry, but I'm not enough of an oddball to study on my own during spring break when we don't even have homework."

"But we'll be taking entrance exams only next year, you know?"

"Entrance exams… Just graduating seems like a shaky prospect for me. It's too late for me, I'm a lost cause. The most I can do is try not to be late for school too often next year."

"…Hm," Hanekawa mumbled, almost as if bored.

Why, I wondered. It couldn't be that she wanted me to come with her. But Hanekawa didn't say anything more.

Oh, well.

I knew she wasn't some proud, self-important character, but I didn't know what she was.

The light had been going from red to green to red again.

Now it was red.

I thought that next time it turned green would be when I should leave—yes, that would be the perfect time.

I was sure Hanekawa thought the same.

She wasn't someone who couldn't suss the mood.

"Araragi, do you have a cell phone?"

"Well, yeah. Of course."

"Can I borrow it?" she asked, then held out her hand.

I didn't know what she was planning on, but I obliged, taking my phone out of my pocket and handing it to Hanekawa.

"Oh, isn't this a new model?" she said.

"I upgraded just the other day. It's my first new one in two years, so it has all these new features I don't even know how to use."

"You're still young, don't be so pathetic. If you're saying things like that now, civilization is going to pass you by all the more once you become an adult. If you're already on the wrong side of the digital divide, you won't even be able to live a decent life in the

31

future."

"Well, in that case, I guess I'll have to go live up in a mountain somewhere. Then, once civilization crumbles, I'll come back to this town."

"Exactly how long do you plan on living?" Was I immortal or what, she sighed.

Moments after our exchange, Hanekawa began messing with my phone.

While she may have been a class president among class presidents, the very picture of a model student, she was still a high school girl, and thus ridiculously fast at typing on a phone.

It wasn't as if my phone contained any kind of personal information that I didn't want other people seeing, but…don't be messing with people's phones, all right?

Or, I wondered, could she actually be suspecting me of having used my phone's camera to sneak a picture when her skirt was flipped? If so, I wanted her to scour the thing. I wanted to wipe out such a disgraceful suspicion.

But at any rate, it must be hard being a girl, worrying about so many things all the time. If a guy had his fly open, all he had to do was claim that he was being a Sexy Commando or something.

…Or maybe not?

"Thanks. Here, you can have it back."

Hanekawa returned my phone to me in no time at all.

"No pics, right?" I prompted.

"Huh?" She tilted her head. "Pics?"

"…Er, nothing."

Oops.

Had I misread her?

Then what exactly had she been up to?

Hanekawa seemed to pick up on my puzzlement, because she pointed to the phone that I still held, unable to return it to my pocket, and said, "I put my number and email address in there."

"You did what?"

"Too bad for you. You just made a friend."

And then…

Before I could say a single word in response, she ran to the other side of the crossing; the light had turned green without my noticing.

That was how I was planning on leaving, and now it felt like she'd stolen my thunder—wait. Wasn't she going to go to the library? No, since she'd decided to go to the library mid-conversation with me, her heading in the opposite direction now wasn't strange at all.

When she crossed to the other side, Hanekawa turned back to me and waved a "See you later."

I reflexively returned her wave.

Once she saw me waving my hand (like an idiot, I assume), she turned back around, made a right in front of the school gate, and walked off in a cheerful mood. She soon turned the corner and went out of sight.

After I was sure she was gone, I checked my phone.

To see it was true.

A "Tsubasa Hanekawa" had been registered in my contacts list.

A phone number, and an email address.

I had never used the contacts feature on my phone before. I remembered all the numbers I needed—though I don't say this to brag about my memory. It's not something I could brag about since the only ones I had memorized were my home phone number and my parents' cell phone numbers. My sent and received call history was enough for any others.

I simply didn't have many friends.

And that's how "Tsubasa Hanekawa" became the first number to be registered on my phone.

"What's her deal?"

Her actions—hovered beyond my comprehension.

A friend?

Is that what she said? A friend?

Did she mean it?

To begin with, while we may have known each other's names, what was a young lady like her doing casually handing her contact info out to a guy she'd basically spoken to for the first time? Or was I just being old-fashioned about this?

I didn't know.

But as much as I didn't know, there was one thing I did know now.

Tsubasa Hanekawa: the model student among model students, the class president among class presidents, not only wasn't a stuck-up, self-important character—

"…She's pretty damn cool."

A class president among class presidents.

Tsubasa Hanekawa: It was her, whom I happened across the afternoon of closing ceremonies, that I would meet again during spring break, though I had no way of knowing it at the time.

I didn't even feel a sliver of a premonition.

003

And then—

And then night came, that day's incident still fresh in my mind. Night.

I was walking around the town after it had become totally dark. While I'd walked, not biked, around school for no particular reason earlier, I now had a clear motive.

I own two bicycles, by the way.

One is a granny bike that I use to go to school; the other is my pet mountain bike.

The latter is my companion to such a degree that I wish I could ride it everywhere, yet at that precise moment, I could not. If my securely locked bicycle, stored in the entrance of my house, was gone, someone in my family would notice that I had left the house.

Putting aside when I was younger, my family's current approach to me could be described as completely hands-off.

You could even say that they've decided to neglect me.

So unlike my two little sisters, I don't have anything like a curfew or a ban on going outside at night (not that my sisters care about such rules), but there are times when I want to go out without my family knowing.

For example, when I want to go buy a porn mag.

"………"

No, uh.

It won't be a pleasant sight, but allow me to defend myself.

I couldn't get the image of Hanekawa's panties I had seen that afternoon out of my head.

...Am I digging my grave in quicksand here?

Either way, that was the truth.

Though I said that I would likely never forget the image, I didn't actually expect it to get seared in my memory so vividly.

Even after I parted ways with Hanekawa that afternoon, her panties stayed with me, never leaving my mind. I had thought at the time that were my retinas to be transplanted to another person, that person would suffer hallucinations of Hanekawa's panties. Over ten hours later, my hypothesis still obtained.

Dammit.

I was sure we'd talked about a lot of things after that, so what was I to make of the fact that her panties had left the strongest impression? While my memories of those panties refused to recede, I'd forgotten nearly everything else.

This, when she was cool.

Hanekawa was a cool person!

That fact only added to a guilt that I had no business bearing.

It needled my heart.

Hanekawa was so cool, yet the feelings that I harbored toward her bordered on lust...

But then again, I wondered.

How long had it been since I'd last seen panties in the wild? While Naoetsu High may be a prep school, half of its students are still high school girls. Some of them wear their skirts short for fashion reasons. While there were close shaves where I got glimpses, I probably hadn't seen panties worn on a girl in such a naked and perfect form...even in middle school.

Thinking back to elementary school... Well, no point in counting those.

Ah, then it was for the first time in my life…

I mean, it had felt like an '80s rom-com manga or something. And in a way I hadn't even imagined, a flag had popped up for me, like in a dating sim, over Tsubasa Hanekawa, a girl I'd assumed stood beyond my sphere of connections.

Dammit.

Wasn't that foul play? As in, I doubt a girl who saw a boy's underwear would start feeling the way I did?

No fair.

Of course, while I likened it to a sign popping up over her head, on further consideration all that had happened was that the two of us passed by each other.

We hadn't even truly met.

Surely Hanekawa didn't even remember talking to me a little past noon that day. So there really was no need for me to feel guilty, but…that's another way I was a petty fellow.

But anyway… As I finished my dinner, I began to think that I couldn't leave things as they were. When I realized that I might be living with a guilty conscience for a long time, perhaps for the rest of my life, I shivered.

A cool person.

And even if she wasn't, as "friends."

See, I thought, this is why I hate having them—my intensity as a human had dropped considerably.

I was having to worry about this?

And that's why once it was completely dark outside my window, I put the "studying" sign on the door and snuck out of the house.

To buy a dirty magazine from the one place in town you could call a major bookstore.

I completed my mission and began to head home, having bought two.

Naturally, I never try to do something as unmanly (?) as buy a dirty magazine together with a regular book to put on a show for

37

the bookstore employee. I'd buy two magazines rather than do such a thing. That's the kind of man I am. If Hanekawa is a class president among class presidents, I'm a man among men.

Though I do check to make sure there isn't anyone I know in the store, at least.

Anyway.

My plan was to read the dirty magazines so thoroughly that the images in my head would be overwritten. It was my own take on the idea Hanekawa must have had when she'd come chasing after me. While I ended up thinking that Hanekawa's ruse never had a chance of working (though I now realize, that probably wasn't her intention), overwriting one dirty thought with another was certainly a plan.

Erasing a memory might be impossible, but overwriting it maybe wasn't.

The issue was that it was the only one, unique. If it was one among many, then its presence would fade as a result. There had to be a large difference between naked flesh and photos, but quantity could make up for that.

Taking the nature of the earlier situation into account, both of the magazines I purchased had a primary focus on high school girls and their underwear. Since I had already bought a number of dirty magazines in the beginning of March, spending any more was a burden on my wallet, to be honest, but desperate times called for desperate measures.

Better a wallet-ache than a headache. I didn't have a choice in this matter. I couldn't allow myself to keep having such indecent thoughts about Hanekawa.

The guilt would kill me.

People talk about dying of boredom, but guilt can kill you too.

Oh, boy.

If only she'd just smacked me then and there…

"Still, friends?" I muttered, holding the paper bag with the two magazines in one hand and my phone in the other, checking through its contacts list. "It's not like...I need them or anything."

Still.

Being told that kind of thing made me think: When did I get this way?

I want to say I played well with others in middle school— to say nothing of elementary school. In that case, was it after I entered high school and turned into a slacker?

How simple.

I overreached in picking high schools, got in by mistake, fell behind, and...didn't see things the way those around me did.

Because I had failed.

No, was that really it?

Even then, I must have had a chance to fix things. My grades may have been poor, but it wasn't as if I was being discriminated against, and I wasn't despised. I should have had more than enough opportunities to make friends.

The party that was rejecting those opportunities was none other than myself.

"Hmm."

Sometimes, I just don't know.

I don't want friends, but is that just me making excuses for myself for not having friends?

Friends.

It's not as if I can't live without them.

People without friends can just hang out with other friendless people. Really, it isn't as if I'm alone—to give an extreme example, this guy who was in my class both my first and second years rarely talked to anyone at all as far as I could tell.

So it's fine. That's one way of living your life.

But...

"I don't feel like I want to make friends, and I certainly don't feel like I want a girlfriend, but why is it that I can't stop having dirty thoughts?"

Such a mystery.

A single pair of panties had shaken me so profoundly that I was ultimately moved to contribute to the circulation of currency.

Didn't I know that it was basically just a piece of cloth?

Before, I had wondered, "Why do girls go out of their way to wear those things and gussy themselves up? What are they, perverts?"

But I'd had it the wrong way around.

It's not like you can't buy those.

...No, wait!

Buying a used pair, that would be a crime!

Even if it's not technically a crime, it's downright criminal!

God, I wish I could turn into a plant.

Then I wouldn't have anything to do with these desires.

But turning into stone or iron? I've never wished it, nor could.

Is that just another way of being small—as a person?

"Ack, this late already."

Though I'd intentionally leapt into the bookstore right before closing time, it was quite late after all of the wandering around I'd done—in fact, the date on the calendar had changed.

It was already March 26th.

Spring break had officially started.

I put my phone back in my pocket and began to hurry home, my pace quick. The large bookstore I had gone to was farther from my home than what I would normally consider walking distance. In fact, locationally, it wasn't too far from school. I had more or less walked a distance that I normally biked.

Of course it took time. But I'd taken a little too much time.

I had no reason to get home early, but still, I couldn't be too late... There was always the chance my little sisters would barge into my room without asking, too.

Knowing those two, they were apt to put everything together if they saw that I wasn't at home but my bicycle was... They're perceptive when it comes to that kind of thing.

Oh, speaking of which, I suppose I've seen my little sisters' underwear before. They walk around in them after getting out of the bath, after all. But I guess that doesn't count.

Putting that aside...

Whether or not I was at risk of being discovered, it was late enough to be even darker out than when I'd left home. It'd be idiotic if I got myself hit by a car.

I think all guys share this anxiety; we are never more careful on our way home from buying a dirty magazine than on any other itinerary.

I mean, what if you got in an accident and your belongings were inspected?

A primary focus on high school girls and their underwear.

If Hanekawa somehow managed to find out about it...of course she'd misunderstand.

But that's not it! If anything, this is a way to safeguard your chastity from me... No, that's not my intention at all!

Well, to be honest, this kind of pointless suspense is more fun than anything else.

I couldn't deny that it was dangerous to be out, as dark as it was, but I lived in a sleepy town. There were few cars on the road to begin with, and they were easy to spot with their headlights. So my fear was irrational—but.

That said, wasn't it a little too dark?

I looked up toward the sky, and I realized why.

There was no light coming from the street lamps.

The lamps that were installed every fifteen feet were barely emitting any light—actually, less than "barely." Only one was lit.

Were they broken?

But so many of them couldn't go out of service at once... Was it a power outage, then? But in that case, it didn't make sense for just one to still be on.

And while I thought this—

While I thought this, I continued walking, with the vague notion that these things happened—no point in giving it too much thought.

I said earlier that I had no reason to hurry home, but come to think of it, my mission required that I return as soon as possible to peruse the publications I'd purchased.

My mission had utmost priority—

"Ye."

And that's why.

"Hail…ye thither. Aye, thee."

And that's why, even if someone called out to me like that, I'd ignore it and keep head—ye?

Who in this day and age called out like that?

Despite my intentions, I reacted.

I looked in the direction of the voice—and it was when I did that I was truly struck speechless.

Illuminated, under the one working street lamp—was She.

"It shall…be thy privilege to aid me."

Her blond hair looked completely incongruous for our provincial town.

Her well-defined face, her cold eyes.

She had a chic dress on her, and it too seemed incongruous.

No, in the case of the dress, I mean it in a different way.

Surely once elegant and refined, it was now anything but.

Ripped to pieces.

Torn asunder.

It seemed like a tattered piece of fabric, in such bad condition that even a dust cloth might look more proper—though to look at it another way, the fact that the dress still exuded a sense of its original extravagance spoke volumes on its own.

"Can ye not hear me? I am telling thee that it shall be thy privilege to aid me."

She—was staring at me.

I felt as though my body might freeze in her sharp, cold glare—but perhaps there was no need to be that afraid.

After all, She seemed to be dead tired.

Leaning on the lamp for support, She lay sitting on the paved asphalt.

No, "lay sitting" isn't right, either. It would be better to say that She'd collapsed. Glaring at me was all She was capable of.

Or rather…

Even if She hadn't been exhausted, hadn't collapsed—She probably couldn't have held me with anything beyond a glare.

To begin with, She had no hands with which to hold me.

Her right arm, from around the elbow.

Her left arm, from the joint of its shoulder.

Each had been—*lopped off.*

"…gh!"

And that was not all.

Her body was in a similar state below her torso.

Her right leg, from around the knee.

Her left leg, from the base of its thigh.

Each had been—*severed.*

Well, only the right leg showed an exceptionally sharp cut—I could see a clear cross-section. It looked nothing like the disgusting, torn state of the other wounds on the right arm, left arm, and left leg.

But the exact state of the cross-sections was trivial. To put it simply, She had lost every one of her four limbs.

And it was in this state that She had collapsed under the street lamp.

Forget about tired.

What She was, was dying.

"H-Hey—are you okay?"

They speak of your heart ringing like an alarm bell. I had always thought that to be a figure of speech, but it was exactly how it felt at that moment.

My heart rang so hard it hurt.

My heart—was running wild. As if it was trying to alert me to an impending crisis.

Like an alarm bell.

"I-I'll get an ambulance right away—"

She wasn't bleeding nearly as much as someone whose limbs had been severed should be.

But at the time, my mind could not process even that fact. I took out the phone I'd just stored back in my pocket—but was too jittery to press the right buttons.

Wait, what was the number for an ambulance?

117?

115?

Dammit, I should've put it in my contacts if this was going to happen—

"An ambulance… I have no need of such."

She—though every one of her limbs had been severed, still conscious She addressed me in her forceful, dated manner.

"*Instead…give me thy blood.*"

"………"

My fingers froze on the keypad.

And then—

I remembered my conversation with Hanekawa early in the afternoon.

A rumor that was only spreading among the girls.

What was it again?

What did we talk about again?

Night.

Something about night, and not walking around alone, and—

"…Blond hair."

Blond hair.

In the light of the street lamp, that blond hair seemed dazzlingly bright—and also.

No shadow.

With none of the other street lamps in the area working, and under the only one lit, She seemed to be basking in the spotlight atop a stage—blond hair truly bedazzling—but really.

She had no shadow.

"Not a shadow" didn't capture it. No shadow, for real.

And She said—

"My name is Kissshot Acerolaorion Heartunderblade…the iron-blooded, hot-blooded, yet cold-blooded vampire."

Her clothes tattered, her body limbless, but her tone domineering.

Beyond her parted lips were two sharp fangs.

Sharp. Fangs.

"I shall consume thy blood as mine own flesh. So—give me thy blood."

"…Isn't a vampire," I said, gulping, "supposed to be—immortal?"

"I've lost too much blood. Neither regeneration nor transformation is possible for me in this state. Unless something is done—I will die."

"………"

"A worthless human such as thee should be honored to become my flesh and blood."

My legs wouldn't stop shaking.

What in the world was going on?

What in the world was I getting dragged into?

Why did a vampire suddenly appear in front of me—to be dying already?

That which is not supposed to exist, a vampire, existing.

That which is not supposed to die, a vampire, dying.

What kind of reality was this?

"H-Hey."

As I stood shaken and speechless, She seemed to scowl at me.

Or perhaps it was a scowl of agony.

After all, She had lost all of her limbs.

"Wh-What is the matter? Thou hast the privilege of rescuing me. Is there any greater honor? Ye need not do a thing—present me with thy neck and I shall do the rest."

"B-Blood? Can't you settle for a transfusion or something?"

It was not a very thought-out question, even by my own standards.

What was I trying to say?

Was I kidding?

She...Kissshot Acerolaorion Heartunderblade, must have thought the same, and didn't reply.

No.

She just might have lacked the energy to reply.

"H-How much do you need?"

She answered this question, possibly because it was specific.

"For the time being, I will be tided over with thy body's worth."

"Oh, just my body's...wait!"

But that'd kill me!

I almost shot back at her like the straight man in a comedy routine—but swallowed my words.

Her eyes had given me pause. Cold eyes. Eyes looking at *food*.

She wasn't being the funny man, and was quite serious.

Worthless human.

She was on the verge of death. And was trying to survive—by eating me.

She wasn't seeking my assistance. She just wanted to *prey* on me.

To survive all on her own, you know?

"............"

Right.

What was I thinking—and doing? Why was my thought process premised on *helping* the woman?

How absurd.

46

We're talking about a vampire, all right?

In other words, a monster.

Who knew how She'd lost her limbs and ended up nearly dead there, but it couldn't be for any respectable reason. What good would come of getting mixed up in it?

Discretion is the better part of valor, no?

Why venture when there's nothing to gain?

She wasn't human, and existed apart from humanity.

An existence greater than humans. That's how Hanekawa put it.

"What is the matter? Thy blood. Give me thy blood. Hurry... Hurry up. Why do ye dally, laggard?"

"........."

Faced with this vampire, who spoke as though I would oblige as a matter of course, never dreaming to do otherwise, my feet took a step.

A step back.

I'd be okay. If I ran...I could probably get away. It didn't matter if she was a vampire, a monster. Her arms and legs had been torn off, and I'd get away—she probably couldn't even chase after me.

I just needed to run.

The same thing that I've always done was all I needed to do to reject this reality, too.

And when I moved my other foot back—

"Y-Ye jest..."

Her eyes grew weak and frail. As if the ice they had held until moments ago had never been there at all.

"Ye...fail to aid me?"

"........."

A monster, in a tattered dress, limbs cruelly shorn, shadowless even under a street lamp—

But I thought her, with her blond hair, beautiful.

As pretty.

I was drawn to her. From the bottom of my heart.

I couldn't take my eyes off of her.

And I couldn't take another step away.

Not because I was cowering in fear, or because my body wouldn't stop shaking.

I just couldn't move.

"N-No waaay."

Her haughty diction crumbled, and from her eyes—the same color as her hair, golden—overflowed large tears.

Like a child, she began to sob.

"No way, no way, no waaay... I don't wanna die, I don't wanna die, I don't wanna die, I don't wanna diiiee! Help me, help me, help me! Please, pleeease, if you help me, I'll do anything you say if you help meeee!"

She screamed, painfully, unabashedly, as if I wasn't there.

Uncontrollably she cried and screamed.

She bawled.

"I can't die, I can't die, I don't wanna disappear, I don't wanna vanish! Nooo! Somebody, somebody, somebody, someboddyyy—"

Who?

Nobody would ever help a vampire.

No matter how much she cried or screamed, I couldn't let myself be moved.

I mean, I'd die.

A body's worth of blood?

I'd always been too scared even to donate any.

It's just this kind of thing that I hated, right?

I hate being burdened by other humans, so a monster? The weight was too much for me to even imagine carrying.

Just try having a vampire as your burden. See how much your intensity as a human drops then.

"Waaaaaah!"

Her tears began to turn blood-red.

I couldn't say.

I couldn't say, but—it seemed to signal death.

A vampire's death.

Tears of blood.

"I'm sorry, I'm sorry, I'm sorry, I'm sorry, I'm sorry, I'm sorry, I'm sorry, I'm sorry…"

Finally, her words had turned from plea to apology.

What was she apologizing for?

Who was she apologizing to?

Whatever the case—I couldn't bear to watch her apologizing like that, for reasons unknown and to an unknown being.

I had a feeling she probably wasn't supposed to be doing that.

A being like her wasn't supposed to die so miserably.

"Unh… Aaahhhhh!!"

At that late stage, I let out a yell and began to run.

I forced my immobile legs into action—turning my back to her with all my heart and all my strength, I took off running.

I could still hear her voice behind me, apologizing.

Was I the only one hearing her voice?

Might someone else not go there summoned by it?

Kissshot Acerolaorion Heartunderblade.

Wouldn't someone try to help her?

…Of course not. They would die.

And in any case, she was a monster. A vampire.

No need to help her—right?

"Of course I know that!"

I slammed the paper bag I'd been carrying into the garbage collection area I'd come to.

The paper bag holding the two dirty magazines.

You're supposed to take your trash out in the morning, but there was no garbage collection on Sundays to begin with. My chucking them there nonetheless was a minimal show of conscience.

Some lucky middle school kid would probably come and pick them up.

It seemed like a waste, but I didn't need them anymore. If anything, they'd be a nuisance.

How could I be holding on to dirty magazines when I was about to head to my death?

Ahh! A guy had to be more careful on his way home from buying a dirty magazine than on any other itinerary—had I not known that damn well?

My intensity as a human had plummeted and crashed.

"........."

As I began to head back and return to that street lamp, tears began to fall from my eyes, too.

My parents.

My two little sisters.

As someone who had avoided human contact, those were about the only people who came to mind—and the fact that there were only four of them was enough on its own to make me cry.

It's not as if my family was particularly close. Especially after I began high school and started to fall behind, a weird, unbridgeable gap seemed to yawn open between me and my parents.

I didn't dislike them or hate them. It must have been the same for them, too.

Simply, a gap had formed.

These things happened during adolescence—I'd explained it to myself that way, but if I knew this was going to happen, I'd have talked to them more.

Snuck away and went missing, eh?

Ahh... My sisters would probably deduce that something had happened to me on the way home from buying dirty magazines, even though I'd thrown them away.

Oh well.

Even they wouldn't air our family's dirty linen.

I loved you, *mes soeurs*.

"......"

I wiped away my tears.

Hey, come to think of it, not having many people to remember was a good thing—if I had friends or something, I'd run out of time. In fact, the choice I was now making seemed possible only because I hadn't built any relationships beyond family.

And so I returned to the street lamp.

The blond vampire was still there, just as I had left her.

She wasn't even crying anymore.

She wasn't screaming anything, either.

Though she was sniffing and hiccupping, she seemed to have given up.

"Don't give up, stupid!"

I ran over to her as I screamed the words, leaned in, and then—

I thrust out my own neck.

"You'll do the rest, I take it?"

"…Huh?"

She opened her eyes. Surprise overtook her face.

"S-So you're good with it?"

"Of course I'm not, dammit—"

Bastard, bastard, bastard…

Why?

How did things end up this way?

"H-How? Of course I know how!" I screamed. "It's because I've wasted my whole life not doing a single worthwhile thing."

I screamed with everything I had.

"There isn't a single reason for me to bother staying alive, not a single reason for me to value my own life over someone else's, the world wouldn't care one bit if I died!"

Neither beautiful, nor pretty.

If that was my life, then to allow this beautiful thing to live…

Shouldn't the choice be for me to die?

Wasn't that the logical conclusion?

I was but a worthless human.

The vampire was a greater creature—wasn't it?

"I swear, I'll make something better of my next life. I'll be reborn as someone who's glib, who dances around relationships, who doesn't feel guilty over every little detail, who can leave things to chance without having to worry so much, who doesn't feel any doubts about insisting on getting his way, and who's able to blame everything bad in his life on others! And that's why—!!"

So I said, at least uttering the words myself my point of pride as a lower being.

"I'll help you. Suck my blood."

"………"

"I'll give it all to you. Don't leave a drop behind, wring me dry."

"Tha…" For the first time since she was born—I'm speculating here—Kissshot Acerolaorion Heartunderblade gave thanks to a being other than herself. "Thank you…"

Sshink.

A sharp pain ran through my neck, and I realized that I had been bitten by her.

I instantly began to lose consciousness.

And with my last wisp of awareness, I remembered.

Tsubasa Hanekawa. Her.

If I had friends or something, I could run out of time—okay?

Now, that was close. If I'd thought about her just a little earlier, I might not have made it—talk about annoying.

Well, fine.

We'd spent no more than ten short minutes together, but if I was going to die embracing my recollections of coming across Hanekawa, that wasn't so bad. And no, in this case, I don't mean my recollections of Hanekawa's underwear.

Seriously, what kind of way to go would that be?

Let me act cool in my final moments, at least?

And so, that is how I, Koyomi Araragi, after seventeen years and change, met my abrupt, unannounced, and unexpected end—

or should have.

0 0 4

I snapped back into consciousness.

It honestly felt as though I had been reborn.

Or rather, as if I had been revived.

"Oh! It was all a dream," I tried and yelled.

Of course, it wasn't a dream—if it had been a dream, I'd have come to in my room.

But this was not my room.

In fact, it was a place I'd never seen before. My little sisters, who woke me up every morning, were not there either.

"……"

Still.

I wanted to try going back to sleep again and again until I finally got the "It was all a dream" ending.

What was this place…an abandoned building?

I knew I was inside some sort of man-made structure, but… thick boards had been nailed across the windows to shut them tight, and all the fluorescent lights hanging from the ceiling had been shattered, without exception…

I turned my attention to my posture.

I seemed to be lying down. The floor was made of linoleum, but was horribly cracked.

I moved just my head around to get a look at my surroundings—

what was that thing on the wall?

A blackboard?

And...desks?

Seats?

...A classroom?

So this was a school... But it couldn't be Naoetsu High. I could tell that much. And...it didn't really feel like a school.

I was, after all, a high school student.

Though it wasn't my school, I could at least tell if I was actually in one regardless of all the trappings.

What was it, then?

What kind of place other than a school had a blackboard and tons of desks and chairs?

Then I understood. The atmosphere—it was a cram school. This had to be a cram school building.

But, uh, judging by how the place looked, it couldn't be in use?

The windows, the lights...maybe it had gone bankrupt? Or did it just look that way because it was so dim in—wait, dim?

Hmm?

Why was I—in a room with blocked windows that not a single beam of light seemed to enter—*able to see so clearly?*

I could tell it was dark. It definitely didn't seem bright. I shouldn't have been able to see the tip of my own nose, it was that dark, but I could see.

I could see clearly.

But...maybe there was nothing to it? Were my senses a little confused because I'd just woken up?

Wondering, I raised my body.

"...Ow!"

I'd bitten the inside of my mouth.

Huh?

Wait, were my canines always this long?

I stuck a finger inside my mouth to see what was going on,

and—

Moving my arm in order to move my finger, I realized, only then, that my splayed arm was being used as a pillow by a little sleeping girl.

"......"

What?

A little girl?

"...Whaaaa?!"

Indeed, a little girl.

She seemed to be about, oh, ten years old?

A blond girl wearing a fluffy dress that matched her, her skin so far beyond white that it seemed translucent.

Exhaling tiny breaths, she was fast asleep.

"......"

All of it was baffling.

Why was I there, where was I, and who exactly was this blond girl? Not a single thing made sense...but I was certain that I was in a bad spot!

That she was a little girl wasn't bad on its own.

But when you start talking about "unfamiliar little girls," things really start to sound criminal!

"H-Hey...w-wake up."

I tried shaking the safest spots on the blond girl's body that I could think of (like her upper arm).

"Nngh."

When I did, the blond girl began to groan with apparent displeasure.

"Just five more minutes..."

Such a scripted reply, little blond girl.

She turned in her sleep, as if she was annoyed.

"C-C'mon, I said wake up!"

I continued to shake the blond girl's body, paying no mind to her reaction.

"…Just 'x' more minutes."

"How much longer is that?!"

"…Four-point-six billion years or so?"

"That'd be enough time for another Earth!"

As soon as I yelled my retort at her, I put my hands to my mouth in a hurry.

Right.

Come to think of it, if I did wake her up, wouldn't I be worse off?

Clearly, searching for a solution on my own was the best course of action. Of course, speaking of solutions, I didn't even know what my problem was…

I decided to start off by looking at the wristwatch on my left arm.

Lessee.

The time was—4:30.

No good. I couldn't tell whether it was morning or evening from my wristwatch. I searched around for my phone…and found it.

The time on its screen stated that it was actually 16:32. The date was…March 28th?!

Umm… I thought back to the last time I'd checked my phone for the same reason, and back then—the date had just changed, and hadn't it become March 26th?

Two whole days had gone by?

"…No."

Even if it wasn't a dream…how much of that was true, I wondered.

That.

Those memories—how accurate were they?

I gently pulled my arm from under the girl's head, careful not to wake her. My first goal seemed to be to figure out where I was.

Sneaking, I headed toward the door of the room (classroom?)—which was unlocked. Well, it was more like it was off of one of its hinges, making it a very shabby excuse for a door. This dispelled my fear that I was being imprisoned in a mysterious facility (it may seem ridiculous, but I was actually quite worried about that possibility).

Sure, a cute little blond girl, but what gain could there possibly be in kidnapping me…

As I exited the door, I immediately noticed the stairs. A marker by the floor read "2F."

The second floor?

There were stairs leading both up and down. I thought for a moment about which to take—but the commonsense choice was the first floor. First and foremost, I had to get out of the building.

On the other side of the stairs was what appeared to be an elevator, but I didn't have to approach it to know that it didn't work.

I climbed down the stairs.

"…Okay, Hanekawa's number and email address is in my phone's contacts list, so I did run into her after the closing ceremony… And my memories before that must be fine, too."

So those panties were no dream. Even if it was like a dream.

"I have less money in my wallet, and I have a receipt…so I definitely bought those youth-oriented magazines on women's fashion, too."

Though my memories were slightly altered, I pretended not to notice and continued.

"But what happened after that…just doesn't seem like it could be real."

Even if it wasn't all a dream.

Maybe I'd misrecognized what had happened.

For example—there was an injured woman who had been hit by a car…and I was so surprised when I saw her…that I passed out on the spot?

Hrmm.

It was a bit of a stretch, but I had to start somewhere.

After that…someone carried me here when I fainted, and… nope. No imaginative tinkering could make sense of it. You'd just call an ambulance.

But the time displayed on my cell phone had to be real.

Crap, I hadn't been home for two days, and it would feel to them like three.

While it wasn't my first time staying out overnight without permission, three days was stretching it. Compared to my little sisters' wild behavior, three days out seemed altogether cute, but... I needed to at least call home as soon as possible.

At that point, I was still entertaining such optimistic thoughts.

The moment I stepped outside of the building, they were dashed. Avoiding rubble and metal and glass fragments and junk like strange signs, cans, and even cardboard boxes strewn about my feet (but really, why was I able to see so well in the dark?), I exited into an audaciously overgrown field of grass—and it happened as soon as I left the building.

My body.

My body, from head to toe—*burst into flames.*

I should've known. Why, despite it being late enough to call evening, the sun seemed so incredibly *bright*. But it was already too late. My body was on fire.

"AAAAAAAAAAAAAAAAAAGH!"

My shriek didn't even sound like a voice.

"Pain" wasn't the word.

My hair, my skin, my flesh, my bones, all of me—was on fire.

I was combusting—at an incredible speed.

"AAAAAAAAAAAAAAAAAAAH!"

Vampires are...

Weak to the sun?

Vampires, creatures of darkness, are weak to the sun, hm?

And that's why they don't have shadows.

But what does that have to do with m—

"You fool!"

The voice echoed from inside the building as I rolled on the ground, making full use of any and all knowledge I possessed about flames engulfing my body (I recalled reading somewhere that doing this would work).

I looked, with blazing eyes that didn't have an ounce of moisture left, looked in the direction of the voice, and there found the blond girl who had been asleep until just moments ago.

With a domineering glare that hardly suited a little girl, she yelled, "Get thee here at once!"

It was well and good for her to say that, but the pain was so extreme that my body wasn't behaving as I wanted it to—and the blond girl must have seen this because she braced and leapt out of the building.

No sooner than she did, her body burst into flames.

But she seemed to not even mind, and running to my side and holding me up by my armpit, she began to drag me right along the ground.

All as her body was covered in flames.

She dragged me—right along the ground.

She didn't seem to be all that strong. Her strength was that of a regular child.

She deserved some praise given how slender her arms were—but they weren't strong enough to hold me up.

All she could do was drag me.

Drag me—with her body in blazes.

It was quite a feat to muster that much strength while on fire—but it took the girl a fair amount of time to drag me back into the building, or in other words, into the shade, where the sun's rays didn't reach.

But what really surprised me was what happened next.

My body.

The moment we entered the shade, the flames that engulfed both my body and the blond girl's disappeared, as if by magic. And that wasn't all—our bodies didn't even have burns on them.

Despite those raging fires.

Our clothes weren't even scorched. Not my hoodie, not my camouflage pants.

In fact, they didn't seem so much as frayed.

Likewise for the blond girl's fluffy dress.

"Wh-Wh-Whaa...?"

"Honestly," the blond girl responded to my confusion, "what sort of dunce runs out under the sun with no warning? I take my eyes off of thee for a moment and look at what ye do. Have ye a death wish? Any average vampire would've evaporated in the blink of an eye."

"...What?"

"Never go into the daylight again. With thy immortality turned to a curse, ye'll be stuck in an eternal loop—burn, recover, burn, recover. Thy powers of recovery exhausting themselves or the sun setting—whichever comes first, ye'd live through hell. If an undead vampire could be said to live."

"Whaaat."

A vam—pire.

So—it really wasn't a dream or some misunderstanding.

"Y-You mean you're..."

Blond hair, dress.

And those cold eyes.

No, I thought, there was a huge age difference. While it may have been hard for me to make an accurate guess because the woman I'd encountered was fighting off death, I'd still say she looked, oh, twenty-seven or so.

She was clearly different from this ten-or-so-year-old girl.

Plus, her limbs. Her right arm, her left arm, her right leg, her left leg, the blond girl had them all. A ten-year-old girl's limbs, straight and thin.

She was clearly different from that limbless woman.

But—

But they had some traits in common.

The white fangs I saw inside her mouth every time she spoke, for example.

"Mm," she nodded, her attitude utterly domineering and proud. "Indeed I am Kissshot Acerolaorion Heartunderblade—you may call me Heartunderblade."

She followed this up with a terrifying statement.

"Four hundred years have passed since I last created a thrall, and this was but my second time—yet it seems to have went well, judging by those regenerative powers. No sign of going into a frenzy, either. Ye spent quite some time asleep, I was beginning to worry."

"Th-Thrall?"

"Indeed. And as a result, ye've…hm. Now that I think of it, I've yet to hear thy name. Ah, but what difference does that make? Thy past name henceforth has no meaning to thee. Be that as it may, servant—"

She laughed. It was a gruesome laughter.

"Welcome, to the world of the night."

"…gh"

And so, that is how I, Koyomi Araragi, after seventeen years and change, met my abrupt, unannounced, and unexpected end—or should have.

But didn't.

In a sense, though, my life really had come to an end.

No wonder it had felt like I'd been reborn. Because I'd literally *come back to life.*

A vampire.

A vein long since mined dry, whether in manga, movies, or games—one of those notions we now consider dated twice over.

But despite that, and despite being a high school student, I was fairly ignorant when it came to vampires.

Or rather, I didn't know anything about them.

The extent of my knowledge was that they're blood-sucking

demons that don't like the sun and don't cast shadows—and even that I'd only recalled while talking to Hanekawa.

What else, I thought—oh yeah, did they hate garlic?

I wasn't sure.

Which is why I didn't know—that *when a vampire sucks someone's blood, that person turns into a vampire.*

Having your blood sucked makes you one of them.

Having your blood sucked makes you a thrall.

I hadn't known that I'd be forced to quit being human.

One of them.

A thrall.

I'd assumed the result would be death. That was the logical outcome of giving away all of the blood in your body—and I had offered her my neck ready to die.

But—this?

I was hardly prepared to be a vampire. But there was no point in saying so now—no point in crying over sucked blood.

I'd been wrung dry of blood by her—and preposterously, had become a vampire.

There was no need for me to prove it to myself.

My body burst into flames under the sun.

My body recovered in moments despite having burst into flames.

My eyes could see well in the dark.

And the canines in my mouth—fangs.

Clear evidence, proof enough.

There was no need for me to search in vain for my shadow.

"Wh-Where am I?"

However. I, Koyomi Araragi, loser and chicken, not wanting to face the truth, started off with a softball question.

Second floor.

The two of us had returned together to the room where I regained consciousness. I seemed to be right about it being an abandoned building of some sort, at least, but the only room across all four of its floors where the windows were closed off with thick boards—in other words, where sunlight wouldn't come in—was this one.

Yeah.

Even if I was able to regenerate, I still wanted to avoid going up in flames.

What was the word she used again? "Evaporate"?

"Mmh," the vampire began, flipping back her blond hair, "they call it a 'cram school'—though it seems to have gone out of business a number of years ago. Now it's nothing more than an abandoned building. Convenient for concealing ourselves as we have been."

"Huh…"

So it really was a cram school. And I was right about it being abandoned, too.

But "concealing ourselves"? Get off it.

That made it sound like we were in hiding. She'd chosen a place out of the public's sight just so she could watch over me while I was unconscious, right?

"Okay, Kissshot. My next question is—"

"Stop," she, Kissshot, interrupted. "I said to call me Heartunderblade."

"But that's way too long. Heartunderblade? I feel like I'm going to bite my tongue twice just saying it. You don't want to mess up saying someone's name, right? Kissshot is shorter and easier to say… Or am I not supposed to call you that?"

"Uh…" Kissshot started to say something but shook her head. Her golden hair floated quietly through the air. "If ye be fine with it, then 'tis fine—I have no reason to deny thee."

What an odd way of putting it.

Oh, but if it wasn't a Japanese name, then was Kissshot her first name? In that case, it'd be weird if I suddenly started calling her that…but did such commonsense rules of human conduct apply to vampires?

"And what is thy next question?"

"Umm...I've been...turned into a vampire...yes?"

This second question was the one I wanted to ask her the most.

Loser and chicken? Well, it was the kind that someone who didn't want to face reality would ask, and as such fell in the softball category too. I didn't have to ask her to know the answer.

"But of course," she stated. "There's no need for me to spell it out to thee now, is there—ye have become my thrall and my servant. Consider it an honor."

"Your servant..."

She'd called me that earlier, too. Hmph...a servant. Strangely enough, the thought didn't bother me.

"So why do you look like a child now? Last night...er, two nights before yesterday? When I met you, you were more—you know, grown-up, and—"

"Excuse me for being childish."

"No, that's not what I mean."

More grown-up. And with all of her limbs severed.

That's what I wanted to say.

"I wrung thee dry to the last drop, even so."

She bared her fangs at me—and laughed. What she was saying was no laughing matter, but she laughed nonetheless.

"Yet that was still not nearly enough—which is why I've taken on an appropriate form. 'Tis better than dying, though I'm only able to sustain the bare minimum of immortality. Most all of my powers as a vampire have been curtailed—such an inconvenience."

Still.

'Tis better than dying, she repeated.

She didn't want to die, she said.

The image of her crying and sobbing floated through my mind. There wasn't a single trace of it in the way she spoke now.

It was then that I realized—long after the fact—that I really did save this woman.

I'd saved a vampire. Tossing away my own life.

"As thou can see, I was able to regenerate my limbs, at least in form. There's no meat in them—but they will suffice for the time being... But let me make our relationship clear for thee, servant. Though I may have taken on this guise, I am a vampire who has lived through five hundred years. Not to mention our master and servant relationship, in truth I am not one to be addressed as an equal by a newly born vampire such as thee."

"O-Oh?"

"What a vague reply—do ye understand me?"

"W-Well, yeah."

"Then as proof of thy submission to me, stroke my head!" she said, domineeringly.

....

I stroked her head.

Sheesh, I thought, her hair's so soft. There was so much of it, but it was like my fingers were gliding across it.

"Hmph. Good enough."

"...This is proof of my submission?"

"Do ye not even know that?" she said haughtily.

It seemed as though vampires operated under different rules.

"How ignorant. But ignorant as thou may be, I am glad to have a pliant servant—a good master attracts good servants. However, servant," Kissshot continued, glaring at me with her cold eyes, "ye saved my life. Saved it, even as I appeared in that unsightly manner to thee. Which is why I am of a mind to grant thee special permission to address me in that uncouth tone and to slur me by calling me Kissshot."

"S-Slur you?"

Had I basically called her by her first name after all? I felt like I'd really messed up...but I couldn't call her something else now, not after all that.

Still.

Kissshot had said another thing that bothered me.

—As thou can see, I was able to regenerate my limbs,

—at least in form.

It was true. While her petite, slender body was a ten-year-old girl's, Kissshot did now have her arms and legs.

At least in form?

They had no—meat in them?

"And…I suspect that I will have to rely on thee in the days to come."

"Huh?"

What was that supposed to mean?

That didn't just bother me, it wholly preoccupied me.

"Uhh…and that means?"

"But don't get carried away, my servant. A servant attends to his mistress as a matter of course. If I command thee to stroke my head, ye shall faithfully stroke it, no matter the time or place. Understand?" she said, puffing out her chest with pride.

Well, I say that, but she had a ten year old's body, which meant she had no chest to speak of. It was more like a child trying to stand her tallest.

…Though of course, the phrase "puffing your chest out" doesn't include "emphasizing your breast size" as a nuance. Then again…no, it seemed pointless to tease her about it. I couldn't see her giving me a proper reply, either.

I'd rib her about that later—I needed to get around to asking her the one thing I wanted to know the most.

I lobbed a lead-in question.

"Why did you—turn me into a vampire?"

"Hm?"

"I was ready for you to suck me dry—for you to kill me."

I'd even seen my life flashing before my eyes. I'd seen face after face—well, just four.

Or wait, had it been five?

I had a hard time remembering.

"It's not as if it was intentional. One whose blood is sucked by a vampire is turned into a vampire, without exception. There was nothing more to it."

"Oh. I see."

If I had known that…would I have offered her my neck?

I'd been ready to be sucked dry.

I'd been ready to be killed, too.

But—

Had I been ready to quit being human?

"Well, it's quite convenient for me. Guess why." Kissshot drew out her pause—and went on in the same arrogant tone as ever, "It is because there is something thou must do for me."

"…You said something about having to rely on me."

—To rely on thee in the days to come.

"Yes. My body could only recover to this point with thy blood alone—I am far from my full power. *Going forward*, thou must act for me."

"G-Going forward?"

"Indeed. I always act looking two steps ahead. For that is what makes me the iron-blooded, hot-blooded, yet cold-blooded vampire Kissshot Acerolaorion Heartunderblade."

"……"

What a long slogan. How many characters long was that when you added in her name? Plus, only the "cold-blooded" part made sense.

"What're you gonna make me—"

What are you going to make me do? I almost asked her the question—but that would derail the conversation. If Kissshot was going to try to make me do something, then that was quite worthy of discussion—but first, there was something I needed to ask.

I had the answer to my lead-in question.

So I asked her—the one thing I wanted to know. More than

any other.

"Can I—" I began, making up my mind and looking straight at her, to show that I had the resolve—depending on her answer.

"*Can I—ever become human again?*"

"...Hm."

That was all.

Kissshot didn't respond in any of the ways I expected her to.

I was sure she'd be mad, or bemused, or perplexed—but all she did was nod, almost like she understood.

"Aye—I thought so."

She even said that.

My predictions had been off—but it seemed as though hers had been spot-on. Even the fact that I'd ask. It was as if she knew all along.

"I understand how ye feel."

"Y-You do?"

A greater existence. Those were Hanekawa's words, but judging by Kissshot's tone, I was certain that she ranked humans below vampires such as herself.

For her, humans were lesser beings.

In that case—

Why wasn't I happy to have become a vampire?

Why would I ever want to go back to being human?

I'd thought she'd reply along those lines, but—

"Of course I understand," Kissshot said casually. "I was once invited to become a god, but I declined."

"A-A god?"

"'Twas a long time ago."

In any case, she said, sounding more interested in changing the subject than getting our conversation back on track.

"I understand—not so much wanting to go back to being human, but wishing *to remain as one is*. I thought thou might ask for that. While I did say, 'Welcome, to the world of the night,' I did not expect thee to wish to stay."

"I see—" I began, before realizing something.

I hadn't gotten a reply yet.

"And so? Can I—"

"Sure," Kissshot said, her voice a notch lowered. Her eyes were still as cold as ever. I might even say her gaze was piercing.

"Sure ye can." Despite that gaze, she declared with certainty that I'd be able to *turn back*.

"I give thee my assurance. Upon my name."

"……"

"But naturally, my servant, to do so thou must do *a few things* for me. I need not hesitate to issue orders to my servant—let's not think of them as orders, but as a threat. If it is thy wish to turn back into a human—obey me."

And then—naturally—she let out a gruesome laugh.

005

Dramaturgy.

Episode.

Guillotine Cutter.

Those were the names of the trio who robbed Kissshot of her *parts*—or so she said.

While Kissshot told me about each of them and their traits, words didn't seem adequate to the task.

It was like she was explaining in a foreign language, so my mental image of all three of them was fuzzy. But the most important point about them was beyond easy to understand.

The man named Dramaturgy: her right leg.

The man named Episode: her left leg.

The man named Guillotine Cutter: both of her arms.

They had taken her limbs. Which was why she'd been on the verge of death—in fact, Kissshot wasn't just on the verge, she would have surely died if she hadn't sucked my blood.

Despite being immortal.

She would have died.

And she understood that better than anyone else. She'd resigned herself at that moment. Though she narrowly escaped, barely alive, from the trio, escaping was all she could do.

"Why—"

As she explained this to me, I couldn't stop myself from interrupting her.

"Why would they steal your arms and legs?"

"I am a vampire. Ye humans—well, not thee, but humans call those like me monsters," Kissshot said matter-of-factly. "It is only right for monsters to be exterminated."

"……"

"Those three specialize in slaying vampires—it is those bastards' profession to kill me. Ye've at least heard of the existence of those who specialize in eliminating those like myself, have ye not?"

I guessed so. They were discussed hand-in-hand with vampires. My memory was fuzzy, and it wasn't like I knew all that much to begin with, but I had at least heard of them.

"So they slew you?"

"Don't be a fool, I haven't been slain yet—but having my limbs stolen hurts. I've nearly none of my regenerative power left, and in my current state, I can hardly fight."

"I see."

"Which is why," Kissshot went on, as if stating an obvious conclusion, "ye shall *contend against* the three and simply return to me my limbs."

"Huh?" I was dumbstruck. "'S-Simply'?"

"Well, though I cannot provide thee with details at the moment, in order to turn thee back into a human, I must be at my full power, in full form, so to speak. And for that, I absolutely require those limbs."

"B-But me, fight? It's totally not my thing, you know?" I hadn't done anything wrong, but I started to sound like I might have. "I guess my reflexes aren't terrible, but they're not great, and you can see how I'm built. I've never been in a fight before... Oh, and, wouldn't they just try to slay me, too?"

I, too—for the time being—was a vampire.

The chances were high. After all, I would be up against a trio whose specialty was slaying vampires. Even if they let me off the hook because I was a former human, why would they simply hand back limbs they'd won in battle?

"Fool. That was when ye were human," Kissshot said, appalled. "As my thrall, and now that I am at my weakest, it would be simple for thee even to slay me."

"Ha, are you weak for a vampire or what?"

"Nonsense!"

I got scolded. Basically, she was a scold, this one.

"How can thou reach such a conclusion from what I've said? I'll have thee know that I sit among the top rank of vampires. They call me the aberration slayer."

"The aberration slayer…"

If that was supposed to sound fearsome, I wasn't, you know, feeling it? To begin with, what was an aberration? Was it like a yo-kai? Whatever.

"Um, even if I'm stronger than you in your weakened form… Even if I am, those three were able to take your limbs from you when you were at your full strength, right? Your full form? In that case—"

"I slipped up only because there were three of them. I'd made light of them and was completely unprepared. I'd presumed I could take even three of their ilk together."

"Huh…"

"In short, faced one at a time," Kissshot said—overbearing-ly—"they pose no problem for thee. To put it plainly, 'tis an easy job, and a cheap price to pay for turning back into a human."

It wasn't as though her vague reassurances had persuaded me, but that was how I ended up walking around town at night.

It was a while after the sun had set that I was finally able to leave that abandoned cram school and grasp exactly where I was. The place's coordinates were on the outskirts of my already provincial town—in fact, I'd had no idea that such a building, some bankrupt cram school, even existed out there. I imagined that it was forced out of business when one of those major cram school chains decided to open up in front of the station. While it was perfect as a hiding spot, I was amazed that Kissshot had found it...

I'd already called home.

Fortunately, it was my little sister, the older one, who picked up. I asked her to tell the others that her big bro was using spring break to go on a journey of self-discovery.

She seemed to buy it.

...But didn't that mean she saw me as the kind of older brother who was at risk of setting out on "a journey of self-discovery" at any moment? Kinda pathetic.

Immediately afterward, I received a text from the younger of my two little sisters.

Both of them were still in middle school and weren't allowed cell phones. She'd sent the message from the computer in our living room.

"Dear big brother,

"I know that, at times, we all have to lose our way. But when you have a moment to reflect, try to remember. Where was it that Mytyl and Tyltyl found the bluebird of happiness?"

....

Chastised by my little sister...

I was honestly upset when I realized that I'd wasted some of my phone's battery on receiving the message.

I did have to recharge my phone somewhere... I couldn't just go home and pick up my charger, and maybe I needed to buy a new one at a convenience store. Since there was no way the electricity was turned on in the remains of that cram school, a battery-powered one. Of course, it wouldn't have to come to that if I wrapped it up before my battery died.

"No problem for me? They aren't *my* problem, okay? I should've told her they're her problem."

But...maybe it was an easy job after all?

While I didn't fully believe her at first, it did seem as though my abilities as a vampire were the real deal—but explaining how I tested them might be incriminating. In light of laws against the destruction of property, permit me to remain silent.

Hey, if a building is abandoned, then a little damage here or there—you get the idea.

"At any rate—I feel like we're overlooking something," I'd said.

Kissshot's words had left me wondering. That, plus the fact that the whole exchange had proceeded at such a clip.

"So, where are these three?"

"I haven't a clue."

"You haven't a clue..."

"Thy concerns are unneeded and uncalled for. Walk around at random, and they shall find thee—these are professional vampire hunters, remember. Finding vampires is what they do."

"Oh, yeah?"

"Aye. They should pose no problems while we rest easy in here, but if we walk outside at night, when our vampiric powers thrive—they will surely come buzzing like insects to a lamp."

"......"

"They must be roaming this town at this very moment, searching for me. With any luck, it will be settled tonight."

Keh heh heh, Kissshot had let out a disconcerting laugh.

Hmph.

Well, not having to look for them was neat... Because how would I even do that? I had nothing, least of all personal connections. No way.

Still—that conversation proceeding at a good clip didn't sit right with me. Shouldn't I be questioning a whole number of things? Even if it was a hard fact that I'd become a vampire? For example. I leapt straight on it when she said it, but...would I really be able to turn back into a human again? What proof did I have that Kissshot wasn't lying?

She could be using me in order to recover her arms and legs. Feeding on me hadn't been enough, so she was literally using me as her right-hand man—not to mention her other limbs.

No, Kissshot was clear from the beginning—these weren't orders, they were a threat. She would be relying on me.

…But if I got nothing in return, there was no way I'd agree to help her. And to get me to, she lied—and said she could turn me back into a human. Was that it?

Luring me. With a lie. I wanted to become human again—and Kissshot had predicted that from the beginning.

"……"

No.

If I was her servant, she didn't need to do anything so convoluted. She could order me, right?

…Mmh.

No.

In her current state, she had lost most of her skills as a vampire—so maybe she had to lie to keep me under her command?

That actually made sense…

While she did look to be about ten now, with that ten year old's body of hers…when I recalled her original visage, she seemed to be quite intelligent. At the very least, if she'd spoken truly, she'd lived for five hundred years.

She couldn't be dim.

And anyway—it felt like I hadn't asked the most basic question of all. It was as if I'd been so caught up in becoming human again that I was neglecting a crucial point: I hadn't asked why Kissshot was even here in Japan, and moreover, in such a provincial town, to begin with.

Yokai really didn't seem to be the right word. But in any case, vampires were Western monsters, right?

As for the three guys—hadn't Kissshot essentially brought them to Japan?

"…Hmmm."

Whatever the case, all I had were guesses. Whether or not Kissshot was scheming, I had no choice at the moment but to believe her, to cling to her words. It was she who had grasped the initiative, without question.

First I would get her limbs back—we could talk after that.

Her story may have been made up of whole cloth, but she couldn't have been lying about the vampire-slaying specialists, too.

And it was then, as I was doing as Kissshot had told me to, trudging along a sidewalk-less street as bait, that I came across a fork in the road—and it happened.

I had to wonder, for someone who had lived for five hundred years, could that vampire called Kissshot Acerolaorion Heartunderblade actually be pretty dim?

Faced *one at a time*, they pose no problem for thee—or so she'd declared, but where did that premise come from? She was the one who lost because *there were three of them.* Her own words!

Far from proceeding at a good clip—what an idiot I was.

But—it was too late.

Or, in a way, maybe I had realized just in time? I did envision that very situation a second before it occurred.

With any luck, it will be settled tonight—that was what Kissshot had said, but without any—it would also be settled tonight.

With me dying for a second time.

"Wh-What am I supposed to do?"

First, from ahead and to the right—

A massive man who looked over seven feet tall was walking my way, a greatsword with a wavy blade in each hand. They talk about a mountain of a man, and I could see his powerful frame all but bursting through his clothes; I could have used each leg of the jeans he wore as a sleeping bag, and you could've made five of my shirts from the material it took to make his.

As if to hold back his unkempt hair, left to grow for God knows how long, he wore a hairband above his forehead.

A grim expression on his face, his mouth shut and perfectly straight, this man slinging two wavy greatswords who seemed to be made of pure muscle—glared at me.

He looked exactly as he'd been described to me.

That man—was Dramaturgy.

The man who took Kissshot's right leg from her.

"U-Uurgh."

And ahead, from the left—

A man was closing in on me who seemed to cut a slim figure, and not just in comparison to Dramaturgy. There was still some youth left in his face, but there was nothing innocent about the look he gave me. While it's a common saying, if looks could kill, I'd have died then and there. That was how sharp his sanpaku eyes were. He wore a white traditional school uniform, which, depending on your perspective, really did make him appear young—but the gigantic cross he balanced on his shoulder with one arm did much to dispel that impression. It looked like someone had taken one of those plain crosses you wore as an accessory and multiplied its size fiftyfold. A lump of silver, the cross was comically large, about three times the size of the man, and probably his own weight cubed. It wasn't a stretch to imagine that the cross was used not as an instrument of worship, but in combat.

The man seemed to look straight through me, and even appeared to have a slight grin on his face. And together with that gigantic cross on his shoulder, he approached me.

He looked exactly as he'd been described to me.

That man—was Episode.

The man who took Kissshot's left leg from her.

"Wh-What should I—"

Then, from behind—

I didn't know since when, but a man wearing priestly robes who looked almost docile, at least compared to the two to my front, was following me. His hair brought to mind a hedgehog, but that was the only part of him that signaled danger, and his demeanor seemed downright peaceful. I couldn't tell what lay hidden in his eyes, so narrow that I could barely tell whether they were open or shut, and at the very least, unlike the other two, he had nothing, be it greatsword or cross, that smacked of a weapon—but that seemed to be the most notable aspect of this priestly man of all. For despite his appearance, he'd taken twice as many parts from Kissshot as the other two.

The priestly man, with his unassuming face and empty hands, closed in on me at a natural pace.

He looked exactly as he'd been described to me.

That man—was Guillotine Cutter.

The man who took Kissshot's right and left arms—both of them—from her.

"Heck, there isn't anything I *could* do!"

Experts at slaying vampires.

Dramaturgy, Episode, Guillotine Cutter.

The three men were converging—on me.

It was as if the forked road had been placed there for this exact moment.

There was nowhere to run. I was a trapped rat.

"Whaa? For real? Gotta love it."

The first to speak was the man shouldering the gigantic cross—Episode.

True to his appearance, his speech was a jumble.

"Ma-a-an, it isn't Heartunderblade. Who *is* this guy?"

"■■■■■■■■■■■■■■■■■■■■■■■
■■■■■■■■■■■■■■■■■■■"

So replied the hulking man—Dramaturgy—to Episode, ignoring me though I was caught between the two. His tone seemed stern and wholly solemn, but I wasn't able to make out his words.

While it surely wasn't out of consideration for me, the priestly man to my back—Guillotine Cutter—said, "Now, now, Mister Dramaturgy." His voice was gentle. "Speak the language of the land you're in. That should go without saying."

"…ck."

I made to look behind me, then realized that would mean turning my back on Dramaturgy and Episode. I was unable to move.

Guillotine Cutter, like the other two, paid me little heed and continued, "But it does seem to be the case, Mister Dramaturgy. I dare say—no, I'm certain—that this young man must be Miss Heartunderblade's thrall."

"Seriously?" muttered Episode, his displeasure evident. "I thought that vampire had a notion about not creating thralls?"

"She did create just one in the past, I've been told."

"■ ■ ■ …, perhaps, we drove her to have no other choice… but to create an underling to act as her arms and legs," Dramaturgy said, now in Japanese.

With his body that looked like a mound of muscle, I'd assumed he was a meathead…but he hit the mark when it came to what I was.

"Are you tellin' me," Episode said, the grin still on his face, the giant cross swaying on his shoulder, "the whereabouts of Heartunderblade, which we've had so much trouble ferreting out what with her faded presence, is something we can just beat out of this kid's body?"

"That would seem to be the case," Guillotine Cutter callously seconded Episode's menacing words—and Dramaturgy joined them with hopeful ones of his own.

"We'd better receive a separate bounty for slaying this boy in addition to Heartunderblade."

What had I been expecting?

Overlook me because I was a former human, after all? How could I ever think that? It went beyond wishful thinking.

From the outset, they were treating me like I was nothing.

Ignoring me the whole while.

They didn't recognize me as a living thing. My very existence seemed to count for nothing.

It was Guillotine Cutter who said, "Hmph. What to do? It will take a bit of work if we're to take Episode's suggestion and learn Miss Heartunderblade's whereabouts from this boy."

"I got this. Whoever smelt it dealt it," Episode said, laughing. "I'll kill him without doing any permanent damage."

"No, let me," Dramaturgy chimed in. "I'm the most suitable one for tasks like these. I get along best with vampires."

"I don't particularly mind doing it, either," Guillotine Cutter put himself forward too, albeit in a modest manner. "The two of you must be tired."

"D-Don't be talking crap!"

Gathering up my courage—I yelled. Not to any one of the three in particular. Avoiding eye contact, I yelled.

"Y-You guys, try to talk things out with me or something—don't be going straight into how you'll put me down… I'm a human, okay?! Are you gonna murder a human?"

"……"
"……"
"……"

While it was only for a moment, they went silent. It made me think my words must have gotten across to them.

But—that was all.

While my words may have gotten across, their meaning didn't. Not one of them attempted to respond to me.

"Why don't we do this the usual way," Dramaturgy said.

"'Kay. So first takes it?" Episode said.

"Very well. Fair competition provides a chance for all of us to hone our skills," Guillotine Cutter said.

And then—nearly simultaneously—the three vampire hunters leapt toward me where I stood in the center of the forked road. It was probably only thanks to my vampire eyesight that I saw their movements. Not only could I see through darkness, my eyes had incredible dynamic vision—but.

What good was being able to see them?

What could I possibly do?

"A…Aaaaaaaahhh!!"

The course of action I took was, in most likelihood, the most idiotic one conceivable. That's to say, holding my head in my hands, I curled my back and crouched down to the ground. I ditched offense, but nor was this defense—my stance was an attempt to escape reality.

It was impossible.

Of course it was.

What was I even thinking?

I wasn't the protagonist of some manga or movie or game—I was a mere high school student, so why was I out trying to fight vampire hunters?

What was this, some superpowered school action series? Of course I couldn't win.

So what if I'd been able to punch through a concrete wall? So what if I was able to jump high and move fast? What good would those powers do me?

Like I said, I'd never even been in a fight before—I had no one to fight with! I didn't know any martial arts or anything!

God damn it.

I'd already thrown my life away. Given it to Kissshot.

So then—why was I clinging to it so dearly now?!

"——ck!"

………!

………, ………

Yet…

No matter how much time went by—no matter how long I waited—none of the three began to rain down attacks on me.

What now—were they going to toy with me? Or was I so pathetic that they were stunned? Did I kill the mood by—no, of course not.

They weren't going to toy with me. I barely registered as there in their eyes. Which is why I lifted my face, buried in my knees—and peeked up.

And then.

"…Ha hah!"

I heard an easygoing laugh.

"You're in the dead center of a residential area…and yet you'd swing swords and hammer down with a cross and say menacing things? You three sure are spirited."

Catching both of Dramaturgy's wavy greatswords, one between the index and middle fingers, the other between the ring finger and pinky of his right hand—

Receiving Episode's gigantic cross with the sole of his right foot like it was all in a day's work—

Suppressing Guillotine Cutter's nimble move with an outstretched left hand, without even touching—

Who was he?

Some older guy just passing by.

Still standing on one foot, he asked, "Something good happen to you three?"

006

Mèmè Oshino.

That was the name given by the dude passing by.

I thought it was a ridiculous name, but there was no way I could tell him that, what with him saving my life.

Even if he did seem sketchy.

Even if he was wearing a psychedelic Hawaiian shirt.

He had saved my life—so I shouldn't say such things.

………

But whatta sleazy-looking dude.

"Umm… Oshino?"

I didn't know whether to call him Mister Oshino, and if I should be more polite in general. I may have owed him my life, but I had no idea who or what he was, so I wasn't stooping to stooping.

Friend or foe? Even if he'd saved me, I wasn't sure yet.

Though I'm sure "stooping to stooping" is an odd turn of phrase.

Nonetheless—I did express my gratitude.

"Thanks, you saved me."

"No need for thanks. You saved yourself, Araragi," Oshino said nonchalantly.

He didn't seem to be taking this very seriously.

In fact, neither did those three—as soon as Oshino got in the way of their initial attacks, all three quickly turned back the way they came, as though they'd decided to beforehand.

They had disappeared before I knew it. Without so much as a parting threat.

While I wasn't able to fulfill my goal of recovering Kissshot's limbs, my life did seem to be intact.

Just as long as this Hawaiian-shirted man—Mèmè Oshino—wasn't my enemy…or Kissshot Acerolaorion Heartunderblade's.

"Still, Koyomi Araragi—the name fits you. Nice and dramatic. Ha hah, but those three really don't pause to think, do they? No one with ordinary nerves would get down to it right here without putting up a barrier first. They must really be going places."

"……"

"Oh, don't be so guarded, Araragi. Your eyes are glaring. So spirited. Something good happen to you today?"

As Oshino said this, he pulled a cigarette out from the chest pocket of his Hawaiian shirt and stuck it in his mouth—I was convinced that he'd come up with a lighter next, but he didn't, simply leaving the cigarette there unlit.

"Anyway, Araragi, let's go home for now."

"Home?"

"That abandoned cram school."

He said it like it was nothing, then began to walk. I reflexively called out to his back.

"H-Hold on a minute, how do you know?"

"Huh? Why wouldn't I? I was the one who told that girl about the place."

The guy let drop incredible stuff like it was normal.

Whaat?

True, I'd wondered how Kissshot had been able to find such a place, but…he was the one who told her?

"Well, I was merely doing the right thing. That girl—Heartunderblade—seemed to be in quite a bit of trouble dragging your body around, so I told her about a good spot."

"Do you and Kissshot...know each other?"

"......?"

Rather than respond to my question, Oshino squinted at me as if my very choice of words was dubious.

"What is it?" I asked.

"Nothing. So you call her Kissshot."

"Huh? Yeah."

"As you heard with those three, most call her Heartunderblade... but I guess you don't, Araragi."

"Yeah...it's too long, isn't it?" What was this about? It bugged me. "It's not like there's a correct way to refer to her, is there?"

"Well, you're right. And if she made you her thrall, then I guess it's not too strange. Regardless of what regular vampires may do, she—Heartunderblade—is a legendary vampire. The aberration slayer, the iron-blooded, hot-blooded, yet cold-blooded vampire—"

"Vampire... So you know."

On further thought, it was awfully late of me to be saying this. It was clear from how he'd appeared out of nowhere and easily blocked the trio's attacks.

"Who are you?"

"Me? At times a mysterious vagabond, at times a mysterious traveler, at times a mysterious wanderer, at times a mysterious troubadour, and at times a mysterious nomad of the high sort."

Mysterious all the way through.

"A lot of times, a chorus of a woman's lowest vocal range."

"A lot... altogether, alto?"

"All too..."

"You didn't think this out, did you?"

Oshino shrugged in a display of irresponsibility and said, coolly, "I'm just a dude passing by."

Yep. He was sleazy.

"That's how it was today—and the other day too. I was just passing by when I saw Heartunderblade in trouble. Don't worry. I'm not an expert at slaying vampires or anything."

"......"

Could I believe him?

No, that wasn't it.

I could only believe him, I had no choice.

"Though I'm no amateur, *my specialty is broader*. People have me do a wide variety of things. But introductions can wait until later. Let's go back for now, Araragi."

In the end, I did as Oshino said. I went back to the abandoned cram school with him. There was still technically a possibility that he'd turn out to be a vampire-slaying expert who was after Kissshot. To say the least, however, he knew about the cram school Kissshot was hiding out in and could have gone straight there instead of wandering the streets.

That is, if he were an expert vampire slayer working separately from the three. Slaying her couldn't be hard then, given Kissshot Acerolaorion Heartunderblade's weakened state.

When I looked at it that way, Oshino was no simple enemy. Though he didn't seem like a simple ally, either.

Oshino and I wasted time on pointless chat (truly pointless, like about old anime. The conversation made me certain that friend or foe, I didn't need to use honorifics with him), and after about an hour's walk, we arrived at the abandoned school. Once we reached its second floor, Kissshot was there to greet me with a big smile on her face as if she had been eagerly awaiting my return.

Ack. The woman hadn't realized her strategic blunder yet... Awkward!

"Hm? Who is that behind thee? I do seem to recall his face."

"I can't believe you. Is that all I am to you?" Oshino chuckled. "I'm the one who told you about this secret base in the first place, Heartunderblade—my little aberration slayer."

"Ah...right. From then," Kissshot nodded.

Hmm.

It didn't seem to be a lie after all—Oshino really had met her that night. So it could be true as well that she learned about this abandoned building from him.

"And?" she asked, cutting off the conversation with Oshino as if she was completely uninterested in him—and addressing me.

Again, all that hope in her eyes! It made her harder to blame.

"Umm…I want you to calm down and listen, okay?"

Subtlety has never been one of my strong points, nor am I any good at euphemisms. As someone who's avoided relationships with others since entering high school, my ability to carry a conversation is unusually poor.

Anyway, how Dramaturgy, Episode, and Guillotine Cutter—all three—ended up attacking me at the same time.

How I wasn't able to recover her limbs as a result.

And how Oshino got me out of a tight spot.

I frankly explained it all to her.

By the by, Oshino took that time to gather all the school desks in order to make what appeared to be a bed.

Was he planning to sleep there or what? How carefree could you get?

"Hmph." Kissshot listened to the end—but didn't seem particularly let down.

I'd almost forgotten. It was easy to get confused by her ten-year-old appearance, but in fact she was far more grown up than me. She wouldn't just throw a tantrum. Even if she was, maybe, dim.

"What a predicament… So those three still act as a unit, do they? Now that they have me cornered, I was sure they would separate and engage in some free competition."

"So you did have a plan."

"They seem utterly determined to destroy me. What ridiculous obstinacy. Haven't they damaged me enough already?"

"They were talking about a bounty or something."

"Hrm? Ah, I see… That was how this age operates. Of course.

How heartless," Kissshot said. She snickered, apparently remembering something. "I can't allow myself to be this addled. Perhaps it's due to the time difference."

"You sound like a frequent flyer or something..."

Hm?

Oh, right—I could use the opportunity to ask her. I had been so busy caring about myself that I'd forgotten.

"Kissshot, why are you in Japan in the first place? And in this town in the middle of nowhere, too?"

"Hm? For a spot of tourism."

"......".

"I want to see Mount Fuji, the Golden Pavilion, and whatnot."

She said it awfully casually.

I thought there was no way she could be telling the truth... How was our town going to greet weirdoes who brandished deadly weapons in public that she might end up bringing with her on such a visit? Not to mention that neither Mount Fuji nor the Golden Pavilion was anywhere near our town.

But on the flip side, it was hard to follow up on a lie that blatant.

"You're not plotting to take over Japan or something, are you?" I said just to make sure before continuing, "Whatever. In any case— those three working together took you down even when you were in full power mode, right? Then how am I, your thrall, supposed to be able to beat them?"

"...As I said, face them one at a time."

"I can't do that if they're working together. You said we'd be fine as long as we laid low, but there's no telling when they'll find this—"

"That's not a problem," Oshino suddenly interrupted me. When I looked over, he was lying down on top of a makeshift bed he had finished building.

There was such a thing as being too free-spirited.

"I quietly went ahead and placed a barrier here while you two were asleep."

"A barrier?" He had used the term earlier, too. But what was it supposed to mean? "Like a force field or something?"

"Well, something like that." His tone made it clear that it totally wasn't and he'd only agreed because explaining it would be too much work. "It'd be a different story if they had an amazing sense of the territory, but those three foreigners won't be finding us here."

"...Listen, you," I said, making my suspicions clear, "what are you planning?"

"What am I planning?" he said, laughing frivolously. So sleazy.

How old was he, anyway? He had to be over thirty, but...was I, too, doomed to turn out like him after living for thirty years? Didn't people all become proper adults past thirty?

"Why are you helping Kissshot...and me? I'm starting to understand that you're not an enemy—even though I can't see you as an ally."

"What a terrible thing to say."

Oshino finally took out the cigarette he'd had in his mouth the entire time and returned it to his pocket.

"But like I was trying to tell you—I'm not out to help you two. There's no reason or need for me to help you. It's not even a matter of friend or foe. If it's a help, then you went and helped yourself."

"I have no idea what you're saying."

"What I'm trying to do is balance things out," Oshino said something more like it at last. "You could call that my job."

"......"

"An intermediary between here and there."

But, he continued—"Vampires may be a bit of a nuisance. They're too powerful, even for that side. Not only that, I have the aberration slayer on my hands. Hearing you talk about this, Araragi, you seem to be implying that those three attacking her all at once was a cowardly act, but that's not the case at all. That's what the girl—Heartunderblade there—is worthy of."

"Such praising words. Ye'll make me blush," Kissshot said, puffing out her chest, the one that was pointless to puff out.

It didn't quite seem like praise to me, but I decided I'd ignore that. The question now was finding out who Oshino truly was.

"Now introduce yourself. You said you would."

"Mèmè Oshino. A free spirit with no permanent address," he said. "Well, you can just think of me as an authority on yokai and the like—ha hah. Though unlike those three, I'm not particularly good at slaying yokai."

"Not particularly good?"

"To be a little more honest, I don't like it."

"But—it's your specialty?"

"Balancing things is my specialty, like I said. Standing in between and finding a happy middle ground. If you had to, you could call me a negotiator."

A negotiator?

An intermediary—between here and there? Where was "here"— and where was "there"? Here being humans, and there being monsters? But in that case—which side was I on now?

"Monsters. I like it. Though I call them aberrations."

"Aberrations—"

"And that girl there is known as the aberration slayer—you get what that means? She's the rare kind of vampire able to drain the energy from aberrations. And that's why the kid's famous—"

"I'll have thee know that I did not choose to be famous," Kissshot said, sulkily this time.

Ten is a pretty difficult age, I began to think, but remembered that she wasn't as young as she looked.

They say not to judge people by their appearances, but getting used to this would take time... Another reason I hoped she'd return to full power mode soon.

"Do not presume to know me, boy," Kissshot said to Oshino.

Calling that dude "boy"? Though if she really was five hundred years old, it wasn't exactly wrong. In fact, it was Oshino calling her "kid" and "girl" that was endlessly disrespectful.

But Oshino didn't seem to give a damn, and apparently not minding being called "boy" in turn, he replied, "You're right, Heartunderblade. I shouldn't judge others based on rumors—whether they're human or not. But listening to a bit of your exchange just now, the two of you seem to be in a pretty tight spot. I never would've expected complications."

"There isn't a thing complicated about it. In fact, 'tis quite simple."

"Maybe if you looked at it from a vampire's lifespan—but it spells trouble for humans like us. Right, Araragi?"

"Wait."

Wow. This guy understood the situation—yet spoke like I was human, like I belonged to this side.

"......"

"Hm? What's the matter, why that reaction? You want to return to being human, don't you, Araragi? Am I wrong?"

"Well, I do, but—"

"If you want to stay human, then you're human."

Oshino added, *Basically speaking.* Then he looked at Kissshot next with a sidelong glance.

"And Heartunderblade, I'm pleased. You made Araragi your thrall, but you do intend to turn him back into a human."

"Hmph."

While Oshino seemed to be offering Kissshot unqualified praise this time, she responded with a pout.

"Negotiator or whatever thou may be—do not speak when it is not thy place to do so, boy. I have never liked busybodies."

"Busybody? Oh, I'm anything but. Honestly, I'm the introverted type. But that doesn't matter. I don't mean to be a busybody, but—" Mèmè Oshino said, still lying down, his posture sapping all credibility from his words, "if you'd like, I don't mind interceding."

"I-Interceding?"

Between…here and there?

"Between us—and those three?"

"Who else?" Oshino nodded. "Honestly, I think that showing you this ruined cram school plus constructing the barrier was more than enough, but maybe we're tied by some kind of fate."

"S-So you'll save us?"

"I'm not going to save you. Just lending you a helping hand," he said. "The balance still seems a little off as things are—like you're being bullied. As I said earlier, I don't really like the kind of 'slaying' that they do."

"Does that mean…you're on our side?"

"Again, no. I'm not a friend, and I'm not an enemy," Oshino said. He was *neutral*. "I said I'd intercede, right? In other words, I'll stand in between. What happens after that is up to you. I'm not the one who's going to act. When life gives you the boot, you're the one who has to pull yourself up by its straps. I don't get involved in causes or results. All I do is tinker with the process in between."

"……"

I looked at Kissshot, but she seemed just as dumbfounded by Oshino.

What was with this guy?

Aloofly and airily—he'd manage this situation?

"Oh, but of course, this is my job, so I wouldn't do it for free. After all, I'm a wanderer, going from journey to journey. You don't want to run out of change on the road. Say, how does two million yen or so sound?"

"T-Two million?!" I shrieked.

Meanwhile, Oshino remained calm. "You can pay me when you have it. I won't ever bother you for the money. But I need to at least charge that much—or else it won't all balance out."

"B-But…"

I had no choice but to believe him. Even so—could I really believe him?

This passerby dude?

Between telling Kissshot about this abandoned cram school and saving me from those three—putting the stuff about the barrier aside—he did seem to have done enough to earn our trust.

Still. Something about him just seemed shady.

"…Tell us your exact plan."

It was Kissshot who, unlike a kid with only seventeen years of time on this planet such as myself, demanded the particulars.

"Ye speak of negotiation, but it could not be easy—there is no way to persuade those three. Given thy position as a neutral party, I cannot expect thee to return to me my limbs, can I?"

"Well, I couldn't do that much—I'd be a busybody. I haven't thought much about a plan, either," Oshino said.

As deflating as this was, it inspired more confidence in me than any talk that proceeded at a good clip. Because the guy seemed relaxed about this.

"All I can do is bow my head and ask them nicely. In good faith, too—if they don't listen, I'll have to fall back on dangerous ideas, but if we're lucky and they do, the game will be on."

"The game…ye say?"

"But the first order of business would be to split up those three. They pose no problem faced one at a time—isn't that your take on it, Heartunderblade? Then we just need to make that happen," Oshino said, as if it were the most reasonable thing in the world. "It will require taking on a little bit…well, quite a lot…of risk on your parts—but go along with that for me."

"I've been prepared to do such from the start. Ye can count on our resolve—mine, of course, as well as my servant's."

She'd gone and resolved for me, too. Hey, that's my resolve…

"Still, boy, how do ye plan on negotiating with those three?"

"Like I said, I'll bow my head and ask nicely—those three seemed like the type you can talk to," Oshino replied with what sounded like a joke.

Those three who didn't listen to a word I said were, of all things, the type you can talk to?

Just how much of a pacifist was this guy?

"The details are a trade secret, but…I'll ready the battleground. Then Araragi, you will get Heartunderblade's limbs back from them. If you recover all four—Heartunderblade regains her power, and you go right back to being human."

"…Recover, huh."

In the end, I had to handle the hard part. They posed no problem faced one at a time—but we were talking about those three.

Dramaturgy, Episode, Guillotine Cutter.

Wavy dual-wielded greatswords, a giant cross, an unfathomable man.

Honestly, I didn't feel like I could win…

It was something I had to do, since it was for my own sake, but I wouldn't be able to challenge them completely unprepared like I had that evening.

Then again, for the entire day, I'd done way too little thinking. I'd pretended to be calm when I was actually flustered. Not just me—Kissshot, too.

So if I was going to go fight them again, we needed some sort of measure.

"My servant," Kissshot said to me.

"What, Kissshot?"

"I can't provide human currency—I'm unsure how much of a debt two million yen is, but is it a sum ye could take on?"

"……"

"Worry not. The boy's skills are real—even if we ignore the fact that he taught us of this place and that he rescued thee. I can tell that much even in my weakened state."

"But—he's neither an enemy nor a friend. He's neutral."

"I'd never any expectations for an ally, and if he, privy as he is to my current location, were foe, then we are done for. There's no use worrying over it… If he says that he is a neutral party, then we shall not wish for more."

"…Oh."

That was one way to look at it. A reasoned, or rather, a harsh view. And furthermore, while there was no point in my saying so outright, it wasn't as if we'd be in any worse of a position if Oshino's negotiations failed.

It wasn't just her eyes that were cold, then.

In that case—there was only one question left unanswered.

The passerby dude.

Just passing by.

But the question was—

Did Oshino really happen to pass by?

He was there when Kissshot was at a loss as to where to go, and he was there when I was being attacked—wasn't that a little too much to call a coincidence?

Even if it was intentional, it didn't change a thing, and I didn't think Oshino had anything to gain by it—but passing by that often?

Yet—maybe that was it.

Observing a coincidence that had come to be, I was perhaps ascribing motive after the fact. Going down the same line of thought, even my encounter with Hanekawa, who left the school gates the afternoon after closing ceremonies while I was wandering around near school, seemed not to be a mere coincidence.

Come to think of it, if I hadn't run into her, I wouldn't have snuck out of the house that night to go to the bookstore, which is to say I wouldn't have run into Kissshot—or was I begining to overthink it?

Maybe I needed to call it all a lucky coincidence and be done with it.

For the time being.

Then again, "lucky" definitely wasn't a word I wanted to apply to encountering such a sleazy dude…

I absolutely don't like saying this about my savior, but to be frank, he's the sort that I'm least comfortable around.

Even so.

I made up my mind and said, "I don't have that kind of money saved up…but if I can pay you when I have it, and you won't bother me for it, and if you also don't need any guarantor or collateral…I'll take it on."

There was nothing else I could do. It was heartbreaking to have to take on a debt at my young age, but desperate times called for desperate measures.

"All right, deeal. Ha hah! Thanks for your business, as they say," Oshino cried, his tone cheerful to the point of being off. "Oh, and I'll be staying overnight here starting today. Hope I'm not too much of a nuisance. Well, actually, I'd had my eye on this place ever since coming to this town. I had to do the right thing and let Heartunderblade have it, but there really is no better abandoned building in town. So, what now? Wanna form a huddle to psych us up for tomorrow and what it'll bring?"

Oshino said this in a most un-psyched posture, still lying down— and of course, neither Kissshot nor I took him up.

Once again, midnight had come and gone without my noticing. It was now March 29th.

Speaking of tomorrow—today was already tomorrow.

007

Dramaturgy.

A massive man over seven feet tall.

A dual wielder of wavy greatswords, apparently known as flamberges.

A mountain of a man—a ball of pure muscle.

The hairband he wore to hold back his hair stood out, too.

And—he was a vampire hunter who had taken Kissshot's right leg from her.

After this and that—though to be honest, only Oshino knew what this and that were, and I had no idea why things turned out as they did—I was facing him first.

"Phew…" I sighed, slumping my shoulders, a little hunched over as I walked around the town at night once again.

The date was March 31st. The last day of the month.

If I took too long, midnight would come and it would be April Fool's Day… I needed to be careful. Don't get me wrong, I was already about to be in my last year of high school, so it's not as if I had any particular feelings about April Fool's Day. It was simply a matter of my mood.

While I have no feelings about April Fool's Day in particular, I don't like days that are like special events.

"Dramaturgy is a vampire."

I'd just been told that.

Moments before I was going to leave, in that second-floor classroom, Kissshot gave me another lecture about Dramaturgy.

This bit was new to me, though.

"V-Vampire?"

So naturally, I was surprised.

"He's—a vampire?"

"…Could ye not tell by the sight of him? Or are there humans who boast his frame? I've never heard tell of any in my five hundred years."

"……"

Well, she was right. He was more than just tall or muscled, he was on a different level. Still, did she have to look at me like I was an idiot?

"But why would a vampire be a vampire hunter? That doesn't make sense."

"Vampires who slay their own kind are not particularly uncommon. An eye for an eye, a tooth for a tooth, a vampire for a vampire, eh?"

"Wouldn't that make him a traitor, though?"

"We've no such concept," Kissshot said.

Even though Dramaturgy had, in fact, stolen her right leg from her, I didn't catch any traces of resentment in her voice.

"Or do ye mean to say that humans do not kill one another?"

"……"

"Listen, as far as I know, no species of animal exists that does not kill its own kind. No, even among plants, trees rob one another of nutrients."

Though strictly speaking, she added, vampires are not living beings.

What a fine detail to point out.

"Even among plants, huh? Anyway, I get it…but you do need to tell me those kinds of things."

"Hmm. I suppose so. In my weakened state and in this form, both my thought and memory must be slightly impaired."

"So, what should I do?"

"Oh, nothing special. Merely have a firm grasp of the characteristics of a vampire. And I've already taught thee, have I not?"

Advice.

Though her offhand remark hardly merited that name.

"I doubt Dramaturgy would use the tactic, given his position, but do be careful not to let him suck thy blood. Vampires who have their blood sucked by another vampire will see their very existence wrung dry."

That was all she said.

…For some reason, Kissshot's attitude ever since I woke up made it almost seem like she thought highly of me.

Like I would win anyway.

Like I just needed to hurry off and fetch her limbs.

Like I ought to, ye imbecile, get off my butt already.

Maybe it was this high estimation of me that kept her from scolding me to any great degree even when I failed. But while I was glad of her high estimation, I couldn't help but feel that she was overestimating me.

Well, the fact was that she saw me as her thrall and servant. She sang her own praises as a legend and the strongest, so she must have conferred that valuation on me as well.

Still, you know?

"……"

I walked forward slowly, stopping and starting intermittently, reading a book.

Its title: *Aikido from Step One!*

It was a martial arts training manual.

"Hmm…"

The first place I'd headed after leaving the abandoned cram school was the one major bookstore in town. The very same bookstore I went to before meeting Kissshot below that street lamp. I was on my second attempt, and possibly what you could call my first serious one, so I'd been expecting more constructive advice from Kissshot. Since I didn't have that to rely on, I needed to see to the matter myself.

And that is why I had the book.

By the way, buying a martial arts training manual on its own was embarrassing, so along with it I purchased a guide on how to play baseball and a book of lists of suggested classical music.

Though...

What did it mean that I was able to buy dirty magazines on their own while I couldn't overcome my shyness about buying such a manual on its own?

Thinking about that, I read as I walked—and soon, I had scanned through all of its pages.

Hmph.

At nighttime, it was convenient having eyes that could see in the dark...but what I was doing seemed far too much like a stopgap solution.

It wasn't clicking at all.

But then, I was reminded that the older of my two little sisters practiced a martial art.

Was it karate?

Right, while I may have had zero experience in real fights, if I counted scuffles with my sister, then I was quite seasoned... She didn't really know how to hold back.

But then, I realized what I was thinking and chuckled bitterly. I was about to fight a vampire, of all things. And not only that, it was a duel with a vampire-slaying vampire, and I was trying to learn from some last-minute cramming and fights with my little sister. I was being absolutely ridiculous.

Sheesh.

I really couldn't act serious, could I?

I was just a devil-may-care kind of guy when it came down to it. When exactly had I given up on living an honest life? And just then—

"Is that you, Araragi?"

I heard a voice from behind me. I turned around—and saw Tsubasa Hanekawa there.

She was wearing her school uniform, even though it was spring break. She looked the exact same as she did when school was in session, down to her glasses and braided hair.

"Oh—Ha-Hanekawa."

Wh-Why was she here?

There wasn't anything special about the location. It was just a point along the shortest route between the bookstore and the "duel site" Oshino had decided on.

A regular residential area, like the crossroads where I'd been attacked by the three.

Huhhh? Did Hanekawa live around here?

Don't tell me she picked up on the trigger word "honest" running through my head and was here to follow up? Was she that aggressive? Well, that couldn't be it, could it.

Naturally—I had begun staring at Hanekawa.

"Hmm?" She tilted her head, then suddenly held down the front of her skirt with both hands. "Oh, no. I'm not giving you a look today."

"……"

This woman…

She delivers a line like that with a straight face?

So adorable, dammit!

"Wh-Wh-Wh-What do you m-m-mean m-mean m-mean mean b-b-b-by th-th-that?"

I tried to play it off coolly, but instead I sounded like I was trying to rap.

"Um, no, stop, are you, I don't know what you're

105

talking about."

My voice was cracking. The reaction of someone who knew damn well.

"Hmm? So you forgot what happened?" Hanekawa said in wonderment, pouting her lips.

Forgot? Me, forget?

If anything, I'd expected Hanekawa to forget about our encounter that day soon afterwards.

"Even after you saw my panties."

"……"

"After staring right at them."

She remembered. Remembered it devastatingly well.

"Panties? Oh, you mean those items of clothing used in this country for protection against the cold, worn below the torso?"

"Don't act like you're from a different culture."

"…N-No! This is a misunderstanding, it's all a misunderstanding! I only saw the lining of your skirt! That was the only thing I was paying attention to, the lining of your skirt!"

"That's pretty perverted in its own way," she laughed at me.

She laughed at me…

No, that wasn't the issue here.

"What are you doing here, Hanekawa?"

"Hmm? Going for a walk? I guess?"

"What, at this hour?"

The time was nine at night. Right on the borderline of when it was and wasn't normal for—putting aside people like me—a serious student like Hanekawa to be out. No?

"I should ask you the same thing, Araragi. Why are you out here at this hour alone trekking like the Magnificent Seven?"

"How do I even trek like the Magnificent Seven all alone?"

"Hmm? What're you reading, Araragi? Is that a book about baseball?"

"Um."

I started by putting my manual away.

I doubted she'd be able to figure out that I'd become a vampire just from my behavior—but since vampires don't show in mirrors (so they say), I honestly couldn't tell how I was coming across at that moment.

Still, I had to hide what needed to be hidden.

First, my canines. I would be fine as long as I didn't open my mouth too wide as I spoke…I bet?

Apart from that—the wound on my neck?

The wound from when Kissshot bit me—but even if Hanekawa spotted it, I would be able to explain it away.

As far as changes outside of my body, being a vampire I didn't have a shadow—but as long as I didn't walk too close to a street lamp, she probably wouldn't notice.

What concerned me more than anything was how my clothes smelled. Being a vampire, I didn't worry about my body odor in the least, but nor did I have a change of clothes or access to a bath in that abandoned cram school.

I really needed to just go and buy a change of clothes…

I wanted to take a bath, too, just because.

But I basically wanted to allot whatever precious money I had in my wallet to the war effort… The phone charger cost more than I expected, and after buying the books, I was essentially out of spending money. Maybe I really needed to go by home at some point?

"What, is that book something you don't want me seeing? Hey, could it be something dirty?"

"Don't be stupid. I've never even touched printed matter as crass as that. I wouldn't want to sully my soul."

It was a blatant lie, but Hanekawa let me off the hook at that— cool person that she was.

"Well, yep, that's about it."

I didn't know myself what I was yepping or what was about it, but I was focused on cutting the conversation short and splitting—partly because I had to hurry ahead after taking longer than I'd hoped to read my book.

But there was also a more concrete fear I had.

Wasn't there a chance that I'd get her caught up in this?

I was a vampire, after all.

And so was the man I was about to meet.

There was no room for a regular person—Hanekawa—in that.

No matter how much of a model student or a class president, Hanekawa was a regular person.

"Hmm? Hold on. You're such a fast walker, Araragi. It's not every day we run into each other, we should take the chance to talk some more."

While I thought I had managed to briskly turn my back to her and walk off, Hanekawa caught up to me.

Just like she'd done that day.

"Talk...about what?"

"Hmm? Right—okay, here goes. Araragi, what did you study today?"

"......"

What kinda small talk was that?

I hadn't studied anything, duh.

Hadn't I told her? I wasn't the kind to study on my own during spring break.

Besides, since becoming a vampire my days and nights had completely reversed themselves, and in my mind "today" had just started.

"I focused mostly on math," she said.

"M-Math, huh..."

Ever since I started high school and stopped caring, I'd failed a test in nearly every subject at least once.

But math was an exception.

It was thanks to my ability to score well on math tests that I was able to cling on to my life as a student at a selective private school.

Even in the teachers' lounge, you could find people who, fortunately, equated being good at math with being smart.

That said, did I have the confidence to take Hanekawa on about math right then? The answer was an emphatic no.

I wouldn't stand a chance.

After all, if the rumors were true, Hanekawa knew her times tables up to five hundred.

Five. Hundred.

In other words, even a dizzying product like 456 times 321 was something she could supply without thinking.

Well, people who use abacuses can apparently do even more impressive things—but ultimately, no matter how difficult, math came down to multiplication and division. If you bypassed the hassle of multiplying and dividing, you spent significantly less time per question.

I was good at math precisely because it wasn't a subject that benefited from a lot of memorization, but even math fell under that category for Hanekawa.

Maybe she was far more of a monster than any vampire.

"U-Unfortunately, all I studied today was Spanish."

"Spanish? …Hunh," Hanekawa said with a surprised expression.

Did that mean she believed me? I hadn't actually expected her to.

"Too bad, I don't know much Spanish."

"Th-That really is too bad."

"Yeah. Just enough for basic conversations."

"……"

So she could handle basic conversations…

"Spasibo!" I yelled involuntarily.

"…'Spasibo' is Russian," Hanekawa shot back. "Also, it doesn't have any connotation of 'wonderful' if you wanna know."

"……"

I wasn't expecting to be hit with that kind of a correction.

Or rather—way to go, Hanekawa, you even guessed I'd used

the Russian word thinking it meant "wonderful"…

"You need to remember what words mean, Araragi."

"Y-Yeah… You really do know everything, don't you?"

"Not everything. I just know what I know."

"Ah."

Letting slip words pregnant with meaning as if it were the most natural thing, eh?

She wasn't a class president among class presidents for nothing.

…When I stopped to think about it, we were neither second years nor third years during spring break, so Hanekawa wasn't really a "class president"…but why split hairs.

She felt like a class president.

"Anyway, who cares what I studied," I said. "Every day is a new lesson for all of us."

"Hm? That's a pretty good one."

"So let's think about something more constructive. Like how to make society a better place."

"You're right," Hanekawa said, taking my makeshift excuse seriously. "Okay, what might we do to get rid of bullying?"

"……"

Like I'd know!

This was supposed to be small talk—spare me the heavy stuff!

She'd toss that at me without any sort of advance prep?!

"I know it's heavy, heavy stuff, but Araragi, we've got to start somewhere. Like they say, Lourdes wasn't built in a day."

"You mean Rome wasn't—"

Wait…didn't "lourdes" also mean "heavy" in French?

A clever one, wasn't she? She ad-libbed that?

"………Um, for starters, placing security cameras throughout a school should get rid of outright bullying at least?"

It wouldn't address the cause, but it'd surely wipe out the effect.

"Hmm. It's not bad as an idea, but there's still the issue of privacy. What about the locker rooms?"

"Guh."

She'd pointed out a major flaw in my plan.

People do get bullied in locker rooms. In fact, private spaces pose the highest risk.

"…Okay, I got it. As the person who came up with the idea, I'll take responsibility for checking the videos of the girls' locker room."

"What's 'okay' about that?"

Miss Hanekawa shook her head in earnest with a teacherly expression. I'd misspoken big time.

"And anyway, I wasn't really talking about the girls' locker room, was I?"

"Yikes!"

I panicked. Hanekawa continued to look at me, decidedly un-impressed.

"You'd peep, Araragi?"

"No, wait, I got it! I'll let you check the videos of the boys' locker room, so just pretend that I never said that!"

"No, thank you!"

…Wait.

That wasn't what was important here. I had to hurry up and get away from Hanekawa—I couldn't stand Dramaturgy up. And I couldn't get her involved.

"Hey, Hanekawa… Why don't you head home already? I was about to do the same, anyway."

"Hmm? Well, you don't have to tell me. That was my plan to begin with."

"Do you live around here?"

"Nope. I was on a walk and ended up here."

"…You shouldn't wander around at night," I said. "You might run into a vampire, you know?"

It was meant as a self-deprecating, ironic remark, but it wounded me far more than I was ready for. I didn't expect my own words to be so cutting, but on top of that—

"Actually, I was kind of hoping I would," Hanekawa said, almost playfully, as I thought that. "I guess it's only a rumor—but I was thinking I just might get to meet a vampire."

"Why?" I couldn't help but ask. "Why would you want to meet a damn vampire?"

"Oh, I don't have anything particular in mind. I'm at that age where you hanker after something out of the ordinary, that's all. I thought I'd meet a vampire, then have a little chat—"

"Bullshit!"

And like that, without even meaning to—I yelled at her.

Oops, I thought. I messed up.

"Huh… Hmm?" With a confused, vague smile on her face, Hanekawa hurried to say, "S-Sorry. I-It seems like I touched a nerve there."

"……"

It would have been easy to say, *Not at all.*

It probably would have been easy. But—I didn't.

Honestly, I was surprised; it wasn't Hanekawa who was confused, but me.

I'd thought I'd come to accept my situation and was keeping my cool as I dealt with it.

"It" being the fact that I'd become a vampire.

The fact that I was out to collect Kissshot's limbs.

I could become human again if I did that.

It was simple to understand, and simple to accept. Or so I'd thought.

No part of me regretted saving Kissshot from the verge of death—even in spite of my predicament, I could confidently say so.

Yet—a few little words from Hanekawa had rattled me.

When was the last time I'd yelled at someone outside of my family?

Oh, boy…

So my intensity as a human was still at an all-time low.

Well—I wasn't even human anymore.

And yet. Or rather, that was why.

Precisely why.

"…No," I shook my head.

Instead of apologizing back to her, I swallowed my words.

"You're the one who gets on my nerve," I continued instead.

"What?"

"You piss me off. I'm sick and tired of you."

As Hanekawa stood there, still with her vague smile as if she hadn't taken my meaning, I started hurling at her the most lacerating words I could think of.

It felt like abusing a kitten. In other words, it couldn't have felt worse.

But I had to say them.

"I'm alone because I want to be alone. Stop following me."

"Wait, A-Araragi? Why are you saying these things all of a sudden? Weren't we having fun talking until just a second ago?"

"It wasn't fun for me at all," I said, doing my best to strangle my emotions. "I was pretending."

"That's—"

"I was only after your fortune."

"M-My family isn't that rich, you know?!"

Ack. I hadn't meant to crack a joke.

I regrouped.

"…I don't know if this is some way for you to get good letters of recommendation, but what's a model student like you doing talking to a washout like me? You might enjoy whatever feelings of superiority you get from this, but I can't bear you standing there and feeling sorry for me."

"……"

Hanekawa's face went blank. But I couldn't falter. I had to keep going.

I took my phone out of my pocket and pointed it at Hanekawa.

"And don't mess with people's phones without their permission."

I made sure she could see my phone as I deleted Tsubasa Hanekawa's name, number, and email address.

"...So get out of my face."

Sst.

Hanekawa closed her eyes after I said that to her.

I wondered if she was going to cry. I hadn't made a girl cry since elementary school.

That's what I thought.

But rather than cry, she opened her eyes and smiled—though it was a weak smile.

Even at this stage?

"All right," she said. "Sorry you had to say all of that to make me go away."

Then, Hanekawa turned her back to me and ran off, leaving me behind.

Sorry?

Did she just apologize there at the end? After everything I'd said to her? Honestly, I had managed to blacken my own mood saying all those things—how was she able to smile at me like that?

...It was obvious why.

She wasn't like me. She was a really cool person.

I had to quickly part ways with Hanekawa before going to the agreed-upon location—I couldn't allow a regular person like her to get involved. That, of course, had been going through my head.

But far more than that, it seemed like I had vented my anger on her. Armed with a host of justifications, I'd taken things out on her.

She wanted to meet a vampire.

I had vented my anger on her for innocently saying so, when it was clear she didn't mean ill.

Maybe I was actually regretting it? Helping Kissshot?

Maybe I actually hated it? Having to get back Kissshot's limbs?

Having to endanger my own person to do it?

And there was one more thing—which truly scared me.

Did I…

Did I really want to return to being human?

I found myself in a living hell if I went out in the sun.

There were lots of other restrictions, too.

But—was I sure that I didn't long to be a vampire, an existence greater than any human, closing my eyes to those details?

In the end.

I had to be feeling nervous.

In that case, it was good that I hadn't simply parted ways with Hanekawa—it was good that I'd cut ties with her.

No, the two of us had probably yet to meet—

We simply happened to pass by, this time too.

And that's why.

That's why it was probably fortunate that we'd parted ways before any ties could form between us.

Was I lucky or what?

"Fine," I muttered. I took my phone, still in my hand, and put it back in my pocket. "That must have done something—to up my intensity as a human."

I was stronger—which meant that my battle with Dramaturgy, my mission to return Kissshot's right leg to her—would surely go off without a hitch.

Right now, that was what I needed to do most.

My heart aching was not a problem.

My heart aching was not the issue.

I stepped forward.

It'd taken me more time than I'd expected, but there still seemed to be no risk of being late—to begin with, my destination wasn't far from the bookstore.

The location of my battle with Dramaturgy, as specified by Oshino, was a spot I knew well.

The athletic field of Naoetsu Private High School.

008

You can't schedule a time or a place for vampire hunting.

The need can pop up whenever and wherever, and searching for the vampire to then slay is the vampire hunter's way—but it'd be quite a problem if such an extraordinarily troublesome, ultra-pragmatic, and dangerous doctrine were put into practice in a modern-day provincial town in Japan.

An intermediary between here and there—Oshino managed to live up to his boast, selecting a location for our battle where not a soul would notice us even if we were to rampage around.

I had to say, the choice of a school's athletic field wasn't a bad choice at all. A school at night was like a blind spot, in a way. A place that noisy and boisterous during the day undergoes a transformation at night—and gets no one's attention. It seemed made for vampire slaying.

Of course, we couldn't enter into the school building. With the teachers' room, the principal's room, and other targets for burglars inside, it was protected by a professional security system.

However—as long as you could scale the school's gates, its athletic field was accessible.

So, for a short period of time, there would be no witnesses.

An excellent spot for a battle.

"...But why Naoetsu High?"

"Because it's where you go to school," Oshino had answered me.

"Yeah, and I'm asking you why you chose the athletic field of the school I go to. I guess it's far away from any houses, so it might be a suitable battleground in that sense. But doesn't it seem obvious that it'll be hard for me to fight there?"

"Hard? You've got it wrong. It'll be easy," Oshino said, wagging his finger. "It'll be easy for you, Araragi. You're a brand-new vampire who turned just the other day, and you'll be facing an expert vampire hunter—wouldn't you want to go around on familiar terrain?"

"Gore Round? Is that some kind of vampire ability? I don't know how to use that."

"Go around. With a locational advantage."

It wouldn't be fair otherwise so he threw that in for free—that was how Oshino put it.

I understood his point—but still, I didn't like the idea of doing something as strange as this at the high school I attended...

Oh well. Let's see some superpowered school action then, quite literally this time.

"Sorry to keep you waiting."

My greeting sounded somewhat moronic. But my opponent had arrived before me, so it was something I had to say, even if I wasn't late.

In the center of the field sat the mountain of a man, cross-legged. With his mouth shut and his eyes closed, he nearly seemed to be in a state of Zen meditation.

In response to my voice, the man—Dramaturgy—said, " ■ ■ ■ ■."

No, I didn't know what he said.

Then—"Ah yes, the language of the land I am in," he said as he stood.

He really was huge. It was like he had to be careful not to hit his head on the moon.

Hm…?

He didn't have his flamberges? Those wavy greatswords?

Not even one?

Wha?

"Do not misunderstand—my brethren," Dramaturgy began speaking to me in stunningly fluent Japanese, though he'd taken so long that I'd gone and entertained suspicions about his unarmed state. "I have not come here to slay you."

"……"

What was this guy trying to tell me now? I flinched into a battle stance.

I mentally flipped through the index of *Aikido from Step One!* which now sat, with the rest of my bag, outside the gates. What moves could I use in a real fight… Umm…

As I was lost in thought, Dramaturgy repeated words to the same effect. "I did not accede to the pronouncements of that man—that frivolous-looking man—out of a desire to slay you."

"If you're not here to slay me—then what?"

That frivolous-looking man.

He had to be referring to Oshino. So he looked sleazy even to guys like Dramaturgy…

"I hope to recruit you," Dramaturgy revealed, forgoing any formalities and cutting straight to the heart of the matter. "I put this to you. Why not don the garb of a vampire hunter—like myself?"

"…What the hell." I put on a brave face in reaction to this unexpected turn of events. "Last time we met, you tried to chop me down, no questions asked—so why are you saying this now?"

"Episode and Guillotine Cutter were there at the time. I could not extend this kind of an invitation in the company of those two. But I would regret having to kill a being as rare as you—a thrall of Heartunderblade, the iron-blooded, hot-blooded, yet cold-blooded vampire."

"If I join you," I asked, "you'll return Kissshot's right leg—is that the deal?"

"…You're quite courageous to call that woman Kissshot, but your conjecture is incorrect. Your first job would surely be to kill Heartunderblade."

"Then it's not happening."

There wasn't any point in talking. In any case, I was going to turn back into a human—how could I become a kinslaying vampire?

Think about who you're talking to.

"I see. That is unfortunate. Truly unfortunate. I currently have fifty-three brethren—and you seemed fit to join them, as someone whose mistress seems to have little control over him."

Little control over me? Was it true, then?

Had Kissshot—failed to make me her servant?

"Fifty-three, that's a pretty big number. If there really are that many vampire kinslayers, then I suppose Kissshot was right. If I'd agreed, I'd have been Buddy No. 54?"

"No. You would have become number one in no time," Dramaturgy said with a straight face. "Incidentally, I am currently number one."

"…Hunh."

I'd never taken him for some grunt, so I wasn't particularly surprised. If such a vampire was so eager to slay her—Kissshot really had to be something.

The iron-blooded, hot-blooded, yet cold-blooded vampire.

The aberration slayer.

I see.

"I see why you wanted to have me join you, paradoxically enough—but next time, try a little harder with the invitation? Shape up or you'd never pick up a girl."

It wasn't as if I was endeavoring to imitate Oshino, but I tried delivering a sleazy line. It felt like the kind of moment where I needed to act cool.

"Ah." Dramaturgy simply nodded.

Of course the quip didn't land. How embarrassing.

…But this was my chance.

Dramaturgy had probably left those wavy greatswords somewhere in order to recruit me. Although I got that I was immortal, blades were scary, period—so I was grateful for this turn of events.

Dramaturgy's greatswords—with which he must have had severed Kissshot's right leg.

Of the four severed limbs, the only wound that had looked smooth, defined.

It actually seemed difficult to slice like that with a wavy edge—but if Dramaturgy didn't have them with him, it was an opportunity for me.

The winds favored me—perhaps.

"Then let us begin, pitiful boy. Thrall of Heartunderblade. You have no time to waste, correct?"

"Wait, before we do that, let's go over the conditions," I said to Dramaturgy, who had begun to loosen his arms, rotating them around and around. "We need to be on the same page."

"Very well. Then make sure we are."

"If I win—you'll give Kissshot's right leg back to me, right?"

"Only if you'd tell me Kissshot's location were I to win."

"Fine by me."

"Then it is fine with me, too."

Let us get to it, he said, rotating an arm—and striking at me.

The sheer speed of it belied his massive physique, his fist barreling toward me with his whole weight behind it like a pro boxer's punch.

I could see it.

I could see it with my vampire eyes.

But—even if I could see it, there was nothing I could do about it.

"Agh… Ah!"

A moment later—my left arm was gone. It hadn't broken, nor had it been torn off.

The impact of Dramaturgy's punch had blown it to smithereens.

"Ee...Eeeeeeeek?!"

It wasn't a matter of pain.

Fear had instantly overtaken my body. I mean—I'd just lost a fifth of it!

Reflexively—reflexively, and instinctively—

I started to run away from Dramaturgy.

But after no more than two steps, I tripped over my own feet and nearly fell—and it seemed to be a good thing that I had. A gigantic fist swooped through the air where my head had been only a moment earlier.

I barely avoided tumbling over, supporting myself against the ground with my left hand.

But my mind was racing—left hand?

Huh? My left arm should have been blown to bits—but it was there?

"..........!"

Vampiric—regeneration!

But really, it worked that fast?

While the fabric that had gone flying along with my left arm didn't regenerate together with it, my bare arm only emphasized the healing powers of vampiric flesh.

I had tried out my physical strength, but I hadn't gone so far as to test my healing powers—so I was gobsmacked. Though upon further consideration, there was the time at the very beginning when I'd experienced pure hell after exposing my body to the sun— so there was nothing surprising about this level of recuperation.

"What's wrong? Are you just going to run, thrall of Heartunderblade?!"

"Don't call me weird names!"

I began to calm down after seeing my left arm regenerate. All of the fear I felt vanished. Yes.

Yes, indeed.

My opponent was a monster—but I was a monster too now.

What was there to be afraid of?

"Raaahhh!" I yelled as I did a backflip.

My athletic abilities had unmistakably improved as well. I'd always thought that you needed a trampoline or computer graphics in order to do a backflip.

Then—I struck a pose and faced Dramaturgy straight-on for the first time.

"Ah ha. So you're ready to make a stand."

"Thanks to you—so I won't ask you to pay for the clothes you ruined."

As I said this, I began to think.

Dramaturgy.

A vampire-slaying vampire.

Kissshot had told me that all I needed was a good grasp of the characteristics of a vampire. If I remembered correctly—

They were weak to the sun. They didn't like crosses. They didn't like silver bullets. They didn't like holy water. They didn't like garlic. They didn't like poison. They died if you stuck a stake through their heart. Those were the weaknesses, right? What other characteristics were there... Well, first and foremost, they sucked blood, which resulted in energy drain. They didn't have shadows and didn't show in mirrors.

And indeed, even under the moonlight, Dramaturgy didn't have a shadow.

Just like I didn't.

Canines—or rather, fangs. I didn't really notice them on Dramaturgy, who tended to keep his mouth shut in a straight line.

And—they were immortal?

They had semi-permanent powers of regeneration?

They had eyes that could see well even in the dark?

There was also that bit about shape-changing, where they could turn their bodies into mist or darkness among other things, as well as the healing powers of vampire blood—but none of it really seemed relevant at the moment, I thought rather belatedly.

I didn't want to make light of Kissshot's advice—but since both Dramaturgy and I were vampires, it appeared as though everything, both our strengths and our weaknesses, cancelled out.

If I was immortal, then so was he.

In that case—was it down to experience and raw ability?

In terms of experience, he had to have a slight edge on me— well, okay, maybe more than slight. I'd only read an aikido manual on the way...

"So be it!"

Maybe Kissshot was rubbing off on me, because I screamed an old-timey phrase that I never thought I'd utter during my lifetime, and charged like a kamikaze at Dramaturgy.

"I had expected some ruse. I commend you for your guileless-ness," Dramaturgy said, meeting me with his own guileless attack.

Guileless. Or to put it another way, one-note.

No matter how massive his fist, no matter its astonishing speed, three in a row was pushing it. Well, it might have worked back when I was human, but now with a vampire's eyes, three times was enough for me to adapt.

Forward.

I ducked forward to evade his fist—then, as his log-like arm followed a beat later, I grabbed the earthen pipe of an appendage.

Using the momentum of my opponent's fist, and in one fluid motion—I transitioned into an arm lock.

Aikido from Step One!

"① Take the opponent's arm. ② Pull it toward you. ③ Slam down your opponent as hard as you can!"

Going back over the words, they seemed a tad breezy for explaining a technique to a beginner. But it worked.

The seven-foot-plus giant fell hard on the more or less unkempt field without so much as an attempt to break his fall.

Well—he couldn't because I was making him fall.

From there, I pressed down on his back with one knee and stretched his joints as far as they would go.

"H-How's that?!"

"…Too clever by half," replied Dramaturgy, his face still buried in the ground. "Guilelessness served you better—it seems you are still clinging to the common sense you acquired as a human. But I suppose that is only natural—*I understand as I was once a human too.*"

"Wha? Cut the nonsense and surrender already! If you don't, I'll break this arm right now!"

Oops, wait a sec.

I sounded exactly like a character who was about to have the tables turned on him.

It smacked of a cue.

…The common sense I acquired as a human?

Common sense—as in my line of thought?

"Oh…"

Right—of course.

So what if I put an arm lock on him?

What good would that do?

I was going to break his arm? Really?

And even if I did manage to break it—he was a vampire. Wouldn't it heal immediately?

"O-Oh sh—"

But that wasn't what Dramaturgy meant, either.

I doubt I'd have been able to do anything even if I'd wised up sooner, but as it was, I only grasped the true meaning of his words after both of my hands, busy twisting his pipe-like arm, had been cleanly severed.

Severed by him?

No, I'd practically severed them myself. *By gripping his hand, which had turned into a wavy greatsword.*

"Ou... Hrnngh!"

This time, I did feel pain—real pain.

Lacerating pain.

I'd be using that figure of speech with some genuine feeling from now on.

I involuntarily leapt back, distancing myself from Dramaturgy's body. My two lopped-off hands disappeared before they hit the ground. I looked again to find them attached to my wrists. They had come back into existence.

My physical regeneration didn't feel to me like I had grown new wrists, like a lizard's tail—it was as if my hands had simply returned.

And the severed ones disappeared... Or to be more accurate, it was like they'd evaporated.

It was a convenient system, so to speak. Leaving my severed hands on the school's athletic field wasn't an option.

Dramaturgy got back up slowly, unhurriedly—you might even say sluggishly.

It was no surprise that it took him time, though. After all, both of his hands had turned into wavy greatswords.

"......"

Shape-changing!

Vampires—could shape-change!

This guy *turned parts of his body into weapons!*

On that day, too!

It may have been at night—no, I could see fairly well at night with my vampire eyes—so my lingering human common sense was to blame. I'd dismissed the possibility because it went against common sense!

Putting his wavy greatswords away in order to recruit me had been an idyllic fantasy.

The two greatswords—had been *one* with Dramaturgy.

"What's wrong? Finished already?" Dramaturgy said.

Despite his advantage, his stern expression remained unchanged—in fact, having bared his blades, he looked to be getting serious only now.

There was too much of a difference in experience. Too much of a gap in general.

We were both vampires—but I could never be like him. His size, the length of his swords... Now that we were squaring off face to face, it seemed impossible even to approach him. His giant body alone must have given him three times my reach.

"I asked if you're finished. Are you not going to answer me? Was that not—the 'judo' of this nation?"

It was aikido.

But I wasn't good enough at it to be able to say that in reply.

It had been a fluke—I wouldn't even be able to repeat it, so if he asked about any variations, I wouldn't know what to do!

Dammit, why had I shown up empty-handed to begin with?

I'd never imagined they were a part of his body, but I was quite aware that my opponent used greatswords.

I should've come properly armed, too! If I'd only brought a cannon...

"Only"? I didn't have those kinds of connections!

"Hm?"

Hold on a second...

Maybe I did have a hand to play.

In that case—

"......"

"I see. So you've given up. Very well, then I will go next. And I will keep on carving up your body until your powers of immortality expire—or you cry out for death."

Dramaturgy began to move—and so did I.

But while he moved forward, I moved backward.

I was making a retreat—in other words, I ran in the opposite direction from Dramaturgy.

"! You would run?!" he yelled.

But I hadn't taken flight, nor was I routed. I was strictly retreating—retreating in order to set up a reversal.

A coherent plan had yet to take shape in my head, but I couldn't afford to hesitate—"so be it," indeed. It was somewhat inelegant, but I had no other hand to play!

I had Dramaturgy beat at sprinting speed if nothing else. By my rough estimate, Dramaturgy weighed over 400 pounds—and now that both of his arms had turned into those wavy greatswords, he could be closer to 650.

No matter how fast his fists, it didn't mean that he could move fast. Punching was a question of shifting your body weight perfectly.

While I was sure that he could run faster than a human, there was no way Dramaturgy could match me and my pure body weight of 120 pounds. I had to use my advantage to its fullest!

Still, I wasn't running away. And I wasn't fleeing at random. I had a destination in mind—it was about "locational advantage."

I wasn't the most serious of students, but I'd spent two years at this school—so I at least knew where to find *the P.E. storage shed*.

I arrived at the shed having put a fair bit of distance between me and Dramaturgy still giving chase—and kicked down its sliding steel door. I knew it would be locked, and even if it wasn't, I didn't have time to fiddle with the latch.

And—bingo.

Yes, P.E. class at our school included *baseball* practice!

I took one of the many balls from inside a cage and then tried to remember the contents—of that guide to baseball that I bought together with the aikido manual!

Thank goodness I'd flipped through it after reading the aikido manual just because I'd had some spare time. I would've been in trouble had my fingers itched for the classical music book instead!

"① Wind up. ② Transfer your lower-body strength to your upper body. ③ Swing your arm through!"

Again, this was too breezy for a beginner. It seemed like I had no talent for picking out reference materials.

Still—the ball flew in a straight line toward Dramaturgy.

As someone with no experience playing youth-league baseball, this was of course my first time ever throwing a ball in this way (unfortunately, baseball was an elective in P.E. class. I'd selected soccer), but as with the earlier aikido technique, this was what they called beginner's luck—the hardball landed right where Dramaturgy's lungs were.

"Guh…"

Dramaturgy, who'd been charging toward me like a freight train, crouched over on the spot as the ball rolled away. He may have been a vampire, but his internal organs seemed to function like normal internal organs, and he was having trouble breathing. Come to think of it, a stake through the heart killed a vampire, so it was natural for the lungs to work as lungs.

That meant an attack on the sensory organs would be effective, too.

Even in the face of immortality, there were ways.

Okay, let's keep this up, I thought as I grabbed the next ball.

I had a full cage's worth of them, an embarrassment of riches.

But my control was an embarrassment as in poor.

I seemed to have exhausted my beginner's luck, as the next five balls I threw didn't so much as graze Dramaturgy's squatting body.

One after the next, they dug into the ground next to him. They dug pretty deep, so much so that I needed to go over the field later with one of those heavy rollers or whatever the baseball team used. But even pitches with that kind of impact didn't serve their purpose if they missed.

And it was such a big target, too!

How would I ever climb the pitcher's mound in the majors like this? Climbing Mount Everest seemed easier.

"…You seem to be a man who is too clever by half and guileless at the same time."

Dramaturgy stood while I kept at it. He began running toward me again.

"But that, too—will only work once!"

".....!"

Dramaturgy and I were now thirty yards away from each other—or thereabouts? Considering his gait...he'd reach me in three seconds! In which case, being partway into the P.E. shed was a minus... Even if I wanted to run, I had nowhere to go!

Out of desperation, half-resigned, I threw what would surely be my last ball—

"Hmph! So long as I know they're coming, one or two balls as squishy as those will do nothing to stop me!"

Dramaturgy was saying this and charging straight at me when the ball crashed into his face.

The ball stopped him in his tracks.

Not that his previous statement was mistaken. No need for a retraction.

Because the final ball I threw—wasn't a squishy hardball.

It was a hard hardball. Almost a cannonball.

The shot used in the shot put.

"......"

Gosh, who left it inside a cage for baseballs?

This did deal some damage—Dramaturgy was covering his mouth with his two wavy greatswords and groaning.

Was it...taking some time to heal?

Didn't vampires heal wounds instantaneously, like with my left arm and my hands?

Was it the shot put?

No, why had I landed a hit with the shot put to begin with? Playing it back in my head, I seemed to have thrown it with some grace, if I do say so myself. But who normally threw a shot put like that?

Why—ah, right, its weight!

I should've remembered upon kicking down the steel door. Having turned into a vampire, I had greater arm strength. A regular hardball used in baseball must have been too squishy, and too light, for me. After the bit of beginner's luck for the first one, that's why my aim was so erratic.

Something like a shot put was just right. No, even a shot put was on the light side.

In that case...

"Y-You!"

Before Dramaturgy could lift his face—

I'd gone to the back of the shed and dragged out the concrete roller they used to smooth the field.

The roller the baseball team used.

Grabbing and lifting it with one hand—I wound up.

"If I can't even hit a big target, I guess I'll have to use a bigger ball!"

Then, transferring my lower-strength strength to my upper body—swing my arm through!

".........gh!"

But the instant before I did—

Nothing had hit him yet, but Dramaturgy crouched down where he was, his wavy greatsword hands raised toward the sky—and I stopped myself from swinging my arm through at the very, very last moment and instead slammed the roller into the ground.

A huge dent formed in the athletic field. I'd nearly crushed my own toes...

"What are you up to, Dramaturgy?"

"It is as it appears. I surrender," Dramaturgy said in his selfsame tone, his stern expression still unbroken. "Smashed with that thing, with your strength, the damage would be tremendous—it would take me two full days to regenerate."

"Wha...?"

"You seem to have misunderstood something. Not many vampires have the ability to heal damage instantaneously. True, amongst vampires I am on the weaker side when it comes to regeneration, but you belong to a wholly different category. After all, you are Heartunderblade's thrall."

W-Was that so?

Still, I couldn't take Dramaturgy's words at face value, so I kept up my guard. I quietly reached for the roller I'd flung to the ground in the nick of time.

"Did I not say that you were number one?"

"……"

"In spite of the gap in raw ability, I thought my experience gave me a chance, for now, to beat you—but it seems impossible. Netting you is beyond me."

"No—wait."

While he had me beat in experience—I had him beat in raw ability?

That wasn't how I saw it, and I still didn't get that sense.

"Would you be satisfied, then, if I said this? I will never lay my hands on you again, so please spare my life."

Dramaturgy said that without the slightest hint of a grin. The damage from the shot put appeared to have healed—he hardly seemed done for.

Was pulling out now the mark of a pro?

A professional. Quitting while both of us were still fine…

"…Kissshot's right leg. You'll give it back?"

"Yes." Dramaturgy nodded, then returned the wavy greatswords that were his hands to their original shape. "I am keeping it hidden somewhere at the moment—but I will deliver it to that frivolous man as soon as I may. Is that enough to make you happy?"

"…Yeah."

"Then we have a settlement," he said—and suddenly *began fading*.

I thought my eyes were playing tricks on me, but they weren't.

While a vampire's eyes could misrecognize, they couldn't be deceived.

His body—was melting away into the darkness of night.

Shape-changing. Turning one's body into mist—and just like that, Dramaturgy disappeared.

But after he had vanished completely, his voice echoed across the field.

"Thrall of Heartunderblade."

"What is it," I replied into the darkness.

"Allow me to invite you once more. Will you not join us?"

"Ain't happening," I flatly turned him down. The answer wouldn't change no matter how many times he asked. "That kind of thing doesn't interest me one bit."

"……"

"I've had my fill of superpowered school battles."

There was no reply to my line. He seemed to have completely melted away into the dark.

Would he keep his promise? I felt a bit anxious, but then reconsidered. It was to make that happen that Oshino had arranged this. And either way, this Dramaturgy vampire seemed like the type to keep his word.

Guileless and straightforward.

Another formerly human vampire, was he?

Well, in that case, it would've been nice to talk to him a little more—a part of me thought that, but nothing would have been more pointless.

The two of us didn't mix.

They were trying to slay me and Kissshot—and I wanted to get her limbs back from them.

It was that simple.

"…That takes care of the right leg."

One fourth of the way there.

It had only taken a few minutes, but it felt like I'd lived five lifetimes—my body may have been immortal, but this was rough work.

Rough work—but only three quarters left.

Right, time to tidy up and head home...

It seemed that thanks to my powers of recovery once again, I wasn't physically tired at all. But I was exhausted mentally. Clean up the balls, then flatten the ground...but what would I do about the steel door on the P.E. shed?

I'd kicked it down.

...Well, it couldn't be helped. I'd try my best to force it back into place.

"Um...so I guess I should start by cleaning up the balls I threw everywhere?"

And then—just as I lifted my face—

I think I've already hammered this point home, but—thanks to my vampire eyesight—I noticed someone in the shadows of the school building, far off on the other side of the athletic field.

"Someone"? Who?

It wasn't Dramaturgy... Could it be one of the remaining two? Episode, or Guillotine Cutter?

No, no way... I was supposed to face the remaining two at a later date. In that case... Could it be Oshino?

Despite all his talk about being neutral, he was actually watching over me from the shadows?

Just like the hero's master in a boys' manga!

I didn't remember ever agreeing to become his disciple!

Ah, but the thought still made me a little happy—

I even made such a mistake, but that someone wasn't Oshino, either. I took a dozen or so steps closer at an angle to get a better view of the school building's shadow, and finally, my eyes made out the figure.

Pupils that silently looked in my direction.

It was Tsubasa Hanekawa.

"......Wha?"

What? Why was *she* here?

She hadn't followed me, had she?

Had she tailed me? Even after I'd chased her away so meanly?

I was too confused to do anything and simply stood there like a statue—but despite the distance, Hanekawa seemed to realize that I'd noticed her and began walking my way.

Stomp, stomp, stomp.

I could almost hear her footsteps.

Ack…

She was three times as scary as Dramaturgy.

Why are girls so scary… Or did I feel that way because I was facing Hanekawa?

A model student. Tsubasa Hanekawa, class president among class presidents.

"What was that just now?" she asked straightaway.

In the time it took for Hanekawa to reach me, I'd decided that my best course of action was to play dumb, but her tone suggested that she wouldn't let it go at that.

She'd seen me…

She'd probably…seen everything.

Not that I'd be in the clear if she'd only seen the last minute… I'd picked up that roller with one hand.

"I went looking for you after that. I lost track for a bit, but then I found this bag in front of the school gates."

As Hanekawa said this, she held up her right hand to show me the very bag containing the aikido manual, the baseball guide, and the book of classical music recommendations.

"So I thought you might be inside school. I did have to climb over the gates, though."

"……"

Awfully aggressive for a model student. Still—leaving the books outside the gates was a misstep, though I never imagined something that minor leading to this fix…

"Hey, Araragi? I was too far away to see clearly, but…weren't you just doing something out of a fantasy novel?"

"…What's it have to do with you?"

It was all I could say.

Dammit.

Right when I thought I'd taken care of things for the time being by winning back Kissshot's right leg and earned myself a breather, I had to do it again.

I had to wound Hanekawa again.

"And why are you tailing me, anyway? I don't get it. I told you not to follow me around—stop pretending to be my friend just so you have an excuse to stick your nose in my business."

"…You're not the type to say that kind of thing, are you, Araragi?"

Hanekawa's eyes were honestly frightening. They weren't cold eyes, like Kissshot's—if I had to describe them, I'd call them probing.

Eyes that bore a hole, that saw through you.

Eyes that forced you to recognize how shallow you were.

"I feel bad that I'm making you say these things—it must mean you're in such a tough spot that your only option is to say them, right?"

Hanekawa held the bag in her right hand out toward me.

I took it.

If she was only here to deliver me some dropped items, our exchange would now come to an end.

"I'm sorry for taking so long to notice. But," she continued, "I want to help if that's the case."

"You're really pushy, you know that?" I said, squeezing the words out of my throat. "You're reading too much into things. I was just bored of hanging out with you. I prefer to be alone."

"Liar. You're not a misanthrope or the world-weary type, Araragi. I can figure that much out. At least, you seemed to be having fun when you were talking to me."

"Like I said, I was only after your fortune!"

"And like I said, my family isn't that rich!"

"Then I was only after your toddy!"

"I don't drink, and you shouldn't either!"

Not what I meant to say!

"No, I'm telling you I was only after your body!"

"Which is it, my toddy or my body?!"

"Your body!" I yelled. I didn't even know what I was saying anymore. "Fine then, I'll make up with you if you show me your panties again!"

"Okay."

Meanwhile—Hanekawa was utterly calm. Unperturbed, not even moving an eyebrow.

In one fluid motion, she turned up her school uniform's skirt, showing me the underwear it hid inside.

The deep-gray article was made of a felt-like material. It had a simple design, featuring neither patterns nor decorations, but that served only to bring out the flavor of the material itself.

"Is this okay? Can you see them all right?"

"......"

"Do you want me to take off my blouse, too?"

Hanekawa said the words quietly, still holding her skirt upturned.

Oh, I thought.

Now, for the first time.

I was finally meeting Hanekawa. We weren't passing by each other—we had met, head-on.

Right. She was a cool person—but that wasn't all.

She was a strong person.

Compared to me—she wasn't even in the same league.

"...I said some horrible things. I'm sorry."

I bowed my head, bending forward as far as my body would let me.

Hanekawa still had her skirt held up, but it should go without saying that I wasn't bowing my head in order to get a better view.

It was to apologize to her.
And to ask her.
"Please be my friend."

0 0 9

There was something I had to do before explaining the situation to Hanekawa, though—not to mention the fact that it was already far too late at night. I had her go home for the time being, with the promise that I'd tell her everything tomorrow night.

I then went back to the abandoned cram school. Oshino was out, but Kissshot was waiting in the second-floor classroom. I told her that I'd managed to get her right leg back for now.

"Well done," Kissshot said. "But of course, I should expect no less from my thrall. As one who has inherited my power, thou must have had no trouble handling the likes of Dramaturgy."

"I had plenty of trouble... He knows when to accept defeat, though."

"Hmph. Well, Dramaturgy is the most understanding of those three—I do not mean to frighten thee, but it won't be the same with the other two."

"Yeah, I bet..."

Episode.

He even looked like bad news, with that gigantic cross slung over his shoulder—and then there was that priestly man...Guillotine Cutter.

Whatever he wasn't showing was bad news, no doubt.

"Still, take this moment to rejoice. Ye've drawn a sure step closer to humanity."

"Have I really…?"

If anything, I felt like I'd become less human.

"Dramaturgy had superhuman strength, but my powers of regeneration seemed to outdo his. Anyway, I wanted to ask you just for my own reference—how many times can I die?"

"A good question," Kissshot replied. "And one we won't know the answer to until we try to find out."

"I'd rather not."

The two of us kept up our conversation, equal parts celebration and review, until before dawn. Around the time I finally began to feel sleepy, Oshino returned.

He wore the same Hawaiian stuff as always. He did seem to own multiple shirts, but they uniformly featured psychedelic designs like it was a political statement of some sort.

He was empty-handed when I met him at the crossroads, but at some point, he had obtained the bare minimum of daily sundries and supplies. He seemed to be no stranger to camping out.

"…Speaking of which, your dress never seems to get any dirtier. How does that work?"

"Hm? Well, vampire clothes are almost a part of our bodies," replied the ever-dress-clad Kissshot, even though I looked like the frontman of a rock band with my left sleeve torn courtesy of Dramaturgy. "He turned to mist along with his attire, did he not?"

"So his clothes are a part of him just like those wavy greatswords."

"Attire owes more to an ability to generate matter. At times I, too, wield a sword in battle, but unlike Dramaturgy, I employ my powers of matter generation to do so, not those of transformation."

"That's amazing…"

Where are you, laws of conservation of energy and mass?

Oh well. Something must have happened to them.

And in due course—

"Welcome back, Oshino."

"I'm ho-o-ome!"

The man waved casually, a Boston bag in his hand—could Kissshot's right leg be inside?

"Good job, Araragi."

"I didn't really do that much."

"What're you talking about? You put in some hard work. I know, I was watching over you from the shadows."

"…You were?"

"Yep," Oshino said, nodding. "So guess what, I also know that you made a girl pull up her own skirt."

"……"

I recalled feeling a bit happy when I'd mistaken Hanekawa hiding in the shadows of the school for Oshino, but now I only felt embarrassed.

But he really was watching, huh…

Still, why say that in front of Kissshot?! Look, she's tilting her head disapprovingly!

"Um…Oshino?"

"Oh, no need to worry. I was watching you from the front, so I couldn't see that girl's panties from my angle."

"That's not what I was worried about!"

"You've got a good friend. Is she a classmate?"

"We're in different classes. But yeah…she's a friend. Her name is Tsubasa Hanekawa. She's a class president among class presidents," I said, though it was embarrassing in its own way.

Huh, Oshino mumbled noncommittally. "In any case, you should properly explain the situation to any witnesses—especially her, since she seemed like a smart one."

"That was my plan. I don't know how to explain it, though."

"There's always the option of pushing her away."

"I've already tried. And failed."

"Did you, now. Well, you are dealing with a girl. There's no such thing as being too sensitive."

"I don't think it matters if I'm dealing with a boy or a girl in this situation."

"What's this, now? Is that really your level of awareness? Unlike girls, boys don't come up with creative dance routines, do they?"

"...Man, you say that like girls have more originality, but it's just that only they have a creative dance component in P.E."

What a way to judge me and my originality.

"But Araragi, you're the one who'll be fretting because you can't dance when the story of our everyday lives gets turned into an anime."

"Why would our everyday lives get turned into an anime?!"

"Because a drama CD can't convey that wonderful face you make when you act the straight man."

"Our everyday lives were a drama CD?!"

"It'll be fun, though. It'll be like the ending of *Demon-Lord Hero Legend Wataru*."

"I don't think I was even born when that was on the air!"

"You say that, but I see your Kyocera phone. The prospect is so on your mind."

"What sort of roundabout appeal am I making?!"

But point taken, it was a mystery to us boys what the girls did during creative dance class... Honestly, I didn't have the first clue.

"Well, being a man myself, I don't exactly know what they do, either," Oshino admitted. "But I bet they could never show to boys the kinds of immodest dances they—"

"What? Now you've got me interested!"

"Why else would those classes only be for girls?"

"Hmm."

I had a feeling he was on the wrong track, but it was also true that boys were always out on the athletic field during P.E. when the girls were inside doing creative dance. Was that like quarantining?

"Oh, but Oshino, speaking of girls only, there's another thing about Phys Ed that makes me wonder. During health classes in middle school, there were just a couple of times when they split up the boys and the girls. These were lectures and had nothing to do with stamina and all. I wonder what the girls were learning then."

"Araragi, that—" Oshino began, but he thought better of it and coughed mid-sentence. "That, I don't know. There are some things even I don't know."

"Yup. I thought so."

"Hey, why don't you ask that Tsubasa Hanekawa girl when you explain the situation to her? I bet she'll tell you."

"Oh, that makes sense. Good idea."

What was it that I was feeling?

The air was buzzing with a faint degree of malice…

"There," Kissshot finally stepped in. "Done chatting?"

"Hm? Oh—ha hah, you seem to be in good spirits too, Heartunderblade. Anything good happened to you lately? Sure it did."

Laughing, Oshino undid the zipper of his Boston bag.

He then stuck his hand inside—and pulled out Kissshot's right leg.

"……"

It had been placed inside as-is. Not kept in a case or wrapped in plastic. Just the bare leg, stuffed inside. Like something a sick murderer would do…

It was an adult woman's leg. Slender—and pretty. Neither bleeding nor rotting, no doubt because it was a vampire's leg…

"He really did give it back."

Dramaturgy. The vampire-slaying vampire.

"That's what a negotiator is for. I wish you'd at least put that much trust in me—there's nothing more important than a relationship based on trust, you know. There's no negotiating without it. They might be expert vampire hunters, but I'm a pro in my own right, and on such a point I'd never let them breach a contract—here, Heartunderblade."

Oshino casually handed Kissshot her right leg, and she took it from him.

What a sight.

"…Wait, what're you going to do? That leg doesn't match your current size… You aren't just swapping them, are you?"

"I do this," Kissshot said.

Cradling her right leg with both arms, she opened wide and sunk her teeth into it.

From there, she simply began eating.

Chew chew. Chomp chomp. Gnaw gnaw.

Meat and bone together.

"……"

Okay, no anime adaptation.

A ten-year-old girl eating the right leg of an adult woman…and apparently finding it pretty tasty.

"Hm?" Kissshot glanced in our direction. "Don't be standing there gaping, fools—leave me to myself as I eat. Where are thy manners?"

"Uh huh…"

Whatever, it wasn't like I wanted to watch.

Hardly needing the prodding, Oshino and I left the classroom, went out into the hallway, and closed the door without looking back.

Oshino was snickering.

What was so funny? All I could do was sigh.

"By the way, Oshino. While Kissshot is taking her meal, there was something I wanted to ask you."

"Hm? What is it?"

"You must already know if you were watching, but Dramaturgy blew away my left arm—but I recovered instantly. So fast that 'recovered' isn't the right word. So why didn't Kissshot's limbs regenerate at all?"

"Don't you think it's because Heartunderblade had lost nearly

144

all of her immortal force by the time you met her?"

"Well, yes, I did think of that. But when my hands were cut off, the old ones disappeared by the time I was healed. So I thought maybe Kissshot's limbs might have disappeared, too—but that wasn't the case, either. I was wondering why. They didn't regenerate, and they didn't disappear…"

"That kid is a rare breed, Araragi," Oshino answered without holding back. "Those guys want her body intact—to steal it and make it their own."

"……"

"Intact, but piece by piece. In other words, it wasn't her limbs that they took from her as much as her existence as a vampire. That's why the severed limbs neither regenerate nor disappear. It's an extremely bothersome thing they're doing. Denying her limbs the opportunity to disappear also blocks their regeneration—when you think about it, it's a very good way to *disable an aberration slayer.* Araragi, you ought to be careful too," Oshino said, his tone turning vicious. "It seems like Dramaturgy actually wanted you to join him, but you're Kissshot's thrall. Who's to say they won't steal your body to make a specimen out of you?"

"R-Really?"

"Ha hah! You bought it. Well, it's a unique technique that can't be used very frequently. Don't worry, they wouldn't try—and it probably took all three of them to do it, anyway. With only two of them left, the risk is already gone."

"…Which one do I face next?" I asked. "Episode or Guillotine Cutter?"

"The order is up to them, so I can't say for sure, but I think it'll be Episode. I'll try to set things up as soon as I can. That way you won't have to waste any time going back to being human."

"Oshino." I felt a little hesitant, but I decided to ask the question—I needed to know for sure before talking to Hanekawa. "Am I…really going to be able to become human again?"

"I don't see why not, as long as you can get back all of Heart-underblade's arms and legs. Isn't that what the kid said?"

"Well, that's the thing—isn't there the possibility that Kissshot is lying? I can see how she might be in order to get her limbs—"

"Hey."

Tap.

I'd been poked in the head.

"You shouldn't distrust her like that, poor girl."

"But…"

"I can't believe how ungrateful you are, saying that about some-one who saved your life."

That's what Oshino said.

Ungrateful? Saved my life? Did he just say that Kissshot saved my life, and not the other way around?

"What's with that face, Araragi? Something good happen to you?"

"…Don't talk like you see through me."

"I do see through you. Yes, you threw your life away for Kiss-shot's sake. You presented your neck to her and her fangs. I think it's a wonderful thing you did—a beautiful act. But you know, Araragi. Normally, you would have died there."

My blood wrung dry.

Not a single drop of my bodily fluids left.

I was supposed to have died there.

No—I did die there once, for certain.

"But you came back to life. As a vampire, of course, but you've been allowed to keep your sense of self."

"Isn't that because there's a rule set in stone? If a vampire sucks your blood, you turn into a vampire, right? Yes, I may not have died for good there, but to say that she saved my life—"

"Set in stone? Where did you hear that one?" Oshino grinned, again as if he saw through me. As if he could see through all the fear and distrust that had settled in my heart like sediment.

146

"That's what Kissshot said."

"It's just what she said, no? Haven't you considered the possibility that that's when she was being a liar?"

"Liar."

Liar?

That's when she was being a liar?

But—why tell such a lie?

"I don't mean to take Heartunderblade's side, so I'll spill the beans here—there are two patterns when a vampire sucks a human's blood. It's either as a nutrition supply, in the way of eating, or it's a way to create a thrall and servant."

The two are completely distinct, Oshino said with a slight smile.

"Well, a vampire does receive a bit of nourishment when creating a thrall—but if she'd sucked your blood simply to feed on it, she surely wouldn't be missing her skills to such a degree, even if fully recovering was still unlikely."

"No, but—"

That may have been true.

Kissshot had said as much—under that street lamp. My body's worth of blood could tide her over.

Her current figure.

A ten-year-old girl's figure.

Did that really tide her over? Did that really nourish her?

She was like a schoolchild without any lunch money.

"At the moment, all I'm seeing are her powers of healing. It looks like she exhausted her skills just to form that body and even lost her all-important power to suck blood."

"What? Really?"

"Really. The form she's taken right now is something of an emergency-use-only one—she's maintaining her vitality at the cost of sealing most of her skills. Must've been the most she could do with all four of her limbs severed. If she'd sucked your blood as simple food, she'd surely be in much better shape."

"So…" I began to think, straining my inadequate brain and nonexistent knowledge to their limits in order to connect the dots, "in order to get her limbs back from those three, she had to make me her thrall, even if it meant temporarily losing most of her skills down to her ability to suck blood?"

"That's not it." Oshino waved his hand sideways. "You could look at it that way, and that's probably what she'd say if you asked her. But I think it would be an excuse she made up after the fact. What I think—is that she couldn't bring herself to kill you."

"……"

"Not only Heartunderblade, but vampires in general don't particularly like to create thralls. Even if they're dying, they'd rather not create a thrall just in order to survive. Heartunderblade—there's a heart under that blade. She seems to be a very different vampire from the one I'd heard about—turning you into her thrall must have been the only way for her to stay alive without killing you."

Saved my life.

If that was true—then indeed, Kissshot had saved my life.

That had to be it.

When Kissshot first called out to me, she wasn't planning on making me her thrall. She simply meant to nourish herself, to feed.

To tide herself over.

But—she said thank you.

To a worthless human.

To me, for sticking out my neck.

"When you woke up here, Heartunderblade was sleeping by your side, wasn't she? Using your arm as a pillow. Doesn't that mean she was nursing you around the clock?"

"Around the clock…"

"A fresh thrall always has the risk of going into a frenzy. She was on the lookout to make sure that didn't happen. Or maybe it would be better to say she was watching over you. And then…afterwards too, when you carelessly tossed yourself under the sun, she didn't hesitate to rush into the sunlight to save you—braving the risk of her own body evaporating as well."

That said, Oshino added, "Maybe it's close to the kind of affection humans feel for their pets—but at the very least, Heartunderblade is true to you."

"True, huh?"

"So you need to believe her. She'd be such a poor little thing if you didn't. Remember what I was saying? A relationship based on trust, Araragi. *Don't worry, you'll be turning back into a human*—in fact, the real trouble might come after that."

"…After that?"

"I'm telling you not to think of yourself as the victim here. Playing the victim—doesn't sit well with me."

Those were harsh words. Unexpected ones, too, putting me at a loss.

"Hey, I don't care how I sit with you…but I'm not trying to play the victim here."

"That's good to hear. I'll keep it in mind, Araragi. But either way, looking at you from my perspective—you're being naivë."

"Excuse me?"

"Oops. I meant naïve," Oshino corrected himself.

Whatta way to misspeak.

"Every aberration has its reasons, they say. Araragi, you need to give some more thought to why you encountered a vampire."

"Well, that'd be…by chance, no?"

"I'm sure it was by chance. What you need to think about is why that chance came about…but for now, maybe it's best if you prioritized getting back Heartunderblade's limbs. I'm not obligated to worry about you, Araragi, but the way you fought makes me a little concerned."

"Well…I won't say you can count on me."

To get back on topic, though.

If that was what Oshino, an expert, said—then I supposed I

didn't need to worry.

Right. Kissshot was arrogant, but she was true to me—she may call me her servant, but she also seemed to see me as someone who'd saved her life.

In that case, I needed to respond in kind. Meeting trust with trust—a relationship based on trust demanded it.

"So, do you think the kid is about done eating?"

"Yeah...I guess. I'll need to ask her about my next opponent... Episode."

I opened the door to the classroom and went back inside.

Kissshot Acerolaorion Heartunderblade, who'd looked like a ten-year-old girl, had transformed, sure enough—into looking like a twelve-year-old girl.

She'd grown.

Already bigger than just the last time I saw her.

010

"So this girl's body grows each time she eats one of her stolen limbs," Hanekawa indicated her grasp of the situation.

The two of us were speaking immediately after sundown on April 1st. Kissshot was still asleep. A vampire's day and night were reversed, and that applied to me as well—but feeling bad about dragging a model student like Hanekawa out of the house at too late of an hour, I'd tried and *woken up early*.

There was a barrier placed around the abandoned cram school. That's what Oshino said.

It not only hid my presence and Kissshot's, it also made it difficult for regular people to find it without a guide—apparently. That's why I had Hanekawa come close by so I could go pick her up after the sun set.

Hanekawa was on time and present at the spot we'd agreed upon. As always, she was wearing her uniform.

"Heya." Hanekawa raised her hand. She was being affable without a shred of awkwardness. It was just the right amount of distance and felt comfortable.

"Did you bring what I asked?"

"Yup. See?"

"Oh. Thanks. This way, then," I said, showing Hanekawa to the school.

Private Property, No Trespassing.

We passed through a fence bearing the sign (the ruined cram school's fence was befittingly ruined and filled with holes) and headed inside the building.

Oshino was out negotiating, and Kissshot was asleep. I had told Kissshot that I'd be bringing Hanekawa, but she hadn't seemed particularly interested. Since our conversation might get pretty involved, maybe it was better to go to a different room, but I wanted Hanekawa to check out what Kissshot looked like.

That's why I decided to speak to Hanekawa in the room on the second floor that I usually spent my time in, with Kissshot enjoying her beauty sleep right by us. Needless to say, the windows of the room were boarded up, and not even the light of the moon and stars filtered in. I was fine with my vampire eyes, but I'd arranged for a flashlight for Hanekawa, who had normal vision—which is to say, she'd gotten it herself.

After a little bit of chit-chat (I'd been deprived of newspapers and TV since spring break started), I told Hanekawa the story up to that morning—and she listened with interest, nodding.

A model student.

Maybe her curiosity about the unknown exceeded most people's.

I told her everything I could. I didn't want to hide anything. Even if it was the first of April, I didn't want to lie.

And it was when I had finished telling Hanekawa about Kissshot's "growth" that she said—

"So this girl's body grows each time she eats one of her stolen limbs... 'This girl' might be an odd way to refer to a five-hundred-year-old vampire—but is that the deal?"

Hmm. She seemed to have a decent grasp of the situation.

Yes, I nodded.

"When she ate her right leg...from the knee down, she aged about two years, so... Yeah, after recovering the rest of her arms and legs, she'll probably be back to her old body...and look like a twenty-seven year old."

"Huh."

"Well, to put it Lord Frieza style, she has two more transformations left, one for her right leg, and one for both of her arms."

"That does clarify it for me," Hanekawa said, glancing at Kissshot snoring away atop the simple bed that Oshino had built.

While she may have been a vampire, at first sight she was just a cute twelve-year-old girl… She and I being together in an abandoned building had a real whiff of criminality about it.

I just had to pray that Hanekawa wouldn't come to that conclusion.

"So maybe—it's my fault," she said.

"Huh? What is?"

"Your run-in with a vampire."

"……"

Why would she think that?

While I said I didn't want to hide anything and told her everything I could, I wasn't a total idiot. Hadn't I skipped over the stuff about her panties and the dirty books?

But as it turned out, I was fretting for no reason.

"Rumors have a funny way of coming true, right? Especially for ghost stories and stuff. They say *rumoring* has a way of—having them find their way to you."

"Hunh. But it's not like I—"

Oh.

Right. That day—I'd heard a rumor from Hanekawa.

A rumor about vampires. Walk around by yourself at night, and…

"But that doesn't make sense. You told me about the rumor, so you'd have to run into a vampire too."

"I don't *have* to, it's probably just that your chances increase… Besides, I have, haven't I?"

"Huh?"

"You, Araragi."

Ah. Right.

I was a vampire too.

So that was it—on my way to fighting Dramaturgy, I'd happened to run into Hanekawa, then and there, perhaps due to such a heightened probability.

Every aberration has its reasons.

The reason that I met a vampire—

"There's another way of thinking about it. That the rumor actually precedes the aberration—that rumors cause them to be born. Like with oral traditions, you know?"

"I see. Are they rumored because they exist, or do they exist because they're rumored. It's like the chicken or the egg, which of them tastes better?"

"Huh? I like eggs better."

I had meant it as a joke.

A dud.

"…You know the answers to everything, don't you?"

"Not everything. I just know what I know."

"Is that so," I nodded before bringing the conversation back on track. "Putting the talk about rumors aside. Hanekawa—yesterday, you were going out of your way to look for a vampire, if anything."

That's when I'd gone nuts. I didn't get mad this time, of course.

"Why were you? Existences greater than humans—was it? You said you wanted to talk to one or something?"

"Well, it wasn't as if I was seriously looking for a vampire. I was stamping my feet for something that I know doesn't exist, more like. How do I say this—maybe I've been going in circles and wanted a change in my life?"

"A change, eh…"

In my case, I'd gotten one, not only in my life, but also in my biology.

It really was too much.

But—a model student.

A class president among class presidents, Tsubasa Hanekawa, feeling like she was going in circles came as a bit of a surprise to me.

Then again, maybe that was normal—she was human.

As for me, I still felt lost even as a vampire.

Actually, I felt a lot more lost.

"It was just my way of trying to escape from reality."

"I'd love to get back to reality, myself."

"I'm sure you'll be able to," Hanekawa said. She had nothing to back up her words—but they made me glad. "Like I said, I want to help—but considering how outrageous the situation is, it doesn't feel like there's much I can do."

"That's not true," I said, pointing at the backpack containing everything Hanekawa had brought. "Those clothes and daily essentials are a great help."

"Oh, it's nothing," Hanekawa said bashfully. "Why don't you hurry up and get changed, then? Your clothes are a mess."

"Guh."

"Honestly, I was shocked when you showed up to meet me looking like that. Doesn't this Oshino person have clothes you could borrow?"

"All he owns are these Aloha shirts…"

"What's wrong with an Aloha shirt?"

"Maybe if they were LOHAS shirts," I said, picking the first similar-sounding word I could think of.

Not that I knew what it meant.

In any case, I couldn't keep going around in the clothes I was wearing. It wouldn't be an issue if I could generate matter like Kiss-shot, but it went without saying that I couldn't.

"Yeah, you're right. Umm…"

Still, it didn't feel right changing clothes in front of a girl… I'd have to take my pants off, too.

"On second thought, maybe there's no rush…ulp!"

I'd just realized something.

The previous night, I'd asked Hanekawa to "buy me a change of clothes" without giving it much thought, but…my situation being what it was, didn't that mean not just shirts and trousers but underwear?

"……"

Whaa…

Whaaaaat?

"I-I guess I could at least change my shirt," I said, putting up a calm exterior as I reached for the backpack Hanekawa had brought.

It was pretty full… Well, it did have more than clothes inside… But when I undid the zipper, the clothes were at the very top.

Actually, underwear was at the very top.

"Was medium okay?"

"Y-Yeah…"

"I got you both boxers and briefs."

"……"

Why bother?

No, actually…this was my fault. It really was. How dim had I been? And because of that, Hanekawa had suffered the worse embarrassment, buying both boxers and briefs…

"? What's the matter? You're not going to change?"

"I will…" I said, grabbing the plain shirt folded under the underwear. It looked brand new, but it wasn't in a bag, and the tag had been taken off. Had Hanekawa washed and dried the clothes once after buying them?

Why go so far?

It was like I had the dirt on her or something!

In any case, I took off my tattered shirt and began wriggling my arms through the sleeves of the plain shirt.

"Wait a sec," Hanekawa said.

I stopped, but, uh, I was kind of topless…

"I knew it—I thought so yesterday too, but your body's a little different, Araragi."

"Huh?" But now that she mentioned it.

Was I—a little more muscular?

No, more than just a little—I had abs.

"I knew it," Hanekawa repeated. "Something seemed a bit off when I saw you from behind yesterday—so it was your muscles. You also seem thinner, more cut."

"......"

Identifying boys she barely knew from behind—Hanekawa, what are you, really?

That was the bigger question.

Then—

"Mumble, mumble."

Kissshot seemed to have suddenly woken up.

If you were wondering, when she "grew," her clothes and hair changed along with her body. As a ten year old, she'd worn a fluffy dress and had short, bobbed hair, but now that she was twelve, she had long hair and her dress looked a little more grown-up.

"Of course thy body has changed, ye've become a vampire. Our powers of healing work to keep our bodies in optimal condition."

"Huh?"

"Gzzt..."

Having supplied that explanation, Kissshot dozed off.

Which was she, awake or asleep...

Still, it felt like she'd dropped a bombshell?

Then again—maybe that's how it was. My fingernails hadn't grown since becoming a vampire, and I didn't have to bathe. I couldn't tell after only a week, but I doubted that my hair was growing, either.

So that was why. My new physique represented the ideal amount of muscle for my body and bone structure.

And if you kept going, you arrived at the muscular heights of Dramaturgy or turned parts of your body into weapons as an application of that ability.

"…She went back to sleep."

"Yeah. Rising and shining doesn't seem to be her thing."

"And she's five hundred years old?"

"According to the lady herself."

"…She didn't seem to notice me at all." Then Hanekawa said, "Excuse me," and touched my upper body.

She began to slowly stroke my abs and chest.

Stroke.

Stroke.

…Uh oh, I was getting mildly aroused.

Was she being naughty or what?

"You still feel the same as a human. But with subtly more muscle elasticity."

"……"

A simple case of intellectual curiosity. Right, of course.

"You say 'the same as a human,' but have you touched other men's bodies?"

"Huh? No no, never." Hanekawa quickly pulled her hand away from my body, shy all of a sudden. "You're right, I was speaking from imagination, not experience. I shouldn't do that… Hurry and put on that shirt."

"O-Okay."

I put on the shirt.

She said it was a medium, but it felt a little on the large side—I figured it wouldn't be a problem, though. I liked that it was a plain shirt, too.

"Hm. So it fits?"

"Yeah. Thanks—or rather, sorry about that. I'll pay you back as soon as this is all over."

"Forget about it. I've been saving my New Year's gift money ever since I was little."

"Don't use that kind of money on me!"

Cash I could reimburse, but not memories!

What an unfathomable woman…

Carelessly requesting something of her could have dire consequences.

"There are two hoodies under that. Oh, were jeans okay for pants?"

"Yeah. Ease of movement is what matters most."

"I eyeballed the waist and inseam sizes, but just tell me if they're too tight or too short. I'll go buy another pair."

"……"

Note to self: put up with it even if they're a little tight or short.

While I wasn't changing into them at that moment, I decided to at least check the jeans and began rummaging around the bottom of the backpack.

Then—I found a bag.

It was a paper bag from that major bookstore.

It felt like ten or so books were inside.

"…?"

When I pulled it out, for no reason really, Hanekawa told me, "Oh, those are presents. You bought an aikido book yesterday, right? The one that you left by the school gates. And judging by your story, you got it in order to fight that big person, right?"

"Well—yeah."

So that was her appraisal of Dramaturgy. "Big person."

She had some guts, didn't she?

"In the end, the baseball guide I bought along with it came in handier."

"Ah. The one you were reading when we met, right?"

"What are you getting at?"

Hanekawa nodded. "Well, you were right to try and prepare in the face of a tough battle—but I also thought that you were going about it the wrong way."

"I don't disagree with you there. You mean cramming will only help so much."

159

She had seen me the day before. My crude style of fighting. How much I relied on luck, how I just took things as they came.

"No one would spend years practicing if they could master it by flipping through a book."

"Oh, no no, that's not what I meant," Hanekawa said. "Aikido and baseball are both things that humans do, right?"

"…? Well, I guess an arm lock was useless against Dramaturgy—but if his regen wasn't very good, breaking his arm might've had some effect?"

"Uhmm. You sound so rough. But that's not it, either. This isn't about who's on the receiving end, but on the giving end. I'm talking about your side, Araragi."

"Huh?"

"Aikido is a human fighting style—and baseball is a human sport. Your strength is clearly greater than a human's right now, Araragi, so aikido or baseball or anything of the sort seems like it would only end up limiting your strength."

"O-Oh."

She was right.

In fact—a baseball was too light for me. The shot put was okay. It wasn't until I grabbed that roller that it felt right.

All of my stats had been lifted at the same time so it was hard for me to be aware of it, but as I was, human techniques might actually just hold me back.

"So I think what you should be reading now are these," Hanekawa said, opening the paper bag I'd taken from the backpack and showing me what was inside.

It was manga.

A straightforward superpowered school action series, at that. A boy in a school uniform was on the cover.

"……!"

"I looked for one with a vampire high schooler as the protagonist, but I couldn't find one, so I went ahead and picked one where the main character is a boy who uses superpowers."

"W-Went ahead and picked..."

"Just like this," she said, opening up to a page where a boy, probably the protagonist, was running up a wall, "you can probably now move ignoring the laws of physics."

"Uh huh..."

I was taken aback for a moment—but hold on. It might not be such a bad idea?

Actually—it was a pretty good one.

I was still clinging to the common sense I'd acquired as a human—according to Dramaturgy. There was weight behind his words, since he was a former human like me. And just like he said, I'd dug myself a hole during our battle because that sort of common sense had too much of a hold on me.

I was able to do a backflip, for crying out loud—surely I could run up a wall.

"Oh...I see."

"I did read through it. It's pretty fun."

"Hm..."

I hadn't heard of the manga before, but it did look fun.

"There's a fantasy novel that I'd personally recommend, but I thought manga might be the most immediately effective solution considering your goals. Learning visually will help you remember better, too."

"That's definitely true."

"Well, try using those as your yardstick. After that, pick out what you think you'd like."

"...Thank you."

And...I had yet to tell Hanekawa that I needed to face Episode and Guillotine Cutter after this. Talk about being prepared...

Gosh, she was no ordinary girl.

"Here. A bookstore gift card for then."

"That's beyond prepared!"

"Hm? Would you have preferred cash?"

"I can't believe this!"

What was I?

In any case...I gratefully received what Hanekawa was considerate enough to offer me. Including the gift card.

I was seriously broke. From buying too many books.

"You're a lifesaver, Hanekawa. I promise I'll make it up to you some day."

"Uh-uh. This is really all I can do, anyway."

"All you can do? It's more than enough."

Honestly, it was heartening. Which, I supposed, also meant that I had been feeling disheartened.

I couldn't call Oshino an ally—as for Kissshot, this was really her business, plus she was a vampire.

I hadn't expected to feel so relieved from talking to someone.

No—it wasn't because I'd talked to just anyone, but to a friend.

"Thank you. I mean it."

"Oh, stop it. That's what friends are for, right? Don't hesitate to let me know if there's anything else you want me to do, Araragi. This is about everything I can do at the moment, though."

"Yeah. I'll be counting on you."

"Oh, right. Do you want me to clean this classroom?"

It looks like a total mess, she added.

Well, the building was abandoned.

No sooner than she'd spoken, Hanekawa began moving—but wait, I couldn't actually let her do this.

"It's fine. It was like this when we found it."

"That's no reason to leave it a mess. We ought to start where we can, and—hm? Hey, what's this?" Hanekawa said, picking something up from the corner of the room.

For a moment, I didn't have any idea what it was either. But only for a moment. It was yet another bag from that major bookstore—but neither the one Hanekawa had brought, nor the one with the aikido, baseball, and classical music books that I'd purchased the night before.

But I remembered seeing it.

And then I realized.

Yes. It was the bag with the two dirty books in it, the one I thought I'd thrown away on the first day of spring break.

"Mumble mumble."

It was Kissshot, sounding half-asleep behind us.

"I had forgotten to tell thee. That bag thou had so preciously clung to was on the side of the road, so I brought it here with me for thee."

"Y-Youuu!"

"Gzzt…"

Dammit, back asleep.

Ohhh no… Hanekawa was staring at the books inside.

A high school girl was staring at dirty books featuring high school girls…

"Um, when you encountered that vampire, you were…on the way back from the bookstore, right? On March 25th? The night of the day we first ran into each other?"

"……!"

Wow!

I couldn't believe how perceptive she was!

B-But couldn't she be misunderstanding the situation in the worst possible way here?!

"Hee-hee."

Hanekawa looked up and turned to me, grinning from ear to ear. The flashlight was illuminating her from directly below, and it felt like I was facing an aberration.

She took one of the books from the bag and opened it to a random page.

Of all things, it contained a stunningly idiotic special feature on "Bespectacled Class Presidents."

She asked me in the kindest of purrs.

"So. What's this?"

0 1 1

Episode. A man with sanpaku eyes and a white traditional school uniform who carried on his shoulder, with one hand, a gigantic cross triple the size and the cube of the weight of his body.

Apparently, he was a vampire hunter. A man who slew vampires in order to collect bounties. A hit man, if you will.

And to add to that—he was supposedly a half-vampire.

Hunter of, and half.

Though he could even look juvenile, contrary to his appearance he was an expert hunter of vampires who'd taken Kissshot's left leg from her. That was Episode.

"…He sure is late."

Three days later—April 4th.

"Four" being homophones with "death" and an unlucky number in Japan, the date felt vaguely ominous to me, but I wasn't complaining about such trifles.

I tried to check my wristwatch, only to realize that I'd forgotten to wear it—I thought I'd check my cell phone instead but had forgotten it too.

No good.

I wasn't calm after all.

It was fine, though—like the vagabond he was, Mèmè Oshino, the man I'd most want to contact in a tight spot, didn't own a cell phone.

To hear him say it, though, it was just that he hadn't a clue when it came to gadgets. True, nothing seemed more far-removed from yokai and aberrations and such as a cell phone.

Either way, it was the night of April 4th.

I had once again come to the athletic field of Naoetsu Private High School at night.

For round two, of course.

To fight Episode, the second of the three vampire hunters.

I had been giving it a lot of thought over the past three days, but my ultimate decision was to show up empty-handed, like the time I battled Dramaturgy.

I'd accepted Hanekawa's view on the matter.

"I think it would be better if you didn't have any weapons. I mean, a normal weapon couldn't handle your so-called vampiric strength, and even if we found one that could, what if the police pulled you over for a stop and frisk?"

"……"

She was all too right, but bringing it up at this stage?

"Hey, if that's the deal, I think the authorities need to be stopping and frisking those three vampire hunters more than me."

"But these people are professionals, aren't they? They must have the know-how to avoid that sort of thing."

"Hmph."

Come to think of it, Dramaturgy could even turn his body into mist.

Plain human restrictions wouldn't hinder them.

And so, that's why I was bare-handed—and though it felt like I hadn't learned my lesson from last time when I'd tried and failed to take on Dramaturgy's dual-wielded wavy greatswords with my two empty hands, Hanekawa, her usual impressive self, had shared with me a number of observations she'd made simply by watching the battle from the shadows of the school building.

They were mostly red marks. But if I could put my experience to use this time…

As usual, Kissshot's advice wasn't very helpful—a flashback scene of how I sought it follows.

"A vampire hunter and a half-vampire—well, even I know that much vampire terminology, but couldn't you give me some more details, Kissshot?"

Her body now a twelve year old's, Kissshot had this to say in reply: "I forgot."

She forgot…

She was puffing her chest out as haughtily as ever—having gone from ten to twelve, which meant the onset of puberty, her chest was budding—but it certainly wasn't a reply to be dispensing haughtily.

"Mm. My powers of recall have weakened. Oh, had I already mentioned that?"

"I do appreciate the humor, but…"

"Hmph. Wait one moment."

With that, Kissshot held the fingers of her right hand in a straight line by her head and, without skipping a beat, dug the four nails into her temple.

The blond girl's tiny right hand vanished into her head down to the wrist. Blood began to spurt out, evaporating and disappearing each time.

"H-H-Hey…"

"One moment. I'll remember in no time."

Kissshot proceeded to rummage around inside her own head, which is to say she was mushing around her brain. Not only blood, but a liquid like spinal fluid was also shooting out of the wound.

"…!"

No no no no no no no no no.

Forget an anime adaptation twice over.

What's more, maybe her fingers were getting caught up in her ocular muscles, because her right eye made idiosyncratic movements

167

like she was under demonic possession.

L-Literally searching through her memories…

I'd heard of some strange mnemonic devices before, but this took the cake.

"Ah."

Kissshot finally removed her reddened hand. She wore a refreshed smile.

"I remember."

"What…" I prompted as I watched the blood that stained her golden hair red evaporate before my eyes, "What did you remember?"

"As thou could surely tell from his attempts to win thee over, Dramaturgy does not hunt vampires out of any sort of hatred. But Episode is different. The fellow detests vampires."

"He detests them? Why? He's half vampire, right? Well, he's a vampire hunter, so I didn't think he'd be on our side or anything—"

"No, though it is difficult to say decisively with such a small sample size, most half-vampires come to hate vampires."

"Why?"

"Well, to put it simply, 'tis because half-vampires are not accepted into the world of vampires. Nor is that reason enough for them to be accepted into the human world. And so—they hate their vampire blood."

"Wouldn't that make them hate humans just as much, though?"

"They do not think well of them, but what use is it hating those weaker than you?" Kissshot replied bluntly. "They may be but half-vampire, but their strength is leagues beyond the average human's. Episode in particular seems to have a strong hatred of vampires. I've no knowledge of his upbringing—but I imagine I would prefer to stay ignorant of it. So do not assume that he will give up easily. While work may have driven Dramaturgy, emotions move Episode."

"Huh."

So he was less of a pro than Dramaturgy.

"While a half-vampire's immortality is not as strong as a vampire's, their breed is notable for their near lack of vampiric weaknesses. They are even capable of walking in daylight—and of casting shadows."

"Huh… They cast shadows?"

"In other words, in exchange for half of their strengths, they eliminate nearly all of their weaknesses."

"Ah…"

Okay. I shouldn't be too quick to draw conclusions—but him not having any weaknesses was kind of rough.

"So, how can I beat him?"

"Eh? Well, by being thy usual self?"

"……"

Thank you, Kissshot, for your excessive faith in me.

And thus—the night of the battle had come.

For the past three days, I had been absorbed in manga. I couldn't blame any onlooker for thinking that I was goofing off or at least slacking off, but I'd covered nearly every superpowered school action series in serialization.

Oddly enough, reading manga out of necessity meant taking it slow no matter how much of a page-turner it was… But every day including that day, Hanekawa came to the abandoned cram school right after the sun set to bring me more manga, so it wasn't as if I could stop. I'd even received a gift card, but I was told that it'd be best if I kept from going outside too much.

It was Oshino who told me that.

On the night of April 1st, right after Hanekawa left to go home, Oshino returned—and that's when he told me. I regretted just missing my chance to introduce Hanekawa to him, but then, he could have been waiting for her to leave, so I didn't press the point.

"I know I'm supposed to stay neutral here, but that's a pretty good idea. Li'l missy class president really has her wits about her," Oshino said. "But I think I might have to oppose the idea of you walking around outside when you don't even have a match. They might seize the chance to go after you."

"Wait—but couldn't you negotiate that?"

"One of the tricks to negotiating is to not give away any opportunities for free. I don't think they'll try to lay their hands on you, but you wouldn't want them tailing you."

"Even if they do, they can't find this place, right?"

While it didn't affect Kissshot and me, who lived within it, and barring Oshino, who'd put up the barrier in the first place, he'd said it was that effective.

"Of course I'm confident about the barrier. But I want to squelch any risks."

"Risks?"

"Missy class president is coming by again tomorrow, no? If you want a wider variety of titles to read, try asking her then. Oh, and while I think the barrier will cause her to get lost even on her second and third trips here, that'll just have to be part of the package."

"B-But—"

"And of course I can't help you, so if she says no, you'll have to ask a different friend."

I didn't have other friends.

I had no choice but to rely on Hanekawa.

"Oh, and let me borrow them when you're done."

With that obnoxious parting remark, Oshino left.

He'd gone back out only minutes after coming home... When did the guy sleep, anyway? I saw him lying around often enough, but I couldn't remember him ever sleeping. Was he hustling that much with his negotiations?

In that case, I supposed I could at least let him borrow some manga.

For her part, Hanekawa continued to be really cool—when I asked her during her visit to the abandoned cram school the next day, the second of April, she agreed to be my "shopper" right away.

For three days straight, until today, the fourth of April, she'd gone and bought for me her recommended manga & my requested manga.

She was way too cool.

"Do your best, all right?"

Even today, as I left the school for the first time in three days, she sent me off with those encouraging words. Simple words that touched me.

"Jeez…if I do get to turn back into a human, how much thanking am I gonna be doing?"

At that moment—I was missing the mark completely.

Even at that point, the strength of the woman called Tsubasa Hanekawa, but also her precariousness, hadn't registered with me.

"I wonder if she's gotten home by now…"

Just as I muttered those painfully idyllic words, considering later developments—Episode finally appeared.

Appeared on the athletic field of Naoetsu Private High School.

Appeared—like a cloud of mist.

"……"

A vampire hunter.

A half-vampire.

No weaknesses as a vampire. Yet—though halved, endowed with the powers of a vampire.

A somewhat frail-looking man—with sanpaku eyes.

White traditional school uniform.

He could look juvenile—but the gigantic cross he slung over his shoulder with one hand worked to dash that impression.

Just like the other day, he wore a faint smile—and glared sharply at me.

Episode.

The man who had stolen Kissshot's left leg.

"Gotta love it," he started in. He offered no apology for being late. "Cracks me up, it really does—old Dramaturgy finding himself on the wrong end of a hunt going after a brat like you. How careless could he have been? I hate all vampires, even the ones that are vampire hunters, but I'd at least thought highly of old Dramaturgy."

"……"

No shortage of hostility or malice. On top of it, he was making light of me.

Well, if he hated both vampires and humans, that would make me, a former human and a fresh vampire, his most hated type of all.

"So? What am I supposed to do, brat?"

"…Supposed to do?"

"We're about to have a match, yeah? What sort of match will it be? It doesn't have to be violent. I feel like I could beat the likes of you at anything."

"Sorry," I said, "if you take away the fact that I'm Kissshot's thrall, I'm just a plain human—even a washout. The only way I could face you is as a vampire against a vampire hunter. The only other thing I could see myself beating you in is rock-paper-scissors."

"Yeah? Gotta love that."

I seriously made him laugh, Episode said.

"You're being awful timid, aren't ya? I've hunted my fair share of formerly human vampires—but they were all more cocky, y'know? Like they'd become omnipotent. They were acting like they were gonna rule the world when all they'd gained were the powers of a mosquito. Gotta love it."

"……"

Maybe he was making a point of speaking "the language of the land," but it felt really weird for a man who carried such a menacing cross to be saying "Gotta love it" over and over…

Whatever point he thought he was making.

"Of course, I brought 'em all back down to reality. There doesn't seem to be any need to do that with you, though—saves me some work. So you get a special treat," Episode said, closing one eye.

Maybe he was winking.

"I'll kill you without doing any permanent damage."

"…You used that line before."

"It's my trademark line. Gotta love it, huh? If you're gonna imitate me, don't just copy it—make it your own."

Saying this, he held out his hand, the one he wasn't using to support the cross.

A handshake?

Was this a pre-match handshake?

Maybe he was surprisingly polite in that way… Wondering, I reached to shake his hand, but just as I did, Episode quickly moved his—into the shape of a pair of scissors.

"There, I win."

"……"

"You can't even beat me in rock-paper-scissors—as a vampire hunter fighting you as a vampire, I'd win too."

"People like Oshino make me uncomfortable," I said, "but people like you—I hate."

"Hey hey, if you're saying that about me, you can't duke it out with Guillotine Cutter. Even I get a little creeped out by how nasty he is. But lucky for you, I'll be beating you here tonight, so you won't have to face him."

"You're pretty confident."

"Sure," he said. "But I agree with you, that bastard Mèmè Oshino is a handful. Gotta love this little farce he set up—whether it's formerly human vampires or true blue ones, I've never had to fight this fair and square."

"…You know the conditions."

"Yeah. If I win, you tell me where Heartunderblade is—and if by some freak chance you win, I give you her left leg back. Have I got it down?"

"Yup—that's it."

"By the way, do you actually know what those conditions mean?" When I nodded, Episode continued with a grin, "*They rule out killing each other.* I can't kill you if I want you to tell me where Heartunderblade is, and if you want that woman's left leg back, you won't be killing me, either. It may seem like a rough-and-tumble way to settle things, but it draws the line at killing. How pacifist."

"……"

A match—that's how Oshino had put it. Not a fight to the death, but a match.

"And—you're right. Old Dramaturgy, Guillotine Cutter, and I are all professionals. This is the only way you can win. We've managed to choose the single one."

Was that…true?

Was that what he meant by "balance"?

Did that sleazy man think through all that in putting together these matches?

As a neutral—negotiator.

To the tune of—two million yen.

"Of course, if I knew where Kissshot Acerolaorion Heartunderblade was, I'd kill you and her both—once again, without doing any permanent damage," Episode said, laughing. "I'm warning you, don't think I'll go easy. I hate picking on the weak—but I love picking on the evil."

"Am I evil?"

"Of course you are. You're a monster."

"…Aren't you—"

Aren't you one, too?

But I couldn't say so. He was—only half that.

"Huh? Aren't I what? If there's something you want to say, spit it out."

"No, it's nothing… There's nothing I want to say. Let's get started."

"Yeah, let's end this."

And with that, the prologue came to an end.

In contrast to the time I faced Dramaturgy, I was the one to make the first move—above all, I was determined to act first.

I lacked actual battle experience. As soon as I was on the defensive, I'd be thrown off-balance and lose myself—I had to try to attack, at least.

Exactly as I had learned in a manga, I stepped forward and unleashed a punch with all my body weight behind it—but all it met was air.

Or more precisely—all it met was mist.

Episode had turned his body to mist in the blink of an eye—and you can't punch mist, not to any effect. I staggered ahead, pulled forward by my arm that now traveled with an awkward amount of momentum.

Oops, he's going to counterattack, I thought—and readied myself, but he was unable to harm me either, transformed into mist as he was.

"Sorry, but you easily outclass me in terms of raw ability, being a thrall of the aberration slayer—I don't intend to fight a close-range battle," Episode, still a cloud of mist, cross and all, said, before returning to his original body a significant distance away from me.

The cross returned, too.

Since it had turned into mist with him—was it a part of his body, just like with Dramaturgy?

No, something was different…it seemed to work more like clothes, both Dramaturgy's and Kissshot's.

"…What are you thinking of doing from all the way over there?"

"This!" Episode said—hurling that giant cross in my direction.

Carelessly—without getting into anything remotely like a pitching form, unlike me against Dramaturgy—he hurled it with sheer force.

"A…Agh!"

It caught me completely by surprise. I never imagined he'd throw that giant cross, three times his own size—sure, I did almost throw the roller at Dramaturgy—but what kind of vampire hunter tossed his cross?!

So little faith!

I'd figured the cross was a weapon—but I thought he was going to use it like a broad ax!

"...Ack!"

I barely got out of its way.

And when I did, I felt like kicking myself.

Stupid me, hadn't I learned anything at all? There was no need for me to dodge attacks! Given my powers of recovery as Kissshot's thrall, I could heal myself in moments—and my plan was to use that fact to my advantage! But thanks again to the common sense I'd acquired as a human, I could not but jump out of the way of what my vampire eyes were able to see. Yet—

Yet this time, it worked in my favor.

The cross I thought I'd dodged had barely grazed my right shoulder—and a moment later, my shoulder began to burn.

It was engulfed in flames.

It—evaporated.

Almost like the time I'd exposed myself to the sun—

"C-Cross!"

I mean—it was totally a vampire's weak point! Even I knew that much!

Episode had been carrying it all too naturally, and its presence had been so overwhelming, that I'd been paradoxically blind to the fact—or rather, because its sight had caused me no problems whatsoever, I'd disregarded that fact.

Now I understood.

Episode being a half-vampire and not having a vampire's weaknesses—also meant he was fine around crosses.

Crosses.

A giant cross.

Since seeing it appeared to do nothing, it must have been a weapon whose effect only manifested itself upon direct contact.

Its tremendous effect.

My skin had evaporated—and it wasn't regenerating.

No, it wasn't not regenerating—just regenerating at an abnormally slow speed. Even my powers of recovery as Kissshot's thrall couldn't keep up.

In that case, it was even worse—than the sun.

Because it involved direct contact, the effect was amplified. A mere graze—had me like this.

What would happen if it hit me for real?!

"Huh…?"

While I was worrying about my wound, Episode had turned his body to mist once more—and was moving while in that form.

I was convinced that he'd take the opportunity to press his attack, but exactly as he'd declared earlier, Episode wasn't going to close in on me. Where he did go was to the gigantic cross he'd just hurled.

Having grazed the tip of my shoulder and flown another thirty feet or so, the weapon had stabbed half its length into the athletic field. Episode restored his body near it—then pulled out the buried cross.

"That reminds me. When you faced old Dramaturgy, you threw things at him from a distance, too—a good idea. If I ever had to go at it with a character like him, I'd probably do the same, like this!" Episode said—before throwing the cross again.

In my direction.

This time, I dodged it cleanly—but it didn't mean I could relax. That's because, at that moment, I perfectly understood Episode's tactic at long last.

My previous fight with Dramaturgy. The red marks from Hanekawa, who'd been watching, came down to two points.

"What if your opponent tried doing the same thing to you?"

That was number one.

"If that big person with his brawn had caught the shot put or the roller you'd sent his way and thrown it back at you, what were you going to do?"

As for number two.

"The scariest thing with long-distance attacks is running out of ammo. You're throwing your weapons—so even with a full cage of balls, throwing them thoughtlessly isn't ideal."

What Episode was now doing to me, a vampire, masterfully avoided both of those red marks.

For one thing, he was throwing that cross.

No matter what, I wouldn't be able to throw the cross back at him—how was I supposed to hurl something that I couldn't even touch? The moment I touched it, that body part would evaporate.

Furthermore, there was no risk of him running out of ammo. He could turn to mist, then go get the cross he'd thrown.

"H-Half vampire…"

He could touch crosses fine—and he could turn his body into mist.

Making the most of his own strengths—he was also exploiting the weaknesses!

"Gotta love it."

As if to confirm my hypothesis, once again Episode reconstructed his body by the cross sticking out of the ground—and yanked it out.

"I'll just whittle you down—please don't mess up dodging it and take a direct hit to the heart. I can't have you actually dying on—me!"

He threw the cross mid-sentence as though to take me by surprise.

I could dodge it—probably because, as he said, I outclassed him in raw ability. While a half-vampire's arms could generate a fair amount of velocity, they were still no match for a full vampire's vision and burst of speed.

But true—at this rate, he could whittle me down.

I had no hand to play—the superpowered school battles I'd

read over the past three days didn't cover this development!

I turned around.

Unsurprisingly, the cross was sticking out of the ground. It almost looked like a gravestone.

A giant cross sticking out of the athletic field!

Then, his body manifested next to it.

"You could surrender, too—not that I wouldn't just slaughter you tomorrow instead. I don't care if you think I'm being repetitive or uncreative, I'll kill you using the exact same method. There isn't a thing a vampire can do about its weakness to crosses, after all."

"……"

He was a professional. While he may have been moved by emotions, he was still a pro.

I looked at the shoulder wound I'd suffered at the outset. It still wasn't done healing—and the pain coming from it was still extreme.

No hand to play.

From the get-go, outside of a quick face-off, there was no way, given my total lack of experience, I was going to defeat a seasoned opponent. If he was going to take his time like this—there was nothing I could do!

I was done for then.

I could run to the P.E. storage shed, but why throw shot puts and rollers against an opponent whose body was mist? How was I to strike back against an opponent I couldn't damage with physical strikes?

Just as I was coming to an oddly calm judgment that fear had fixed my body in place and that I probably wouldn't be able to dodge Episode's next attack, I heard a loud voice.

"A-Araragi!"

No auditory hallucination could be that loud—and upon looking in the voice's direction, who do I find but…or actually, I already knew who it was after all the conversations we'd had. It was Tsubasa Hanekawa.

She'd appeared—from out of the school building's shadows. Had she been hiding there, just like the other day?

Ridiculous, Hanekawa had gone home…

"You can't give up yet! The opponent turns into mist—" Putting both of her hands to her mouth like a megaphone, Hanekawa continued to yell, completely ignoring my confusion. "He turns into mist, so that means—"

"…Gotta love it," he said.

Episode didn't even seem to hesitate as he threw the giant cross he'd readied towards me—*in Hanekawa's direction.*

Hm?

Huh?

Why do such a thing, the bastard…

"H-Hanekawaaaaaaaa!"

I'd heard that Hanekawa's reflexes were by no means poor. She was a model student. Even her P.E. scores were appropriately off the charts—but of course, within the bounds of human common sense.

Needless to say for a vampire—she was no match even for a half-vampire.

She wasn't blessed with the necessary vision or burst of speed to dodge the cross—and barely managed to get half a step out of its way.

One corner of the cross gouged her flank.

Naturally, since she wasn't a vampire, she neither burst into flames nor evaporated from coming in contact with the cross, but the giant crucifix was still a hefty mass of silver.

What was a soft human flank to it?

"……gh!"

I ran over to Hanekawa using every ounce of strength I had in my legs. It felt like I was able to reach her in a split second—and in fact, I was able to catch her before she fell backward to the ground.

But—it was still all too late.

Hanekawa's uniform was torn, her skin was torn, her muscles

were torn, her ribs were torn, her organs were torn. Crimson blood gushed out from her—and wouldn't stop.

The wound was simply too big to stop the bleeding.

Naturally, neither the pieces of flesh that had scattered from her body, nor the flowing blood, evaporated.

It just seeped into the field.

Taking its time staining it red, red.

"H-Hanekawa, Hanekawa, Hanekawa, Hanekawa!"

"…Hee-hee."

She laughed—bashfully.

In this situation.

As if she were embarrassed that I'd seen her organs.

A shy smile.

"Be quiet, Araragi."

"……!"

"Y-Your phone."

Hanekawa's complexion was growing worse and worse. But she didn't let her smile fade.

She only continued to smile as she added, "Forgot your phone, didn't you? I came—to give it to you."

"Wh-Who cares about a phone!" I yelled.

But Hanekawa had to know that too. This bit about my phone was just an excuse for her.

Plain worried—she must have come here, instead of going home.

And unable to stand by and watch any longer—she'd showed herself.

She had to have known how dangerous that was!

"Get it together…you're dealing with mist." Though the ground grew redder and redder, Hanekawa's tone remained firm. "Mist. Which means water."

"…? …Ha-Hanekawa?"

"Araragi." Her voice still firm, she slowly began to shut her eyes. "What's your long jump record, roughly?"

Sink.

As if on cue, Hanekawa's body suddenly grew heavy. But she'd lost so much blood—did human beings grow so heavy just from losing consciousness?

In that case…what happened when they lost their lives?

"Hah. Gotta love it. How long are you going to keep me waiting?"

When I saw him, Episode had already picked up the giant cross that had pierced Hanekawa—and had it readied in my direction.

"If you don't move, that girl's body is only going to take more damage."

"Y-You…"

"Let me just say that you're the one who broke our promise, thrall of the aberration slayer. This was supposed to be one on one. But I'll agree to call it even since I laid my hands on a third party."

"Hanekawa—is a normal human."

She wouldn't have counted. What could she have done?

"How could you, to a normal human!"

Or…are humans your enemies as well?

More than targets of hatred—but enemies?

Not just vampires—but humans too!

Still, why lay his hands on Hanekawa—even the advice she'd given me, in a firm tone to the very end before she faded into unconsciousness, sadly passed over my—

"……!"

Mist?

Water?

Long jump?

Oh. Never mind.

Never mind. I understood.

Yes—my "locational advantage."

I take it back, Hanekawa did count.

Now I could beat him!

182

"Raaaaaahhhh!"

I screamed with all my might—and charged.

Having gently laid her body on the ground, I was taking Hane-kawa's suggestion and acting on it immediately without so much as revising it.

I drew a straight line from Episode's current location to "that place"—and came to a halt atop it. It was at the exact same time that Episode hurled the giant cross in my direction. I'd made it—or no, not yet.

The conditions wouldn't be met unless I dodged the cross!

Instead of leaping out of its way, I ducked—and passing above my head, the cross took a tuft of my hair with it.

Continuing along its path, the cross pierced "that place."

"What, really? You get mad, but you're just going to run away? Gah! Lame to the bitter end. Gotta love you!"

Wasting no time, Episode turned his body to mist and chased after the cross.

But I wasn't idly staying where I was. Still crouched, I used my knees like a spring and leapt up into the air!

The impact from this didn't simply cause the field to sink in— it cracked. I'd have to flatten it back out later again.

But now wasn't the time to be worrying about that—it was my first time attempting to maintain my posture in mid-air, and it was fairly hard.

A vampire's powerful leap.

I had probably jumped about sixty feet up.

And the same distance forward—sixty feet.

Exactly what I had aimed for.

"That place" is where I landed.

"That place"—like the P.E. storage shed, I couldn't not know about it, having attended the school and taken P.E. classes for two years.

Namely, the sand pit at the edge of the field—I landed there.

With a long jump.

Though without a running start. Not that I needed one.

Either way, it was undeniably a long jump.

I landed right by the cross buried deep in the sand—once again, just as Episode reached the pit.

"Hah—gotta love it! That's some real power, but you think such a sloppy kick would hit me when I'm a cloud of mist?"

Episode laughed, his body still transformed into mist—when it was no time for him to be laughing.

"You're mist. Water, in other words," I said. "*What would happen if I dumped sand on you?*"

Long jumps sent up magnificent sprays of sand when you landed. Even a regular one, but this was a vampire's long jump. Nearly all the sand held by the pit danced up from the sheer impact of the landing.

Prior to this, the cross thrown by Episode piercing the pit had whipped sand into the air. My landing there dealt the final blow.

Indeed—Episode's body manifested.

Just as Hanekawa's blood seeped into the ground, one might say—not as an intentional act, but as a simple natural phenomenon, Episode showed himself.

"Wh-Wha?!"

"…Ah ha!"

Taking advantage of Episode's bewilderment, I sprang on his frail-looking body—and as the flying sand began to rain down on us, I used my full weight to pin him down.

I was sitting on Episode's back, but he still writhed and resisted—I continued to hold him down by force.

I held him down, and strangled his neck.

Episode wouldn't be able to turn his body into mist for a while.

Then me, with my superior raw ability, would win.

Me.

Me. Me. Me. Me.

"……e!"

I'd *kill him*!

There was another me, detached and elsewhere, observing me as my mind went blank.

Completely blank.

That I had become a vampire, that I was facing a half-vampire, the stuff about Kissshot's left leg—

All of it disappeared from my mind.

Just…

Just Hanekawa's organs. They stuck in my blank mind—and that was why.

I had to do it to him.

This guy—I had to kill—

"Okay, enough."

Plop.

Right then—a hand landed softly on my shoulder.

"Keep going and you won't be a human anymore."

"……!"

I turned around, my hands still on Episode's neck—to find the man in the Hawaiian shirt, Mèmè Oshino.

As sand rained down, he just stood in it.

"A—Ah."

For Dramaturgy as well—he said he'd been watching from somewhere. He must have been doing so this time too. I'd completely forgotten—but in that case!

"Y-You could've! You could have stopped Hanekawa!"

"Don't yell. So spirited, Araragi. Something good happen to you today?"

Even at a time like this—Oshino laughed. He wore an obnoxious smile.

"Well, I'm sorry to dampen your spirits, but the fight's been decided. Just look, he's passed out."

"Wha—"

I only noticed after he told me. Episode's eyes had rolled back in his head. I let go of him, startled, but clear impressions of my fingers remained on his throat.

"Wh...Wha?"

What had I been about to do?

Had I been—trying to kill the guy?

This half-vampire...half-human guy?

But... But Hanekawa.

Hanekawa.

"Hanekawa!"

"Yeah, I saw."

"Y-You saw? Why didn't you stop her?!"

"It's not included in the bill. I've only taken on negotiating with three vampire hunters. Anything beyond that requires a separate fee. I can't get mixed up with ordinary people."

Two million—his fee, his compensation.

The balance.

"Then tell me that from the beginning! If you had—"

"You would've paid another two million yen as missy class president's fee?"

"Two million? I would've paid three!"

"How—how stout of you."

"You're joking around at a time like this, Oshino? What's your deal?!"

"The one you've just proposed, Araragi. We have a deal. Three million yen," Oshino said calmly. "I'll give you a hint, then. Try using your head, Araragi—what's that immortal body of yours for?"

"Huh?"

"You're right, a lone human inserting herself into a battle between a vampire and a half-vampire is no call for murder. That's going too far—so I'll use my additional fee to teach you something neat. You shouldn't be strangling his neck here. Try to remember?"

"Remember..."

What?

I didn't have the time to be asking myself.

Like Kissshot had done earlier—I flattened my fingers and thrust them into my temple.

So what if we never see an anime adaptation!

I fiddled around inside my brain like mad, sensing every nauseating bit of blood, spinal fluid, and cerebral tissue until I felt sick. And then—

"......!"

Soon enough, I remembered.

A vampire characteristic—I made my decision on the spot. With my hand still stuck in my head, I left Oshino and Episode behind to run to where Hanekawa's body lay.

Five minutes.

If no oxygen reached the brain for five minutes, it stopped functioning—but that meant if I made it before then, it would do even if her heart had stopped.

It would do. Not even three minutes had passed.

I pulled my fingers out from my temple—and then, I dripped the blood stuck to the hand into Hanekawa's gouged-out flank, her oversized wound.

Yes, Kissshot had told me. *Vampire blood has the power to heal*—and in this case, it was my blood, that of the thrall of the iron-blooded, hot-blooded, yet cold-blooded vampire Kissshot Acerolaorion Heartunderblade.

Of course, being a vampire, my blood evaporated almost as soon as it left my body, and I had to wound myself over and over to keep bleeding—but as I did so, it happened before my eyes.

Hanekawa's wound began to heal.

Her organs regenerated, her bones regenerated, her muscles regenerated, her skin regenerated—and finally, she returned back to the way she was, with hardly a scar left.

It didn't even look like regen—more like someone had rewound her.

I tried touching, gingerly.

I stroked Hanekawa's flank.

Pale, gently sloping, less fleshy than her age warranted—it was so soft and smooth that I was afraid it might crumble if I pressed too hard, but for all that, it existed, without a doubt.

"...Ah, aaah!"

All at once, the emotions that I had been stifling began to flow. My heart was brimming with them all of a sudden.

"Ha-Hanekawa!"

I clung to Hanekawa's abdomen with everything I had. Even though I'd end up back where we started if I destroyed her slender body by hugging it with a vampire's strength.

"...Araragi," Hanekawa said abruptly, having regained consciousness.

No—she seemed to have come to a little sooner.

"Araragi, why are you rubbing your cheek against my stomach, and so fondly too?"

"Uh."

"Also, my uniform is torn—should I chalk that up to you?"

They say people didn't always remember the moments before they lost consciousness, and that seemed to be the case here with Hanekawa.

Forget her uniform, her internal organs had been torn.

"My bad, Hanekawa," I replied without budging, my face buried in her flank.

She was alive, and I just wanted to feel it.

"Stay still for a bit more."

012

It was probably due to the difference in volume between her right leg, which had been severed at the knee, and her left leg, which she'd lost whole. The change Kissshot underwent after consuming her left leg was a dramatic one. Her going from looking like a ten year old to a twelve year old had been a surprise—yet, despite already knowing that her body would change, I think I was even more surprised this time around.

Having recovered her left leg, Kissshot suddenly grew to the point where she looked roughly the same age as me.

A seventeen year old.

She may have had me beat in height.

Of course, between twelve and seventeen, from puberty to adolescence, is a period when appearances change the most amongst humans, too—but to give a specific example of her growth, her breast size had become something else.

If she puffed her chest out with pride as she'd been doing, it'd be almost frightening now.

Her face also looked far more grown-up, and accordingly, the design of her dress looked more chic. Her hair had grown even longer and was tied into a ponytail.

Such stunning results.

True, whatever form she took, Kissshot was actually five hundred years old.

"Mm."

She sounded pleased. Just like when she'd gotten her right leg back, Kissshot didn't bother trying to hide her feelings of satisfaction or joy, which made me, who worked as her "limbs," happy as well. She made it feel worthwhile.

"My body feels quite a bit better—I dare say that my immortality has nearly returned."

"Oh…so are you at a point where you might, you know, take care of the next battle?"

"Unfortunately, I seem as yet unable to use my skills as a vampire. It has become harder for me to die, but that is the extent of it. Perhaps I would be able to fight Dramaturgy, but even Episode might prove too much for my current state," Kissshot said, her tone cautious. "Let alone Guillotine Cutter."

"………"

She was saying the same thing—that was my reaction.

After that battle.

I began by having Hanekawa, now recovered from her wounds, go back home. I thought it would be best to have her do so while Oshino kept an eye on Episode.

In addition, Oshino didn't seem to want to meet Hanekawa (Even after the first day, their timing was perfect in terms of not meeting each other—since Hanekawa wasn't capable of avoiding Oshino, if anyone was doing the avoiding, it had to be him), and she picked up on this and agreed to go home.

Saying see you again tomorrow, she went home.

After that, Episode, who had woken up, and Oshino and I cleaned up the athletic field we'd utterly trashed. With our bare hands we filled in the holes where the giant cross had plunged into the ground, returned the sand pit to normal, gathered Hanekawa's scattered chunks of flesh (which of course would never evaporate, wait as we might) and took care of them. (It may seem a little lurid, but we buried the collected bits in the flower bed and put up a sign reading "Here lies Tweety." It was Mèmè Oshino, the expert, who came up with the idea, but his using twigs to mark the grave with a cross seemed to be going too far even as a morbid joke.) While I wouldn't say we restored things to the way they were, we managed to get it to the point where most people would be fooled.

Oshino and Episode then left me to go somewhere on their own.

"You got me," Episode said as he left. "Sheesh, gotta love it—I must be losing my edge, too. Upset by a total amateur like you."

"……"

"Don't glare at me like that. I apologize about the chick. I got needlessly excited. Plus—I might've been playing it off like it was nothing, but a battle with a thrall of the aberration slayer is no cake walk for me. I couldn't afford to let even a regular human pitch in—though I look real bad since I lost anyway. But don't think you'll be able to defeat Guillotine Cutter with some stupid little trick. I may be pretty crazy, but his crazy is on a completely different level."

Then, as promised—well, between Hanekawa running in, Episode attacking her for running in, and me trying to kill Episode, our fight got pretty messed up, so I wouldn't say that it was exactly as promised, but—he gave back Kissshot's left leg.

And so, just as he had done the other day, Oshino brought Kissshot's left leg home with him, packed inside a Boston bag, in the early hours of April 5th.

Kissshot immediately took it and ate it.

She devoured it like a starved animal.

And assumed the form of a seventeen year old.

"So, Guillotine Cutter."

The priestly man with the hedgehoggish hair.

The only one who was unarmed.

"What's his deal? Both you and Episode seem to be super cautious when it comes to him."

"I've already explained, have I not?"

"Your explanations tend to be too vague. There are so many things I'm realizing after the fact. Can't you teach me properly? I'll listen properly, for my part."

The sun was about to rise on the fifth of April.

We didn't have to worry about sunlight as long as we were in the second-floor classroom, but I wanted Kissshot to tell me before she went to sleep.

Actually, I was sleepy too.

Meanwhile, Oshino had left the Boston bag behind and set out again. He'd gone for the final negotiation—for someone as sleazy as him, he was a decently hard worker.

Well, I was paying him. He needed to earn it.

I really had no idea when he was sleeping, though...

"So ye say, but what practical use would there be in my explaining everything from α to ζ?"

"I'm sure there'll be some... Also, if you're going to put it that way, wasn't 'omega' supposed to be the last letter, rather than 'zeta'?"

Be that as it may.

"Guillotine Cutter... Am I right to think that he's 'human'?"

"Indeed. He is neither a vampire like Dramaturgy nor a half-vampire like Episode, but a plain, pure and simple, human."

"He didn't seem all that plain to me."

And "pure"—I didn't know about that part, either. The word just didn't seem to suit him.

"Mm. True," Kissshot said. "He's what ye'd call...a holy man."

"Hah. Don't tell me he's some kind of Christian spec ops."

"So close, yet so far."

Kissshot shook her head in reply to my offhand comment.

...I'd been fine before, what with her coming across as being only ten or twelve years old, but now that she looked about the same age as me, I did feel somewhat nervous speaking to her.

Kissshot looked beautiful and doll-like, like she was a foreign model or something.

192

Or—like she was a medieval noble from a movie, though maybe it was just the dress.

"How would I say it in the language of this country? Well, a literal translation should suffice."

"A literal translation?"

"Guillotine Cutter is the archbishop of a new religion, one with little history."

"A-Archbishop?"

So he was a big shot.

An archbishop at his young age? He was human, so he had to be roughly as old as he looked, right?

"The religion has no name—I understand little of the organization myself. But one thing is certain—the faith's dogma denies the existence of aberrations."

"Huh…"

A new religion with little history.

Of course, Kissshot had lived for five hundred years. I couldn't rely on her sense of time. For all I knew, she might call a religion formed before World War II a new religion.

How many archbishops had come before him? He couldn't be the first, could he?

"Within his church, Guillotine Cutter has tasked himself with eradicating aberrations, which supposedly do not exist at all. In other words, in addition to being the archbishop, Guillotine Cutter doubles as their captain of 'special ops,' to use thy term."

"Ah ha."

"He is the Shadow Team Leader of the Black Squad Belonging to the Dark Number Four Group of Secret Special Operations."

"Yeah, that sounds like a very literal translation."

Couldn't she come up with a smoother gloss on it? That was as rough as you could get.

"But… Whatever else he may be, he's still a human, right? No matter what methods he uses, won't he still be no match for a vampire?"

"Consider the situation. Neither a vampire, nor a half-vampire, but a 'human' has taken on vampire hunting as his specialty. If anything, it should be cause for concern—and in fact, has he not taken both my arms from me?"

"That is true."

Dramaturgy, her right leg.

Episode, her left leg.

Guillotine Cutter, her right and left arms—twice as many parts as the others, if you looked at it that way.

"Still, it was because I erred in not taking them seriously. I felt a tad under the weather, too," Kissshot mouthed a lame excuse.

I decided against needling her about it, though.

"If work is what drives Dramaturgy to hunt vampires, and emotions Episode, then 'tis duty that spurs Guillotine Cutter. As odd as it for me to say this, faith is quite a handful."

Work. Emotions. Duty.

Sure, I could see how a sense of duty might be more of a handful than emotions.

"So, what should I do?"

"Do as ye see fit. I leave it in thy hands."

"……"

Legendary vampire or not, it felt like she was taking the reigning champion, no gimmicks style too far.

But saying no more, Kissshot lied down on top of the makeshift bed and went straight to sleep.

Hrmm.

Not only did she appear to be my age, she was quite beautiful. Kissshot exposing her sleeping figure to me so unguardedly put me in an awkward spot.

It almost felt like an invitation.

Like it'd be rude if I didn't do anything.

But like I was being overly self-conscious.

194

An endless spiral of delusion.

"…Oh, whatever."

It was about that time (early morning), so I could just go to bed. I understood all too well from my fight with Episode that planning ahead didn't count for much in the end. Having a flimsy plan only plunged me into confusion when it inevitably failed.

I had to fight with room to breathe, though that was asking for a lot.

Hanekawa was visiting again after sundown—and I needed to talk to her. Until then, I might as well get plenty of sleep so that I'd be in top shape. Even without any sleep, of course, my vampire body, "always maintaining its healthiest condition," would be in top shape, but this was more about taking care of myself mentally.

It was already April 5th. Before I'd even noticed, spring break was drawing to an end.

Was I safely turning back into a human before the new school year? Because loopy talk like "going on a journey of self-discovery" wouldn't do then—I faded into sleep thinking such thoughts.

Vampires may normally sleep in caskets—but like Kissshot and Oshino, I slept on a bed made of desks.

By the time I woke up, it was already evening.

I'd had no dreams.

Vampires didn't dream, apparently.

Come to think of it, when I did the math, I was sleeping about twelve hours a day. But what could I do? Not much while the sun was out.

They say that nothing rears a child better than sleep.

Kissshot was still sleeping—not that sleep was rearing her, but waking up beside a blond beauty was more unsettling to me than sharing a room with a little girl.

As for Hanekawa—it seemed like she hadn't arrived yet. Nor had Oshino come back. He knew that Hanekawa would be visiting, so he wouldn't be around for a while if he really meant to avoid meeting her.

I wasn't trying to review the material or anything, but while I waited for Hanekawa, I started rereading a superpowered school action manga that Oshino had borrowed and returned after my first time through it.

Hanekawa arrived around when I was done with volume five. She said she'd gotten lost on the way.

This always happened—as Oshino said earlier, it was an effect of the barrier. What an annoying barrier—but on the flip side, it made for an ideal hiding place for Kissshot Acerolaorion Heartunderblade to regain her strength.

It must've been covered—by the fee.

Scratch that, Oshino had just gone ahead with it. For the sake of balance, as he put it.

"Good morning, Araragi."

Putting her flashlight to the side, Hanekawa sat in a chair.

She was in her school uniform.

Both her blouse and her sweater had been ripped apart by Episode the day before, so I was secretly hoping to be treated to my first sight of Tsubasa Hanekawa in street clothes, but it seemed that my hopes had been betrayed.

"Traitor."

"Hunh? Wait, what? How? I haven't betrayed you, Araragi."

"Sorry, just talking to myself."

More like talking nonsense.

Well, she'd have a backup uniform, wouldn't she. I'd heard that the girls' uniforms wore out more easily, too.

"Hanekawa, how's the wound on your stomach?"

"The wound—well, there's nothing left of the wound."

"Ah. Here, show me."

"What 'here'?"

I got scolded.

I was being pretty serious, though. Then again, we'd made extra sure the night before, and if Hanekawa said she was fine, she probably was.

Healing with vampire blood.

I'd begun to worry afterwards that it might end up turning Hanekawa into a vampire too, but when I checked with Oshino, an expert, he said there was no risk.

It seemed that vampirism and immortality were two different systems—or rather, they weren't really interrelated. One wasn't the byproduct of the other, they were independent.

"For a moment there, I thought maybe being a vampire isn't all bad if I can heal injured people—but then, if I hadn't turned into a vampire, you wouldn't have been maimed like that."

"Yeah, I guess so."

Ahaha, laughed Hanekawa. She then looked toward Kissshot, dozing the time away atop a line of desks, and said, "Oh. So it's true. Miss Heartunderblade has gotten bigger. Wow, and she's become stunningly beautiful. I can still see traces of how she looked before, but…she's almost a different person."

"You'd agree, speaking as a woman?"

"Anyone would, just look at that. Her hair is in a ponytail… I guess she keeps it like that even when she's asleep?"

She went, *Hnmm.*

There seemed to be something on her mind. Well, maybe women were more sensitive when it came to women's appearances.

Hanekawa sat there for a while longer, seemingly in thought, before facing me again and reaching inside her bag. "Here you go, Araragi. I bought you a Coke," she said, holding out a drink that she'd probably bought from a vending machine in the area.

I took it.

"Hey, thanks."

"And a Diet Coke for me, if you were wondering."

"Huh."

"If your body naturally puts on muscle, does that mean you can take as many calories as you want without getting fat? That'd make any girl jealous."

"Nah, I wonder. If anything, it's that I don't feel hungry. Like I'd be fine if I didn't eat."

Kissshot didn't eat much either. It seemed like we ate as a luxury, for the taste of it, not because our stomachs were empty.

"Don't vampires feed on blood for their meals?"

"Oh yeah, that's right."

"Speaking of, Araragi. Do you ever get urges to suck blood or anything?"

"Hm? Well, now that you mention it—no."

Despite being a vampire.

Oshino said Kissshot didn't seem to have the ability to suck blood right now—was it the same for me?

I hadn't even thought about it.

"…Can you tell the difference in taste between Coke and Diet Coke, Hanekawa?"

"Well, yeah."

"I can't, really."

"Huh. Okay, I just thought of something."

"Hm?"

"A new product is developed by a beverage company. They've managed to create a diet cola that tastes the exact same as Coke."

"Nice."

"But the color is Blue Hawaii."

"Then it isn't Coke!"

I found it mildly funny and laughed. After laughing for a bit, I calmed down.

A class president among class presidents.

A model student.

Excellent grades.

With phrases like that overshadowing her, my mental image of Hanekawa was of a prim and proper stickler, a self-important class president, but when I actually spoke to her, she wasn't like that at all.

She said interesting things and was always considerate.

Despite what she went through the day before, she had yet to blame me in any way.

We'd seen each other every day since April began—if she hadn't done that for me, I would most likely have lost heart.

My unease that maybe I wouldn't be able to turn back into a human. My unease over having to fight it out with expert vampire hunters—feelings of uncertainty assailed me when I let my guard down even for a moment.

I doubted that Kissshot, who basically considered herself the strongest vampire, could understand such feelings—but Hanekawa helped me cope with them.

It wasn't just the night before. Hanekawa had rescued me, saved me many times over.

I thought I knew, but until the previous day's events I hadn't realized for real what it meant, vacuously enough.

That's why—I had to talk to Hanekawa.

There was something I had to talk to her about.

"Hanekawa."

"Hmm?"

"You should stop coming here."

"…Hm!"

With a cheerful smile still on her face, Hanekawa stood up from her chair and walked over to me.

"Well, I thought you might say that."

"Please, I don't want you to feel hurt—it's not like last time. Well, last time was partly about not wanting to get you mixed up in it, of course, but…a lot of it was my not being able to keep my emotions in check. I took it out on you, and I regret it. But this time is different."

"…How's it different?"

"When Episode's cross took a chunk out of your side yesterday...I lost myself. I could feel the blood rising to my head... I thought I'd die."

"You, not me?"

"Me."

My body was immortal—yet I thought I was going to die. Her wound hurt as if it were my own.

"I talked to you about my intensity as a human, right?"

"......"

"Your getting wounded hurt like it was me who'd gotten wounded. No—it hurt more. Hanekawa, I'm—" Since the night before I'd been thinking of all the different ways to say it, but in the end I could only be direct. "I'm not so desperate to become human again that I'd do it at your expense."

"...At my expense?" Hanekawa said, sounding a bit confused. "I don't feel like you're treating me in such a way, Araragi."

"But don't you wonder what you're doing? Wasting your spring break for my sake at an important time in your life—and nearly dying in the process. Doesn't that make you wonder what you're doing?"

"Not...at all?"

Hanekawa shook her head from side to side as if being asked such a thing was the bigger quandary.

"I've forgotten what happened then, but it was my own fault that I nearly died, right? If anything, you were the one who saved me."

"I'm not able to see it that way."

I knew that Hanekawa was being honest when she said what she said. I knew that she wasn't just trying to consider my feelings.

She wasn't being insincere.

She was sincerely a good person.

But—she was that strong, and therefore precarious.

"I just don't get it."

"......"

"I'm not confident that I'd be able to help you in the same situation. I'm not confident that, if our positions were reversed, I would be able to go that far. I'm not confident that I'd be able to show myself to a loose cannon like him if I had a body that could die—but you did it like it was nothing."

I tried to choose my words—but to no avail.

I had no choice.

There was only one word that could express the way Hanekawa was.

"You scare me."

"...I'm scary?"

"Honestly, you creep me out," I said, my eyes downcast. "Please, I'm not saying that to hurt you—I just can't understand why you're going this far for me. I can't figure out how you'd be this devoted to a classmate you only got to know the other day. It's like you're a saint or something."

A saint.

Or perhaps the Madonna.

"But your self-sacrifice is way too heavy a burden for me. I'm not big enough to bear it. Healing or not isn't the issue—when I think of you being wounded for my sake, I...just freeze. It scares me so much that I can't face Guillotine Cutter like this."

"It's not self-sacrifice."

That was Hanekawa's reply—

And she sounded a little angry.

"It *isn't* self-sacrifice."

"Then what is it?"

"Self-satisfaction," she said quietly. "You're misunderstanding me, Araragi. I'm not that good of a person, and I'm not that strong of a person. I'm just doing whatever I feel like doing... I doubt there are many people out there as self-absorbed as I am."

"......"

"If you came to know the real me, Araragi, I bet you'd feel

disillusioned."

Stop putting a girl on a pedestal, she laughed.

"I'm sneaky, and I think I'm tough. Enough to creep you out, actually."

"…How?"

"How? In every way, I guess? Even with you, Araragi, I'm only doing this because I feel like it. There's absolute no reason for you to feel bad."

"Hanekawa…"

"But," Hanekawa said, clapping her hands in front of her chest, and continuing with her hands still together, "if my presence is making things harder for you, then that really is putting the cart before the horse. You already have a pretty nice collection of superpowered school action manga, so maybe I'm done being your shopper. Reading more might cause everything to overflow. It does look like there's nothing left for me to do."

"No, there is something you can do."

I was staring at Hanekawa.

With my eyes still fixed on her, I said, "Wait for me."

"……"

"At that school, once the new year starts. Wait for me."

I realized I was asking for a lot. It wasn't like I had no idea how much pain and anxiety accompanied waiting for someone who might never show up. Even if I fought the most dangerous vampire hunter of the three, this man whom everyone was cautious of, and beat the next stage, it wasn't a given that I could turn back into a human—and I wanted her to wait for me.

"I'm looking forward with all my heart to chatting with you again."

"…Whoops." Hanekawa took a step back at that moment for some reason. There was a playful look in her eyes. "Bi-bi-beep, bi-bi-beep, bi-bi-beep."

"Huh? What's that the sound of?"

202

"My heart throbbing."

"What? Girls come with a sound effect for that?!"

A sound like any old alarm clock, too!

"Phew, I nearly developed something for you just now."

"What do we mean by 'developed' here, like a new drug or a beach resort?"

I was rich, then. A tycoon.

"So that's the line you use to sweet-talk girls."

"Huh? No no no. I don't even know what you mean, I barely even talk to girls."

"Listen to you, acting all tough and uninterested. Like you never bought those dirty magazines."

"Urk…"

But I'm a guy. What's a guy to do?

"Sheesh," she said.

Then, after giving her body an exaggerated stretch, and putting on a determined look, she thrust both of her hands underneath the hem of her school uniform's pleated skirt.

I thought she was going to pull up her skirt again, but no, Hanekawa wouldn't do something so illogical.

Instead, she took off her panties.

She lowered her peach-colored, lace-rimmed panties and carefully stepped out of them, the elastic parts staying clear of her soles.

I think it goes without saying that I was dumbfounded.

Prime-grade illogic.

"Mm…kay."

It had been enough to make even Hanekawa blush. She shyly held out her balled panties.

"Like just before the climactic fight in a superpowered school action series, if I may," Hanekawa said, still looking bashful. "I'll let you borrow these. Give them back when we meet next school year."

"…Hold on, hold on. Yes, there was a scene like that in the first manga you bought for me, but the item there was the heroine's necklace."

"I don't wear a necklace," Hanekawa said, awkwardly holding down her skirt. "Araragi, you like panties, don't you?"

"………!"

I won't deny that!

I'm not denying it, you know?!

Denying it would call into question Koyomi Araragi's very identity, so I'm not denying it, okay?!

A Koyomi Araragi who can't say no!

But—but still!

"U-Um."

"Well, if you don't want them."

"No I did not say that. Wanting it or not isn't the issue here, is it. Yup, yup. Er, what was that, so I give these back to you when we meet next school year?"

Quite at a loss, and somewhat surprised at how compact panties were once removed, I accepted them.

A soft warmth spread within my hands.

"…Sorry. I can't give these back."

"E-Excuse me?"

"I mean, I'm never giving these back. I'm passing these down from generation to generation as the Araragi family heirloom."

"I certainly didn't sign up for that!"

"These panties have been parted from your flesh for eternity."

"How dare you!"

"I won't give them back, but mark my words," I said, trying my best to strike a brave pose, "I will return this favor. If there's ever a time you need me, and even if there's nothing I can do, I promise, I'll be there—as of today, it will be my life's mission to repay you."

"Just give those back."

My very best effort to sound cool, and it didn't work.

Hmph.

Words—so powerless.

Hanekawa spoke next. "So, now I'm going to have to go home panty-less, in a skirt, with its low security rating... Compared to that, beating this Guillotine Cutter person can't be that hard, right?"

"Point taken."

No matter how grueling the battle—I would overcome, if I kept that in mind.

I'd win handily.

"Then good luck."

"Good luck to you, too."

Until next school year.

The two of us smiled as we bumped fists.

I looked forward to it—meeting Hanekawa in the new school year, once spring break was over.

Hoping I'd be in the same class as her, I looked forward to it.

Renewing my determination to become human again—but.

About three hours after she went home, when the memories of our parting were still fresh in my mind and Kissshot had finally woken up, Oshino returned to the abandoned cram school—looking uncharacteristically distraught.

"Sorry, I messed up," he said in an equally dire voice.

"Missy class president got kidnapped."

013

Guillotine Cutter.

The priestly man with the hedgehoggish hair.

Narrow eyes that, on first glance, appeared gentle.

A human.

A human who denied the existence of aberrations.

A human who eliminated the existence of aberrations.

He carried no weapons.

A vampire hunter by creed.

According to Kissshot, he was the archbishop of a "new religion" as well as the Shadow Team Leader of the Black Squad Belonging to the Dark Number Four Group of Secret Special Operations.

Episode, the half-vampire, described him as nasty, and even Kissshot warned me to be careful of the holy man.

And—it was Guillotine Cutter who had stolen both of Kissshot's arms from her.

"Ah, have you run over? Why, you must be exhausted. Though if you are unable to turn your body to mist, you must be a novice with regards to such abilities," Guillotine Cutter said. He spoke in a ridiculously polite tone—and with narrowed eyes.

"……!"

Speechless. I had no reply.

We stood on the athletic field of Naoetsu Private High School.

I found Guillotine Cutter waiting for me at the same place where I'd faced Dramaturgy at the end of last month and where I'd battled Episode the previous night.

And he held Tsubasa Hanekawa's body in one arm. His hand, which wielded no weapon—was clasped around Hanekawa's neck.

"A-Araragi…"

Hanekawa was—okay for now. She hadn't been hurt, and she was still conscious.

Of course she was.

She was there to be used against me—as a hostage. It would be meaningless if she wasn't okay.

For now.

"I-I'm sorry, Araragi, I—"

"Please don't speak without permission," Guillotine Cutter said, tightening his fingers around her neck—silencing her.

Kufff, I could hear her breath escaping from inside her neck.

"H-Hey!!"

Provoking him could turn out poorly, but I couldn't stay silent—so I'd yelled.

"Yes?" he asked in an utterly gentle and meek voice. "Is something the matter, monster?"

"Th-That's a girl, you know!"

"I abhor gender discrimination."

"But—she's a normal person."

"Why yes, she is. Otherwise she wouldn't be a hostage."

"D—" Our conversation had stopped making sense to me. "Don't…be a jerk."

"A jerk? Like this, you mean?"

With his fingers still digging into the base of her neck, Guillotine Cutter hoisted up Hanekawa's body. It almost looked like she was being hanged.

"Ugh… Uurgh!" Hanekawa moaned in pain.

This drew a response from Guillotine Cutter.

"You're a noisy one, aren't you?" he said, putting her back on the ground.

Even then, Hanekawa couldn't allow herself so much as a cough—if she did, even as a physiological response, there was no telling what Guillotine Cutter might do to her.

She just stood there—limp.

"Y-You…"

I didn't feel as though I'd taken it all lightly. I thought I'd taken both Episode's and Kissshot's words seriously—but as always, I hadn't understood a thing.

Guillotine Cutter.

Or perhaps, upon hearing that he was "human," I'd relaxed a little. I'd gone and relaxed. At the very least, he wasn't monstrously strong or immortal like a vampire or half-vampire—which made me think that the difficulty would be turned down for this fight.

But that was not the case.

He hadn't hesitated to take a hostage—and that was his way of challenging me to this duel.

"No, I'm entirely to blame here," Oshino had said, truly apologetically, after coming back to the second floor of the abandoned cram school—as Kissshot was finally waking up—to tell me that Hanekawa had been kidnapped.

His sleazy, frivolous tone was gone.

"It would be one thing if this happened two days ago or before that, but I promised to take missy class president on last night. Still, I didn't see this coming. It was a problem that Episode threw his cross at her, but that could be said to be a part of combat. The truth is, humans who move in this world, including those in my kind of position, tend not to want to affect regular people…"

"Is that why you were avoiding Hanekawa?"

"I wasn't really avoiding her, but I didn't have any intention of meeting her face to face. I thought she and I shouldn't exchange words—yes, well, even I don't care to actively bring regular people, not just missy class president but in general, into this. I won't try to stop them, but I won't encourage it—that's my position. But as for Guillotine Cutter…"

He didn't even seem to hesitate, Oshino said.

"He wasn't the least bit shy—it was a complete blunder on my part. I'd totally misjudged the opponent's capabilities and powers."

"…But how'd he get Hanekawa? He wouldn't know this place, right?"

"He must have been watching. Probably—the fight with Episode. He may have been watching your fight with Dramaturgy, too—I'd negotiated with the three separately so that sort of thing wouldn't happen, but he outsmarted me."

Just like how Hanekawa had been watching from the shadows of the school building.

Just like how Oshino had been watching from somewhere.

Guillotine Cutter, too, had been watching from somewhere.

"The barrier is still effective even if you're being followed, but it's not as if missy class president lives here—he could find her if he looked."

So it was after she'd left the cram school—and the barrier—behind. He'd found her on her way back home. Or had he waited for her in front of it?

"…What should I do?" I asked Oshino. "What is it that I need to do?"

Strangely enough, I wasn't leveling words of blame. I was more concerned about what to do next.

It was all I could think about.

"Aside from that, the conditions are the same—you and Guillotine Cutter will go at it one on one, and if you win, Guillotine Cutter gives back both of Heartunderblade's arms. If Guillotine Cutter wins, then you tell him where Heartunderblade is."

"…What about Hanekawa?"

"She must not count for him. He probably sees her as a tool—

no, as a weapon."

"A weapon..."

Like Dramaturgy's greatswords.

Like Episode's cross.

Tsubasa Hanekawa—was Guillotine Cutter's weapon. He was armed with her.

"Wh-What about the time and place?"

"He chose them. The location will be the same as the other times, Naoetsu Private High School's athletic field—and since he specifically asked for this location, we could consider that proof that he was watching your other fights—while the time is the night of April 5th."

"What?"

"In other words, tonight."

While the request made him seem terribly impatient, it was understandable when you took Guillotine Cutter's view, the man's nauseating view.

Hanekawa was a regular human.

Not only that, she wasn't a washout like me. She was a model student—her walking around at night was enough to worry even someone like me. If she didn't come home for just one night, her parents would probably contact the police.

Guillotine Cutter wanted to settle things before that happened. It was a rotten way to go about it, but it was in its own way—professional.

He wanted to settle things before an uproar ensued—though I doubted Hanekawa's safety was guaranteed once the fight was over.

In fact, I didn't see how he'd let Hanekawa off unscathed now that she knew too much. But there had to be some way for me to take advantage of his wanting to avoid trouble before the fact.

"Exactly," Oshino said. "Good, Araragi. That's the spirit."

"Oshino—"

"...This is my mistake at the end of the day, paper over it as

I might. So I'll give you a little more of a hint this time. A way to rescue missy class president. If you can do *it*—then you should be able to beat Guillotine Cutter."

"...Even though he has a hostage?"

"Yeah," he said, nodding. "First—start by forgetting everything you read *about how heroes act in superpowered school action manga*. Also, forget about your humanity."

There was so little time. Not even enough for worrying.

So my only option was to go along with the tactic that Oshino described to me after that preface—I was accepting the risk of coming up with a plan in advance of a fight, in other words, the risk of finding myself confused if it failed—but this time around, I had no choice but to swallow it.

This was already my third fight, but I still wasn't managing to make good use of my experience.

"Unfortunately, Mister Dramaturgy and young Episode have already left for their home countries—facing your camp alone was a bit much for me. Without a hostage or two, how could I ever balance the situation?" intoned Guillotine Cutter, completely unashamed of his actions.

He smiled with his thin eyes like it was funny.

"Mister Dramaturgy, who had Miss Heartunderblade's right leg, and young Episode, who had Miss Heartunderblade's left leg, returned them like honest fools. Chivalry? How bizarre."

"......"

"In other words, Miss Heartunderblade must have recovered to a reasonable extent. Once-human boy, my dear thrall of Heartunderblade. I can't allow myself to be injured in a head-to-head fight with you."

After all, he wasn't immortal, he proclaimed serenely.

"Wh-What are you going to do to Hanekawa?"

"I'm not going to do anything. As long as you don't do anything," Guillotine Cutter shot back. "If you plan on doing something to this girl, then I will do something to her, too—dealing with just-turned humans is nice and easy because hostages work on you as they should. Not so when I'm dealing with pure vampires—or perhaps it's different when the hostage is a thrall? Would you like to try being a hostage against Miss Heartunderblade?"

"…Cut the crap."

"I'm being entirely serious."

Sst.

Guillotine Cutter thrust Hanekawa's body out toward me like a shield.

Like—a tool. A tool, plain and simple.

"While I may not have superhuman strength like your kind, I have trained quite a bit. A single girl? Killing her would be easy."

"Ngh…"

I could tell that he was strong. That much was clear from the way he was moving Hanekawa around with one arm. But even more so than his body—he had trained his mind.

He was far too strong mentally.

He wasn't showing anything like an opening—in as fraught a situation as this.

"By the way, I don't plan on killing her in a way that would give you enough time to resuscitate her, like what happened with young Episode. I'll crush her brain with one blow. Even the blood of a thrall of Miss Heartunderblade wouldn't be able to perfectly restore a destroyed organ as complex as the human brain. Wouldn't you agree?"

"…And you call yourself human?"

"No. I am God," Guillotine Cutter declared, placing his free hand on his chest. "Therefore your kind, who would stand against me, should not exist. I swear to God, namely myself—I will not allow your kind to exist."

"……"

"Though if, like Mister Dramaturgy and young Episode, you

213

choose to join me…I suppose I could let you live."

"…I'll pass," I instinctively replied. Just the invitation was enough to make my skin crawl.

God? Really?

You, sir, are far more the monster than I'll ever be.

I was sure Mèmè Oshino was watching us, just as he had the other times—but no matter what happened, he wouldn't be able to interfere. A one-on-one battle: the result of his negotiations.

Hostage-taking—just had to be overlooked.

There was the option of getting Kissshot out here, but it would all be meaningless if Guillotine Cutter defeated her. She still wasn't at full power.

And even if Kissshot won, we probably wouldn't be recovering her arms that way—something had to give.

That meant one thing.

I would have to prioritize Hanekawa's life.

"Is that so." Guillotine Cutter nodded, hardly sounding disappointed. "To be honest, I never thought you, freshly turned, would defeat Mister Dramaturgy or young Episode. Those two are surprisingly pitiful."

"Look who's talking… You waited until the end to show yourself because you wanted to test the waters with those two first, right? When it was finally your turn, you used that information to come up with a plan that might work."

Oshino had negotiated with the three separately, but they had decided the order: Dramaturgy, Episode, Guillotine Cutter. Dramaturgy had volunteered to lead off, while Episode had shrugged that it was all the same to him.

Guillotine Cutter's wish had been to—bring up the rear.

"Oh, it wasn't the result of any deep thinking. Young Episode must have simply ceded to Mister Dramaturgy and me, his seniors, and Mister Dramaturgy, seeking his bounty, preferred to go first. Actually…I suppose Mister Dramaturgy tried to befriend you, correct? Then he must have been wary of young Episode or I beating you. Of course, your line of reasoning wasn't outside my consideration either, but if one of those two had slain Heartunderblade, the credit would have redounded to my church all the same."

"…You wanted to take it easy."

So he was the one who had put out the bounty.

And what was his goal?

If Dramaturgy was after the bounty and recruits, Episode was likely moved by emotions first and prize second—which was why he hadn't cared about the order—but what was Guillotine Cutter's goal?

I didn't even need to ask.

Duty—that's what it was.

"Still, this is just as well. I am not one to avoid getting my hands dirty—I begrudge no labor if it is done to better the world."

But we've chatted for long enough, Guillotine Cutter said.

He did talk a lot.

He was probably a talkative man by nature, but maybe his loquacity was also a sign of overconfidence.

There are two ways to defeat a superior opponent. Win by making them overconfident, or win by making them nervous.

It seemed clear that the former was the only option here. That was how I'd beaten both Dramaturgy and Episode.

And at that moment—

Guillotine Cutter seemed overconfident.

While he may have had no openings, he took me lightly.

I had a chance of winning. But to do that—

To do that, I had to abandon my humanity.

"Hanekawa." Ignoring Guillotine Cutter's words, I spoke to Hanekawa, whom he still held in his arm. "It'll be okay."

Hanekawa didn't reply.

She couldn't, because she was being choked.

She only—looked at me.

"I promise I'll save you," I added.

"...How unpleasant," Guillotine Cutter said, in the same calm tone. "I am not so tolerant as to allow myself to be a willing participant in your show of high school friendship. God, which is to say me, has spoken—let it begin."

"Begin?" I said, now looking at Guillotine Cutter. "How? There's nothing I can do as long as you have Hanekawa hostage. And I don't plan on doing anything, either. I absolutely need to submit to you—under those circumstances, how can we even fight?"

"God, which is to say me, has spoken—all you need to do is put your hands up and say 'I give up' the moment the battle begins. In other words, the match will be decided as soon as it begins."

"Okay." I nodded without so much as a pause. There was no reason to pause. "So start by releasing Hanekawa."

"Do you really think I'd make it that easy for you? The hostage will be freed after the battle is over. What kind of fool lets go of his weapon in the middle of a fight?"

Was that God speaking, too?

Gimme a break.

Hanekawa? A weapon?

No—she's different. She's different from you—and me. She's not someone you should be allowed to touch!

"Araragi!" Hanekawa cried out then, her neck still in his clutch.

Even as her neck was on the verge of being snapped. Even as she was being threatened with the destruction of her brain.

She still cried out.

"You don't need to care about me!"

"How could I not care about you?!" I shouted back.

And that—signaled the start of our battle.

Of course, Guillotine Cutter didn't move—he didn't do anything. Except inch open his narrow eyes—and laugh at me hysterically.

It was a loud, shrill laugh.

I didn't want to have to hear it, so I went on shouting. "I told

216

you I'm not so desperate to become human again that I'd do it at your expense. There's no point in becoming human if I can't ever see you again!"

And I—hardly even needed to raise my arms.

The battle was over as soon as it started.

Just as Guillotine Cutter had said.

"…What?"

Only—I had won.

I shoved away Guillotine Cutter's body as hard as I could—and managed to recover Hanekawa's body in the process.

It was simple.

Extremely simple…and convenient.

"Wh-What are you?" Guillotine Cutter groaned. "That, too, is your vampire power?"

"Nope. That was the power of friendship."

However—he and I were thirty feet away from each other.

Guillotine Cutter wouldn't have allowed me to get any closer—and I didn't trust myself enough with projectiles, be it a shot put or a roller, not to hit Hanekawa whom he'd been using as a shield.

Which was why—I hadn't moved.

I'd closed the distance without moving.

By transforming my body.

"…Yeah, I don't see a superpowered school action hero ever doing this."

Of course they wouldn't. In fact, it was what an enemy would do.

Just as Dramaturgy had transformed his arms into wavy greatswords—I had turned my arms into plants, stretching them forward as far as they'd go. I'd considered various scenarios, but the image of "extending my body" was hard for me to visualize in a short period of time, so instead, I'd pictured replacing my body with *plants*.

Plants I could do.

I'd thought every day about how much I wanted to become a plant.

True, I'd never wanted to become a monster—but it had gone exactly as I'd envisioned.

I had doubts about pulling it off like Dramaturgy, even if I was a vampire like him—but Oshino had shot me down.

"You can run up walls, and you can jump sixty feet."

In which case.

"You can pull off a little transformation—the rationale is the same. They say crabs dig holes to match their size and shape, but there's no need for you to stick to looking like a human. Since Guillotine Cutter thinks you're a noob vampire, he'll never expect it—just picture a non-human form and change your body accordingly."

I repeated that it was impossible.

His answer was, "Oh, but abandoning missy class president isn't?"

......

Oshino. You bastard.

My two arms had *grown*, not into greatswords, but like great trees flourishing in an old-growth forest on a lonely island, splitting off into countless branches, every last one of which I was aware of and able to freely control.

Shoving Guillotine Cutter's chest.

Ensnaring his arms.

Even retrieving Hanekawa had been within my means.

Maybe I'd gone overboard with my image.

Looking at myself—I certainly wasn't human.

I had abandoned my humanity.

In the end, when I complained I couldn't do what Dramaturgy did, I was refusing to let go of my humanity—rather than just clinging to the common sense I'd acquired as a human.

It wasn't something I was supposed to be capable of *if I hoped to become human again.*

I couldn't picture myself as anything other than a human

218

being.

But those illusions were just that—illusions.

I was already a monster.

From there, I slammed Guillotine Cutter to the ground, restrained him, and shut him up. I didn't care if it was God speaking or whatever, I didn't want to hear him spew any more lines, and so I bound his mouth shut with ivy—and knocked him out.

Of course, I didn't go so far as to kill him.

I had to get Kissshot's arms back from him, for one, and I'd been able to do something so outrageous—

Thanks to you, Guillotine Cutter.

Thanks to you.

I thought never turning back into a human was maybe fine.

"…Phew."

I returned my arms to their original form, which took no time at all.

No mental images or anything required.

These were arms I'd been seeing for seventeen years…so remembering them was enough. I'd gone and come up with the reckless idea, in the worst case, of cutting off both of my arms if it didn't work, so I was more than a little relieved.

I pulled Hanekawa toward me as I did this.

"Hanekawa—are you okay?"

I held her close and looked at her neck—clear and painful impressions of fingers were left on it, but there seemed to be no internal bleeding. In that case, the marks would disappear soon enough. I checked to see if anything else had been done to her—but no, she seemed fine.

Thank goodness…

Thank goodness, really.

Nothing could make me happier.

"Ah—ah, um, Araragi."

Hanekawa used both of her hands to push against my chest. I

wondered what she was doing until I realized that she seemed to be trying to get away from me.

"C-Could you let go?"

"Uh… Okay."

When I relaxed my arms, Hanekawa moved even farther away. She was putting some distance between us.

"Um… Ha-Hanekawa?"

"Th-Thank you, Araragi," Hanekawa mumbled, her eyes avoiding mine. "B-But, um—please don't come near me. J-Just don't come close. And don't touch me."

"…What?"

Was she—afraid of me?

Because I got her involved in this?

Because she nearly got killed?

Or was she frightened—because my arms had transformed?

Was she scared of me—because I'd abandoned my humanity?

But—I mean, I was…

"No, it's not like that," Hanekawa said bashfully as she fixed the hem of her skirt. "Just, I'm not wearing panties right now."

014

Next day, April 6th.

Afternoon.

Night, in other words, for a vampire, so as usual both Kiss-shot and I were sleeping in the abandoned cram school's second-floor classroom, the one with the blocked windows.

I was roused out of bed. By Mèmè Oshino, who hadn't come home the previous night or even shown himself to us. Who knows where that humble attitude of his from yesterday had gone, as he was now laughing away in his usual, sleazy way.

"Morning, Araragi."

"…I can't begin to describe how sleepy I am."

"Yeah, yeah. Over this way."

I was pulled out into the hallway, my eyes still blurry—while Kissshot dozed away, not even turning over in her sleep, despite our chattering.

What a peaceful soul. Did she never worry?

"What is it, Oshino?"

"Hm? Er, I don't know about the hallway… I'm sure Heartunderblade won't wake up, but let's go upstairs, just to be safe. Up to the fourth floor."

"The fourth floor…" As drowsy as I felt, I was still capable of making judgments. "The windows are open up there. What do you think is going to happen once the sun hits me?"

"Don't worry. It's raining today."

"Raining?"

Huh.

Now that I thought about it, it hadn't rained in a while. Unless it had been while I was unconscious before turning into a vampire, this was the first time during spring break.

Or maybe it had rained during some of the twelve-hour afternoon stretches that I slept through… I wasn't looking at the weather report, so I wasn't sure.

"So it's fine. And with your healing abilities, even in the off-chance that the sun hits you, it's not like you'll die on the spot, eh?"

"Tell me that after you've had your body evaporate once."

"C'mon, let's go."

Oshino began to wander up the stairs, and I followed him, careful of my step. It didn't seem to matter what classroom we went into as long as we were on the fourth floor, and Oshino chose the closest door. Once he finally got the thing, with its broken knob, to open, we were greeted by a tragically messy room. He didn't have the luckiest fingers.

"Hup!"

But he seemed to ignore this fact entirely, dragging a random seat over and sitting on it backwards.

I did the same. Out of a vague impulse to imitate him.

"…That."

I pointed at the Boston bag Oshino held. My eyes were focused at last. It was the same bag that had held Kissshot's right leg and Kissshot's left leg.

Which meant…

"Yep," Oshino nodded. "Absolutely correct. Both of Heartunderblade's arms are inside."

"…I see."

Relieved, I took a deep sigh. After Oshino hadn't returned by morning, I was concerned that just maybe Guillotine Cutter didn't intend to return Kissshot's arms.

For her part, Kissshot barely seemed to care and went to sleep with a "Morning, is it? Time to sleep."

A peaceful soul—without a single worry.

That, or I was faint-hearted.

But this was Guillotine Cutter, the man who had called both Dramaturgy and Episode "honest fools" for returning Kissshot's right and left legs, respectively. It seemed entirely possible that he'd renege on his promises.

No matter how much I fretted, my only option was to hope Oshino could take care of it—

"Hm? Oh, I know what you want to say, Araragi. You're surprised that Guillotine Cutter kept his promise, right?"

"Well, to be direct about it, yes."

"That's where my skills come into play. I am a negotiator, after all—though to spoil it, Guillotine Cutter didn't actually seem to be interested in returning them."

"After all."

"He was being pretty stingy—no surprise there. Unlike the other two, Guillotine Cutter was acting out of duty."

"Duty, huh." I recalled the many lines he'd delivered. "Still, is that how you act when you think you're one of the good guys?"

"Everyone has their own definition of good. You shouldn't be so quick to repudiate others—he was a villain to you, that's all. And, despite all he said, in the end..."

Oshino tossed the Boston bag in front of me. Roughly, like it was luggage.

"He did give it back."

"I'm amazed he did."

"Like I said, I had to convince him."

"How? He's basically a fanatic—or maybe a fantasist to my non-religious eyes. For him, isn't returning a vampire's limbs like abandoning his faith?"

"Like I said, these guys will listen if you talk to them. They're pros, after all."

"Pros, you say."

"Yes, professionals."

My cross-examination must have been starting to annoy Oshino; he tried to bring an end to it with that word.

"Specifically, I told him about how you wanted to turn back into a human after collecting Heartunderblade's limbs—and how Heartunderblade had agreed."

"…So you're saying Guillotine Cutter backed down for my sake?"

"That's one way to put it, I guess," Oshino said somewhat vaguely. He seemed to be insinuating something, but then I remembered that this was a guy who spoke in an awfully insinuating tone no matter the time or place. It didn't seem very meaningful to take it at face value.

His know-it-all pose could be just that—a pose.

In any case, it was a good thing that Kissshot's parts had been returned. Normally, that would be all, no further discussion necessary. I didn't want to have to think of Guillotine Cutter again.

I undid the zipper of the Boston bag. Inside were—her right arm, from the elbow down, and her entire left arm, torn off from the joint of its shoulder.

"I did at least make sure he could save face. Of course, I also gave him a very strong warning about kidnapping missy class president. If this were a game of soccer, that would've earned him a yellow card."

"A red card, you mean."

"Maybe a red card if he'd killed her. Episode would've received one if she'd died after what he did—but then, you tried to kill Episode, so let's call it even."

"It wasn't like I was trying to—"

To kill him, I wanted to say, but stopped myself short of the end.

That was a lie, plain and simple.

I'd lost my temper and couldn't help it—or actually, I didn't even care what happened.

If Oshino hadn't stopped me, I probably would have—killed Episode.

I did try—to kill him.

"Er, well."

"What? You're so spirited today, Araragi, raising your voice one second and muffling it the next. Something good happen to you today?" Oshino said as if to sweep things under the rug, before taking a peek at the arms inside the Boston bag and pointing to them with his unlit cigarette. "Anyway—I guess this makes all four of her limbs that you've fetched. Congratulations, Araragi. Mission complete. I'm as happy for you as if this concerned yourself."

"A little more empathy, please?"

"Well, it's not my problem, is it."

"……"

Sure. It wasn't his problem.

"I'm impressed, I really am—a mere high school student with no combat experience whatsoever took on three veteran vampire-hunting specialists and defeated all three in a row. I must take my hat off to you."

"You don't wear a hat."

"It's a figure of speech," Oshino said, putting his cigarette in his mouth. He didn't light it.

"…I know this might be a pointless question, but—Oshino, why don't you ever light your cigarettes?"

"Hm? Well, if I did, it'd be harder to adapt into an anime, right?"

"……"

Why did he care so much about an anime adaptation? It was a complete mystery to me.

"Now now, Araragi. I'm telling you congratulations, but you

seem awfully sullen. You accomplished your goal, that's something to be happy about! It's like you're at a wake or something."

"I still feel doubtful, Oshino," I said.

It was about—one of the things that bugged me.

I'd been going back and forth on whether to ask Oshino, but now, face to face with his carefree attitude, it felt idiotic to be mulling it over.

If there was something I wanted to ask, I needed to go ahead.

If he wouldn't give an answer, then that was that.

"It's about Guillotine Cutter."

"Hm."

"Well, I understand in theory—he underestimated me in yesterday's battle, and as a result I was able to beat him without even getting wounded. I understand that in theory, but Oshino, it's like you just said. A single attack from a mere high schooler who'd transformed his body for the first time ever—that was all it took to defeat someone as dangerous as him? A man who stole both arms away from a legendary vampire?"

"Mm."

"And actually, it's not just Guillotine Cutter. It's the same for Dramaturgy and Episode. They each took Kissshot's right leg and left leg—but when you look at what ended up happening, they were easily defeated by me, someone who, as you said, has no combat experience, who's only ever been in scuffles with his little sister—how could that be?"

I got lucky, you could say.

That it was a fluke.

But—wasn't there a more constructive answer?

"*Is it that they're weak? Or am I—too strong?*"

While I asked the question, I had no guess as to what the answer might be. It baffled me, plain and simple.

But—and I didn't know why—I felt like Oshino knew the answer. Because he was more neutral than anyone else. Because he was someone who tried to maintain a balance—

"It's both," he said, sure enough. "From their perspective, you're just too strong—and from your perspective, they're just too weak. After all, you're the thrall of none other than Kissshot Acerolaorion Heartunderblade."

"But is that really the only reason?"

"It's the only reason," he, Mèmè Oshino, asserted. "If you're looking for a reason why an amateur like yourself was able to defeat them, that's the only one—still, there was a very real chance you'd lose. In fact, the odds were heavily stacked against you. You were quite impressive out there, Araragi."

"Heavily stacked against me? You brought the situation back to fifty-fifty, didn't you?"

It was about balance.

I had been granted the locational advantage, killing had been forbidden—and when Hanekawa was kidnapped, I was alerted to a tactic to make up for Guillotine Cutter having that much of an edge.

He made sure that things were fifty-fifty.

But.

"But I'm saying it doesn't make sense if that's true. If you start off with that premise—it stops making sense."

"Stops making sense, how?"

"I'm this strong as a thrall. If Kissshot was in full power mode—how could those three stand a chance against her even if they all attacked at the same time?"

That was my gut feeling.

Even if you went with the lowest possible estimation of Kissshot's power as a vampire in her regular form, there was no way she could be weaker than me—and on top of that, she had five hundred years of experience.

Five hundred years of experience.

Combat experience.

Dramaturgy's wavy greatswords, Episode's giant cross, Guillotine Cutter's fearsome underhandedness—even together, could they rob Kissshot Acerolaorion Heartunderblade of her limbs?

I could only arrive at one conclusion.

It seemed—impossible.

Like there'd be no way.

"You've got good intuition, Araragi—keep at it, and you might turn out to be quite the expert," Oshino said with a sly grin.

Just as I thought that he had no intention of answering me seriously, he proved me wrong.

He continued—and answered my question. "You're exactly right, Araragi. Those three must have decided to attack her together because they knew they stood no chance of defeating Heartunderblade individually, but even together, they still would have had no chance of defeating Heartunderblade. Only…"

"Only?"

"If Heartunderblade wasn't at her full power at that moment—things would be different, yes?"

Not at her full power.

Those words began to summon something from within my memories. I didn't even need to mess with my brain to remember—Kissshot had mentioned it herself.

She had felt under the weather—or something along those lines.

I had thought it was an excuse.

But what if it wasn't?

"So when Heartunderblade faced those three—it was a *fifty-fifty* fight," Oshino said.

"……"

"Well, I was planning on giving this to you whether you asked or not—but I'm glad, Araragi. Giving this to you after you've asked me makes things flow smoother. You can be pretty sharp sometimes, Araragi."

Then, Oshino pulled *something* out of his Hawaiian shirt pocket and tossed it in my direction. I thought he was throwing his box of cigarettes at me, but that wasn't it. At any rate, I couldn't see how the pocket of Oshino's Hawaiian shirt could fit something *that big* inside of it.

It was a chunk of bright red meat—it was a heart.

"Eek…!"

I cowered and nearly let it fall from my hands—but somehow managed to maintain enough composure not to. I maintained it but found myself frozen to the spot.

Yet while I stood there, frozen—

Badum badum, the heart continued to pound.

"The heart of Kissshot Acerolaorion Heartunderblade," Oshino said. "She'd fought those vampire hunters one-on-three without it—so it's understandable that she got her limbs torn off."

"……!"

Of course it was understandable.

Even I understood that a vampire's power owed to her blood. So without a heart, the most vital element in the delivery of that blood—it was more surprising that all she did was lose her limbs.

"…She hasn't noticed, has she," I said.

"Probably not. She thinks that all she's missing is her limbs—and probably that it really was her not feeling her best that had nearly gotten her killed. She's too confident—the thought that the rug had been pulled out from under her would never cross her mind."

"Ah…so that's how it was." Huh. "I knew Guillotine Cutter was a crafty one, but stealing Kissshot's heart from under her nose? So they piled on her afterwards? Well, taking Kissshot's heart without her noticing must have been pretty hard work. Maybe I should be more impressed by that?"

"No, no, Araragi," Oshino disagreed. Pretty smoothly. "It wasn't Guillotine Cutter who took her heart."

"Huh? What? So did Dramaturgy or Episode steal it and give it to Guillotine Cutter for safekeeping?"

"No, no, no, no. It wasn't Dramaturgy or Episode, either."

"Then who was it?"

The spine-chilling thought ran through my head that perhaps a fourth vampire hunter would make his appearance—but Oshino's reply consisted of a single syllable.

"Me."

"……"

For a moment, I was speechless.

A number of lines came to me, but I kept them all to myself, none of them seeming cut out for the occasion. Then, without any prompt, Oshino began explaining—and he sounded like the villain of some historical drama giving his soliloquy.

"Yes, I did really start out as a passerby—wandering the streets at night, I found an incredibly powerful vampire, one who was certainly no laughing matter. It wasn't hard at all for me to guess that she was the aberration slayer, so I plucked out her heart—*in order to balance things.*"

Because he also guessed, he noted, that a number of vampire hunters would have come to this town as well.

"I plucked out her heart—quietly, so that she wouldn't notice."

"You're…up to such a task?" I asked, recognizing how stupid the question was as soon as it left my mouth—why, the proof was right in front of me.

Moreover, Oshino had stopped a triple attack from Dramaturgy, Episode, and Guillotine Cutter in a jokey pose, looking like a one-legged scarecrow.

It was because he had such skills that he could—negotiate with those three.

"I am," Oshino replied. "I'm not saying that it was easy or anything—and it wasn't just hard work, it was absolutely backbreaking. It was especially hard to do it so that she wouldn't notice. I brought a cross, some garlic, and holy water as my weapons and somehow managed to conceal myself. But even after all of that, I still didn't know how it would shake out. The odds were no greater and no lesser than fifty-fifty—the dice just happened to fall in the favor of those three."

"…And after Kissshot, all four of her limbs torn off, barely escaped with her life—she met me."

"And held onto it thanks to your blood," Oshino said. "And you became a vampire."

"…I see. So—it's not strange at all that I could defeat those three."

Forget about it not being strange, it made more sense. The difference in raw ability was absolute.

"So was telling Kissshot about an abandoned cram school she could use as a hideout your idea of atoning for it? Even going so far as to put a barrier around the place while we were inside—"

"Atoning for it? I didn't commit any sin. Again, it was a question of balance. Your participation changed the state of the game."

"The state of the game?"

"I never expected the aberration slayer to make a human her thrall. That was far afield of my expectations. I'd thought the story had ended for me at the point when I removed her heart, but that reset everything."

"Reset…"

Now that he mentioned it—those three had said something similar. That it was totally unexpected for Kissshot to create a thrall—

A notion, or something. She had some notion about not creating thralls.

"But while the situation may have been reset, Heartunderblade had now become too weak. One against three, or two against three even if we included you, her thrall, wasn't lending itself to any equilibrium."

"…So, happening to pass by Kissshot as she dragged me, happening to pass by as I was being attacked by those three, that was all on purpose? Your coming on stage didn't seem to have any rhyme or reason, so I was wondering—but that was how it was?"

Teaching Kissshot about this abandoned cram school, saving me from those three, all in order to achieve a balance—so that's how it was.

"Oh no, that was just by chance," Oshino said in a teasing tone. "It just means you two were lucky."

"......"

While I thought there was no way that could be true, part of me also thought that maybe it was.

A phenomenon could only be observed after the fact.

"So—even if Kissshot gets all of her limbs back, she won't be able to return to full power?"

Even if she got them back. Her right leg, her left leg, both of her arms. If she still lacked her heart—that was fatal.

"But of course," Oshino agreed with a nod. "Which is why you were going to get her heart back from me next—because even with the aberration slayer's arms, you'd have been the more powerful vampire. It was with the fourth fight—the one between me and you—that the balance was to be restored."

"...I-I have to—fight you?"

"You were going to."

"Going to?"

"Constantly being referred to as 'a slob' by you, I turn out, in fact, to be the 'last boss'—but my careful foreshadowing went to waste."

"Where is the care in that?"

It didn't pan out. Even if they had a number of letters in common.

Plus, I didn't recall ever calling him a slob. Sleazy, maybe, but still not to his face.

I guess he knew he came across that way, without having to be told...

"I'm skipping that part."

This time, Oshino lazily used his lips to move his cigarette, still

232

in his mouth, downward to point at the heart in my hands.

"See, I've already given it back to you."

"Wh-Whaa?"

"If you want to talk about atonement, now that's atonement. I really am sorry about missy class president. I wasn't joking when I said it's rare for regular humans to get themselves this involved in a situation. Normally, humans run from aberrations. There's something a little off about that girl. You can't explain her actions through goodness alone—"

"......"

Tsubasa Hanekawa.

Not self-sacrifice—but self-satisfaction.

Even after she was nearly killed by Guillotine Cutter...

She was considerate.

After it was over, too, she didn't have a single word of blame for me. In fact, she said something ridiculous like "Sorry for getting captured so easily, I should have kept my eyes open."

"To be completely frank with you," Oshino muttered, almost to himself, "I find that degree of kindness creepy."

"...Seriously? That's no way to put it."

"I'm sure you feel the same way. Don't you?" he asked, once again acting like he saw through me.

But yes, it was true. I'd said something similar to Hanekawa.

And despite the fact that I had—Hanekawa hadn't changed a bit.

"...It's like she's forcing herself to be a good person. Of course, that doesn't mean I can blame missy class president for what happened to her. In the end, it was my plan that saved her, but it was you who carried it out, Araragi, and I don't believe yesterday night is enough to atone for it." During the brief moments he spent saying these words, Oshino looked solemn—just like the day before. "What a blunder. That was so bad that you could hold every Oshino who lives in Japan accountable for it."

"It was your mistake, don't drag every Oshino living in Japan into it."

"Ha hah. Anyway, consider that heart as reparations, Araragi. My way of showing you just how sincere I am."

"Reparations..."

"It's part of our trusting relationship. And with this, balance has been restored—though there are still a few kinks here and there."

Saying so, Oshino stood from his seat.

"Her right leg. Her left leg. Her right arm. Her left arm. And her heart. Now you've recovered all of Kissshot Acerolaorion Heartunderblade's lost parts. In other words, now you can go back to being human. Allow me to congratulate you once more. It's okay for you to be happy, you know?"

"...Honestly, I feel conflicted," I said. "It's almost like it was all fixed."

"You're overthinking it. If someone fixed this whole situation, then I probably belong to the fixed side."

"I don't see it that way."

"Whether you do or don't, that's the reality. You overestimate me a bit in ways, Araragi. Even I have things that I can and cannot do. I may be the genius type, but I'm not actually a genius."

"......"

What an annoyingly misleading type.

"I may have prepared situations, but I didn't preordain them. Oh, and by the way. This is simply out of curiosity, Araragi, but haven't you felt hungry lately?"

"Huh? No—I think I told you earlier, but I haven't felt very hungry since becoming a vampire. I think it might be the immortality?"

"I see."

"Why do you ask?"

"Hm? Oh, do mind."

"So I should."

"I think it's time you started to feel hungry. It's already been two weeks—ha hah. That was rough, eh... All right, Araragi. Be careful not to do anything rash again after you turn back into a human. Once a person has encountered an aberration, he gets dragged in more easily henceforth, so do be careful."

With that, Oshino began heading to the exit, leaving behind me as well as his chair, which he didn't even bother to return to the original position.

"Hey, what's your deal? Don't make it sound like you're done with this place."

"But I am done. My work here is over—it ended in failure, but what's done is done, what's over is over. Oh, Araragi. That's right. About your two million yen and missy class president's three million, five million yen in total. Consider it paid 'n done."

"L-Lazy…bum?"

"No, that's me. Paid. And. Done. Offset, canceled out. I'm making up for my mistake with Heartunderblade's heart and—well, that might already be enough, but consider it a bonus."

"……"

"No need to look at me like that, I don't have any secret motives. I'm more generous than you might think when it comes to money. I'm not going to complain as long as we have balance. So send my regards to missy class president."

"You're going to go without ever meeting her?"

"Yep. I guess this is gonna end without us ever meeting—but there's no need for us to go out of our way to meet each other."

"Maybe so. But now that everything is over with those three, it's not like there's any danger of getting her mixed up in anything, is there?"

"Even so, it'd be awkward for us to meet at this point."

Plus, Oshino added.

On top of that.

"That girl does creep me out," he said, unambiguously—and harshly.

Oshino laughed a merry laugh as if to change the topic.

"Well, I still plan on wandering around this town for a while longer. Say hi if you see me. If you can't stop yourself from feeling indebted to me because I called off your payment—well, why not look into tales of aberrations that have been handed down in this town, so you can teach me about them? That's what my real specialty is supposed to be. I want to be done with all the hack and slash—it's not my style, it really isn't."

Oshino kept walking at the same pace, opening the door with the broken knob, exiting out into the hallway, and closing the door again even as he said all that.

He didn't say goodbye.

Now that I thought about it—I'd never seen him utter parting words to anyone. Even for the most innocuous of partings, all he ever did was chuckle and smirk.

"Is he serious?"

Feel indebted to him?

Was he serious?

Of course I didn't feel indebted—whether or not he'd fixed everything, he was part of the reason we'd gotten into this fix.

Of course—he'd saved us too.

No. If I said that to him, I knew what he'd say in reply.

We just saved ourselves on our own.

"…So now I've got her right arm, her left arm, and her heart."

Both of her arms from Guillotine Cutter.

Her heart from Mèmè Oshino.

All of the missing pieces had been collected.

At last, it was time for the iron-blooded, hot-blooded, yet cold-blooded vampire Kissshot Acerolaorion Heartunderblade, the aberration slayer—to be fully restored.

015

"Yyyyyyyyyyyyyyyyyyyyyyyyyyyyyyyyyyyyyyyyyyyyyyyyyyyyyyyyyyyyy
yyyyyyyyyyyyyyyyyyyyyyyyyyyyyyyyyyyyi—ppee!"

That was the first cry to come from Kissshot in her perfect form.

After she woke up that night, I gave her the three parts I had received from Oshino—I had to think about it for a while, but I decided to tell her the whole truth about her heart. Kissshot simply replied with a happy-go-lucky "ah ha" before taking the kind of bite out of her own bright red heart that you would expect from someone eating an apple.

It's only polite not to bother a lady with one's presence while she's eating. So I exited into the hallway.

And after a little while—I heard that shriek of joy. Filled with happiness, from the bottom of her heart.

I opened the door and went back inside the classroom. Standing there was Kissshot in her perfect form.

It was she—the woman I'd met under the street lamp that day.

Her golden hair. It was now even longer and loosely tied together at her nape.

A chic dress—and she was far taller than me.

She was simply beautiful.

Not just "cute" or "cool"—it seemed like the first time in my life that I was struck by actual beauty.

No.

I'd felt the same way that day, too.

She truly was perfect. Her form was one of perfection.

"Woo-hooo! I'm back, I'm baaack!"

"......"

Well, if she weren't skipping around in the classroom so wildly in her perfect form, perhaps I'd have felt even more struck, even moved.

She really was whooping it up. Forget dignity.

"By the way, Kissshot...it seems like Oshino took his leave this afternoon."

"Hm? So what?"

"Well, your heart. Aren't you going to get mad at him?"

"'Tis a trifling matter, I shall grant him forgiveness—I mean, I don't care!"

Kee hee hee, she laughed girlishly in spite of her current form, still hopping and skipping around.

Hrmm.

I hadn't noticed when she was under that street lamp, given the circumstances...but Kissshot's breasts were huge.

Every time she skipped, they bounced and bounced, bounced and bounced.

The bust of her dress was fairly exposed, as well.

Ah, so that (ten years old), by way of that (seventeen years old), finally ended up like this (twenty-seven years old)...

A grand mystery.

"......"

With her feeling so happy and hyper, maybe she'd let me touch those breasts if I asked—the low thought passed through my mind, but I didn't have the courage to put the plan into action.

It certainly didn't mesh with being moved.

"Hm."

Halt.

Kissshot stopped moving.

Wait, had she read my mind?

I suddenly felt uneasy and asked her, "Wh-What's wrong, Kissshot?"

I felt like my voice was quivering slightly, too.

"........."

Kissshot didn't move for a while, only causing my discomfort to grow, but after a bit, she replied, "Huh? What is it? Were ye speaking to my afterimage?"

"Y-Your afterimage?"

"I just circled the Earth seven and a half times."

"What are you, light?!" I interjected for what would probably be the first and only time in my life.

"Just kidding, just kidding! If I had circled it seven and a half times, I would be in Brazil right now!" Kissshot cackled.

Sheesh, she really was being hyper.

"Mhhm. It is truly a wonderful thing to be myself and complete—my dear servant."

Kissshot frolicked for another two hours or so, but at last she began to calm down.

Once she did, she said, "Allow me to give my thanks once again. Of course, I had expected thee to do a splendid job of gathering my arms and legs, but even to collect my heart, which I had not even noticed was missing, was quite unanticipated. I bestow my praise upon thee."

"I dunno about that."

Though she thanked and praised me, something still didn't feel right. I just couldn't get rid of the sense that everything had been fixed. That I'd danced to someone's tune.

"It feels like all I did was wander around aimlessly—rather than me gathering them, they just gathered together," I said.

If anyone deserved credit, it was probably Oshino. But he wouldn't like my saying so. In that case, it was thanks to Hanekawa.

Tsubasa Hanekawa.

By the way, she wasn't visiting that night. The next time we met would be during the new school year—as we'd decided. Together.

Of course, now that all three of the three vampire hunters had been defeated, it seemed unthinkable that coming would put her in danger all over again—but we'd judged that it was best for her to stay away from the abandoned cram school.

Plus, it hadn't been a given that Guillotine Cutter would return Kissshot's arms when we'd agreed on that.

I say the new school year like it was some far-off event—but it was only two days away.

Just around the corner.

The next time we met—I'd be human.

Should be, at least.

…Oshino left having avoided Hanekawa, openly at the end, but perhaps Hanekawa had wanted to at least meet him? In fact— I'd forgotten to ask her.

Whatever. There was nothing I could do about it.

At any rate.

"Kissshot. I'm sorry to have to ask this when you're celebrating— but I'd like you to hurry up and turn me back into a human."

"Ah yes, there was that matter. Calm thyself, I shall turn thee back—but, my servant. Won't ye have a little talk with me first?"

"A talk?"

"There is so much—well, not much to talk about. Only, in turning thee back into a human, there is something I wish to discuss," Kissshot said in a perfectly cool tone. Her cold eyes had returned as well.

She seemed to be serious now.

"Sure, I guess."

"Mm. Then let us change our venue."

"We can't do it here?"

"Doing so would pose no problem, but, well, I'd like to create the right mood."

Let's go upstairs, Kissshot said.

I did as she said, leaving the classroom and climbing the stairs—it looked like it had stopped raining, but it was now night. No matter where I went, there was no danger of evaporating.

Kissshot overtook me partway up the stairs, and she ended up climbing to the fourth floor. She chose the same classroom Oshino and I had entered that afternoon. Just as I was fully expecting to begin our talk there, Kissshot asked in a sullen voice, "Can we go no higher?"

"They probably don't have a usable rooftop. I didn't see anything like an emergency exit up to it, either," I said.

"Hmph."

Kissshot glared at the ceiling.

Sharply.

When she did, a portion of it blew off.

Concrete began to crumble down on us, but making no effort to dodge, she said, "Come with me, servant."

Then (as if it were the most natural thing to do) she sprouted bat-like wings (!) from her exposed back—her dress being just as revealing there as it was on the front—and flapped her way outside through the hole that her gaze had punched in the ceiling.

"……"

I didn't know where to begin with that one.

Her biology seemed to be made up of plot holes.

Wait, so Kissshot was able to destroy things with her gaze… Even Episode's mean stare paled in comparison to that.

She outclassed Dramaturgy's abilities of transformation, too. She'd sprouted those wings.

I attempted to do the same, but while I could do plants after my years of visualization practice, I'd never even imagined myself with wings before. It wasn't happening.

So I just jumped up through the hole.

Making that kind of jump is still pretty impressive, you know?

We were on the rooftop floor of the abandoned, ruined cram school—well, "rooftop floor" might not be accurate. We were just on top of a roof.

And there, on top of that roof, Kissshot sat, her arms around her legs.

Under the starlight, sitting there looking almost melancholic, she had a strange sensuality to her. I began to feel kind of nervous.

Somehow.

I grew timid and shrank.

Her perfect form—a perfect figure.

A perfect existence.

A greater existence.

I felt reminded of the fact that, after all, I was nothing more than her thrall.

"Hm?" Kissshot abruptly looked my way. "What is the matter? Approach me."

"…Okay."

I did as she said—and sat down next to Kissshot.

Then, suddenly, she hit me with a head-butt.

Nailed me, forehead to forehead.

"Wh-What was that for?!"

"Why cower so? Thou art my precious servant. I won't eat thee."

"O-Oh…"

Her words showed that she knew exactly how I was feeling.

But she was right—seeing Kissshot laugh, I felt stupid to be cowering. The thought helped me relax all at once.

"Now, what do I talk about with thee?"

"Wasn't there something you wanted to discuss?"

In turning me back into a human. She'd said so.

"Ah, that was not quite accurate. It is not that I wish to speak to thee of something. I merely wish to speak with thee of something."

"? That's an odd thing to say."

Let's chat.

I recalled Hanekawa saying something along those lines to me once.

Well, vampire or not, I guess she was a woman?

Maybe she enjoyed chatting.

Perhaps this was like her full-recovery party.

"And this is something necessary in order to turn me back into a human?"

"Indeed it is. For me."

"Hmph. You've lived for five hundred years, though. You must have tons of things to talk about."

"Nothing in particular," Kissshot said. "All of these years, I have been battling the likes of those three—and before I knew it, I'd become a legend. True, a man like that boy is rare—"

"By 'boy'…you mean Oshino."

"To steal away my heart unnoticed is quite the feat. I've no memories of ever being inattentive—I don't so much as know when the two of us crossed paths."

"Who is he, exactly?"

"A good question. But even I shiver at the thought of what would have been had the boy decided to devote himself wholly to the hunting of vampires. Thankfully, he is an opportunist who only tries to secure himself a middle ground."

"An opportunist…"

Part of me thought it was a nasty thing to call him, but it also seemed like a surprisingly fitting title. So much so that I could see Oshino gleefully taking it on if I told him.

"Which is why these events have been a reasonably stimulating experience for me—but mostly it has been five hundred years of boredom… Let me see. If there is anything for me to speak of, that man would be it."

"'That man'?"

"Thou art the second thrall I have created, as I trust I have told thee. This would be about my first thrall."

"Your first…"

Um, how long ago did she say that was? Four hundred years?

"Yeah, you did mention it. Something about it being your second time, and the first in four hundred years—like you were some team getting to the World Series."

"The World Series?"

"Er, never mind. Just trying to find an example. Anyway, what was that first thrall of yours like? I'm interested."

"Very well, then I shall tell."

"Was he like me?"

"? Why do ye think so?"

"Er, because—"

I hadn't told her this yet. Oshino was gone, so I guess it'd be fine.

"Oshino actually taught me something. He said that vampires suck blood for one of two reasons, and that you don't necessarily become a thrall when your blood is sucked."

"Mmf." Kissshot knit her brows. "…Don't be mistaken. It was not as if I wanted to spare thy life—I simply needed a thrall and used thee to collect my limbs. I suppose I can reveal this now, but had I told thee, ye might not have obeyed me, so I lied."

"Oshino also said that you'd probably say that."

"……"

Kissshot fell silent. And remained silent.

Was it because I was right on the mark, or was it because I'd missed it? I didn't know which.

"W-Well, anyway, that's why I thought he might be like me—after all, we're the only two you chose to be your thralls."

As I tried to backtrack, thinking that maybe I should've kept mum after all, Kissshot refuted my hypothesis. "The only trait I'd say ye share with him is thy race. He was a warrior—a warrior so mighty I could entrust my back to him."

"Huh… Well, I couldn't be entrusted with that, I suppose."

Entrust me? Maybe with her keys or something.

Nah, not even her keys.

"Hey, that was four hundred years ago. Unlike now, all the men were warriors, basically."

"Thy view of history is quite prejudiced and warped, I must say."

"Guh."

I do suck at world history.

"I mean, you know how I am. I'm not good at..." I said, fishing for the English word, "at thinking *hysterically*."

"I was not aware that 'in a *historical* manner' was the subtle connotation of that word."

Now she knew that I sucked at English, too.

"Be that as it may, this country has grown quite peaceful since I last visited long ago—as if it has been cut off from the rest of the world."

"Well, excuse us for being so blissfully civilian."

I didn't see it as a bad thing, but it was certainly true that I was no warrior.

No matter how much I tried to mimic the heroes of those superpowered school action titles, I was just a regular person. Whatever skills I may have gained as a vampire, it was like a middle schooler getting his hands on a butterfly knife.

Kissshot must have felt let down.

Especially if the first person was so incredible.

"Well, whether you made me into your thrall out of consideration for my life, or if you did it so that I'd collect your limbs, in the end, it was just an emergency measure... I guess there'd be no reason for me and that first person to have anything in common. But you did say that we were the same race, right?"

"Indeed."

"So, what, he was Asian? Surely not Japanese, though. Continental Asian?"

"No, a Japanese," she said unexpectedly. "I was gallivanting around the world, my youth getting the better of me, and I met the man here in this country. And that is when I learned Japanese as well—though much seems to have changed with the language since then."

"Japan four hundred years ago…"

That would be the Edo Period? I think?

I suck at Japanese history, too.

Well, I'm bad at everything other than math.

"So he wasn't a warrior, he was a samurai…"

"Hm? Ah, perhaps he was." Kissshot nodded. "Either way, he was strong."

"Huh—but in that case, you should've gotten him to help you this time around, too. If he's your thrall, that would make him like another one of your servants, right? Then you wouldn't have had to take the risk with me and—"

"It wasn't possible. He is already dead," Kissshot said as if to cut me off.

Actually, she did cut me off.

"That too happened in the distant past… Remember I said that I sometimes wield a sword in battle?"

"Hm?"

She did?

Wait, that's right, we'd been talking about Dramaturgy's great-swords then. She could use her power to generate matter to create a sword, or something.

I'd completely forgotten. Still, I was glad I remembered without messing around in my brain.

"The sword is a keepsake from him."

With those words, Kissshot flattened the fingers on her right hand and thrust them into her own stomach. Her hand pierced her dress, and her nails dug straight into her innards.

Just when I'd avoided picking around my brain…

Unconcerned by my stunned expression, Kissshot pulled her right hand out from her abdomen—and she was gripping what appeared to be the hilt of a sword.

What's more, judging from the hilt—was it a Japanese sword? I'd guessed right.

The sword Kissshot drew from her own stomach was a great katana more than six feet long.

"The enchanted blade Kokorowatari—it may be by an unknown swordsmith, but apparently it is a fine piece. Of course, I'm not very familiar with these—a sword serves its purpose for me if it cuts well."

"Wow…"

The wound on Kissshot's stomach was already healing—so I could focus on the sword. It was long…but not as long as Dramaturgy's. Still, while Dramaturgy's flamberges did have somewhat of an artistic shape, I couldn't deny that a katana had its own unique flavor.

To be frank, a Japanese sword didn't seem to match the blond, dress-wearing Kissshot at all—and to begin with, fine or not, could any such weapon withstand a vampire's supernatural strength?

"Don't move," she said.

Fwip, Kissshot swung her sword, Kokorowatari, as if to flick dust off of it.

But that wasn't her intention.

"Hey—"

"Don't move. I just cut thee."

"Uh, what?"

"Does it hurt?"

"N-No—"

"Hm. Then my skills do not seem to have dulled—ye may move now. Ye've already healed."

"Wh-What? Are you following up that going around the Earth seven-and-a-half times thing with another lie? Even if I heal, I'm not able to heal my clothes, remember? Where did you cut me?"

"Through thy torso, sideways. Ah, the happy things I slice."

"You mean 'sorry'!"

"Worry not about thy clothes, either. Kokorowatari's edge is inarguably sharp—so much so that whatever it cuts pulls itself back together with time. Of course, only because it is wielded by one with my skill at arms."

"……"

She didn't seem to be kidding.

Seriously?

"But how is that sword able to withstand your skill—and your arm strength? It's just a regular sword, right?"

"It is not the original. My first thrall created this with his flesh and blood using the original as material. Furthermore, I inherited it. Well, a too-sharp blade presents its own problems since what it slices sticks back together no matter how many times I cut. One might say that the blade is suited to cutting down aberrations and nothing else."

"The aberration cutter, huh?"

"Indeed. 'Kokorowatari' is slightly difficult to pronounce, and it is by the name 'aberration slayer' that my foes came to know it. That was not always my moniker, but the blade's," Kissshot said—as she stored the sword back in her stomach.

It looked like she was committing seppuku.

She sure was immortal.

But then, she said the sword was a memento from her first thrall, who should have been just as immortal… Yet he was already dead.

"If an immortal vampire died, does that mean—he was slain by a hunter?"

Dramaturgy, Episode, Guillotine Cutter—did people like them exist four hundred years ago?

But Kissshot replied with a no.

"He was not a man to be slain even on his worst day."

"Then how did he die?"

He was immortal. How else could he die?

"Suicide," Kissshot said dispassionately.

Her cold eyes were downcast, facing the town spread out below her.

"A common reason, one accounting for nine-tenths of vampire deaths."

"......"

"Incidentally, the remaining tenth succumb to vampire slayers—any other reasons fit within the margins of a rounding error."

"Suicide? Why?"

"Do they not speak of dying of boredom?"

Boredom—was a killer.

Guilt could kill too—but boredom was absolutely lethal.

"While it of course depends on the situation and the age, most vampires, whether pure-blooded or formerly human, wish to die after living for two hundred years."

"But—how does a vampire commit suicide? We're immortal."

"The simplest way is to throw one's body under the sun as ye did that first day. They throw themselves to their deaths."

"Well put, I guess…"

But—was that how it was?

I thought back to that day, and sure enough, Kissshot had asked me if I had a death wish.

"If there was anything odd about that man, it was that he chose death only a few short years after becoming a vampire—when barely anything changes in such a short time."

He died before my eyes—Kissshot said.

By throwing himself under the sun.

He made a display of it. He flaunted it.

"And after that," Kissshot muttered, "I created no thralls. Until I met thee, that is."

"…Didn't you get bored yourself?" I asked, though maybe it was inappropriate. "You've lived not just two hundred years—but five hundred."

"How could I not be bored?" Kissshot replied without drama.

"I've had nothing to do."

"……"

"Nothing—absolutely nothing for me to ever do. When there is, those vampire hunters respond by swarming to me like flies—just as those three followed me here on my sightseeing trip."

"Sightseeing."

That, I thought, was probably a lie. But then again, maybe it was true—if it was here in this country that she created her first thrall—

"…Yet I was not bored by thee, my servant. Thy actions, every one of them—were absurd."

It must have been the first time in history that a human had offered his own neck to a vampire, Kissshot observed with an amused laugh.

Compared to the age she looked now, it was such a childlike laugh.

"Ye also dared to call me Kissshot from the beginning."

"Oh… I never got a good chance to ask about it, but everyone sounds surprised when I call you by that name. Even Oshino. Am I not supposed to or something?"

"It is the rare fool who calls a vampire by her true name."

"True name? Is that like a first name?"

"…To try to explain it would be foolish as well. But perhaps 'tis generational, or rather, epochal. I speak not only of myself, but of those three as well. Out of fashion and out of date. If we wanted to match the current age, perhaps we need to appear as that boy does."

"You think you need to dress like Oshino? No way, I'd never accept anything about that sleaze ball as being ideal."

"I speak more of reality than ideals."

In any case, Kissshot said.

"That is about all I can speak of. And now I am more interested in hearing thy story. Seventeen years, correct? Ye can't have spent all of it idly. Try to amuse me."

"Ack."

Whatta way to put me on the spot.

Plus, she'd set the bar very high for interesting stories.

"U-Umm… Okay, then how about a funny little story. There was once a man. While he was a decent young man, he had a weakness for drink. If that was all, you could write it off as a personal foible, but one day, he drove drunk and struck a young girl crossing on a green light, her hand up in the air. Drunk as he was, he didn't notice that he'd hit the girl until the next morning, when he saw the blood on his car's bumper in his apartment's parking lot. He then learned through the newspaper that the name of the girl he struck was 'Rika.' Turning himself in would be the right thing to do, but the man hesitated. There should have been no witnesses, so if he never spoke up… While he wrestled with such thoughts, night came—and that was when the phone in his apartment rang. 'My name's Rika. I'm in front of your apartment,' the voice simply said, before the line died. 'Rika?! That's impossible!' The man began to tremble. The voice was unmistakably a young child's lisp. Could it be the girl he ran over, the one that should be dead? Then the phone rang for a second time. 'My name's Rika. I'm on the first floor now.' The man's room was on the fifth! Surely, that was where 'Rika' was headed. Upon realizing this, the man's trembling gave way to terror. Then, a third call. 'My name's Rika. I just got on the elevator.' What—too lazy to use the stairs?!"

"……"

I'd bombed.

And after I'd gone on for so long, too.

I'd tried to mimic the style of a raconteur, which may have been incredibly grating.

"No, not that kind. A regular, interesting story," Kissshot said.

"Urk…"

My pride was wounded!

I was more used to playing the straight man…

But I couldn't turn back, not after being dismissed like that!

251

"O-Okay, then part two!"

"Oh?"

"An old proverb: 'Where there's a will, there's a yaaay!'"

"………"

She didn't even grin.

One-liners weren't working out, either.

"Fine, then part three! Let me tell you an embarrassing story. That bit earlier about world history reminded me of it!"

"I'm expecting quite a bit of this."

"Once, on a test, I was asked the following: 'Prior to World War II, Japan faced the ABCD line. Give the names of the countries corresponding to each of the letters in ABCD.' So this is how I answered! 'A: U.S.A., B: Great Britain, C : China, and…D: Deutschland'!"

"……"

Kissshot cocked her head to the side.

She wasn't even going to laugh at my embarrassing stories?

"Um… Well you see, what's funny is that while I correctly answered 'U.S.A.' and 'Great Britain' though they don't start with those letters, I couldn't figure out what 'D' stood for and went with the first thing I could think of, even though it was in German. But like, Germany was on the Axis side?"

I was now being reduced to explaining my own jokes.

In response Kissshot said, "What sort of line is this ABCD line?"

"That's right, our common sense means nothing to you!"

What a sad way for a joke to fall flat.

And then we continued, until, at last, the clock ticked to midnight, bringing the date to April 7th—which meant that Kissshot and I spoke on top of the abandoned building's roof until the last day of Naoetsu High's spring break was here.

. While I'd felt like Kissshot's cold eyes were brimming with an intent to stifle my parade of silly jokes, partway through, the two of us found ourselves in one of those moods where anything is funny, and both of us started to erupt in laughter at whatever either of us said.

I think most of it was meaningless talk.

I think most of it was empty talk.

But probably—

When I look back on that spring break, the most vivid memory from it, the one I'd never forget, was going to be chatting with Kissshot that day, that time there.

It would be the fact that we laughed together.

"All right," Kissshot said, standing as she wiped tears of laughter out of her still-cold eyes, "I suppose it's about time to turn thee back into a human."

"Oh. Yeah."

That was right—I had somehow forgotten.

I surprised even myself... How does someone forget something that important?

I'd spent too much time having fun, but, well—the party was winding down.

"Speaking of which—didn't your first thrall ever say that he wanted to turn back into a human?"

"...Mmm, that's iffy."

"Iffy?"

What an uncharacteristically contemporary word for her.

"At that time I was in fact unable to turn him back into a human—and I plan to use the lessons I learned then this time around. Are ye ready?"

"Er... Well, I'm actually a little hungry. I think it's because I laughed so much. Could I get a bite to eat first? I'm pretty sure we're out of food, so can I quickly go get something?"

"Hm? I am famished too, after suddenly returning to my perfect form—but is thy hunger so pressing?"

"Uh, not really."

"Will ye bring back thy rations here?"

"Rations…"

What a weird way to put it. Was it just her dated sensibility?

"Well, it's my last night as a vampire. I think it's me being reluctant to just quit being one. Is there anything you want?"

"I've neither likes nor dislikes."

"Huh."

Only a convenience store would be open at that hour, of course, so it wasn't like we had many options.

"Very well. Follow thy heart, servant. I shall humor thy sentiment of wanting to remain my servant for a while longer—I will make preparations on the second floor."

"'Kay."

And with that, our conversation on the roof came to an end.

While I said only convenience stores would be open, the closest one was pretty far away—it would take an hour, round-trip, from the abandoned cram school.

That is, if I didn't run there using the leg speed of a vampire.

But—I didn't feel like running. If anything, I walked at a deliberate pace.

Phew.

What to do.

"I suppose it's about time to turn thee back into a human," she'd said. I couldn't deny that I'd balked after her all-too-casual words.

After all, I was a chicken, and I was a loser.

However—my telling Kissshot that I was "reluctant to just quit being one" was a convenient lie. Of course it wasn't that I wanted to be her servant for just a little more. How could I?

But…

I was reluctant to say goodbye to her.

"…Hrrm."

And probably…Kissshot felt the same way.

Something to discuss in turning me back into a human—in the end, there'd been nothing.

All she'd wanted to do was talk to me. Finish with a little get-together.

"I dunno."

Kissshot Acerolaorion Heartunderblade.

The iron-blooded, hot-blooded, yet cold-blooded vampire.

The legendary vampire.

The aberration slayer.

"I guess—she's going to go off somewhere."

She'd recovered all of her body parts. There'd be no reason for her to stay any longer in this town—or country.

Sightseeing, she'd said.

Considering the story about her first thrall, this was probably like a trip down memory lane for her—only, this visit had left those memories plastered over with unimaginably awful ones.

A stolen heart and four torn-off limbs.

She created a second thrall out of desperation, but he was a regular person. Not only that, he told her he wanted to become human again.

At least she said I didn't bore her.

"She said she'd been invited to become a god, but declined—what a contrast with Guillotine Cutter."

She would leave this country, and then what? Wander the world again?

No, she said that she only gallivanted around because her youth had gotten the better of her. So maybe she didn't travel that much lately.

Could she even ride planes, to begin with? Wait—she could just sprout wings and fly through the air. What a convenient body.

Still, I wasn't reluctant to quit being a vampire.

Probably the only thing that bound me and Kissshot was my being one, and I'd simply gotten cold feet about losing our tie.

I felt like I understood why Oshino, despite being such a joker, never said goodbye.

"What can you do, though?"

Meetings and partings. That was life.

It may have been two weeks full of horrible memories for Kiss-shot, but looking back on it, maybe it hadn't been such a bad spring break for me.

Maybe it hadn't been so bad.

And because I could think so—

"All right."

I decided to follow up our get-together with our farewell party.

Wanting to go out with as big of a bang as possible, I scraped together what money I had left to buy all the cakes and sweets I could at the convenience store, and then headed back to the abandoned cram school with a newfound spring in my step.

On the way back, I swore I'd say my goodbyes to Kissshot—and then arrived at the second-floor classroom.

The date was April 7th.

The time was past two in the morning.

"I'm ho-o-me!"

Trying my best to sound cheerful, I opened the door.

Kissshot was eating.

Chomp chomp. Chew chew. Gnaw gnaw.

Chomp chomp. Chew chew. Gnaw gnaw.

Chomp chomp. Chew chew. Gnaw gnaw.

Chomp chomp. Chew chew. Gnaw gnaw.

She was eating—a human.

"…Wha?"

The convenience store bag fell out of my hands.

The sound it made caused Kissshot to turn around.

Still in her hands.

A human head, gnawed halfway through.

"Ah, my servant—back earlier than I expected. But did I not tell thee? Have some manners and excuse thyself when a lady is eating."

I had seen the head somewhere before.

One of the three—one of the vampire hunters.

The one human among them.

It was Guillotine Cutter.

His body, his flesh, had been torn to pieces—minced into bite-sized fragments.

Served open and whole.

"He came by as I awaited thy return—it seems that even this barrier fails to hide my presence now that my powers are at their fullest. Then again, he came at the perfect time, just as I was feeling hungry. A handy restorative."

And then.

Kissshot seemed to be looking for someone behind me.

She tilted her head quizzically.

"What is this? Had ye not gone out to fetch those bespectacled, braided *rations*?"

016

I didn't know of a place to put myself at a time like this—I couldn't go home, of course, but I also didn't have the mental or emotional composure needed to find another place like the abandoned cram school, if it even existed in the first place.

The clock was ticking. Time was inching closer and closer to the moment day broke—inching me right into a corner.

Eventually, I decided to stick not just one, but both hands into my head, mixing and messing up the brains it held, thinking of every possibility I could—until I decided to use Naoetsu High's P.E. storage shed as a temporary shelter.

A temporary shelter—for someone who needed exactly that.

But the windowless P.E. shed, separated from the outside world by steel doors, seemed to be a suitable place for someone like me—a vampire—to hide even during the day. Not such a bad spot, considering my desperation. I found myself truly glad that I'd done everything I could to force the steel door back into working shape the day I fought Dramaturgy—okay, maybe not.

There wasn't a thing to be glad about.

It was all wrong.

"Uunh... Uuuuunnnnnhhhhhhh..."

You could hear my teeth chattering.

My body wouldn't stop shaking.

Why?

Why?

Why hadn't I realized?

Kissshot Acerolaorion Heartunderblade—a vampire.

A vampire.

Weak to the sun.

Didn't like crosses.

Didn't like silver bullets. Didn't like holy water. Didn't like garlic.

Didn't like poison.

Died if you stuck a stake through her heart.

Didn't cast a shadow, didn't show in mirrors.

Fangs.

Immortal.

Semi-permanent powers of regeneration.

Eyes that could see well, even in the dark.

The ability to transform.

Had blood with healing powers.

And—*ate humans.*

"Uuuunh…. Uwaaaaaaaaagh!"

I moaned and groaned and wailed—

But all I found myself with was regret.

I stuck my hand in my head and kept messing around with my brain, thinking over and over—where did I go wrong, how did I go wrong, how did it turn out this way?

But in the end…it was all wrong.

"Uunh…. Uuuuuuuunnnnh!"

Humans were food to vampires.

As greater beings, humans were below them, located at the very bottom of the food chain.

Didn't I know that? From the very beginning of it all?

In fact—she'd tried to kill me, right?

She tried to eat me, right?

She tried to drink my blood until I was dry, right?

Worthless little human.

Ultimately, even I—

Was just food to her.

Even if it did feel like I understood her.

Even if I felt a bond between us, on my part.

In the end—I was food.

"……"

To Kissshot, all humans were.

Every human was the same to her.

Of course, she did speak highly of Oshino's skills. That's just how impressive they were.

Perhaps she'd discussed them with him when I wasn't around—but still, humans were humans.

Food was food.

Even Oshino knew that.

As proof, didn't he leave the ruins before Kissshot could regain her perfect form and skills as a vampire?

Plus.

When I really thought about it—Kissshot had barely said anything to Hanekawa. It wasn't just that she was ignoring her—

Right.

Hanekawa was food to Kissshot.

Not my friend.

She saw her as rations.

My rations, vampire rations.

Hanekawa could have fallen victim to Kissshot's powers had the two met after she regained them.

Just as Guillotine Cutter had.

She could've been cut into pieces and eaten.

"Ye often hear that holy men taste dreadful—but he was quite the delicacy. While I don't have likes and dislikes, an empty stomach truly is the greatest sauce of all."

"Er…"

As she coquettishly licked away the blood and meat stuck to her mouth, I mustered an answer. I had to muster my bravery and suppress my fear before I could tell her.

"Y-You can't—eat humans."

"Hm?"

She seemed honestly confused as to what I meant. Kissshot's head was cocked far to the side.

"But, my servant, don't ye know I'll die if I don't eat?"

She was right.

She was exactly right.

It was such an obvious reason.

Almost too simple.

And Kissshot seemed to have no doubts concerning that reason—she didn't even feel the need to persuade me, a former human who was trying to become human again soon.

She thought it was common sense.

It probably was common sense.

I was sure it was something she'd always done.

They'd always been eating humans.

Vampires.

Her first thrall—and then her second thrall.

How could she have only sucked the blood of two people in her five hundred years alive? Every other human she'd fed on, she'd eaten like that. She tore them into pieces and left neither flesh nor bone behind.

That was how she nourished herself when she wasn't creating a thrall.

I'd been told.

Apparently, the idea that humans turn into vampires when their blood is sucked by another vampire isn't entirely wrong. Unless proper measures are taken after their blood is sucked, people do turn into vampires.

All it took was a drop of blood sucked.

That was enough—it turned any human into a vampire.

And those "proper measures"were to—eat every fragment of the human's body. Doing so would nourish a vampire more than any other method—plus, it prevented the human's body from rising as a vampire after the bloodsucking.

That seemed to be how it worked.

Because I only had my blood sucked, I turned into a vampire.

But Guillotine Cutter?

He was eaten as food—flesh and all.

And not just Guillotine Cutter. It was something Kissshot had done over and over again in her five hundred years.

An obvious fact.

It was as clear as day—yet I hadn't realized or tried to realize. All I'd done was avert my eyes, for all this time.

Right. It was just that I'd been clueless.

Even when I first met her, when I didn't try to help Kissshot despite her being so close to death—she hadn't understood right away.

She didn't understand why I wasn't helping her.

Why a human—food—might not help a vampire.

Predator and prey. That was the only relationship between the two of us.

"Unh, uuuunh… Aahh…"

Guillotine Cutter.

I hated him.

A cowardly, base man that I was loathe to call human.

But still—

I hadn't wanted him to die.

Though he was awful to Hanekawa—it was my fault.

My fault, for being a vampire.

Guillotine Cutter. He didn't care about the reasons or means just as long as it meant another monster exterminated.

"N-No. No, no, no! No. I don't want to think about this— I don't want to think about this!!"

I pulled my hands out of my brain and clutched my head. "No!"

But my brain wouldn't stop thinking. And not just about Guillotine Cutter.

Dramaturgy. Episode.

Even those two, who'd already gone back to their countries, had been here to slay a vampire—and it was no one else but me who'd gotten in their way.

After all the trouble they went to.

They fought to take Kissshot's arms and legs from her—but I stole them back. And then, of all things, I restored the legendary vampire—to her perfect state.

To say nothing of Guillotine Cutter, any humans whom Kissshot ate after this—every time she fed—

The fault would lie entirely on my shoulders.

If she ate Hanekawa.

If she ate my sisters.

If she ate my parents.

It would all be my fault.

My fault for helping her.

It wasn't just about her limbs and her heart.

It started with that first day.

If I hadn't helped out Kissshot when she was under that street lamp—if I'd only been able to abandon her—the story would have ended there.

I understood only now, but it was because I was a weak person that I couldn't just leave her there.

It wasn't anything like Hanekawa's strength.

It was a kind of weakness that bore no resemblance at all to her kindness, which Oshino called gross and I thought was scary.

That, if anything, was self-satisfaction masquerading as self-sacrifice.

Leading a devil-may-care life—didn't mean I should take the

same attitude toward death.

What if I'd been eaten there by a vampire and died?

How would my sisters feel, for example?

Did I really think they wouldn't cry?

"—Gurfft—!"

I somehow kept myself from vomiting.

I was about to cry, but I kept myself from doing that as well.

I was able to hold myself back because I had no idea what would happen if I let my defenses crumble.

I was afraid of losing control.

At that moment, I wanted to maintain my autonomy. Whatever little bit I could.

Kissshot and I had quarreled and argued until we didn't know what we were saying—and I'd ended up storming out of the abandoned cram school despite having nowhere to go.

And that's how I arrived at the P.E. shed.

The one dark place I could find in my memories.

The sun had to be rising by now—while it was spring break, kids that were in sports teams still came to school to practice during vacation. Fortunately for me, though, it was the last day of spring break. Extracurricular activities were prohibited.

I didn't have to worry about any sports teams opening the door to the shed. Of course, I'd barricaded the entrance from inside, just to be safe.

"It's my fault."

I didn't mean to speak out loud, but my thoughts began to escape from the edges of my mouth.

"It's my fault that more people are—going to be eaten."

By that vampire—whom no one could stop.

That iron-blooded, hot-blooded, yet cold-blooded vampire.

By Kissshot Acerolaorion Heartunderblade!

"It's my fault—it's my fault, it's my fault!"

When I thought about it, Oshino must have seen this coming.

While he'd gone on about balance and whatnot, he hadn't stolen Kissshot's heart because someone had hired him to—her confrontation with those three came afterwards.

That meant it had to be an independent decision on his part. An act that deviated from his job, his role as an intermediary between here and there.

In other words—at least he'd made a judgment on behalf of the human side to steal Kissshot's heart.

He wouldn't go so far as to slay her. Establishing a balance was his way of doing things. An opportunist—I recalled the term that Kissshot used to describe Oshino.

And I had taken that balance that Oshino established—and destroyed it.

If it was unexpected for Kissshot to create a thrall, then it must have been equally unexpected for a human to save her when she was on the verge of death.

My being so foolish and toolish—

No one could have expected it.

I'd ruined all the work that those three had done.

I'd even won over Oshino, who had stolen her heart.

The one making everything complicated—was me.

I felt like someone had fixed things? What was I going on about? At this rate, I was the one who'd put in the fix. Every last aspect of this situation, every nook and cranny—was all my fault.

It was all because of my rash decision.

I'd been too weak to abandon a dying vampire—and this was the result.

Guillotine Cutter was dead.

Eaten and dead.

She'd bitten through his head and eaten his brain, skull and all—there was no way he was coming back. It didn't matter if someone used vampire blood on him or not—he wasn't coming back.

He was dead.

Death.

There was no turning back the clock now.

"How did this—"

And Guillotine Cutter wasn't the end, but just the beginning. He was nothing more than a new start for the vampire Kissshot Acerolaorion Heartunderblade.

She'd continue to do what was normal for her—and eat.

I think someone once told me that you never escape the "mal" in "normal."

Stopping her would be impossible now—Guillotine Cutter, the all-important hunter standing at the top of that three-man pyramid, had been eaten, and it wasn't as if those three together could have slain her on their own.

Not Dramaturgy.

And not Episode.

No matter how much work or emotions drove them, they wouldn't try to take on Kissshot now that she was in her perfect form—a fact that made me realize just how strong Guillotine Cutter's sense of duty must have been for him to confront her alone.

I didn't want to praise him. Not under any circumstances.

But still, he showed just how strong a human could be.

Though he knew it could be him that didn't survive the encounter, he didn't grow timid.

If anyone was being timid—it was me.

Mèmè Oshino—Oshino, the man who was able to steal Kissshot's heart from her without her noticing, could just maybe stop her. But I doubted he would.

He was already done balancing everything out.

The game.

The situation—had come to a close.

Humans had lost.

Lost—to Kissshot.

And anyway, how could I possibly ask him after all that? "Please stop Kissshot Acerolaorion Heartunderblade"? There was no way I could utter those words.

If any request was off-limits to me now, that was it.

"—I just hate it."

This spring break.

I'd never imagined that everything I'd done over it would turn out to be a mistake. And I'd even thought that despite all the twists and turns, it hadn't been a bad spring break in retrospect—that it wasn't so bad after all.

In reality, it was the worst spring break possible.

It was hell, plain and simple.

It was all a big joke that felt like hell.

And I was nothing but a clueless fool.

"I hate it, but…"

But.

Something else was also giving off smoke inside of me.

It made me feel regret and remorse, and I did everything I could to avert my attention from it—but I'd noticed one more terrifying fact.

And I could only avert my eyes for so long.

Right. There was one more obvious fact.

"I hate it, but I—"

It was too obvious, self-evident.

"I'm—a vampire too."

No matter how I feared, loathed, and hated vampires—I was one myself.

Yup.

I could feel the weight of Oshino's words.

Words that weighed heavily on my heart.

Words that weighed heavily—on my stomach.

—Oh, and by the way.

—This is simply out of curiosity, Araragi—

—But haven't you felt hungry lately?

"............!"

My stomach—was empty.

I now felt hunger.

—I see.

—I think—

—It's time you started to feel hungry.

—It's already been two weeks—

"Dammit, dammit, dammit, dammit...!"

I could still hold out—for now.

It was just a little rumble in my stomach.

But—if Oshino's words were meant to suggest what was happening to me now—*soon, I would want to suck a human's blood.*

I would feel the urge to suck blood.

And I would want to eat a human being.

Why wouldn't I? I was a monster.

I was a greater being.

"Dammit!"

Her first thrall.

There was no way for me to know what kind of man he was—but I began to think that this, or something like it, was the reason he took his own life after only a few years. I knew he was different from me—but in the end, we were the same. Unable to bear himself after being reduced to a monster—no, after being raised into one. Kissshot seemed to be unable to understand these emotions—but how could she?

They were human emotions.

And now, four hundred years later.

I, her second thrall—found myself in the same position.

"Heh... Hahahaha."

At last—I began to laugh.

All I could do was laugh.

When I thought about it, it was a pretty comical situation.

It'd make for a great funny story.

I'd gone every which way and found out in the end that everything I'd done was a mistake—an audience, if I had one, would rate me a talented jester.

One person could only be so stupid. And I'd been so stupid that it was funny.

"What am I going to do now? My only option now is death."

Obvious, one might say. It was the obvious conclusion.

Because what was the point?

Now? I didn't have any desire to turn back into a human now.

To have my hopes fulfilled after the mess I made would be utter selfishness—or no.

Talking about selfishness was whitewashing the truth.

My thoughts weren't as laudable as that.

I was simply scared.

Scared that the moment I turned back into a human—Kissshot would eat me.

Of course she would.

I was afraid of falling to the bottom of the food chain, that was all.

But it was no reason to stay a vampire.

I didn't want to suck blood or eat people, either.

I even found myself detesting my immortal body.

And so.

"My only option is to die."

And not in a devil-may-care way—I really had to die.

The cause of death for nine-tenths of vampires.

I wasn't going to be dying of boredom.

But guilt—was absolutely lethal.

And so, I had no choice but to choose death, just as her first thrall did—it was the only path left to me.

Really, though—why had I decided to hide in the P.E. shed? Why had I tried to continue living, during daytime?

For example.

For example, I could clear the barricade, open the steel doors, and hurl my body onto the athletic field—and die there.

A death wish. Is that what she called it?

Of course, considering the recuperative power of a thrall of Kissshot Acerolaorion Heartunderblade, I wouldn't die easily even if I threw myself under the sun—it would be an endless cycle of evaporation and regeneration, but still.

I'd surely die before the sun set.

Surely, if I took off my clothes and bathed naked in the sun, in what would be my first and last try at public streaking.

The Vampirer's New Clothes.

I agree, not even funny.

I told you I prefer playing the straight man to the funny man.

"…Oh jeez."

I messed up.

Messed up big time.

I thought I could do a better job—and I thought I was doing a better job.

But look at how it actually turned out.

Hard even to look at.

Idiot, now all I could do was go and die.

"…Oh, right."

The moment I made my decision, I grew calm again as if I'd been exorcized.

I needed to call home.

It had completely slipped my mind, but I was supposed to be on a journey of self-discovery—though in reality, I had managed to do the opposite and lose myself entirely.

Or maybe it would be better if I didn't call them.

How'd I ever tell them that I was about to go off and die? It wasn't like I could explain why. Maybe it was best to let it be— the eldest brother went missing while on a journey of self-discovery.

I didn't know how they would take it, especially my parents.

As for my little sisters, they might be able to joke about it—their brother, the runaway boy.

This wasn't a fun little case of a runaway, though—it was as serious as you could get. But again, I thought, maybe that wouldn't be so bad.

"Still—I wish I'd told Hanekawa."

Besides, the right thing would have been to tell her.

Hanekawa didn't deserve to be left in the dark after all of her involvement, after all I'd dragged her into—but unfortunately, I was currently in a P.E. shed to avoid both the sun's rays and Kissshot, and I had no way to contact her.

I'd deleted her cell phone number and her email address myself.

In front of her.

To wound her.

While Hanekawa and I began meeting each other after that, it had felt too awkward to ask her for her contact info again. I was probably the only one feeling awkward about it—but I still felt bad.

What a chicken, what a loser.

While I was good at math, I wasn't great with numbers. There was no way I could remember an eleven-digit phone number, and an alphabetic email address was hopeless. Her info would be on my phone if I'd contacted her even once—but I hadn't a single time, nor had she. When I thought about it, Hanekawa didn't have my number or email address either.

She still didn't have my contact info.

If only I'd told her then.

…If only I'd told her—then what?

Did I think that Hanekawa was going to call me at this exact moment?

How ridiculous.

No matter how amazing Hanekawa was, she didn't have ESP— life doesn't unfold that conveniently.

If God liked stories to be that convenient, then I wouldn't be in my position to begin with—and I wouldn't have committed all those blunders.

While I realized it was an empty act of resistance, I still decided to pull out my cell phone, in part to check the time.

It was five in the afternoon. I'd been holed up for over twelve hours—though it didn't feel like it at all. That was the only reaction as the empty indication of the time of day entered my field of vision and my brain.

Meanwhile, the pointless struggle of opening my contacts list—actually wasn't pointless, and the fact struck me like a hammer blow.

Because there.

I found Tsubasa Hanekawa's name.

"Like I said…" the words slipped from my mouth.

I found myself suddenly moved, despite my situation—I never imagined that I, of all people, would ever be moved by the inorganic screen of a mobile phone.

There wasn't a thing to be glad about.

It was a spring break filled with nothing but misery as far as I knew.

"…Don't mess with people's phones without permission!"

She'd had plenty of opportunities.

It could've been when she came to the field to give me my phone while I was fighting Episode, or any other time. I was pretty lax about holding on to my cell phone and didn't even keep it locked.

It's not like I had much personal info at all on it—but.

My once-empty address book had an entry for Tsubasa Hanekawa's name once again.

Her phone number—and her email address.

"……"

I'd thought it was fine.

I did want to talk to Hanekawa, and I thought I owed her a talk, but another part of me had thought that it would be fine if I never got to.

273

Not to say I thought it was fine to keep her in the dark.

But at the same time, I didn't want to have to tell her anything.

So—while I went on about this turn of events being far too convenient, it might've been more convenient for me the other way.

But this was too much. I had no choice now.

Or rather—I did choose.

I sent a text to Hanekawa.

Because I was afraid I might cry if I called her.

I wondered what Hanekawa was up to on the last day of spring break—studying at the library, maybe? I didn't know where the library was, but if she was, she might have her phone turned off.

Oh well.

I'd be patient and wait for her reply.

Or so I thought, but her reply came immediately.

When I checked the time on the message, it had arrived with the same timestamp as my outgoing one. It hadn't even taken her a minute.

No way…

That meant she'd responded in less than sixty seconds.

I checked the message, assuming that it would be a brief reply, only to find an honest-to-goodness letter, beginning with a "Dear Araragi" and ending with a "Sincerely yours."

Unbelievable.

I knew that girls were fast at texting, but…

I was reminded of the day of closing ceremonies, when she first entered her personal info into my phone. Hanekawa was a fairly fast typist then, but…

Wow.

Actually, though I didn't know for sure because I really only ever sent them to my family, were text messages supposed to be this formal? Weren't they more a tool for no-frills communication?

In any case, to summarize Hanekawa's message, it said, "Wait there, I'll be right over."

Unable to summarize the situation well, I'd only been able to convey a rough outline of what had happened. But true to form, Hanekawa seemed to have figured out the entire situation.

Honestly.

If only Hanekawa had met Kissshot instead. "Rumors have a funny way of coming true," was it? Hanekawa had spread a rumor about vampires—but in the end, I was the one who ended up encountering both her and Kissshot.

A thought suddenly came to me.

According to Hanekawa, rumors were going around the girls about Kissshot—could someone else entirely, neither me nor Hanekawa, but a girl who went to our school, or even another, have encountered Kissshot?

If someone had, what happened when they met?

Did they just pass each other by?

Or did the girl have her blood sucked—and her body eaten?

While it seemed like it would be huge news, if her body had been eaten with not a scrap of evidence left behind, then the talk may not have spread beyond her family and friends.

A journey of self-discovery. Running away from home lite.

Maybe that's how people would see it. Maybe not if the number of victims began to pile up—but Kissshot didn't seem to need that much "food," perhaps owing to her elevated rank as a vampire...so it seemed within the realm of possibility.

"Oshino said about two weeks, didn't he? Then maybe that means one person a month for Kissshot...so, including Guillotine Cutter, just two or three victims?"

Of course, it wasn't a question of numbers.

But if true—it wouldn't have surfaced.

"...What could it be? It feels like I'm still overlooking something..."

Overlooking something, or maybe forgetting to do something.

But now that I'd contacted Hanekawa, there shouldn't have been anything left for me to do—and that was when.

Hanekawa showed up.

I heard someone knocking on the steel doors of the P.E. shed.

Clang, clang.

"I'm here to deliver a girl."

"......"

Not funny.

She was trying to be considerate, but in the wrong way.

In any case, I took apart the barricade (both building it and taking it apart were easy for me, with my vampire strength) and told Hanekawa to slide in sideways while cracking open the door as little as possible. I pressed my body to the wall so that no sunlight would hit me as she entered. Judging by the time, it would be dark soon, but the late-afternoon sun was still probably out.

I'd be taking in sunlight sooner or later, though. Every inch of my body would be taking it in.

But that would be after I talked to Hanekawa.

As always, Hanekawa was wearing her school uniform. I wondered if showing me what she looked like in her street clothes just wasn't on her to-do list... Or maybe she really didn't want me to see her like that... Well, not that I care, mind you.

Hanekawa grinned with the same smile as always.

Was this her being considerate, too?

"I dunno about this..." On top of that, she began to speak to me from behind in an unusually high-strung voice as I barricaded the door once more. "I've gotten myself locked into a P.E. shed. What am I going to do if you tried something naughty?"

"...Naughty?"

Wait... How much of a pervert did she take me for? I admit, I may have shown her that side of me more than once, but I wasn't the type who actually enjoyed that kind of talk.

If anything, I was a gentleman.

"Flashlight, on!"

She turned on her light and put it on top of a gymnastics vault. It was rectangular in shape, which kept it from rolling off. Then, Hanekawa sat down on top of a gym mat, while I sat directly in front of her.

"Oh my. There you go sitting right in front of me to sneak a look at my panties."

"You're getting who I am as a man all wrong," I finally said, unable to take it any longer, while Hanekawa pulled on the hem of her skirt. "If a naked girl was in front of me, I'm the kind of guy who wouldn't look at her if she said not to!"

"That's normal."

"Ulp!"

Seriously?

Since when had that become standard?

"No, Hanekawa, I don't think you understand just how gentlemanic I am at heart."

"Gentlemanly," Hanekawa corrected. "But if that's true, I can't wait."

"Can't wait for what?"

"Won't I be treated to oodles of your gentle behavior once the new school year starts?"

"……"

Wait a sec. How could she be so perceptive?

I didn't so much as hint at it in my email—my plan was to hide it until the very end.

Because I knew that Hanekawa would try to stop me.

"So you can't die on me."

"…Hanekawa."

"You can't die," she said.

She looked at me head-on in the dark.

"Those thoughts of yours are proof your heart is trying to run away from everything."

"…You're incredible."

After taking time to digest her words, I replied with my unfiltered thoughts.

"You're incredible. Seeing you—I feel so terribly lame. I probably would've died a lot sooner if I hadn't met you. There were more than enough situations where I could have."

"You're not listening, I just said you can't die—do you hear what I'm saying?"

"This is all my own doing," I said. It almost felt like I was confessing. "We're in this situation all because of how thoughtless I am—I hadn't even considered that things could end up like this when I gave blood to Kissshot that day, you know? It would've taken nothing more than a moment of thought to realize what it meant to give my blood to a vampire, but I went and…"

It hadn't even crossed my mind—that she ate people, that people would die because of her. I'd run away from those thoughts. Even after I'd given my blood to her, no matter how preoccupied I was about having become a vampire—I still had more than enough time to think about it.

No.

I'd said it myself at the very beginning.

To Hanekawa, on the day of closing ceremonies.

I was the one who'd spoken the words.

She'll suck your blood—and kill you.

And that's exactly what happened.

Guillotine Cutter had his blood sucked.

And then he was killed.

He died.

I should have known—but didn't.

"Someone died because of me."

"It's not your fault, Araragi. Plus, for a vampire…for Miss Heartunderblade, it's probably a very natural thing to do. It's the same as when we eat cows or pigs—right?"

"……"

She'd die if she didn't eat.

That's what she told me.

"But—she even thought of you as my rations. You never counted to her—she never saw you as among our numbers."

"But you were an exception for her, right?"

Saviors.

Each of us had saved the other's life.

I saved Kissshot—

And Kissshot saved me.

Maybe ours was a relationship based on trust in that case. But still.

"She was just being good to me the way you or I might be to a smart cow... Well, maybe not a cow, but you know what I mean. Like one of those genius dogs, or a genius monkey."

"You mean a pet?" suggested Hanekawa.

She was right.

And Oshino had said something like that too.

The kind of affection humans feel for their pets...

"But it must all be natural for her—including how she sees me."

"Yeah. Which is why Kissshot isn't to blame. It's all my fault. I was in the wrong here—no one else."

"I don't think you were in the wrong, Araragi. All it takes is a shift in perspective for what's right and what's wrong to be flipped all the way around."

"I agree."

Oshino—had touched on that too.

We all define justice in our own ways.

That was why Oshino did what he did. He chose the middle ground—and stuck firmly to it.

"It seemed impossible to me at the time. Dramaturgy, Episode, Guillotine Cutter—those three were *the human side of justice*."

"That's because you were being a vampire then, Araragi. You couldn't help it...but I guess it's not that easy to rationalize."

"Easy or hard, I can't. I've become an enemy to humanity."

"And that's why you're giving up on becoming human again?" Hanekawa's tone wasn't accusatory, but the question weighed heavily on me. "Have you given up on being human, Araragi? I thought you wanted to go back to being one—you said you wanted to return to reality."

"But we ended up with a dead body. For me to have my wish granted at this point is just too selfish."

"Speaking of selfish, isn't that what you're being now, Araragi?"

"Huh?"

Hanekawa touched her glasses as if to make sure they were in place and took a brief pause—before saying, "You're trying to leave the big mess you made and run away from it all."

"No…" That's not it, I tried to say, but the words wouldn't come out.

Hanekawa kept going.

"You're running away emotionally, and you're running away physically."

"……"

"You're trying to run away from here. Trying to reset everything all because you failed. Life doesn't have a reset button—so you're trying to pull the plug instead. No?"

"…No."

No. I didn't think so.

"It's not that I want to run away, I want to take responsibility. The only way I can atone for it is to end my immortal life with my own hands."

"That's not atonement. You'd just be piling sin on top of sin," Hanekawa said. "Suicide is a sin, you know."

"What, Hanekawa… Are you one of those anti-suicide people?"

"I don't have a firm stance on the matter either way, but we probably have the same opinion on that kind of thing."

"The same opinion?"

"It feels awful when people die." After letting that sink in, Hanekawa continued, "I don't mind if I die—but it feels awful when people die."

"......"

"No matter who that person is."

"...You're talking about Guillotine Cutter?" I began to think about him, though we'd only met a couple of times. "Some people ought to die—but people dying can't ever not matter. That's how I see it, and that's how I define it. And from that perspective, I'm a person who ought to die."

"But you're not a person at the moment, are you?"

"Now you're just nitpicking."

"I'll pick as many nits as I need to, if it's for a friend."

"Hanekawa."

I realized there was no need to say what I wanted to say, and that even if I did say it, she'd have some retort, but—I still said it.

"True, I'm not human at the moment. I'm a vampire. And that means—just like Kissshot, I eat people."

"......"

"I tried imagining it just now, but...just the thought makes me sick. I don't want to live so badly that I'm willing to eat people."

Which, I explained, is why I needed to die.

If I wasn't turning back into a human, my only choice was death.

"Unlike you, I'm a weak person. If I don't die now, I'm sure I'll gradually slip—and some day, I won't be able to resist my hunger."

Rations.

Kissshot's word.

"Hanekawa. Eventually, even I'm going to end up seeing you as nothing more than food."

And that was what scared me.

Guillotine Cutter's corpse was scary—but so was Kissshot's comment about Hanekawa.

Her understanding of Hanekawa.

Her common sense would some day become my common sense, too.

Some day, the common sense I'd acquired as a human would leave me, and it would be replaced by a vampire's common sense.

And when that happened, it seemed likely that I'd see Hanekawa merely as food.

I'd want to eat her.

"Then eat me."

As if she had no desire to shoot me down, Hanekawa didn't attempt a retort of the kind I'd expected—instead, in a composed tone, she said *that*.

"I think it'd be fine if you ate me."

"…What? What are you even saying?"

It was an honest question. I didn't know.

Not what her words meant, but how she felt.

"I wouldn't call someone a friend if I wasn't ready to die for them."

"…Er."

I knew people had their own definitions for everything, but this one went a little too far.

Who could keep up with such a definition of friendship?

"Yeah, that's what I thought," Hanekawa said with a smile. "I told you, if you got to know the real me, you'd feel disillusioned."

"…Who exactly are you?"

"Hmm? Your friend, Araragi. At least, I'd like to think so."

"Would a plain old friend go so far for someone like me? How are you able to do so much for my sake? What, are you the reincarnation of a cat I saved when I was in elementary school? Some inseparable childhood friend who moved away years ago? Are you a war buddy from my previous life?"

"Nope, not at all."

"Didn't think so."

If you were wondering, I never saved a cat as a kid.

I didn't have any friends who moved away, either.

My previous life I wasn't so clear on, though.

"Like I said before—how are you able to do all this for me, someone you just met? If you went this far for everyone you knew, you could have all the lives you wanted and it still wouldn't be enough."

"Well, I don't go this far for everyone I know," Hanekawa said. "I'm doing this because it's for you, okay?"

"I hope you know that however much you do for me, I'm still a minor. I can't co-sign for you on anything, all right?"

"That certainly wasn't my plan all along."

"And I'll probably be unemployed even as an adult, so I still wouldn't be able to co-sign on anything for you."

"Well, about that, I do hope you end up with a job."

"Don't actually be worrying that I might not!"

"Fine, then you worry."

But at any rate, Hanekawa said.

"One life is all I need to save you, Araragi."

"…So you're saying that you dying doesn't matter?"

"I don't want to die, but you already saved my life twice—so I wouldn't complain if you ate me, Araragi."

Though she'd probably say that it hurt or something, Hanekawa said casually.

She hadn't shot me down—but I didn't have a reply for her.

She was amazing—she really was.

Honestly, she was so amazing that it didn't make sense.

"So you can't die," Hanekawa repeated. "Don't die."

"…Then who's going to take responsibility?" I couldn't help but ask. "I was the one who revived Kissshot when she was on the brink of death—and I collected all of her limbs, then gave her back her heart, which she hadn't even asked for. Who's going to be responsible for that? Even if dying is a means of escape, how am I supposed to take responsibility without dying?"

"So you'll be able to take responsibility if you do?"

"I don't know, but..."

It was already all over. There was nothing that could be done—the situation was set. No one could stop Kissshot Acerolaorion Heartunderblade now that she had her full powers. It was my fault that she'd recovered—and I knew she was going to keep eating humans without so much as a second thought.

Just as she had done until now.

But from today on, it would be my fault.

"Guillotine Cutter couldn't do it—in the time it took me to go shopping at the convenience store, she tore him to pieces and ate him as a snack. Dramaturgy and Episode have gone back home, but there's no way they'd be any match for her. If I had to come up with someone, it'd be Oshino—but he would never do anything beyond striking a balance. He's drawn a firm line—this business with Kissshot is over and done with in his mind. He's not going to go and steal her heart on a whim again. No one can stop that vampire now."

"Even you, Araragi?" Hanekawa said, cutting to the heart of the matter. "Wouldn't you be able to stop her, Araragi? In fact—aren't you the only one who can stop her now?"

Her words struck me almost entirely by surprise.

And—that's what I had been overlooking.

"Kissshot Acerolaorion Heartunderblade...the iron-blooded, hot-blooded, yet cold-blooded vampire, right? And you, Araragi, her one thrall—aren't you actually the only one who can stop her?"

"...Oh."

What I'd overlooked.

What I'd forgotten to do.

Absolutely. How had I missed something so simple? If neither Dramaturgy nor Episode nor Guillotine Cutter nor Oshino could do it—

Then I, who collected from them her right leg, her left leg, both of her arms, and her heart—I, Koyomi Araragi, had to do it.

I could just be the one to do it.

That—was taking responsibility.

Whether or not I could pull it off didn't matter.

Right, I may have made a big mess of things.

But—I hadn't done anything yet!

"I'm going to be the one to *slay* Kissshot," I said aloud.

As I did, it began to feel real.

This was it.

It was something that only I could do.

The aberration slayer—I would stop her!

If that's what I needed to do—then I had no choice but to!

Click.

It felt as if the gears had met and finally started to turn in my head.

"Your expression changed. Want to hear some good news on top of that, Araragi? Well, maybe it's bad news," Tsubasa Hanekawa lost no time to add.

"Huh? Which is it, good news or bad? Don't be so vague."

"It might be inconvenient for you right now, but it would've been convenient for you a little earlier."

"Now I'm even more confused…"

"So, I went to the library yesterday and looked something up. When you beat Guillotine Cutter the night before last to finish collecting all of Kissshot's parts…well, maybe you didn't have her heart yet, but anyway, you were supposed to turn back into a human then, right? But—I felt a little anxious."

"Anxious?"

"Would Miss Heartunderblade really turn you back into a human? I was anxious."

It wasn't that she doubted her, Hanekawa said, but…

"I was thinking about what would happen in the off-chance she didn't turn you back into a human—so I did some research to see if there was any other way."

In other words.

She'd looked up how a "formerly human" vampire made into a thrall by way of a vampire bite might turn back into a human being.

"…So, was there a way?"

Hanekawa nodded. "There was. But just one. It said that while servants are normally supposed to follow their master, if they actually caused the master harm, then the master-servant relationship would break down and they'd be stripped of their nature."

"…? I don't get it…"

"In other words, if you attack Miss Heartunderblade—you'll be able to return to being human, regardless of how Miss Heartunderblade feels."

"I see."

First and foremost—I was surprised by such a simple rule.

"S-So that's how it works."

The master-servant relationship would break down.

It seemed to me that it had already broken down—but that would make it decisive.

I'd be able to return to being human. That's what it meant.

"I found the same thing written in multiple books, so it seems like reliable information—I know *it might be inconvenient for you* now that you're saying you don't want to become human again and that you want to die, but I had to tell you. You're the only one who can defeat Miss Heartunderblade, after all."

"Yeah, that is inconvenient."

Man. Always be prepared, huh? A cliché like "killing two birds with one stone" didn't begin to describe how truly—

"How truly inconvenient this is—for me. It means that everything works out exactly as you want."

"You might say I'm 'fixing' things. It's a nasty trap, if I do say so myself."

"You—know everything, don't you?"

"Not everything. I just know what I know."

So, Araragi, continued Hanekawa.

"You'll just have to return to being human, yes? Given your current mindset, you can't possibly let Miss Heartunderblade be."

"I can't possibly—"

"Or are you going to run away?" Hanekawa asked, delivering her final blow. "If you're still going to say that you're going to escape, then—I'm going to do everything I can to stop you."

I'd rather...she spared me.

I'd still be responsible—my responsibility for bringing the situation about would remain, never to go away.

But.

What I could do—was settle it.

I could settle it.

And if I could, I needed to.

It was a far greater act of atonement than simply dying—mercifully dying—could ever be.

I looked at Hanekawa once more.

And I thought again—amazing.

My head had been full of thoughts of dying until moments ago. No matter how I rationalized it, all I could think of was how to punish myself. But a short little talk with Hanekawa, and before I knew it, I'd put those thoughts aside.

I couldn't die until I'd spoken to Hanekawa—but now that I'd spoken to Hanekawa, I couldn't die.

If I slew Kissshot and became human again—Hanekawa still wouldn't let me die, no doubt. She'd use all of her powers of persuasion to keep me from doing it.

I'd made a bothersome friend.

And—I'd made a good friend.

"Then the question is whether or not I can beat her."

I was the one vampire who approximated Kissshot—but our positions as master and servant seemed like a fatal distinction. If I wanted this act of rebellion to work, I'd have to do something out of the ordinary.

"That's the thing. While I may have fixed things—there are a lot of gaps. If you were to lose, it would be the worst possible outcome, at least for me. Not only would you get your wish and die— Miss Heartunderblade would still be out there as an aberration... Miss Heartunderblade might even eat me. She did identify me as your rations, so she probably remembers my face at the very least."

"Do you have any plans for dealing with the situation if that happens?"

"Huh? No, I haven't thought it out that far," Hanekawa said, shaking her head with a troubled expression. "What was she called again, a rare breed? Miss Heartunderblade doesn't seem to fall under any traditional category of vampire. Just as you and Mister Oshino said, her immortality is so powerful that her weaknesses seem to stop being weaknesses."

"Even if that's basically true for me, too—the problem is the difference in our fight records..."

"And your mental preparation."

"My mental preparation?"

"You spent all of spring break together with Miss Heartunderblade—so whether or not you can bring yourself to kill her is an issue here."

"......"

She nursed me.

She sat by my side and cared for me.

She exposed her own body to the sun to save me as I was being fried by its rays.

And—she'd spared my life.

The life I'd tried to cast away and give to her.

She intentionally didn't suck me dry. It was close to the kind of affection humans felt for their pets—

But still.

Despite the time we'd spent on top of the roof, for instance.

That time we spent laughing together, for instance.

"I'm mentally prepared," I answered—even accounting for all that. "I'll be able to slay her."

"I see."

Hanekawa nodded. There seemed to be something else on her mind, but it looked like she was leaving it unsaid.

"All right, then," she said instead. "I'll cooperate. I came up with this plan, so it's my responsibility as well. Don't hold back, let me know if there's anything I can do."

"Don't hold back, huh?"

"Ahaha, but I can't think of anything more perverse than what I did the other day, m'kay?"

Perhaps to lighten the mood now that we were on the same page, Hanekawa laughed cheerfully—wait, hold on.

Please, she had me all wrong... Had she said that stuff at the outset to ease me into my decision?

Why was she offering to be cooperative in that kind of way?

If she wanted to help, she could help by coming up with some tactic. Honestly, what a silly thing to say to the gentleman known as Koyomi Araragi. Don't hold back? Come on.

"Hanekawa."

"Yes?" she replied.

As she tilted her head, I addressed her in an impeccably gentlemanly tone.

"Might you let me touch your breasts?"

"......"

Hanekawa's expression froze in place on her still-tilted head. The fact that she was still able to keep smiling spoke volumes about her strength of character.

An oppressive mood began to fill the P.E. shed. Was this really the time to be making things awkward?

"Your breasts—"

"No, I heard you."

Umm.

Hanekawa looked up, then down. Then she looked at me once again.

"Is that something you just have to do?"

"It's something I have to do," I said, trying to look as deadly serious as I could manage. "You haven't seen Kissshot Acerolaorion Heartunderblade in her perfect form, have you."

"Hm? No…but I've seen her at twelve and seventeen, so I think I can imagine what she looks like at twenty-seven."

"It exceeds your imagination," I said, holding up my index finger. "Her breasts exceed one's imagination."

"…Her breasts?"

"I fear that she might defeat me while I'm being distracted by those breasts. They will jiggle all over the place during battle. So to be ready for that, I want to train in the 'way' of girls' breasts."

"Ohhh," I heard Hanekawa say. "That's an even stupider reason than I expected…"

"B-But it does make sense, doesn't it?"

"Mmf…"

Hanekawa shut her eyes and scowled, as if she was trying to withstand a pounding headache.

"I guess it's fine."

"Wha?! Really?!"

Why?

What about my argument actually convinced her?!

"Hold on a second," she said.

Hanekawa began by untying her scarf. Then, taking off her uniform's sweater, she untucked the hem of her blouse from her skirt. Just as I began to wonder what she was doing, she brought both of her hands behind her and stuck them underneath her blouse.

A few seconds passed.

And then.

Hanekawa pulled her now-undone bra out from under her

290

blouse. She quickly folded it up with practiced motions before hiding it under the gym mat she sat on.

Then, she looked at me.

"Now, touch them," she said.

"......!"

Hold on, I wasn't asking her to go this far!

What was even going on here?!

I wasn't prepared for this, emotionally!

Wh-What did she just undo?!

She didn't have to undo anything!

"Wh-Whaaa?"

Plus, there was something else.

Upon taking off her sweater and undoing her bra, Hanekawa's breasts seemed to grow bigger—was it some kind of optical illusion?

No. A vampire's eyes couldn't be deceived.

As Hanekawa was now, at least as far as I could observe from over her blouse, her breasts hardly paled in comparison to Kissshot's and even rivaled them.

Not only that, they were so wonderfully shaped.

Now that she had taken off her bra, they should have been without support. But instead, they seemed to defy the laws of physics. Was Hanekawa ignoring the effects of gravity despite being a regular human?

Now this—this exceeded my imagination.

Of course, I'd made this request of Hanekawa precisely because I'd judged that she might be thus endowed. Even then, to call it "training" had been horribly rude.

Tsubasa Hanekawa.

Pound for pound, she could definitely stand up to Kissshot!

Who knew Hanekawa had such breasts!

B-But...

Hanekawa stood up and began walking in my direction (each step she took caused her chest to move in such an unimaginable way that my eyes were nailed to them, my body freezing in place like I was suffering a bout of sleep paralysis) before sitting down right in front of me—putting both arms to her sides, sitting up perfectly straight, and throwing out her chest.

This posture caused her breasts to look even larger.

Now this was drawing attention to your chest.

Not only that, her blouse was a fairly thin one, making clear what was just about the full, entire shape of her breasts.

"Araragi."

"Huh? Er, yeah?"

"If you're going to fondle them, do a proper job of it."

"A-A proper job?"

"I think you ought to fondle them for at least sixty seconds."

"S-Sixty seconds…"

Hold on, now.

She was setting the bar way too high.

Plus, somewhere along the line, "touching" had become "fondling."

Oh no, I thought. I couldn't say it was all a joke now…

What was I making my precious friend do?

"No holding back!"

"Y-Yeah!"

I reflexively held my hands up when I heard her words. But after that, I couldn't move them any further.

After all, I did have a vampire's grip, so I'd have to hold back when it came down to it. But I didn't know how strong was strong enough. And to begin with, I didn't know whether it was right to touch them from the top or from the bottom… There was the initial question of how to begin, but what came next? I didn't even know what the follow-up question was.

They definitely wouldn't fit in my hands…and so I hesitated to take a frontal approach.

I could just go from the side and bring them together—no,

not that.

Agh, but there was a far more compelling issue.

"U-Um, Hanekawa?"

"Hm? What is it?"

"Would it be possible for you to turn around?" I said in a fleeting voice. "I don't know if I can do this while I'm looking at your face."

The shed was lit only by the flashlight, which may not have been enough for Hanekawa to get a good look at my face. But for a vampire, Hanekawa's expression was as clear as day.

Her face was bright red, and she was biting her lip.

It was too much for me.

"......"

Hanekawa made a small, silent nod and spun around.

I could now see the base of her braid.

I had never looked at her hair that carefully before, but I couldn't believe how beautiful it was... It seemed completely undamaged. I could see that she cared for it properly every day.

"Ack..."

I realized that it would still be difficult.

Now that Hanekawa had turned her back to me, my hands would have to make their way around her body. But in that case, her arms, stuck firmly to her sides, were kind of in the way...

"R-Raise both of your arms?"

"Are we doing stretches now?" Hanekawa asked as she raised them.

Now I had a clear path.

So then I passed my arms under hers—of course, this meant our bodies were now inches away from touching. Actually, now that Hanekawa was facing the other way, trying to touch her breasts would basically be the same as hugging her from behind...

Furthermore, this distance complicated things—should I be crossing my arms? No, it would be easier to feel where everything was if I did things normally.

I spread my fingers.

Hanekawa had barely moved an inch since sitting down—but even from behind, I could tell that she was nervous.

But of the two of us, I had to be the more nervous one.

I could feel my heart racing.

"Y-You're not going to get mad at me later, are you?"

"Don't worry. I won't."

"Promise?"

"I promise."

"…Okay, well, just in the off-chance that this ends up going to court, could you say something for me like, 'Araragi, please, I beg you. Fondle my braless boobies'?"

Snap!

I thought I'd heard such a sound.

Was it one of Hanekawa's veins bursting?

Or maybe it was one of the tensed muscles in her face.

"A-Ah, Araragi, p-please! I-I b-beg you! Fondle my braless boobies."

"I can't have you saying it in such a quiet voice. It's almost like I'm forcing you to say it against your will. You need to say it louder. I want it to come from you, so tell me what you want me to do to you, and where."

"Araragi! P-Please, I beg you, fondle my braless boobies!"

"…'It's a great honor to have my breasts fondled by you, Araragi.'"

"It's a great honor…t-to have my breasts fondled by you, Araragi…"

"Okay… 'I've worked hard to grow these lewd breasts all so that you could squish them one day, Araragi.'"

"I've worked hard to g-grow these l-lewd breasts, all so that you could…s-squish them one day, Araragi.'"

"Huh. You know, I never expected you to be this dirty."

"…Y-Yes, I'm a very dirty girl. I'm sorry."

"Oh, there's no need to apologize. It's not like you're causing anyone any trouble by being dirty."

"I-I guess you're right, heheh!"

"So, how exactly are the breasts of our dirty yet hard-working class president lewd ones?"

"I-I take pride…in my belief that their s-size, and their s-softness…could not be any lewder!"

Oh.

Now I saw. I understood.

Like many adolescents, I, too, once struggled with the question of why I'd been born into this world. But now, at the age of seventeen, I was shown the answer.

Enlightened.

I was born for today.

My life existed for this moment in time.

The human known as Koyomi Araragi was born into this world solely in order to experience this day… No, it was bigger than that. It was wrong to speak of it on merely a personal level.

This world must have existed to this point so that I could experience this day.

The rest of history would be nothing more than an afterthought!

"Hold on, squeezing a friend's boobs? That kind of thing just isn't supposed to happen!"

I ran away from it.

I was the one who threw up my arms, who took three steps back and begged for mercy.

I was nearly prostrate.

"No, it doesn't happen! This kind of thing shouldn't happen!"

"…Chicken," Hanekawa said in the deepest of voices.

She didn't even turn to look at me.

She didn't so much as attempt to look at me as I kneeled there nearly prostrate.

"Chicken. Chicken. Chickenchickenchickenchickenchicken."

"Yes, I am a chicken. I am a loser. I'm sorry. There's nothing I can say to you right now. Seriously, please forgive me. It was my fault. I got carried away. I let myself take advantage of your kindness, but it was your fearlessness that made me snap out of it."

"You think that's all it's going to take? Do you have any idea what kind of determination it took for me to sit here like this?"

"N-No, a measly being such as myself could never begin to understand, but w-well, if I may entreat you to share with me the depths of your determination…"

"Honestly, I was convinced you were going to do more to me than just squish my breasts… Oh, I thought, so that's how it's going to be, my first time is going to be here, in a P.E. shed, on top of a gym mat."

"Don't you think you were being a little hasty in making up your mind?!"

"I actually figured it'd be okay."

"You did?!"

I knew that girls tended to be better at making up their minds about these things when it came down to it, but…really?!

"And despite all of that, after you teased me and humiliated me, you didn't lay a single finger on me!"

"A-And that's why I'm apologizing."

"So that's all it takes, an apology. Huh. So that's where I stand. I'm supposed to forgive you as long as you apologize. Huh."

"I am so sincerely and honestly sorry about this. Please forgive me, my stylishly bespectacled class president!"

"…I've never been this insulted in my life."

"Eeek!"

Did she mean the stuff about her breasts?

Or was it the stuff about her glasses?

Or could it have been the class president thing?

"Araragi…am I that unattractive to you?"

"………!"

Stop it, stop it, stop it!

Please, don't torment me with that perfect of a line!

"B-But if I fondled your breasts like this, I'd probably regret it for the rest of my life!"

Though I might regret not fondling them too.

Still, I made my decision. If to fondle would be to feel lost, then better never to have fondled at all!

"W-Would it be acceptable if I were to touch your shoulders instead?"

"My shoulders?"

"Yes. Your shoulders. I'd like to rub your shoulders, Miss Hanekawa."

"…Okay, we have a deal."

We came to an agreement.

I rubbed Hanekawa's shoulders.

Rub, squeeze, rub.

I was amazed. They weren't even remotely stiff.

I'd heard that people with poor eyesight were more likely to get stiff shoulders, but…she really must have been a healthy one. In that case, getting a shoulder rub from someone with no talent for massages like me probably didn't feel the least bit good…

Well, I could definitely say there wasn't any meat to squeeze around her shoulders.

I could feel the shape of her bones—were those her collarbones?

Urk… In its own way, this wasn't so bad.

Wait, no. Focus.

Rub, squeeze, rub.

And then, sixty seconds had passed.

"Th-That's it. Thank you very much."

Not only did I find myself rubbing her shoulders, I was even thanking her.

Talk about a slave mentality.

"You've had enough?" Hanekawa asked.

"Y-Yes. To be continued on our website."

"I don't see an online back rub feeling very nice."

"Th-Then, to be continued in the new school year."

"Yeah. That sounds good."

Hanekawa nodded, shaking her braid in the process.

"So now that you've made a girl do this much for you..."

As I let go of her shoulders, Hanekawa stood and walked back to the mat she'd originally sat on. But instead of sitting, she turned to face me.

"You wouldn't dare lose, would you?"

"I will win, Miss Hanekawa."

It felt like if I didn't go back to how I normally talked, I'd end up speaking politely to Hanekawa for the rest of my life.

But even so. I was able to say it clearly.

"I'm gonna win. I'm returning to you victorious. I'll come again! I swear to you, on your chest!"

"No, it's fine. You don't need to do anything on my chest."

There seemed to be a bit of a gap between how excited each of us were.

"Anyway," Hanekawa said. Clearing her throat, she continued, "So this time is really going to be the final battle."

"That's right—the big finale of our superpowered school action story."

And then, just as I said that.

From outside the P.E. shed—roared a thunderous noise.

017

Kissshot Acerolaorion Heartunderblade.

The iron-blooded, hot-blooded, yet cold-blooded vampire.

The legendary vampire.

The slayer and empress of aberrations.

A vampiress.

Adorned with dazzling gold hair and a chic dress, a beautiful, blood-chillingly beautiful vampire—no other words were needed, but if I were forced to find them—

She was the final nemesis of her thrall, yours truly.

"Kissshot…"

I shoved the barricade away and opened the P.E. shed's steel door—only to find that the sun had already set outside and that she stood there in the middle of the athletic field.

The ground under her feet was cracked.

It must have been from the impact of her landing.

In fact, the field had caved in around her to the point where her ankles had been swallowed by it.

Those bat-like wings were nowhere to be found on Kissshot's back—as her thrall, I could intuit that she must have traveled from the abandoned cram school's roof to here in a single, standing leap.

She'd waited for the sun to set.

And then—she'd jumped to where I was.

Still, her feat could only be described as tremendous. I'd congratulated myself for a standing jump of a measly sixty feet—but Kissshot had jumped miles like it was nothing at all.

Of course, it wasn't fair to compare her jump to mine since I'd been aiming to land in that sand pit, not trying to break any records—but if you asked me if I could jump from the field back to the abandoned school, my answer would be no.

I closed the shed's steel doors behind me.

With Hanekawa still inside.

The door probably didn't pose even a minor obstacle to Kissshot—but closing it still afforded some comfort.

Don't say a word, I whispered to the other side.

Then, I took a step forward. Toward Kissshot.

"…Hey," I said as I approached her. "I didn't think you'd be the one coming to find me."

I'd assumed it would be the hardest part.

Figuring out a time, figuring out a place.

Unlike my bouts with Dramaturgy, Episode, and Guillotine Cutter—Oshino wouldn't be there to mediate.

But we were both vampires.

A master and a servant—her thrall.

That Kissshot came to me at almost the exact moment the sun set seemed to mean that in her perfect form, she was thoroughly aware of my every deed.

Where I was.

What I was thinking.

She was thoroughly—aware of it all.

Kissshot now looked at me with even colder eyes than usual—and began by pulling her legs out from inside the field, first right, then left.

"But once, my servant," she spoke next. "I understood thy feelings in the time the sun was out—the cause of thy anger too. While I wished to sleep, I forced myself to think. I believe I acted thoughtlessly—and that I had not paid thee the consideration due a former human. And that is why I will apologize to thee but once."

"……"

"Return to my side," Kissshot said.

Her voice was beautiful.

And it was with that alluring voice—that she tempted me.

"Live with me. I had my life saved by thee—and while I may think thee a strange creature, that is precisely why I trust that we could live together. Rather than return to being human—will ye not live with me, for eternity?"

"…I refuse."

I looked back into Kissshot's cold eyes, preparing myself for the worst—and said the words.

"You ate a human. That on its own is enough for me."

"Had ye known that—would ye not have saved me? Ye'd have abandoned me, leaving me for dead?"

"Kissshot—I didn't know anything then. No…"

I shook my head.

"I did know from the beginning. I was just keeping myself from looking at the facts. I had thought to die for your sake—which meant that I was permitting you to eat humans. But I didn't actually picture other people dying. While my actions may have been beautiful, they weren't right."

It didn't matter if I died—but it felt awful when other people died.

That was an idiosyncratic view, come to think of it.

How could I possibly expect it to stand up to scrutiny?

"…I thought ye might speak thus," Kissshot said with a smile. "Those were the words I wished to hear from thee."

"Kissshot…"

"And now I am free of doubt, my servant. I, too, had an inkling from the very beginning—that thou were such a one."

"Such a what."

"I had known—that thy kindness would only last while I was weak."

I'd have no interest in her once she became a perfect existence, she had suspected.

There was even a tinge of bitterness in Kissshot's words.

"It was not because of who I am—ye'd have saved anyone, so long as they were weak."

"……"

I don't go this far for everyone I know. You realize I'm doing this because it's you.

That was what Hanekawa had said.

But me? Even if it wasn't Kissshot there, I would have—

"And so, aye—I had thought it may turn out like this. Incidentally—know that I saved thee as thyself. A heroic soul ready to cast away his own life for my sake deserved better than death by my hands."

"…I deserved better?"

"And my gratitude is thine for doing thy share to repay the favor. Now come closer, my servant. Do ye know already, to judge from thy expression? Indeed. By slaying me with thy hands, ye return to the ranks of humans that ye love so."

"……"

I gulped.

I realized anew that she saw through me—and also just how vast the difference in power between us two was.

Facing her here, one on one—would be different.

It wouldn't play out like any of my fights against the trio— I felt intimidated and overwhelmingly tense, like I was being strangled by the air around me.

That was it.

The battle that was about to unfold was, in no uncertain terms, a fight to the death—the biggest difference of all.

Nothing prevented it now.

On top of that—I was facing the aberration slayer.

"Don't feel too despondent, my servant," Kissshot said.

She looked the slightest bit…happy?

"I'm in the best condition I've been in during my five hundred years alive—when I faced those three at the same time, not only was I under the weather, they took me by surprise. I certainly hadn't expected my heart to have been stolen… It is rare for one of my class."

"…What is?"

"Having to try," she said, beckoning me. "In all honesty, even I am unsure of what will happen—but as I face the most powerful of all the foes I have fought until today, there is no need for me to hold back. It is that I am happy about."

"I can't promise I'll be able to meet your expectations."

I worked up my courage and began to walk toward her.

Normally, I would have run away instead—but this was different. I had a dear friend at my back, sitting inside that P.E. shed. There was someone I needed to protect—I couldn't run away.

I had to face it.

Just watch, Hanekawa. I'm not going to look pathetic in front of you.

"After all, I'm a former human—formerly food for you."

"…Fret not. While I will be killing thee with malice and enmity, I shall give myself a handicap—what was it that boy liked to say? Ah, yes, a fifty-fifty fight. I shall set such rules."

'Tis a game.

Kissshot hopped as she said the words.

A moment later, she was directly in front of me—so close our legs nearly became entangled.

In her perfect form, she was taller than me. She looked down on me from where she stood.

"I will not fly. I will not hide myself in the shadows. I will not turn to mist. I will not turn to darkness. I will not vanish. I will not transform myself. I will not use the power of my eyes. I will not even generate matter. Needless to say, I will not use my enchanted sword Kokorowatari…the aberration slayer. In other words, I will not use any of my active abilities as a vampire—ye have my word. Of course, feel free on thy part—but transforming thy body from the arms forward is about all, is it not?"

"……"

And that I was only able to do because Hanekawa had been kidnapped—now that my mind was closer to the human side, it seemed unlikely that I could even transform my fingers.

The story would be different if I had Dramaturgy's force of will, or experience—but I was a beginner who had neither.

"Normally, as thy mistress, I would be able to exert some degree of control over the actions of my servant—but I shall not do that either. I promise not to do such a boorish thing. We shall fight only with our refined, pure powers of immortality—that should negate any need for experience. We will stand here at this distance and fight to the death—would that not make it a fifty-fifty fight?"

"…You must really be bored."

I glared at Kissshot's face, which loomed over mine.

"You're going to do all that just so you don't have to hold back? I mean, isn't that exactly what we'd call letting your guard down?"

"Letting my guard down? Unfortunately for thee, I am not so foolish as to let my guard down against my own thrall—but if I did not offer thee a fighting chance, there would be no game, would there? I do not wish to hold back. But my foe abandoning the fight in the middle of the match would not do at all."

Then she held out her hands, ready to fight. Her hands were open and flat, set to chop—she prepared herself to fight at our super-close range.

I tried doing the same.

An open hand was better for this situation than a closed fist. When you have the physical strength of a vampire, the difference in damage that a fist can inflict compared to a chop is practically negligible. In that case, an open hand is more versatile and easier to use—

"......"

I then looked at my surroundings.

While the sun may have set, it was not late into the night—no one would be inside the school, but there was no guarantee that we wouldn't have witnesses, as far as we were from houses.

I had to settle this quickly.

But as I thought that, Kissshot spoke.

"What nerve, my servant—taking thy eyes off of me at this distance. Do not worry, those three are already gone, and as for any regular human, none could even approach me at my full power. If someone does see me, I shall be no more than a rumor around this town—"

"—A rumor."

A street rumor. An urban legend. Idle gossip.

Rumor would give rise to rumor—and rumors had a funny way of coming true.

"Of course—that doesn't go for those rations in the shed behind thee."

"…Kissshot. I have something to ask you too. One last question of my own."

"Oh? Then let us have it. A souvenir to take with thee to the underworld—I'll answer anything. Just ask."

"What are humans to you?"

"Food."

"I see."

She answered without a hint of hesitation, and the answer undid the final knot that held me back.

"And I wanted to hear that from you, too—I wanted to hear those words come out of your mouth!"

Then I moved—and so did Kissshot.

"I need you to die, master!"

"Prepare to die, servant!"

Perhaps it was to keep the situation at fifty-fifty—though Kissshot appeared to move at the same time as me, she'd allowed me the first move.

The edge of my open hand swept sideways toward her face—decapitating the top half of her head, sending it flying, blond hair and all.

But then, as if she'd anticipated the move, Kissshot unleashed a chop that caused my skull to explode. We had both used the same technique, but the power she displayed seemed to be on a different level—while the point of impact was far smaller than Dramaturgy's fist, that smaller size seemed to concentrate the force behind it to one spot.

Each of us had sent the other's head flying. Normally, the fight would end at that point.

But—neither Kissshot nor I was human.

We were monsters.

It didn't matter if our heads went flying or if our brains were destroyed, and there was no time limit. My consciousness and my vision were severed just for a fraction of a moment—and I immediately regenerated back to my original state.

Neither of us showed any signs of damage.

"Hyaa-hah!"

Kissshot was laughing.

"Hah!" "Haha!" "Ahaha!" "Hahaha!" "Aahahaha!"

Joyfully she laughed, with such vibrato it sounded as if she was trying to harmonize with herself.

"How wonderful! This is it—this is the thrill of two vampires fighting to the death! More, more, more, servant!"

"Shut your mouth!"

Chops crossed paths with chops.

They were not only aimed at the head, but at the body and the limbs as well.

My chops gouged pieces from Kissshot's body—

Kissshot's gouged pieces from mine.

Each of our bodies continued to barbarically bore through the other.

Of course, I wasn't numb to the pain.

Pain came across to me as pain.

My thoughts halted when my brain was destroyed, my breathing halted when my lungs were destroyed, and my circulation halted when my heart was destroyed.

While I'd become a vampire, my body's makeup hadn't changed.

My regeneration, recuperation, immortality—it was just that those things were something else.

But. That was enough.

"Raaaaaaaahhhhh!"

"Haha! Yes, keep screaming! How I love to hear the virile howls of men!"

Just as I'd expected, Kissshot's breasts were bouncing wildly—but her barrage of attacks was even wilder. And throughout it all—she roared with laughter.

I felt pain—and surely Kissshot must have too. It wasn't as if she was divorced from her sense of pain. Yet she betrayed no signs of it, not even a blink of the eyes. She didn't grit her teeth as I did, nor did she scream as I did.

It didn't matter what part of her I destroyed—

Her brain I destroyed, her lungs I destroyed, her heart I destroyed, but she seemed not to care and continued her deafening laughter.

Her eyes were cold, yet she looked happy.

It was a gruesome laugh.

"D-Dammit!"

"Hold now, servant, it is too early to utter such a line—why so vexed when we appear to be evenly matched?"

Did that mean she was used to the pain?

Was the pain of her body being torn to pieces nothing more than a familiar sensation?

If so.

These last five hundred years.

What kind of carnage and bloodshed had she seen? What did she survive?

Our difference in experience—difference in combat experience!

"Grraaaaaaaaaagh!"

But!

I would use my sheer willpower to close that gap—or at least, that's how these stories usually went!

"Aye, aye! That's it, scream—I want to hear thy roar!"

"Stop acting like this is easy for you, Kissshot!"

"How sad it makes me to know that I'll never hear ye call me that again!"

Our fight went nowhere.

No matter how much blood was sprayed, no matter how much flesh was scattered, it all evaporated before hitting the ground and regenerated in the time it took to do so.

And so, neither of us incurred damage.

For my part, death by shock from all the pain seemed within the realm of possibility—but perhaps a vampire's immortality brought you back to life even in that case.

Still…it was strange.

Our powers of immortality were evenly matched.

Kissshot had the edge in attacking.

This in itself wasn't strange.

But honestly, I hadn't thought my chops were capable of wounding Kissshot to such an extent. I'd been convinced that I was at an overwhelming disadvantage when it came to that—but in truth, my attacks were destroying her body without even landing that hard.

It was like destroying a chunk of tofu.

"Hahahahaha!"Haha!"Ahahahaha!"

She looked like a ghoul as she smiled with her cheeks torn away—and as she did, she answered my question.

Master and servant.

She seemed to know exactly what I was thinking.

"In fact, my servant—a vampire's defenses are not terribly high! Of course, they are leagues beyond our food's—mere human defenses—but so low they seem inversely proportionate to our outstanding offensive powers! Were we to rate a vampire's offenses at a hundred, our defenses are capped between ten and twenty! Guess why, my servant!"

"......h!"

Even Kissshot's dress was being restored each time—because she was creating it at will. The same did not go for me, though—my clothes were plain clothes. My torso was now nearly bare.

"Because our immortality equals our defense?!"

"Exactly!" Kissshot said. "So there's no need for thee to defend against my attacks in this battle—focus only on offense, and tear my body apart!"

"What are you, a masochist?!"

"I shan't deny the charge!"

At times, our hands would run into each other.

When this happened, my hand was the one that was destroyed.

There was no room for little tricks here—but that wasn't to say there was any room for big ones.

We would go until her or my immortality gave out.

If not, we'd go until her or my spirit broke.

That was how this battle was being fought—or no.

Not really.

This barren fight was nothing more than an opening skirmish—it was like play to Kissshot, and while it may not have been play to me, it still felt like I was only just getting ready.

I knew.

I understood.

And—I could feel it.

How I could kill Kissshot Acerolaorion Heartunderblade.

The way to slay her.

Now that I was actually facing her, my instincts told me how.

Whether it was my human ones or my vampire ones, I didn't know—but in any case, I intuited the way.

Upon further thought, Kissshot had pretty much told me herself—which meant that the method would work for sure.

I knew exactly what I had to do.

But—I wasn't being given the chance.

Why, you ask? Because while it was the way for me to slay Kissshot, it was also the way for Kissshot to slay me.

That was why this was fun for her.

It was a game.

Kissshot could probably kill me—whenever she felt like it. Of course, this didn't mean she was letting her guard down—she just wanted to relish her famous full powers for as long as she possibly could.

And that meant there was a chance—that Kissshot would show an opening.

Until then, I needed to trade blows standing in place and keep up the futile exchange of death for death and regeneration for regeneration.

"Hah! I like it, servant—ye've grown quite the backbone! Regardless of thy power as my thrall, most vampires with thy inexperience would not be able to disregard their lives so easily!"

"That's how it's supposed to go, right?! Well, I'm happy to hear that you're pleased!"

"And all the more reason 'tis a pity! Perhaps ye could have become a legend like me!"

"A legend? Why would I want to be a legend? Just the thought of someone I've never met knowing my name creeps me out!"

"I agree with you wholeheartedly!"

The two of us conversed as we continued to fight to the death. We talked as we gouged chunks from each other's body.

Almost completely unlike the previous day's conversation, up on top of the roof of the abandoned cram school, this was a wild, reckless exchange where we seemed to be saying whatever came to mind.

I wasn't able to laugh.

While Kissshot laughed, her smile, devoid of affection, was nothing like the night before's.

Though it felt like I was on the verge of being blown back by her attacks—I planted both of my feet and stood my ground.

The punishment I took was hellish.

My body, smashed into dust, was mended back to its original state by the time the wind carried it away, only to be smashed again, mended again, smashed once more, and eternally mended—that kind of hell.

It was like one of the circles of hell.

When I looked at it that way, it didn't seem like an overstatement to say that I was in hell.

"By the way, servant, perhaps ye'd be interested to hear this! There is no point in thy knowing, as ye'll soon be departing this world—"

"What is it?!"

"Dramaturgy, Episode, and of course Guillotine Cutter—all of the vampire hunters who have ever tried to kill me, as well as that floridly shirted boy—never seemed to know, but in truth, I, too, am a former human!"

Kissshot said this and laughed. She said the words as her head was severed and regenerated.

"A former human—like thee and Dramaturgy!"

"Wh-What? You weren't a pure-blooded vampire?!"

I'd been convinced she was. But now that she mentioned it—

she'd never said so.

"I've forgotten nearly everything that happened to me during my time as a human—but it seems I belonged to a reasonably well-off family! The aristocracy, as they say. And this dress seems to be a vestige of that time! Hah! Though once a vampire has been alive for over three hundred years, pure or thrall hardly matters!"

"Okay—so what?!"

"Well, I had forgotten for quite some time—and only remembered yesterday as I spoke with thee! I was reminded that, I, too, hesitated before eating a human for the first time!"

"Yeah, and?!"

"Thou, too!" Kissshot said as she stopped attacking me for a moment. "All it takes is eating one human—and thy guilt will vanish."

"......"

I stopped attacking as well. The wounds we had suffered healed in the blink of an eye.

"Dramaturgy was a former human as well... And while he was a hunter of vampires—he, too, ate humans. True, he stuck to the ones bound for execution provided to him by Guillotine Cutter's church—"

"Just because they were going to be executed doesn't mean it's okay to eat them...especially if they were only judged guilty by Guillotine Cutter's church."

"Indeed. But if we are to speak of what is right to eat and what not, why limit that standard to humans? Thou shalt not eat cow, thou shalt not eat pig, thou shalt not eat whale, thou shalt not eat dog—not to mention Guillotine Cutter, do humans not disagree on these points across cultures? Furthermore, I am a vampire who slays aberrations. Eating one human is enough to sate me for a month—a mere dozen in a year. That is but six thousand humans over my five hundred years alive. Is that such a large number in view of history? How many humans have other humans killed in that time?"

"…That's just sophistry."

"I am by no means a threat to this world. The effect I have on it is miniscule. And yet, ye insist that I die because I eat humans?" asked Kissshot. "A human's hunger is far more insatiable than mine."

We die if we don't eat.

Not just vampires. Humans, too.

Not just humans, but animals too.

Even plants, which I wanted to become.

Unless you're inorganic, unless you're stone or iron—you sacrifice other lives.

"That's not the problem, Kissshot," I said. "And you're right, I insist. You eat humans, so you must die."

"……"

Ah, Kissshot replied.

And her cold eyes slowly began to narrow.

"Kissshot. I'm human."

"I see. I am a vampire."

Then, our battle—was supposed to resume.

We were futilely returning to our futile exchange of death for death and regeneration for regeneration—but then.

"Hold on a second!"

A voice rang out to my back.

It reverberated through Naoetsu High's athletic field.

I knew immediately that it was Hanekawa's voice—and now that I heard it, I realized that I'd also heard the steel door of the P.E. shed opening just moments earlier.

"A-Araragi! Something's not right here!"

As Hanekawa spoke to me from behind, my only thought was that if anything, there was something wrong with her.

How could she leave the P.E. shed under these circumstances—did she have no sense of fear? I knew in my mind that my body was immortal, but even then I felt like I was on the verge of a nervous breakdown just standing in front of Kissshot—hadn't I told her Kissshot could destroy concrete blocks simply by looking at them?

So why? Why was she showing herself?

"Hanekawa! It doesn't matter, just hide!"

I knew how risky it was, but I turned around.

"No, actually—run away! Just run away! Leave this place! Get as far away as you can from here!"

"N-No, Araragi—!"

Hanekawa—seemed flustered.

Hanekawa, always calm and composed, even when I'd done my best to hurt her, even when Episode blew a hole through her flank, even when Guillotine Cutter had her hostage—was clearly shaken.

"Something's been all wrong, for a while now. Araragi, I-I think we're still overlooking something hugely important—"

Overlooking?

Could we possibly be overlooking something even now? No, there was no way.

Only one thing remained for me to do—

"Shut up!" Kissshot yelled.

Kissshot seemed flustered as well.

This was quite the unexpected reaction.

Well, I'd seen Kissshot act flustered just once—that time when I was still human and made to abandon her.

That time when I made the right decision.

That was when she became flustered.

She cried, she pleaded, she apologized—

"This isn't thy place to speak, ration!"

Kissshot glared.

And with that one motion, the steel door of the P.E. shed behind Hanekawa went flying.

That was the power of her eyes.

Unlike when I'd kicked it down, it seemed impossible to salvage—scrunched up like a ball of aluminum foil, the door had

314

disappeared into the shed.

The ground around Hanekawa was now cracked into pieces. Everything around her and behind her had been erased.

Just by being looked at.

With just a single look.

The iron-blooded, hot-blooded, yet cold-blooded vampire—the aberration slayer!

"…Ah."

This display left even Hanekawa speechless.

But I understood.

I already understood.

I knew.

I knew how precarious she could be.

Tsubasa Hanekawa.

I knew that something like that wasn't going to stop her.

She glared right back—firmly, even—at Kissshot Acerolaorion Heartunderblade.

"Miss Heartunderblade. Could you be—"

"Stay out of this, lowly human!"

Kissshot looked at Hanekawa again.

She looked at her.

She was using the power of her eyes, the power of a vampire's eyes—but!

An opening!

An opening, which hadn't even been hinted at during our futile fight to the death—finally showed itself!

Of course, unlike me, Kissshot certainly had room to take her eyes off of our fight—but right now was different.

Now was different.

As she looked at Hanekawa—she was flustered.

Openings everywhere.

"…Kissshot!"

Screaming her name, I jumped in between her and Hanekawa.

I took the full brunt of her eyes.

As my entire body was blown away and scattered—

I sunk my teeth into her throat.

I sunk my teeth into her, my elongated canines, my fangs.

"......!"

A way to slay Kissshot.

A way to slay a vampire.

A way for a vampire to slay a vampire—

Once you thought about it, it couldn't be more self-evident.

My instincts told me how.

I didn't know if they were my human ones or my vampire ones, but still.

In fact, she'd told me.

Kissshot's not-quite-advice to me before my fight with Dramaturgy.

—I doubt Dramaturgy would use the tactic—

—But do be careful not to let him suck thy blood—

—Vampires who have their blood sucked by another vampire will see their very existence wrung dry—

Back then, I wasn't interested in sucking blood—but things were different now.

I was feeling a bit hungry.

Gulp.

I began to suck her blood.

I'd sunk my fangs into her soft, white skin.

No one had to teach me how to suck blood—I just knew.

Precisely as a human fed.

"Guhh—"

Kissshot began to moan.

While her spilt blood returned—her sucked blood didn't.

It was because I was draining her energy.

One aberration was simply turning against another.

You couldn't even call it feeding on her.

Sure, feeding on her was what I was doing, but you couldn't call it that.

All I was doing—was slaying an aberration.

I'd used my body to block Kissshot's glare—it shouldn't have made it to Hanekawa.

If I could keep going and suck Kissshot dry—if I could wring every last drop from her, just as she did to me that day—

"Ha."

Even as she fell backwards, with me leaning over her—Kissshot laughed.

"Haha"Hahaha"Hahahaha"Aahahaha"Hahahahahahaha"Haha"Hahahaha"ha"Hahahahaha"Haha"Ahahaha"Aaaahahahahahahahahaha—!"

So she was going to die laughing.

That was fine with me.

But I had to admit. Her blood—Kissshot Acerolaorion Heartunderblade's blood—tasted better than anything in the world.

I felt like I could go on drinking forever no matter how much of it there was.

I wanted to go on drinking forever.

It was delicious.

Kissshot.

Just like this, without feeling a hint of fulfillment or an inch of accomplishment, but with unfaltering determination—

I will kill you.

The life I once saved—I would now end.

It was my responsibility. But even after she died and I returned to being human, I wouldn't feel any sense of fulfillment or accomplishment—her death a bare result!

"...Huh?"

And then.

And then, it suddenly came to me.

Was I overlooking something?

If I was—then what was I overlooking?

If it was so important that Hanekawa had to leap out of the P.E. shed to tell me—what in the world could it be?

And why did Kissshot become so flustered? Why did the foolish ramblings of someone she considered no more than "rations" enrage her?

She'd shown so much composure up until then.

Plus, I'd heard her say that before.

"This isn't thy place to speak."

That line—I had heard one like it come from Kissshot's mouth before—

—Negotiator or whatever thou may be—

—Do not speak when it is not thy place to do so—

—Boy.

That was it.

Kissshot had said that to Oshino—but what had we been talking about?

I remembered.

Oshino had said—

—And Heartunderblade, I'm pleased—

—You made Araragi your thrall—

—But you do intend—

—To turn him back into a human—

"……!"

I'd pushed Kissshot over and had her trapped between my legs—but suddenly, without thinking, I sat up. Of course, this meant removing my fangs from her neck.

Then I looked at her expression.

I looked at her.

Kissshot's eyes were still cold but now blank, even seeming a bit cloudy—but she was still able to twist her mouth at me.

"What's the matter, servant?" she said. "I still have nearly half of my blood left."

"......"

"While I may not be able to move for now, having lost so much blood, I will recover in no time unless ye make haste."

She was probably right.

Both about being unable to move and about recovering right away.

But more importantly—

There was something I had to ask her.

I thought I'd asked her my last question—but there was something I needed to ask her.

Even if it might not be a good idea to ask.

"H-Hey. Kissshot."

"What is it?"

"*How*...were you going to turn me back into a human?"

Kissshot clicked her tongue and said, "What does it matter to thee now?"

"It does matter to me. It's important."

"That damned ration. She should have kept her mouth shut," Kissshot castigated Hanekawa—then held her tongue.

The castigated Hanekawa—slowly walked toward me and Kissshot. She'd put her sweater back on and retied her scarf. Meanwhile, I could tell by her jiggling breasts, worthy of sound effects, *boing boing*, were this a manga, that she hadn't had time to wear her bra.

But Hanekawa seemed not to care as she approached us.

"Miss Heartunderblade," she said solemnly. "Were you...planning on having Araragi kill you from the very beginning?"

"......"

"So that you could turn Araragi back into a human?"

I'd overlooked something.

What if it hadn't turned out this way—for example, what if I'd never witnessed Kissshot eating Guillotine Cutter?

How was Kissshot planning on turning me back into a human

then? What method existed outside of the one that Hanekawa had discovered?

It had never even occurred to me.

I had overlooked it. Entirely.

"That's enough foolishness from thee, ration. On what grounds—"

"Then could you please tell me how you were planning on turning Araragi back into a human? I looked it up—but I couldn't find any other way of turning a vampire back into a human."

Any other way.

Any way outside of killing one's master.

Any way outside of causing the master-servant relationship to crumble.

"Hah. As if I would know—I never had any intention of turning this servant of mine back into a human. It was a lie I told to make him gather my arms and legs. I could not tell too many if it was to return to my perfect form—and indeed, I only made him my thrall for my own convenience."

"That's not true. You gathered your missing parts because Araragi wouldn't be able to turn back into a human if you weren't in your complete state, even if he killed you, right? It wasn't going to work unless he killed you after you were whole again—"

I thought back to Kissshot's excitement.

So it wasn't because she'd returned to her perfect form—but rather because that meant the conditions had been met to turn me back into a human?

"Fool. It was nothing of the sort."

"If that's true—then why did you come here?" Hanekawa asked Kissshot in an utterly calm voice.

Predator and prey.

A greater existence and a lesser existence.

But Hanekawa spoke like an equal.

"Araragi had a reason to fight you, but you didn't. I know

you came up with some labored reason like wanting to use your full powers or whatever—but you came here to be killed by Araragi, didn't you? That was all, wasn't it? You even made it a fifty-fifty fight—you intentionally provoked him."

"Ha-Hanekawa—"

"You stay quiet, Araragi," Hanekawa interrupted me. "Of course, I don't have any grounds for it—something just seemed strange, that's all. But just now, when you *didn't try to kill me as I came to put a damper on your fight*—that's when I knew. Your—"

Kissshot had used her vampire eyes.

She blew away everything around Hanekawa.

Yet, she didn't harm Hanekawa herself.

When Hanekawa had interfered in the same way during my battle with Episode, he didn't think twice about hurling his cross at her—but Kissshot didn't attack Hanekawa, the girl she'd called my rations.

All she did was try to intimidate her.

"Your plan is to die."

"...Ye should have kept thy mouth shut," Kissshot said, repeating herself. "What good will it do—ye think this servant of mine could kill me after hearing those words?"

"What?"

"As this servant's mistress, I know quite well—he is the kind of fool who would rescue a vampire on the brink of death. Knowing what I 'do intend,' as that boy put it, do ye think this one could suck my blood?"

"W-Well—but—" stammered Hanekawa.

Kissshot gave her a cold look.

A cold look—with her two blank eyes.

"I had thought it would be the hardest step of all—I was vexed by how to make him kill me. That is why I kept mum about the way to turn him back for as long as I could. I was afraid we simply had to plunge into it... But in what I will admit was an unexpected turn of events, the stage was set thanks to Guillotine Cutter. Had I known that eating a single human sufficed to render him so irate, I'd not have worried so."

Kissshot looked at me before continuing.

"—If only I could have simply been the villain, the despised, and slain thus. There was no need for thee to be privy to my intention."

"Why not?" I muttered, stupefied.

But at the same time—if I looked at it that way, everything did check out.

"Why would you…want to do that?"

"My servant," replied Kissshot, "I had been searching for a place to die."

"A place to die—"

The cause of death for nine-tenths of vampires.

Suicide.

Boredom—killed vampires.

She was—so bored.

"And that is why I came to this country—I had not returned since the death of my first thrall. It was not for sightseeing—"

"B-But, you…"

She didn't want to die.

That's what she said—crying and screaming.

Her heart had been stolen—her limbs had been severed—

She'd just barely escaped with her life.

"I thought I was ready to die. That is what I had told myself," Kissshot said.

But.

"At the very end, I grew scared of death."

"……"

"The thought that after five hundred years alive, I would vanish—it began to scare me. That thought, that I would be gone, scared me so. That is when ye came along—and when I sought thy help."

"And—I helped you."

I hadn't been moved by any grand notion.

What would happen next, what the future would hold—I'd had no notion.

I was moved by one thing alone.

Her crying face. I didn't want to have to see it.

I couldn't bear seeing it.

"It was the first time in my life that anyone helped me."

"……"

"No one ever helped me, neither human nor vampire. And as I sat there, sucking thy blood—I began to wonder, what was I doing? And so—once I was done sucking thee dry, I decided against devouring thee and made thee my thrall. My second one ever."

Though I'd taken quite some time to awaken, and she thought I'd go into a frenzy, Kissshot said.

She'd stayed by my side the whole time. She was there to nurse me.

"Yet somehow ye awakened. Of course, I would not have objected if ye wished to remain a vampire—but as I had expected, thy wish was to turn back into a human. While I had mulled it over while ye were unconscious, it was then that I decided."

Her tone was infirm yet firm.

"I would die for thy sake."

"...For my sake?"

"I would have thee kill me, restoring thy humanity while dying at last. I'd felt as if at last, I had discovered a place to die—a place I had been seeking for the past four hundred years."

"Four hundred years—"

That was when—her first thrall.

She had told me.

About restoring his humanity.

—At the time I was in fact unable to turn him back into a human—

—And I plan to use the lessons I learned then this time around.

"I was unable to die for his sake. Unable to die for another. Unable to restore his humanity—and so."

"You'd do it for me."

She would do it to restore my humanity.

To help me.

For that, she was going to—give up her own life?

"But don't let it get to thy head, servant. This was my responsibility from the beginning—none of this would have happened if not for my disgraceful behavior, and I would have died then if not for thy help."

"......!"

Huh? Wait...hold on a second.

This situation—was impossible.

At this rate, my mental preparation—

I'd promised Hanekawa that I was mentally prepared!

"...What is it now? Crying, are ye?"

"Ah..."

Then I realized—my cheeks were wet.

Why?

After all, it didn't matter. None of this changed what I had to do, right?

Even if she was trying to die for my sake—she ate people!

"What a crybaby I have as a servant. Pitiful."

"N-No. These aren't tears. This..."

This, I repeated.

"This is—blood."

"Oh?"

"It's my blood flowing—"

How in the world were things turning out this way?

Kissshot was a vampire.

She had eaten Guillotine Cutter.

She had eaten six thousand people until now.

But even so.

"—And it flows in you too!"

She was alive.

Wasn't it the same, then?

What I had done.

What she was trying to do.

What she had done.

What I was trying to do.

All the same—wasn't it?!

"Now look at this mess, ration," Kissshot said. "I'd planned to show him an opening whenever the fancy struck me, so he could slay me—ah, but what does that matter. Because, my dear servant, the only choice left to thee is to kill me."

"Wh-Why would you say that?"

My preparation.

My mental preparation.

"Kill me here, or starting tomorrow I shall eat, oh, let's say a thousand people a day... Now that I've said that, ye must kill me. No? If I poached thy rations to prove that this is no idle threat, would it move thee into action?"

"......"

"Ye saved my life, so be the one to snatch it away. Isn't that the 'responsible' thing to do?"

"Kissshot—"

"Only one other called me by that name before thee. And ye shall be the last."

I looked toward Hanekawa, as if to ask for her help.

But—all Hanekawa did was bite her lower lip in response. It seemed to me like a sign of how hopeless the situation was.

Even Hanekawa was out of options.

Yes.

Kissshot was right.

She hadn't had to divulge her plan until Hanekawa came leaping out of the P.E. shed—but her intentions didn't change what I had to do. They only made the situation worse, as I could now see.

But.

Had I not found out—had I gone on being mistaken about Kissshot for the rest of my life—I would have been deprived of even regret and remorse.

It would be as a clown if I turned back into a human.

How was that acceptable?

My wish would come true, but that would be it.

It wasn't a happy outcome for anyone.

It was just pinning everything on Kissshot.

"Come," Kissshot said, laughing. "Come. Come—kill me, servant."

"—Dammit!"

She was searching for a place to die?

She wanted to kill herself?

All she was trying to do—was escape!

It was proof she was trying to run away!

It didn't matter how gallant she tried to make it sound, the real her—the real her was the one I heard that day under the street lamp!

No way, no way, no waaay!

I don't wanna die, I don't wanna die, I don't wanna die!

Help me, help me, help me!

Please!

I can't die, I can't die!

I don't wanna disappear, I don't wanna vanish!

Somebody,

Somebody, somebody, somebody, someboddyyy—!

I'm sorry!

"Oshino-o-o!"

And so.

I looked up to the sky—and screamed with everything I had.

I used the full capacity of my vampire lungs to release the loudest roar I could.

"Mèmè Oshino!"

And I called his name.

The name of that Hawaiian-shirted, frivolous, sleazy man.

The name of the man who had known everything from the start, but said nothing—brazenly, with an unlit cigarette in his mouth.

"I know you're out there watching us—so stop acting so important and show yourself! I've got a job for you, bastard!"

Hanekawa was looking at me, shocked.

Kissshot was looking at me, shocked.

But I paid them no attention—and continued to scream.

"Oshino! I know you're there—you'd have to be watching us, with all that crap about being neutral! Now I understand—I don't need any more explanations from you! So come out here—now that I understand, I know damn well that I'm not the victim and that it's my fault! So come out here—Mèmè Oshino!"

"—You don't have to yell, I can hear you fine."

And with the same aimless attitude as always—Oshino was there, sitting on top of the roof of the P.E. shed.

He sat there cross-legged and his face in his palm.

He looked like he found it all a big pain in the ass.

I don't know when—but he'd suddenly appeared there.

"Araragi. Imagine meeting you here, what are the chances?"

"…Oshino."

"Ha hah, how so spirited—something good happen to you?"

"I have a job for you," I repeated.

I focused squarely on him—and repeated myself.

"I want you to do something."

"'Something'?"

Oshino jumped down from the roof of the shed and laughed sarcastically—while he didn't look to be the least bit athletic, he made a clean landing without the slightest bend of the knees.

Then, he began to approach me with a carefree stride.

"That's a tough one."

"I'll pay."

"It's not an issue of money."

"Then what's the issue?"

"A personal one, what else?"

Stop trying to force this on him, he complained, as if refusing.

Actually, refusing was exactly what it was.

"Hey there, missy class president."

Oshino raised a hand to Hanekawa.

"This would be our first time meeting, right? Nice to meet you."

"…Yes," Hanekawa replied with a nod, "nice to meet you too—my name is Hanekawa."

"It was a good thing I decided to stay around this town even though all that business with Heartunderblade had wrapped up. If I'd left, I never would have had the chance to meet you."

"…Is that so? I was convinced that you hated me, Mister Oshino."

"Oh, stop. I could never hate a girl. If Araragi told you something weird, take it from me—he's just making up gossip," Oshino said shamelessly.

How phony was this guy?

"You really are amazing, though—getting this deeply involved when aberrations don't concern you? High school girls really are spirited—something good happen to you lately?"

"They do concern me," Hanekawa asserted. "If it's Araragi's problem, then it's my problem too."

"Wow, ain't that friendship."

Oshino stifled a laugh. I didn't know if he could be any more infuriating and insulting.

"Or maybe it's youth."

"Boy," Kissshot said. "Stay out of this. Wasn't that our agreement?"

"I don't remember ever making an agreement with you, Heart-underblade—I just wanted to set things up well. You deciding to die so that Araragi could become human again was convenient for me, that's all. And by me—I mean mankind."

That was it.

It was probably the same with Guillotine Cutter.

When he meekly turned over Kissshot's arms, I was puzzled, but Oshino told me how he'd explained the situation—Kissshot was agreeing to help turn me back into a human.

That's why Guillotine Cutter returned them.

Oshino must have used that to forge a compromise.

It's how he convinced Guillotine Cutter—that was why he agreed.

In that case, he could return her arms without going against his creed.

Plus, he'd be able to save face as his religion's archbishop.

But, feeling sad about having to part with Kissshot, I took my time to talk to her, went to the convenience store, and so on—and because I kept dragging things out and made no moves to kill Kissshot, Guillotine Cutter, who thought he'd been tricked by Oshino, proceeded to march into the abandoned school alone.

Even Oshino's barrier couldn't conceal Kissshot in her perfect form.

"So things did play out more or less as I expected, but... You know, missy class president, you did make a grand mess of things. Araragi really didn't have to know about that."

"I—" Hanekawa said, still unfaltering, "I think that's wrong."

"Oh dear. Well, I've gotta admit, you do have one big chest on ya."

"E-Excuse me?"

Hanekawa held her arms over her breasts, flustered.

Bounce, bounce.

Upon seeing this, Oshino laughed and replied, "Oh, my mistake.

I meant to say you've got one big heart in ya."

Yeah, right.

It was sexual harassment, plain and simple.

"Either way, that's a very wonderful, model student-like thing for you to say. But in that case, li'l missy class president, what do you suggest we do here?"

"That's for Araragi to decide," Hanekawa shot back. "It'd be so awful if he were to end things without knowing the truth, to say the least."

"You catch that, Araragi? What a tough spot you've been put in—missy class president is so kind she's cruel. There really is something off about her. What exactly does she see in you that lets her trust you like that?"

"......"

"So, what'll you do?" Oshino said, looking at me—and popping an unlit cigarette into his mouth as always. "My original plan was just to watch the aftermath play out—but it looks like just as I thought the ship had sailed, I found myself on it. So fine, I'll listen to your request. This is a job for me as a professional, correct? The fee can be—ah, that's right. That five million I called off, you can owe it to me again."

He made a grin.

"So, what is your heart's desire?"

"...I want you to tell me a way to make everyone happy," I told him.

That was what I desired, from the bottom of my heart.

"A method that will keep all of us from being unhappy."

"How could something like that possibly exist?" Are you stupid or something, Oshino shrugged. "There's convenient, and then there's that. That's an essay topic for an elementary school ethics class. It's unrealistic."

"Oshino, I—"

"However," Oshino said, taking the cigarette out of his mouth and putting it back in his pocket. He looked at Hanekawa, then Kissshot, then finally me before saying, "I can think of a way that will make everyone miserable."

As I looked at him, dumbfounded by this reply, he quickly went on to explain.

"In other words, the grief created by this incident will be split among everyone evenly—no one's wishes will come true, but if you're okay with that, there is a way."

"……"

Everyone would be miserable—everyone would bear the misery. It would be split.

Parceled out—and borne by everyone.

It wouldn't be all forced onto one person.

"To be specific… Well, okay. Araragi, you'd stop just short of killing Heartunderblade. You'd take away nearly all of her traits and skills as a vampire—leaving just enough to keep her alive. For your part, Heartunderblade, you will come even closer to death than you were before. So close that you'll be left with nothing—no shadow, no trace, no game, not even a name. You'd become like lowly human mockery of a vampire—unable to eat a human, no matter how hungry."

Oshino continued, "And you, Araragi. That wouldn't allow you to turn back into a human, either—but you'd be extremely close to one. You, Araragi, would be like a vampiric mockery of a human. You'd have a few traits and skills as a vampire left—and while you wouldn't technically be able to call yourself human, you would be infinitely far from being a vampire, making you infinitely close to human. You'd of course be nothing like a half-vampire. Instead, you'd be an ill-defined, half-baked creature. How fitting."

"'F-Fitting'?!"

"And of course, you wouldn't be able to eat humans if you got hungry, either. However… If that were the case, regardless of what happens to you, Araragi, Heartunderblade would starve to death from lack of nutrition. So, Araragi, you would have to constantly be giving Heartunderblade your own blood. The one source of nutrition that would keep Heartunderblade alive would be your flesh and blood, the very thing that will have reduced her to her vulgar state. You would need to devote the rest of your life to Heartunderblade, and Heartunderblade would have to spend the rest of hers nestled up to you."

"In that case—" Hanekawa interrupted. "In other words, we humans—"

"Yes. We would have to give up on slaying this dangerous creature we call a vampire. Any plans to wipe out the aberration slayer, the iron-blooded, hot-blooded, yet cold-blooded vampire, as well as her thrall—would have to be abandoned. If her powers were taken away to that extent, then hunters like Dramaturgy and Episode wouldn't even be able to locate her anymore. In other words, the risk would still remain. Heartunderblade and Araragi could become vampires, and they might begin to eat humans. That risk would still remain, and it would be very real."

If we did that—

Everyone would be miserable.

No one's wishes would come true.

Kissshot would be unable to die.

I wouldn't be turning back into a human.

Two vampires would be left alive.

"...H-How dare ye spew such ridiculous thoughts, boy!" Kissshot yelled below me.

She was raising her voice. Since I'd already sucked half of her blood, she was unable to move—so yelling was all she could do.

"What do ye know, boy?! Ye've not spent a tenth of my time alive! I have had enough of thy self-serving nonsense—I have no wish to go on living in such a form! I will not abase myself and live in disgrace for all to see! This place is where I shall die! I have finally found it—I can finally die! I will die—for my servant's sake! Allow me to die for his sake! Kill me, kill me—hurry and kill me now! No part of me wishes to live!"

"That's what I'm saying, you'll be miserable. Your wish won't come true. Of course, Araragi is the one who gets to make the decision. Missy class president is exactly right."

"Servant!"

Kissshot turned to me, apparently having decided that she'd get nowhere with Oshino.

"As I just said—do not fall for that boy's cajolery. No part of me wishes to live."

"…Yes, but I…"

I was clear-eyed and determined as I replied to her. I was fully aware of my responsibility, of what would happen next and in the future.

"I want you to live."

"……"

And then—

I stroked her hair. Her golden, her soft, her gentle hair.

Yes, the certain proof—of my submission to her.

"I beg you—and I will as many times as you want, as your servant. So please, stop trying to die in style—live on, awkwardly. Stop trying to find a place to die, and look for a place to live."

Kissshot's expression was one of despair.

But she couldn't move.

She couldn't even struggle.

Tears began to well in her eyes—

Blood-like tears began to well in her eyes as she did the only thing she could, which was to plead.

"P-Please, servant…I implore thee. Please…find it within thyself to kill me. Find a way to kill me and become human again. Think of it as helping me—"

"I'm sorry, Kissshot," I said, calling her by her true name.

A name I doubted I'd ever call her again.

"I'm not helping you."

And that was how my spring break came to an end.

My nearly hellish spring break.

The curtain fell on the last spring break I would ever spend as a high school student—with misery for all and redemption for none, an unhappy ending that was a cruel sight to behold.

018

Epilogue.

Or rather, my life from now.

The next day, Karen and Tsukihi, my two little sisters, roused me from my bed for the first time in a while, and I headed to school. My parents said nothing in particular to me, the eldest son of the family who'd allegedly returned from a two-week-long journey of self-discovery, and my sisters simply had a big laugh at my expense. Since what I'd been up to indeed went beyond words and invited ridicule, I felt like I had no choice but to accept their reactions.

In any case, the new school year was starting today.

I got on my bicycle and began pedaling toward school. It was also my first time riding one in two weeks, but I supposed it took more than a little trip to hell and back to forget how to ride a bike.

I arrived at school.

Class assignments had been posted in the gym.

"Whoa."

It was a miracle. My name and Hanekawa's were there inside the same box. Well, a miracle might be an overstatement, but my heart leapt a little. I hadn't felt anything close to the same emotion looking at class assignments for my second year. Though I couldn't describe the true nature of that emotion even if I tried, marvelously enough Hanekawa and I were going to be in the same class.

I picked out Hanekawa from among the throng of students scrambling to check what class they were in and called out to her— such textbook examples of model students were rare even at Naoetsu High so I had no trouble finding her.

She had changed her hairstyle.

Actually, all she'd done was split her one braid into two, one on each side, but even that had quite an effect on the impression she gave off.

"Oh, if it isn't Araragi… Howdy!"

Hanekawa looked tired. Her shoulders were slumped, and she even seemed to be stooping a little.

What a torpid way to start off the new school year.

"I-Is something the matter, Miss Hanekawa?"

What could it be?

Did she not like our being in the same class?

Although I was beset by paranoia, that didn't seem to be the case.

"Agh!"

Hanekawa pulled on the sleeve of my uniform to lead me outside the gym.

Once we reached a place where we could talk in private, she groaned, "I forgot my bra in the P.E. shed."

"Okay."

"They've probably found it by now…"

While I had tried to clean up the athletic field as best I could, there was simply nothing I could do about the door that had been crumpled up by a vampire's eyes like a ball of aluminum foil, so I'd left it behind and gone home. I hadn't gone to the field yet, but the door had disappeared entirely. How could there not be an uproar over that? They'd surely conduct a thorough investigation of the area around the shed.

And that's what seemed to be causing Hanekawa distress.

"While it was no time to be worrying about that kind of thing, I, Tsubasa Hanekawa, made my mistake of a lifetime…and it will be my lifelong shame."

"Don't worry, Hanekawa."

"? Why not?"

"I made sure to grab it."

"What did you just say?!"

"I would never let you embarrass yourself like that."

"How did you keep it in mind under those circumstances?!"

"Hey, hey, don't say such sad things. During all of spring break, your underwear was always my top priority."

"That's the saddest thing I've ever heard!"

"So yes, top and bottom, together now as a set in my room."

"Give them back!"

Hanekawa and I spoke there for a little while since we still had time before the first bell. The topic of our conversation was, of course, vampires. Hanekawa exhibited for me a tidbit of her vast knowledge on the subject.

"It's just a theory," she began, "but vampires sucking human blood—apparently means completely different things depending on whether they're feeding or creating a thrall."

"Yeah, I feel like I've heard that before, either from her directly or from Oshino."

"When it's for food, well, it's for food, but it seems that creating a thrall is more like intercourse."

"I-Intercourse?"

"I'm being serious," Hanekawa said. "We speak of sexual appetites and those two desires being similar, don't we? And when you think about it that way, doesn't it make sense that vampires don't like to create thralls too often? As far as her—just two in five hundred years. I don't really know the vampire take on chastity, but she seems to be a very modest woman."

"Modest?"

"It makes me wonder if her first thrall could've been her lover."

A notion against creating thralls—

That's how it had been put to me.

A modest vampire.

One who wouldn't create a thrall just in order to survive, was it?

In that case.

When did she create a thrall?

That was the question.

"...But we're talking about a human and a vampire," I said.

"And couldn't that be why she made him her thrall? The existence of half-vampires seems to confirm such couplings...or maybe those cases are different. Either way, this is just speculation. But isn't that precisely why she tried to redo things with you? To atone for the other time, so to speak."

"To atone—"

She couldn't turn her first one back into a human.

Hence she overlaid me, her second—on her first.

That could have been it.

"I'm sure she didn't want to be killed by those three expert vampire hunters—but maybe when she came across you, she truly did find the right place to die. It was when she encountered—her second thrall."

"Place to die, huh?"

"When you think about it, the moment she relinquished almost all of her abilities as a vampire by making you her thrall—when she relinquished the ability to suck blood, she may have already been prepared to starve to death. I mean, vampires die if they don't suck blood."

"That's...right."

"But in order to turn you back into a human, she couldn't allow herself to starve to death."

"...You know, last evening, she started out by inviting me to live with her for eternity, but...if I'd accepted her invitation, I wonder what she had in mind."

"Exactly that, I think."

"Exactly that?"

"Even if you can't live alone, if it's with someone else, you can."

"……"

"Two's better than one—and apparently just two is better than three. That sort of thing."

Dunno, Hanekawa said.

Ditto, I said to that.

"The wound."

"Hm?"

"It's still there," Hanekawa said—looking at my neck.

The two fang marks on my neck.

"Oops. Isn't my collar hiding them?"

"Hmm. People in the know might notice." Crossing her arms, Hanekawa examined my neck from all sorts of angles. "Plus there's gym class and stuff… I think it might be better for you to grow out your hair a bit."

"Ah… Taking care of it's gonna be a pain."

"How vampiric are you still, anyway?"

"I still have to find out the extent for myself, but…well, my body seems to heal a lot better than before. I think my gums bleed less when I brush my teeth."

"What a drab—"

"It is what it is. If we're to give it a positive spin—I'd say I was able to turn back into a human, but not without some lasting side effects."

"I see… Side effects, huh."

"Well, whether or not I'm human now—just being able to be out in the sun like this feels like a world of difference."

"How forward-looking."

As she said that, Hanekawa's bashful smile, too—looked much more dazzling under the sun.

"Well, don't ever hesitate to ask me if you need help with something. I'll be happy to lend you a shoulder to rub any time."

"All right. I'll let you know if I ever want to rub them. You bet I'll be doing some research before next time, and I'm going to be emotionally prepared for it as well, because I want to make sure it feels good for you when I get my hands on them."

"...W-We're talking about my shoulders, right?"

"Huh? Er, yeah, sure, I guess."

"That's an awfully vague answer..."

She grimaced. But at any rate—Hanekawa held her right hand out toward me.

"Now that we're in the same class, I'm gonna make sure you turn your life around."

"What am I, a juvenile delinquent?"

"You lost your life and turned once, didn't you?"

An apt expression for an undead guy, Hanekawa deadpanned.

"Let's make this a good year, Araragi."

"Yeah. And not just this year. Let's make this good, for now and ever."

Maybe not as long as an eternity.

But a good now and ever.

I clasped Hanekawa's right hand.

We shook hands like true friends.

We then headed to class, where our homeroom teacher gave an outline of the school year and trimester to come—but that part was the same as ever.

He told us that class representatives would be voted on tomorrow, and that we should think about who would be suitable. Of course, I would be voting for Hanekawa—as for which of the boys was getting my vote, who cares.

And after class.

I headed to the abandoned cram school alone.

I'd told Hanekawa where I was going. I considered going together with her, but then, this was my responsibility and mine alone.

After about twenty minutes on my bicycle, I arrived.

I entered onto the property through a hole in the fence, as if it was a friend's familiar house, or rather, my own. Come to think of it, this was my first time studying the building from the outside during the day.

Looking at it under the sun—it was even more dilapidated than I expected.

It was decaying and exhausted.

It was a corpse of a building.

So that's how it appeared to human eyes.

Casting mine down, I entered the ruins—and then climbed the stairs.

I got to the second floor—and kept going.

I was headed to the fourth floor.

She was no longer vulnerable to sunlight.

Because She was no longer a vampire.

I checked the classroom with the hole ripped through its ceiling, but no one was there. When I opened the door to the next classroom over—though the door seemed to have its own mechanical problems—I found Oshino inside.

"Hey there. You're late, Araragi—I've been waiting for ages," he greeted me in a carefree tone.

He wore, as always, a Hawaiian shirt.

Lying on a slapdash bed made of desks, he hardly seemed to have been waiting for me, but there was no point in taking this guy to task about every little thing.

"Ha hah. That uniform suits you, Araragi. I thought you were someone else."

"Well, I am a student, after all."

"Oh, right. It'd slipped my mind. Yeah, yeah, you were the hero of a superpowered school action series."

"That's so long ago that I don't even know if it really happened."

And in any case, I wasn't cut out to be the hero.

I wasn't even fit to be the villain or the monster.

What I was now was a simple high school student.

After all, and all in all, I was a student.

Even if I wasn't entirely human.

"I see. And missy class president isn't with you?"

"Nope, I'm alone. Would it have been better if she came?"

"Nah, it doesn't matter either way for this."

By the by, continued Oshino.

"If you don't mind me voicing my concerns, beware missy class president, Araragi—don't take your eyes off of her. That girl is a little—too precarious. Even this time around…she gave every last one of us the run, you and me included. If things were to ever center around her, to be quite honest, even I don't know what might happen."

"Yeah…you don't have to tell me to keep an eye on her," I answered. "We're friends."

"Are you, now. Well, it's not like I sold you a warranty on my services or anything, but I'd like to see how you're going to hold up, so I'm staying here in these ruins for a while—I looked all around, but this abandoned cram school still seems the comfiest place. Come talk to me if you ever need help."

"Your help is pretty expensive."

"It's not expensive. I'm properly compensated," Oshino said before pointing to a corner of the classroom with his unlit cigarette. "All right, why don't we get round number one started?"

In the corner of the classroom—

There sat a blond girl.

She held her knees in her arms.

A petite girl—who looked to be about eight.

Not twenty-seven.

Not seventeen, not twelve, not even ten—

A blond eight-year-old girl.

And.

She glared at me—with threatening eyes.

"…Really."

I didn't know what to call her.

This girl with no shadow, no trace, no game, not even a name.

A husk of a vampire.

The dregs of a beautiful demon.

And—

An unforgettable being, for me.

"Really… I'm sorry."

I approached her.

I sat next to where she sat and hugged her.

"If you ever want to kill me, go ahead."

She said nothing.

She wasn't going to say anything to me anymore.

As if to sulk even harder, she struggled a little—but soon she calmed down and went for my neck, still not saying a word, and chomped down.

I felt a prick of pain.

Along with an intoxicating feeling.

"I don't think this is right, either," Oshino said airily behind me. "I guess you could call it human egotism? The disgust you felt over vampires eating humans is really no different from a cute little kitty eating a mouse turning people off. And now, in a way, you've chosen to keep a vampire as a pet—having filed down its fangs, plucked out its claws, crushed its throat, and castrated it. You, who were made a pet, turned around and made your master your pet. That's all there is to this story. It's certainly no heart-warmer."

"……"

"A human who tried to sacrifice his life for a vampire, and a vampire who tried to sacrifice hers for a human. Sounds like blood begetting blood—but I guess blood is thicker than water. I don't intend on inserting myself into this situation, since this is just work for me—but if you ever begin to hate yourself over this, Araragi, just let me know and I'll do something about it."

343

"I'm never going to start hating anything about this," I answered as the girl sucked my blood. "I'm doing this because I want to."

"Then do as you want."

Even as Oshino's uncaring repartee came from behind me, I embraced the girl's petite body, which seemed so fragile that mere human arms might crush it if I held it too tight.

Having wounded each other, the two of us licked each other's wounds.

Damaged goods both, we sought out each other.

"If you want to die tomorrow, I'm ready for my life to end tomorrow—if you care to live for today, then so will I," I vowed out loud.

Thus begins the tale of the wounded ones.

A tale of blood that splattered red and dried up black.

The tale of our never-to-heal, precious wound.

I will tell it to no one.

Afterword

Some people like to tell fortunes or judge personalities based on blood types, saying, for example, that type Os are natural leaders while type As are highly strung, that type Bs are free spirits while type ABs march to their own drum, but then, you should probably want your leaders to be a little on the highly strung side, and really, "free spirit" is just another way to say "marches to his own drum," and if you substituted "self-centered" for "free spirit," what's the difference between a self-centered person and a very fussy highly strung person, not to mention that if you think it's good for leaders to have strong, unshakeable wills, they'd need to march to their own drum, and once you start thinking about it that way, you have no choice but to point out that, hey, wait a second, they all mean the same thing. Of course, the same could be said of all fortune telling, none more so than zodiac astrology, but they only split blood type fortunes into four types, and that simplicity paradoxically seems to be lending the whole affair its credibility. If you've ever subjected yourself to it, I bet when you gave your blood type you were told, "Ah, I knew it," but that's the trick, and it's not hard to imagine being told "Ah, I knew it" no matter what type you say you are. Also, I bet the simplest way to guess people's blood type, in Japan at least, is to ignore everything about their personality and to declare, "You're a type A, aren't you?" That's because A is the most common blood type among Japanese people. I guess a little further in the future, we might have things like DNA fortunes or genetic fortunes, but to be honest, I don't think they'll be any better than the blood type fortunes we have today.

This book consists of "Koyomi Vamp," the story of Koyomi Araragi, the narrator of my previous work *BAKEMONOGATARI*. Though I called it my previous work, I don't mind at all if you read this one first. In fact, chronologically speaking, this one comes first, so I dare say the *KIZUMONOGATARI*-first order is just as legit as the opposite order. It's the tale of Koyomi Araragi and the vampire Kissshot Acerolaorion Heartunderblade. It's also the tale of Koyomi Araragi meeting Tsubasa Hanekawa for the first time. If *BAKE-MONOGATARI* is the novel I wrote entirely to entertain myself, then *KIZUMONOGATARI* is a novel I wrote entirely-and-a-fifth to entertain myself. In fact, these stories should have been sealed off forever, never to be espied, their author fully satisfied the moment he put down his pen, but by some mistake, they were turned into books, beautifully adorned with the illustrator VOFAN's impressive skills, and published for the world to see. When I confront myself with this fact, I don't feel the need to thank various people as much as the need to do some very serious reflection on my own professionalism. Then again, the occasional book like this doesn't seem like it could hurt, so I would appreciate your magnanimity.

Of course, if you do find the *MONOGATARI* series, which I have written so exhaustively I feel there's nothing left I could possibly add, to be even the least bit entertaining, then there is no greater joy for me. Fueled by that joy, I'll get back to actual work starting tomorrow.

NISIOISIN

Palindromic **NISIOISIN** made his debut as a novelist when he was twenty. A famously prolific author, he is known to publish more than a book per month at times. With his inexorable rise, he has become the leading light of a younger generation of writers who began their careers in the twenty-first century.

Titles by him previously published in English include the first two books of the *Zaregoto* mystery cycle and the novelizations *xxxHOLiC: AnotherHOLiC* and *Death Note: Another Note - The Los Angeles BB Murder Cases*. The *MONOGATARI* series, widely considered his masterpiece to date, makes its first appearance in English with this volume.

Illustrator **VOFAN**, lauded as the "magician of light and shadow," hails from Taiwan.